Evil unleashed

They were coming.

Annat ran down the embankment, anger hurling her forward. The mist split and she saw them: dressed in rags, four men and a woman bending over a prone figure that writhed on the ground. It was—it had been—Pyotr.

Yuda stretched out his right arm, sending a surge of power into the group. Annat felt the impact from where she stood, but it seemed to have no effect on the five. Scorpion fired a blue jet of charge ozone that struck one of the men under the chin, spinning him backwards. For an instant the group wavered—then Annat felt them gathering force for their counterattack. . . .

Praise for *Children of the Shaman*

"A fantastic world with some refreshing differences from the norm of fantasy. . . . Rydill does a fine job of placing the reader in a vividly imagined world . . . worth following . . . along the bumpy track of adventure to a supernatural finale."　　　　　　　　　　　　*—Locus*

"A very accomplished debut . . . [Rydill] vividly evokes texture and atmosphere. . . . I'd welcome more adventures involving the plucky Annat and her father."
　　　　　　　　　　　　　　　　　　　　—Starburst

"Haunting and elegant, this is a masterful first novel. An enchanting story blessed with genuine magic."
　—David Gemmell, author of *Ravenheart* and *Stormrider*

CHILDREN
of the
SHAMAN

Jessica Rydill

A ROC BOOK

ROC
Published by New American Library, a division of
Penguin Putnam Inc., 375 Hudson Street,
New York, New York 10014, U.S.A.
Penguin Books Ltd, 80 Strand,
London WC2R 0RL, England
Penguin Books Australia Ltd, 250 Camberwell Road,
Camberwell, Victoria 3124, Australia
Penguin Books Canada Ltd, 10 Alcorn Avenue,
Toronto, Ontario, Canada M4V 3B2
Penguin Books (N.Z.) Ltd, 182–190 Wairau Road,
Auckland 10, New Zealand

Penguin Books Ltd, Registered Offices:
Harmondsworth, Middlesex, England

Published by Roc, an imprint of New American Library,
a division of Penguin Putnam Inc.

First American Printing, February 2003
10 9 8 7 6 5 4 3 2 1

PUBLISHER'S NOTE
This is a work of fiction. Names, characters, places, and incidents either are the
products of the author's imagination or are used fictitiously, and any
resemblance to actual persons, living or dead, business establishments, events,
or locales is entirely coincidental.

For my parents, Eve and Louis

ACKNOWLEDGMENTS

Thanks to my editor, Tim Holman, for his wise words without which I doubt the manuscript would have seen the light of day. All my friends helped throughout the history of this project, especially Debbie, Gillian and Jonathan. I would like to thank my readers, David Coles and Annette Chaudet, who nobly read the drafts and offered their advice; and my erstwhile therapist, Deirdre Moylan.

Chapter 1

The steam coach with its terrible springing seemed to jolt over every bump and rut, rattling Annat's teeth. She was wedged between her aunt and the side of the carriage, but the window was so smeared with mud she could not see out. It was getting dark, and it would soon be time to kindle the oil lamp that swung from the roof. They must be about an hour from Masalyar. Except for the old woman sitting opposite, whose droning voice and complaints had been a refrain for much of the journey, the three of them were the only passengers. Her brother Malchik was leaning in the corner on the opposite side of Aunt Yuste, sleeping or pretending to sleep. Annat wriggled uncomfortably in the leather seat, drawing a glance from her aunt.

"It'll be the end of our civilisation, you mark me," said the old woman. She was not from their village, and the coach had picked her up about halfway to Masalyar.

"I wouldn't know. We are Wanderers," said Yuste, sounding out of patience. Annat focused on the old woman, waiting for her reaction.

"Are you so? Don't meet many of your kind out here. Most of 'em prefer to stay in the City."

Your kind. Annat put a fringe of her hair into her mouth. They always said that, the Doxoi. She did not need to ask if

the old woman were one. All the country people believed, all
the villages had their temple with its blue-gowned priest.
Where she came from, her family had been the only Wanderers. It was different in the City. Her people. Her kind.

"My father has a farm in Sankt-Eglis—he's the village doctor there," said Yuste.

The old woman's mouth chewed on nothing, as she thought
this over.

"I've heard of him. That would be the doctor Vasilyevich.
His wife had twins, I heard. And that's not all I heard—"

"I'm one of the twins," said Yuste, with a fleeting smile, interrupting the old woman before she could divulge the rumour.
Annat was disappointed.

"So you are," said the old woman, without embarrassment.
"And these must be your children."

"Not mine. My brother's. I'm taking them to meet him."

Annat looked out of the blind window. She could see a faint
reflection of her face, the delicate bones and pointed features,
her eyes two brown shadows. *They say I look like him.* She
knew that Malchik remembered their father, for he had been
five years old when *Tate* walked out of the family house, leaving them and their mother for ever. Malchik was cast in their
mother's likeness, slender and fair, except for his strange hazel
eyes with their flecks of green. He had the height of a tall man,
but his limbs were fine and delicate. Annat had always been
the one who liked to climb trees or the cliff, to swim and run—
but alone. She wondered what was in Malchik's mind as he
dozed in the corner of the carriage. Though she had known
him all her thirteen years, he was often an enigma to her. She
was so different. If there was something in her mind, she said
it. Perhaps that was another reason she had no friends of her
own age.

"And is he a doctor too, their father? I've heard that many
of your sort are doctors."

"Not a doctor. A healer."

The old woman's eyes were glass beads in the twilight.

"You mean a sorcerer," she snapped.

Yuste shook her head slowly. "No, I don't mean that," she
said.

The old woman's lips became a sour purse. She said no more, but took some knitting from the heavy bag beside her and took to muttering over purls and plains. Yuste turned to Annat and gave her a secret, mischievous smile.

Tate was a shaman, as Annat was. He would teach her healing when they were together. Annat felt the faint crackle of power as she flexed her fingers. Sometimes it was good that people thought you were a sorcerer. They were afraid of you, and they respected you. Other times it was bad. They threw stones after you in the street, and talked under their breath of burning.

Yuste clasped Annat's wrist with her warm, thin hand, as if she had read her mind. Perhaps she had. Yuste still had that one power left, though she had lost the others. When Annat met *Tate*, she would be able to talk to him silently, and he would answer; they called it *sprechen*. She would not be cut off and alone, a Wanderer and a shaman amongst people who did not understand or like either.

The last hour seemed the longest. At first, Annat thought that she was seeing a reflection of the oil lamp in the window pane, its image multiplied as it swung to and fro. Soon there were too many lights, some distant and far, like stars, others so close that they threw a warm glow into the carriage. They had street lamps in Masalyar, kept burning by the householders to make the streets safer, Yuste had told her. And now the story was becoming reality, and Annat was moving into the dream. They would meet their father, and he would take them far away into the north, through the country of bandits and Soul Men.

She clutched the hard wooden body of the doll to her chest. The doll had been her mother's, and her mother's mother's; it was old and smooth, though Yuste had made a new dress for it out of green silk when Annat was a little girl. When it had been time to pack, Annat had taken the doll and her *vyel* and a few clothes, white blouses, black skirts and black pinafores. The Doxoi had made a law that Wanderers must dress in two colors, black and brown, to remind them of their dirt and shame. White was allowed because it was no color. Yuste and Malchik both wore brown, but Annat preferred the crow-darkness of black, which made her face look pale and her eyes large.

For some time now, the thin tyres of the steam coach had been rattling over cobblestones, making a tinny melody. There were people in the street outside, the people of Masalyar, but Annat could not see their faces. Yuste unpinned the watch from her blouse to peer at its dial in the dim light.

"Ten of the clock," she said, in her dry voice. "We're late, of course."

Malchik twisted his head towards her, and the light flashed across his glasses.

"How much longer is it?" he asked sleepily.

Yuste leaned past him towards the window.

"I have no idea where we are," she commented. "The Central Station is quite near the port. We could be on the moon for all I can see."

Malchik gave a croaking laugh. His voice still sounded as though it had recently broken, for all his eighteen years. The old woman looked up from her knitting, sniffed, and raised the needles closer to her face. Annat saw the lines of Yuste's amusement. Her aunt was almost an old woman, thirty-six, and not married yet. Most girls in the village married when they were sixteen, straight from their dolls to the marriage bed. They called Yuste a spinster. When Annat had whispered this to her grandmother, *Bubbe* had shaken her head. It was not customary for Wanderers to marry so young.

Annat slipped her right thumb into her mouth, hoping that Yuste would not notice. There was a rough callus below the knuckle, she had been sucking it so long. She was not sure that she wanted to meet *Tate*. What was it that Malchik had whispered to her, last night after they had said their prayers? It had been unlike Malchik to tell her anything; if he wanted to confide in anyone, he chose Yuste or their grandparents. *You know he doesn't really want us. If he cared what happened to us, why did he never visit? It's not so far.* Annat had never asked herself such questions. She had grown up accepting her father's absence as part of the landscape, like a distant shadow on the horizon. There had been Yuste and *Bubbe* and *Zaide* and even *Mame*, though she had not showed much interest in

Annat. That had been the picture of Annat's family, sheltering together on the cliffs like storm-blown petrels.

The carriage jolted to a halt, almost throwing them into a heap on top of the old woman and her knitting. Yuste sank back in her seat, adjusting the pins that kept her brown velvet hat in place on her hair. Almost before Annat had recovered her breath, the driver wrenched open the door next to Malchik, who leaned out to see where they were. Then he jumped out of the carriage, moving with the eagerness of a small boy and his usual clumsiness. Once outside, he turned back to the coach to see whether Yuste would follow, but Annat was first, clutching her doll to her chest. The silver aura of the huge lights made her blink. They were in a vast shed, higher than the tallest barn, which seemed to stretch into infinite and promising darkness, marked with silver lamps. The shadows of the first trains that Annat had ever seen lurked in the distance, dwarfing even from there the steam coach with its long funnel; it was parked at its buffers next to the shallow platform where she had alighted. She turned on the spot, dazzled like a moth, focusing on the lamps until Yuste brushed past her.

Three men appeared. They moved towards Yuste and there was a moment of hesitation, of wordless pause, before the foremost clapped his hands together and bowed. Yuste mimicked him. Annat stared at this puppet show. She was seeing a new Yuste, one who was not just her aunt, but a woman whom strangers recognised and greeted. The first man was little, mostly bald, with bright eyes dark as wine and cheeks the color of old leather. This was Annat's first Darkman, from Ind, far in the east, and she knew his name: it was Sival, Yuste's teacher, whom she wrote to every week. They were embracing now, with the close lock of long-lost friends, ignoring the others, who eyed each other with cautious glances.

Annat stood apart from Malchik. Her stomach felt hollow and queasy-sweet, full of bird's wings. One of the two other men was her father, Yuda, Yuste's twin. The two men were dressed much alike, in City clothes; black jackets with the sheen of leather, open-necked shirts of fine cotton, not like the coarse stuff that Yuste bought from the village weaver to make Annat's blouses, and dark trousers cut close to the leg, very

different from a countryman's trews. She guessed which was
her father at once, for his companion was dark-skinned, tall,
and his shirt was red, a color forbidden to Wanderers. He was
gazing at Annat, almost smiling, but she had already fixed on
her father, so small, scarcely taller that Yuste. It was the image
of his shaman's power that marked him out to her inner eye, a
vivid, coruscating blue that dimmed Annat's own, uncertain
flame. She hardly saw his face before Yuste's warm hand took
hers and brought her to Sival. Her father waited at a distance
with his dark friend.

"Welcome to Masalyar, Annat and Malchik. You are tired,
and a little frightened. So are we. We have been waiting for
weeks to meet you."

"How do you know what I'm thinking? You're not a
shaman," said Annat.

"I told you she was rude," said Yuste.

Sival smiled at Annat, and she had to smile back. He was
little and leathery and full of a shy warmth that she might trust.

"I study people just as I study books. Their faces, their
movements tell a story. You are a shaman, I saw that at once."

Annat looked for her father. She was not afraid. Only that
strange feeling, like fluttering below her chest, that made her a
little breathless. *Speak*, she willed him, sending a message into
the silence.

—There is One in Zyon.

It was not a voice, but clear as black script on white paper: a
reply, which Yuste had never been able to give her.

Sival beckoned the two men.

"Here is your father, Yuda, and Shaka, his friend."

Both men wore their hair long, like women: Shaka's was
knotted into many plaits, bound at the back with a thong;
Yuda's was loose and smooth, like black feathers. Annat
leaned closer to Yuste, wishing she was young and small and
could bury her face in her aunt's clean-scented skirts. She felt
Yuste's arm encircle her shoulders.

"Hallo, Yuda," Yuste said, with a gentle wariness. She extended her free hand to Shaka, who bent to kiss it with a flowing gesture.

"You brought the *kinder* then," said Yuda, as if he had not yet noticed Annat or Malchik. His face was jet on ivory. Like *Zaide*, so dark and so pale, the face of a tall clock, who had looked down at Annat with sad-sweet eyes. Her father's eyes were not sad-sweet. His gaze on Yuste was dangerous: mocking and fierce and inscrutable. Annat relished the wildness from the safety of her aunt's embrace. It promised adventure, not the dull severity she had feared from Malchik's stories.

"I brought them up for you, Yuda. I wouldn't part with them now if I wasn't sick."

"By God, it's been so long," he said, and hugged her, somehow enveloping Annat. She smelled his jacket: *tabak* and leather. Yuste's body shook as she sobbed, once. Annat looked up, disentangling herself, at her aunt's half-seen face. It would be strange to feel so much for Malchik. She loved Yuste, *Bubbe* and *Zaide*; her brother was just there, mostly ignoring her. Annat observed how much grey was in Yuste's hair beside Yuda's. She wanted to stroke her aunt's hair, to gently pluck out the grey strands so that the brown crept back. Now Yuste was going away to be healed, and Annat must travel with her stranger-father to a place she had not heard of. Even her grandparents had agreed that it would be good for them to spend some time with Yuda, who had asked leave to take his children with him to his new posting.

"What do you think?" Yuste asked Yuda as they stepped apart. "They were so small when you left. Annat was only a baby."

"She hasn't grown much," he said, looking down at Annat. She glared back at him.

"I'm small like you."

"You hear that, Shaka? Small like me. Look at the other one; I hope he doesn't get any taller."

As Malchik blushed an angry color, Yuste held out her hand to beckon him closer.

"Malchik takes after his mother's side," she said, a remark that Annat knew to be fraught with hidden meaning. At home, their talk was full of these hints that were understood, not spoken, partly because Malchik was touchy, and partly for other reasons.

"I thought you'd have a beard," said Malchik, approaching with folded arms. He did not look his father in the eye.

"No beard, and too short. What did you tell them, Yuste?"

"I thought they should make up their own minds."

Sival interposed, with quick, fluttering hands. "You young people don't feel the cold, but my old bones are frozen. If you can wait until tomorrow to continue this, I will take Yuste and the children back to the *Shkola*. The train doesn't leave until mid of the day."

"The children should be in bed," said Yuste. "At home, they get up at dawn to do their farm work and say morning prayers."

"I'm not tired," said Annat.

"You look like a ghost. Besides, Sival is right. This isn't the place to talk. Are you coming back with us, Yuda?"

"It's a little early for my bedtime. I'll see Shaka home."

Shaka gave a smile of white teeth that made his face look boyish. Annat longed to touch his glossy skin to see what it felt like. Did he darken in the summer sun in the same way that she did? She would have liked to ask him, but was afraid that he would think her stupid. She did not want to admit that she had not met any Darkmen before. His forefathers must come from Morea, the great continent that lay below the Middle Sea. Annat wished that they were going to travel there, not north into the lands of cold and wildness.

Yuste was right; Annat was sleepy. She would have liked to draw in the sights and sounds of the City as they walked to Sival's house, the *Shkola*, through the streets, having left her father and Shaka with a promise to meet them there next morning, but all she saw were the dancing street lamps: cressets burning on street corners, rows of pale green gas lamps and, where the house owned a generator, the uncertain flickering of an electric bulb. In some of the streets were tram lines, and once a tram rattled past with a noise like a chain of milk carts, making a green flash across Annat's sight. The air was perfumed with the smell of soot from generators and stoves; it hung heavy in the yellowed mist, causing Annat's throat to feel sore. Once or twice the shadows of Doxan temples reared up unlit, except where there was a glow of candles from the long, slender windows. She could not see the stars above their spires.

The *Shkola* stood in a square off one of the main streets where sycamore trees grew slanting towards the cobbled space at the centre. There were no street lights here, but windows lighted rose and gold made rectangles of color like paper lanterns hung from the trees. The bells of a clock tower rang twelve notes as Sival unlocked the street door. Annat drifted drowsily up the stairs, there were so many. When Yuste had kissed her goodnight and the door was closed, she was left in a small room under the eaves where she would sleep alone for the first time. She put the doll on her pillow and lay down beside it fully clothed, staring at the white ceiling. Before she was quite asleep, the doll spoke to her.

Take care, Annat. There is danger waiting for you in the north. Danger for you and your brother.

Annat kept her eyes shut. She did not want to look at the doll for fear of silencing it.

What danger? she thought.

Let me go home. Return me to where I belong.

Annat sat up, convinced she had been dreaming. She looked down at the doll's worn face with its painted mouth. Something made of wood could not speak, yet she knew in her heart that it had.

Chapter 2

The smell of roasted *kava* drew Annat downstairs. Looking over the banisters, she saw the stairs spiral down to a floor of black and white tiles. This was the address to which Yuste had sent her letters for so many years. Barefoot, Annat walked over wood and marble in the thick white night-dress that she had put on in the middle of the night. Her home had only two storeys, and the loft, which she shared with Malchik. The walls were of roughly cut stone, and the kitchen floor was earth. This house with its painted doors and smooth wooden floors seemed rare and fantastic.

Two floors down, Annat found an open door shedding sunlight on to the landing. She entered a white room, clean as an egg, where Sival, dressed in a turquoise satin tunic and loose pantaloons, sat at a table laid for four. A white *kava* pot stood in the centre like the Crown Dish at the Journey feast: Annat was tempted to bow to it.

"Good morning," said Sival.

"There is One in Zyon," Annat responded.

Sival nodded. "One, and One only."

"Are you a Wanderer, Mister Sival? I thought you were a Darkman."

"Darkmen have their own religions, as different as Doxoi

are from Wanderers. I am no-faith. Sit down and have some of this delicious *kava*. I made it myself."

"Will there be food?" said Annat with hungry hope.

"Yuste has gone to the baker's. There is an excellent one close by."

"*Bubbe* makes our bread at home. She bakes a white loaf every Kingsday."

"Kingsday starts tomorrow, doesn't it? You'll be on the train."

"We'll have to get off."

"I don't think Yuda will allow that. The train stops for nothing, not even Kingsday, and he is the chief guard."

"You mean he breaks Kingsday?" said Annat, shocked. Yuste had taught her that all Wanderers, however lax, stopped work on their holy day.

"All the time," said Sival, with a solemn mouth, though his eyes laughed.

"We can't go, then. We'll have to stay here."

"I wish I could keep you here, but Yuste and Yuda have agreed. You have to understand that she doesn't want her sickness to affect you."

"Is she very ill?" said Annat.

"She fought with another shaman when she was a little younger than you, and was badly hurt. You know she lost her powers. Now some of the old injuries have become cancers. We don't know yet whether she can be healed."

Annat felt cold shock spreading through her veins. She did not want Sival, still a stranger, to see what she felt. "Why didn't she tell me?" she said.

"She thinks of you as a little girl, but I think you are strong enough to know the truth."

Annat stared at him as he poured the *kava* into a bowl for her. The thought of Yuste's death tasted like tin in her mouth, as if she were going to be sick. She took the bowl in both hands and said a blessing over it in *Ebreu*, the ancient language of the Wanderers. When she had finished, and set the steaming bowl on the table to cool before she drank it, Sival mused: "Yuda observes your faith in many ways, but he has had to adapt. You cannot live in the old way in this city. The

Doxoi here are tolerant of strangers, less strict than those who live outside Masalyar. Darkmen are friends with Lightmen. Your father even married a Doxan." His voice with its unfamiliar accent seemed like a balm offering comfort without speaking it aloud.

"He left *Mame*," stated Annat, staring at him. He had soft, almond-shaped eyes and long lashes.

"Are you angry with him, Annat?"

Annat shrugged. "Don't know. I'd rather stay with Yuste. I hope she gets back soon, I'm hungry."

She picked up the *kava* bowl and started to drink, conscious that Sival was watching her. He must think her stupid to talk so freely. Yuste called it babbling. She ought to behave like a young woman and be careful what she said to strangers. Yuste, whom Annat was leaving in the City alone.

"I want to go home," she said.

"You won't be away for long," said Sival. "Your father's posting only lasts six months. By the time you get back, Yuste should have recovered."

"Please don't tell her I said that."

"Trust me," said Sival. "When I left Ind to travel here on the boat, I was very scared. I thought all Lightmen were barbarians and I was afraid that the ship would sink. I can't swim, you see."

"Everyone can swim. *Mame* taught me to swim while I was still a baby. Even Malchik can swim, and he's useless."

She stopped, seeing Sival laughing silently. He covered his eyes.

"My dear girl. I think many people you meet will disappoint you. You must forgive us, we are all imperfect."

"Why?" Annat demanded, just as the sound of the street door shutting below announced Yuste's return. Annat sprang to her feet and ran for the stairs on light feet. She met Yuste halfway down and threw her arms about her, shopping and all.

"Don't die, *Tante*. Promise me you won't die."

Yuste cupped Annat's face in her smooth-skinned right hand.

"I don't intend to do so just yet, if the One wills. Help me carry the loaves. I bought some extra to make a meal for you and Malchik on the train. Yuda will surely forget."

Yuste had purchased a selection of crescent-shaped rolls still smelling of warm butter, a round loaf with a rough crust dusted with flour, and three long bread sticks. After the blessing, which seemed to last longer than usual, Annat finished two crescents before Yuste had wakened Malchik, who came down in his night-shirt, sleepy-eyed and cross. Annat wriggled in her seat, waiting for him to finish; he was always so slow, but Yuste expected her to sit at table until the closing prayers were said. Outside, the Doxan bells rang with a harsh, sweet note, announcing the first Gathering of the day. Annat remembered the temple at Sankt-Eglis, where a white haze of incense misted the image of the Mother, Megalmayar, cradling the dead man's body of her Son, who died on the Wheel. Painted tears ran down the Mother's face; the dark vaults were full of her silent weeping. On the walls, faded paintings told the story of the Wanderers' guilt. Annat shivered at the remembrance, or perhaps it was because a sudden draught of cool air in the room chilled her, as the street door banged downstairs. Yuste paused in her benedictions.

"Are you expecting visitors?" she asked Sival.

"Students come and go as they please, but it is a little early."

There were muffled sounds from the hall below, and a stifled masculine giggling.

"I hope they're not drunk," said Yuste.

"Sival! Is there any *kava*?" called a deep voice from below.

"It's Yuda," said Sival.

Malchik and Annat exchanged involuntary glances. Could that voice come from such a small man? There was the sound of bare feet on the stairs, then Yuda and Shaka made an exuberant entrance, bringing cold air and the smell of *tabak* on their clothes. Their looks were bright and fresh but conspicuously unshaven, and they wore yesterday's clothes. Shaka found a free chair, turned it and sat leaning on the back with folded arms; Yuda plucked another from a corner, sat down and placed his feet on the table.

"Yuda! You're abominable," said Yuste.

"Hallo," said Malchik, with a shy grin. It was his first sign of friendliness towards their estranged father.

"I'll make some more *kava*," said Sival, with emphatic resignation, and disappeared from the room with the *kava* pot.

"Thanks, Teacher," called Shaka, smiling his perfect white smile.

Yuda picked up a small spoon and struck a ringing note from an empty bowl.

"I see you're all ready to go," he observed.

"Zyon, Yuda! The train doesn't leave till mid of the day. I wanted to show the children a little of Masalyar."

"It can wait. Shaka's driving the early train. We'll get there on the morn of Kingsday, and the *kinder* can observe it—if they want."

"I suppose that's good. I thought there would be more time . . ."

"I'd heal you myself if Sival would let me. After all, I screwed things up for you in the first place—"

"Please, Yuda, the children—"

"They'll get used to it."

"I don't want them coming back talking like brigands or— or loose women."

"That'll be tough for Malchik."

Annat gave a laugh that was partly a hiccup and covered her mouth with a guilty hand. It was strange the way that Shaka and Yuda had filled the room with a warm maleness that she had not encountered before. They were as cheeky as some of the boys Yuste taught at home, who she found too amusing to punish, at least with any strictness.

"I hope I'm doing the right thing," said Yuste, shaking her head.

"You've made them too mimsy, Yuste. They need to run wild a little."

"That's not what Annat needs."

Yuda glanced at Annat. He had extraordinary eyes: pitch-black, a little slanted, and ferociously bright. Annat swallowed. He wasn't even the slightest bit safe. She did not know whether she was going to like him.

"I mean in wild places, where they don't have to watch what they do for fear of offending the Doxoi."

"Gard Ademar is a Doxan settlement. Most of the inhabitants must be Franj. It doesn't sound so different from home."

"I don't think it has much in common with Sankt-Eglis. It's a frontier town on the edge of our maps. The Railway only reached the settlement a few years ago, and the people there had never seen a train before. Between the river Kron and the big mountains to the east lies a forest that no one has explored since the Thaw. The Forest of Ademar."

As Annat sat up, startled to recognise the name, Yuste said, "I wish you had chosen a posting nearer to Masalyar. There must be plenty in towns in want of a healer."

"Not many towns have Sergey Govorin as their Sheriff. He asked for me. And it sounds as though there'll be plenty of work."

"Yuda likes trouble," said Shaka.

"Trouble likes him," Yuste retorted.

"It won't affect the *kinder*. The village is miles from the tunnel, and it's there that most of the deaths have happened. But I'm going to be working as a doctor, not a guard, *meine schvester*!" and he grinned at Yuste.

Annat and Malchik stared at each other. Yuste had never mentioned why their father had chosen to go to Gard Ademar, only that they would accompany him on his posting, so they could get to know him. Annat had been expecting boredom and embarrassment as a stranger tried to pretend that he cared about them.

"Who died?" she said, leaning forward across the table.

Before anyone could answer, Sival returned with the *kava* pot.

"I see you've made yourself comfortable, Yuda," he said, placing it in the middle of the table. Her father swung his feet down.

"I was just telling them about the mission, Teacher," he said, with a sheepish grin.

"Railway business," said Sival, raising his eyebrows. "How goes the five-year plan?"

Shaka snorted, and Yuda said, "That's a joke, Siv. Nearly

three years building the tunnel. We're already way behind schedule."

Yuste leaned forward. "You could at least explain to the *kinder*, since they will be living there."

Yuda glanced at his sister. "You wanted to show 'em Masalyar. Why not just take them to a Railway committee meeting?"

"You know perfectly well what I mean, Yuda!"

Shaka opened his mouth in a slow smile. "I'm sorry, Missis, but every member of the Railway People has had the five-year plan rammed down their throats. Any idealism we had in the beginning wore off long ago."

Sival sighed, resuming his seat. "I believe the idea was to build the Railway north into the interior, to link Masalyar first to Yonar, and thence to Priyar, the old lost capital. A worthy dream, save that no embassy from this city has ever visited Yonar, let alone Priyar. No one really knows what lies north of the Forest of Ademar; all that territory was cut off during the Great Cold."

"He's right," said Yuda. "They're building the big tunnel to cut beneath the forest. Nice work if you can get it. Steady employment. Three large meals a day."

"Yuda, are you drunk?" said Yuste.

Shaka chuckled. "We spent the night down at the docks."

"They gave me a good send-off. One of the boys was in tears."

"Very nice," said Shaka. "Smudged his paint."

"Madam is jealous," said Yuda, pouring two bowls of *kava*. There was no response. He looked up. "What? Have I said something wrong?"

Yuste had put her hands over her ears.

"She is rather devout," said Sival.

"So am I. She overdoes it. You mean, she hasn't told the *kinder* I'm a *divko*?"

"I would doubt it," said Sival. "The law of the Wanderers forbids it."

"Remind me," sneered Yuda. "Half of the old men leave the *Beit* when I go to pray."

"You'd better tell them yourself."

"Tell them like how? That I screw men?"

Sival winced. "Concise, but offensive."

"What does he mean?" said Annat, who could not help enjoying her aunt's confusion.

"Good grief," said Malchik, turning rosy from neck to forehead.

"The boy understands," said Yuda to Shaka.

Annat was disappointed that no one troubled to explain this shocking secret to her. She would have to question Malchik about it afterwards.

"Have you finished?" said Yuste, lowering her hands. Yuda gave her a sly and dimpled smile.

"You should have told them. Saves trouble later."

"I didn't want Zaide to find out. You know it would break his heart."

"I did that already when I married a Doxan," said Yuda, losing his smile.

"Listen to me," said Sival. "It could not hurt the children to know that you love Shaka. The rest is irrelevant."

"But very enjoyable."

"I am thirteen," said Annat, sitting up straight in her chair.

"More like three," said Yuda. "Catch," and he threw her a folded bundle of black cloth. It was a pair of loose trews like the ones Sival wore, with a drawstring waist, but cut to fit someone Annat's size. She held them high in surprise.

"What are these for?"

"You'll wear them on the train. Better than a skirt."

"She's not wearing those," said Yuste.

"I like them," Annat protested.

"She'd better, unless you want the whole train seeing her knickers."

"Who's to see her knickers?" said Yuste.

"All the women guards wear trousers. It's more practical."

"That's different. They ride outside."

"So will the kinder. They're not going as passengers."

Annat clasped the trews to her chest. She was afraid to tell her father that Malchik would never be able to ride on top of the train. She wished he would speak up for himself, or there was sure to be trouble later on. Yuda used the word 'passengers' with contempt.

"Surely it's too dangerous," said Yuste.

"I'm not expecting trouble this run," said Shaka. "The bandits mainly attack in the summer months. Soul Men are more of a problem, but Yuda is a match for most of them. Some of the other guards are shamans as well."

"I don't like it," said Yuste.

"Leave the worrying to me," said Yuda. "I've been doing this run for ten years."

"Run along then, children," said Yuste. "Get dressed quickly. We don't have much time," in a voice that suggested she would continue the argument in their absence.

When Annat was dressed and packed, wearing her odd new leggings under her skirt as a concession to Yuste, she met Malchik on the landing, with the swathed shape of his harp like a hump on his shoulder. An uncustomary warmth towards him made her shy, though she did not want him to see it.

"Are you scared?" he said, and his defiant tone told Annat that he was.

"No," she said, for what she felt was less simple than fear; fear would have been easier to ignore.

"Nor am I. He acts very hard, but there's nothing behind it. He's just a bully."

"He's weird," said Annat, anxious to be noncommittal for her brother's sake. She rather liked what she had seen of her father, who had found the time to get those leggings for her; they fitted quite well.

Malchik seemed unsatisfied by her response, as if he had wanted her to agree with his statement without reservation. "You don't remember how he treated *Mame*," he challenged.

Annat resented at once the familiar insistence that she accept Malchik's hagiography of their mother's life. His unquestioned version of events had irked her ever since she became aware that it was not the only truth. She shrugged her body into angry, bony stiffness, much like a cat on guard.

"Yuste says *Mame* drove him away," she said.

"She killed herself."

"So what? It wasn't all his fault she was a bit mad."

"She went mad because he left."

"I think he left because she was mad."

They glowered at each other without any real animosity; Annat knew she would not convince her brother, she was not even sure that she believed what she said herself, but it was important not to give in. "It's only for six months," she found herself saying, as if she were Yuste being sensible. "He probably won't bother us much."

Their aunt called them downstairs. Yuda and Shaka had already left for the station, and they had to hurry. It was coldly bright in the city streets, and the tram-lines were silver like a sword. Plane trees curled upwards, shedding bark and round seed clusters, and the sidewalks were deep in leaves. The City was full of stuccoed walls, grey or saffron, and the shuttered windows cloistered the buildings from the street outside. Passers-by did not greet them or seem to see them, and Annat wondered how many strangers there could be living here. Their clothes were not homespun, with the lumpy seams that marred garments made by her aunt or grandmother. Though the colors were plain, grey, dark blue, or brown without warmth, the occasional woman wore a skirt cut off at the knee, which the village elders at home would not have permitted. Yuste in her ankle-length brown skirts looked a little dowdy and out of place. It was not even possible to tell who were Doxoi and who Wanderers. The citizens hurried past, in their unfriendly, dreaming worlds, seemingly unaware of the wild freedom and lawlessness that their conduct implied. How could they not realize how lucky they were to live in a place where no one cared who you were, where no one frowned at your obligatory black clothes or muttered half-heard curses when you went by?

The station loomed above the surrounding houses, its arched roofs grey as clouds against the blue sky. Having only seen it in the dark, Annat was surprised at the sculpted elegance of the high vaults, taller than the tower of a Doxan temple. Smoke and steam from the hidden trains escaped lazily through the vents, drifting away towards the sea. Gulls circled and shrieked over the square before the entrance hall, diving for scraps and crusts and fighting the pigeons which surprised Annat with their grimy feathers and crippled feet. They looked as if they had been fashioned out of rags and wire. Amongst them limped a couple of crows, which seemed to watch her with their clever eyes. Their blackness was like a hole in the sunlight.

She became aware of her heartbeat as they approached the high entrance with its carved portico of over-large statues flinging themselves away from the heaped stone weapons and the erased armorial shield at the centre. The City had once been part of a great country called Neustria, an empire ruled by the Franj before it fragmented into city states and palatinates; even at home, Yuste was obliged to mention Neustria in her history lessons. Annat did not much like these stone reminders of an imperial past. That empire had made the laws marking the Wanderers out by their costume and restricting the work they could do.

Yuda came walking out of the great double doors with their huge glass panels which no glazier could make today, and Annat noticed that, in spite of his slight build, he walked with an assurance and grace that contrasted with the stance of the other men loitering in the piazza, who were mostly taller than him. This quality intrigued her, for she had not noticed it in a man before, especially not in Malchik or *Zaide*, who tended to fade into the background. To be invisible was a useful trick for a Wanderer, especially a man, for instance when the Doxoi chose to commemorate the Son's death too enthusiastically. Perhaps because *Zaide* was a doctor, they had not been harmed, but they had heard of other families driven from their homes, even killed. Yuda held himself with the confidence of someone who had no need to hide.

"Where's Shaka?" said Yuste.

"Cosseting his engine, as usual. I'm only the second love of his life. He doesn't trust the firers with it, even his usual mate."

"I'm leaving the children with you now, Yuda. It won't help them or me if I stand on the platform weeping and waving my hanky."

"What a picture! I don't see you doing that, Yuste."

He put his arms round her and gave her a forceful hug, which seemed to leave Yuste a little winded.

"I don't expect you to write, but ask the children to drop me a line sometimes."

"I will," said Annat at once. Yuste stooped to kiss her, and her tears wet Annat's cheek. "A long goodbye is a bad idea, Natka. Write soon."

When Malchik had been duly embraced, they accompanied their father into the station, from quiet into noise, Annat hugging the doll's hard figure to her chest, trying to crush the sadness inside her. Yuda walked quickly, without looking back, but Malchik kept glancing behind him at the place where their aunt stood, a small, neat figure, holding her hat in place with one hand.

Inside Annat was plunged into a roil of smoke, tarry smells and loud echoing voices. She had to hurry to keep pace with Yuda, to avoid losing him in the crowd, where people rushed and shoved in opposite directions. Yuda became aware of her discomfort and scooped her against him with an arm round her shoulders. The crowd certainly cleared a way for *him*. Malchik followed them with long strides.

"Aren't you a bit old for dolls?" said Yuda, observing Annat's small bundle.

"*Mame* gave it to me. Anyway, it isn't just a doll. It talks to me."

"And I'm the Empress of Neustria," was his comment.

The tall engine with its sooty column appeared, shining with oil and black as grime, not like the pictures Annat had seen in her books. It had a rank smell, like a tomcat. Shaka, who was leaning out of the cab, wearing red dungarees, already smeared with oil, over a blue shirt, waved as he saw them appear out of the thinning crowd. There were fewer passengers at this end of the platform.

"I see you're childrened up, Vasilyevich," he called.

"Give me a kiss, you fat bastard," said Yuda, climbing on to the footplate for the purpose. Annat and Malchik watched with the curiosity of botanists discovering a new *phylum*. "What are you staring at?" growled their father.

"I don't reckon they've seen many men snogging back home in Sankt-Eglis."

"You two, get up on top. It's the first wagon behind the ten-

der. You can put your bags in the guards' van." When they did
not move, he added, "Move yourselves. We'll be leaving
soon."

Annat turned away to look up at Malchik. She could tell
from his face that he had not believed they would truly have to
ride on top of the train. It was difficult to argue with their father, who was clearly used to being obeyed. She feared that if
they hesitated any longer, he would lose his temper, making it
even harder to explain.

"Malchik can't—"

"I can't—"

Yuda gave a small, impatient sigh. He was leaning comfortably against Shaka, who prompted them. "Speak up, *kinder*.
We won't even eat you."

"Sir, it's just that I can't, I haven't got a head for heights. I'll
have to ride inside."

"What, like a bloody passenger?" said Yuda. Shaka whispered in his ear. "All right. There isn't time to argue. But don't
forget you're a guard's son, and a man. I don't want any other
nonsense from you."

"You see what I mean?" hissed Malchik, as they hurried
back along the train to the guards' van. Annat stopped in her
tracks.

"You could just try," she said.

"Give me your pack, I'll put it in a safe place for you. You
ought to come inside with me. He can't force us to ride on the
outside. If we both do it, it won't seem so bad."

"But he got me the trousers!"

Before Malchik could reply, a whistle blew, and they both
ran off frantically in opposite directions, Malchik towards the
rear, and Annat to the front of the train.

Chapter 3

But it was a train on the opposite platform that pulled out. The carriages were painted a garish red, and there were no guards on the roof. The crowd on the platform cheered, and some threw carnations at the departing train. Annat sagged against the nearest wagon of her own train. She felt as if someone had played a trick on her. At least Malchik would have time to discover the guards' van, stow their bags and find himself a seat on board. Judging by the number of passengers leaning out of the open upper windows and smoking, the train was already pretty full. A man with brown eyebrows and a brown moustache leered at her as he drew on his cheroot. Annat slouched sullenly back towards her father's carriage, hands in the pockets of her black coat, wondering what his fellow guards would be like.

Three figures sat cross-legged on the roof, wearing what seemed to be a uniform of baggy camel coats, thick beige cloaks or ponchos, and grey trousers. Long guns of green metal were propped on their knees. Two of them wore hats cut from thick, dun-colored felt; the third was bald except for a tattoo which showed a man and woman in athletic copulation.

"Hallo, little girl," said the bald man in a deep voice. His face was very pink, like a pig's snout, and his lips were thick and rubbery. In contrast, his eyes looked surprisingly blue, with no lashes.

"Hallo," said Annat warily.

"Have you lost your mum and dad?" said one of the two hat-wearers. He was much younger, perhaps no older than Annat, and his smile squeezed his eyes into thin, vanishing lines. Wisps of curly brown hair protruded from under his hat.

"Not recently," said Annat; she did not want to be too obliging.

The third guard laughed, a woman's laugh, comfortable and rich. Annat stared at her in astonishment. A square, smooth jaw, blunt nose, small grey-green eyes; her head was shaven under the hat. Just as Annat had never seen men wearing their hair long until she met Shaka and Yuda, so she had never seen a woman with short hair, let alone a bald one. Her mouth dropped open and she stared, forgetting to pretend to be city-wise.

"You must be one of the Chief's *kinder*," said the young man.

"Nah. Chief doesn't have *kinder*. He couldn't do it with a woman," said the bald man.

The youth snickered. "He doesn't know which end of a woman is which," he said.

"I'm Yuda Vasilyevich's daughter," said Annat, indignant.

"Miracles do happen. Praise the Son!" intoned the bald man, with mock piety.

"Leave her alone, Pyotr," said the woman. She leaned down from the roof and reached out a long, bony hand to Annat, who took it and clambered easily up the side. The roof of the carriage was wide and flat. She sat down amongst the three guards, who made room for her.

"Looks like him, doesn't she, Lyude?" said Pyotr. "She's got the nose."

"Ooh, yes, she's got the nose. And the eyebrows. Even a moustache, which is more than he's got."

Annat's hand flew to her upper lip. She was rather hairy, but it was a soft down, though dark.

"At least I've got hair," she snapped.

The bald man twinkled at her. "You'll have a fine beard when you're older, darlin'," he said.

"Honey," said the woman, "they're full of shit. This is Scorpion telling you. If you listened to half the things they said your brain would drop out of your ears."

"Hers dropped out long ago," said Lyude.

"Not just her brain," said Pyotr.

Annat was saved from further confusion by her father, who arrived from the direction of the engine, having climbed over the tender. Annat noticed that, though he wore a knife at his belt, he carried no other weapons. He smiled at her as if he had overheard some of what had passed before he arrived, and she knew with unexpected certainty that he had. His mind was not closed to her as others' were; if he willed it, she could share his thoughts. He crouched down beside her with the conscious ease of a feral cat.

"I see you're making my daughter feel at home, lads," he said. Annat understood that he had sensed her chagrin as clearly as she had read his mind. She had not learned how to cover her emotions; she had not needed to at home, where she was the only active shaman.

"We treat her like one of us, Chief," said Pyotr, with a grin.

"The loco is chafing at the throttle. I've given the signal to go when the road is clear."

As he spoke, someone on the platform bellowed, "All aboard!" There was a panicked rush as those who were trying to leave the train fought those who wanted to board at the last minute. There was much scuffling and throwing of suitcases through open windows; Annat saw a terrified chicken fluttering down the platform towards the exit until the old woman who owned it caught it nimbly by the tail feathers and stuffed it up her jumper.

Yuda stood up and signalled with his hand to the unseen ground staff. Someone blew the whistle, and the train started to pull out of the station under a hail of carnations. Women ululated, men lifted children over their heads to see the spectacle, and there was a strange atmosphere redolent of both a festival and a funeral.

Annat picked up a red carnation.

"Why do they do that?" she asked Scorpion.

"Because no one knows whether we'll reach our destination alive. Last year a train was raided north of Axar and no one survived—except those who were taken as slaves. We all lost mates on that run. But that train was less heavily guarded than this and they had no shamans on board."

"Is Gard Ademar north of Axar?"

"About as far as it can be. Gard Ademar is the northern terminus. It's wild country up there. No one has explored it since the years of the Great Cold."

Yuda was sitting down once more, smoking *tabak* and talking to Lyude and Pyotr. After a moment of sunlight, thin as silver leaf, as they left the station, the train plunged into long tunnels where lights flashed and klaxons sounded. There was a rank smell of soot and oil, and grit stung Annat's face and caught in her hair. She was relieved when Scorpion swept her cloak over her head, protecting her from the worst of the smoke. She clung to the roof, losing sight of herself amidst the echoing sounds, the roiling, bitter smoke and stench of tar. The train was alive! She felt the carriage juddering beneath her as it jerked its way over the points, and for a moment she wished that she had followed Malchik to nestle in the warm safety of the carriages.

When they emerged from the tunnels, the fresh sun cut sharp as a sword. Scorpion pulled back her cloak, and Annat felt the wind lashing her face and driving back her hair. She gasped, wiping stinging grit from her eyes, and saw the tall plume of steam that rose from the smokestack and gushed back over their heads, like the pall of cloud that the One threw over the Wanderers to protect them in the wilderness. Annat gazed up at its colors, the pale and swirling greys, and felt real tears. She was Eliahu, swept up to Paradise in the fiery chariot; she was the Maiden sitting astride the Dragon's back, riding beneath the stars. She was hardly aware of her companions; the moment was for her alone, borne in triumph from the darkness of the tunnel into the brilliant day.

Beneath her, the carriage rocked more gently. In spite of the wind that seemed to pluck at her, trying to brush her into the air like a cow's tail flicking at insects, her fear had gone; she found herself laughing breathlessly, and pitying her brother who had chosen to stay below, cramped in the smoky, stuffy interior. Leaning on Scorpion without asking permission, she struggled to her feet, and let the full force of the head-wind drive against her, streaming out her hair like a comet's tail. It was cold! She shivered, spreading her arms to aid her balance, and wished she were alone, without a small audience that seemed to find her joy amusing. They were sitting together in a huddle, but Scorpion glanced up at her and smiled, and Yuda looked pleased.

The vine harvest was going on in the fields outside Masalyar; Annat saw grey donkeys like snails under their panniers loaded with fruit. Away to the left, the Kron river spread out in a lazy blue yawn. Annat could make out the slow barges drifting upstream, their saffron lateen sails unfurled to catch the breeze. Ahead, the engine's bulk moved beneath the whirling vortex of smoke, effortlessly swallowing up the silver-grey tracks. To her right, the golden slopes of great hills studded with rock bounded upwards, slipping away even as she tried to study them. She sat down next to Scorpion, wiping her runny nose and shivering.

"Is it far to Axar?" she asked.

"We'll be there at sundown. I'd sleep now, if you can, girl. This part of the run is dull, but it's also safe. You won't get much rest tonight."

Annat could hardly believe that Scorpion thought the journey dull, when there was so much to see in the landscape, as ramshackle villages sped past, their red roofs glowing in the morning sun, and spindly temples held up glinting gold weathervanes. But she remembered something important. "Malchik's got my lunch," she said.

"Never mind. There's a galley in the guards' van."

Annat wrinkled her nose. "Is it Clean?"

"The cook's a Wanderer. Your dad saw to that when he was made Chief. Before that, he lived on sunfruit and apples."

"And in winter he ate salt and turds," interjected Lyude.

"And was grateful for it," said Pyotr. "You Wanderers have been getting your own way too much. Having it soft."

"He misses his pork," said Lyude.

"He is pork," said Scorpion.

Annat saw Yuda relax. There had been just a moment of danger, when banter exposed something like hatred. *Never trust a Doxan, Bubbe* had said. Now Pyotr was grunting like a wild boar digging for truffles while Lyude made suggestions about where to put the apple sauce. No Wanderer, however lax, would eat pig, even if it meant starving. The prophets and prophetesses had declared that pigs still had a fragment of the soul that the One had put into all animals at the Beginning; their squeals were like the screams of a human child. Annat had heard of martyrs who took their lives after being forced to eat the unclean meat.

She settled down beside Scorpion, with no intention of sleeping. Every moment, every sight was new, and she wanted to remember and record them, each flash of color as they passed washing spread out to dry on bushes, each surge of movement as startled horses galloped away from the coming of the train. She wondered how anyone could be bored when there was so much to see and savour; but they had not lived all their lives, thirteen long years, in Sankt-Eglis, with its slow oxen-carts and too-well-known green fields.

Yuda took Annat to the guards' van around mid of the day. As Annat thought of her aunt, eating alone with Sival in that big house, the buffeting of the wind seemed like cruel hands dragging her away from everything she knew. She walked behind Yuda, her arms stretched out to keep her balance, as he strolled back towards the tail of the train, pausing to exchange a few words with the guards on each carriage. When he came to the narrow gap between the cars he jumped it. Annat hesitated before following him in an ungainly, panicked leap, and he caught her. She felt the strength of his arms as he set her down, laughing. Annat fidgeted the hair out of her face, glaring up at him.

"You'll get used to it," he said, without remorse. "You've got good balance."

Annat's legs felt like soft jelly after that first jump, but she would not let him see that she had been frightened. She ran ahead to the next gap and took a flying leap, landing asprawl on her hands and knees. By the time they reached the guards' van at the end of the train, she was breathless and aching. Her hands were numb with cold on the metal rungs of the ladder that clung to the side of the wooden van. Yuda opened the door and stepped inside, and Annat found herself in a warm, crowded space, badly lit and thick with the smell of food. Most of the guards inside were standing, leaning against the walls, balancing their plates on a shelf that ran along one wall. At the far end, a small door gave access to the privy.

Yuda introduced Annat to the cook, a woman in Wanderers' black and white, her hair covered with a white bonnet. She served them with mugs of strong black *chai* and plates loaded with green lentils cooked in onions. It was too noisy in the wagon for them to talk out loud, but as they sat on the packing cases near the stove Annat discovered that they could converse in silence. She was a little surprised when Yuda spoke a blessing over the food before touching it. The next moment, her father's thought invaded her mind, the alien words slipping neatly in amongst her own reflections.

—*I may not be as pious as Yuste, but I haven't forgotten myself.* He sipped his *chai.*

—*Will you keep Kingsday?* Annat found her own thought unwieldy, like a shout, and saw him wince.

—*I hear you, girl. I'm having to shut your thoughts out. You've got no control. I'll keep it if I can. That depends how the run goes after Axar. We may be too busy.*

—*I'm not scared.*

—*That's because you don't know what danger is. If the boy thinks it's safer inside the train, he's wrong. They can get inside.*

—*Won't I get in the way if there's a fight?*

—*You'd better not.*

He put his plate back on the counter half-finished. Annat, who found the food delicious, went on eating. He watched her, and once again she felt the cautious voice in her mind, like an echo that she alone could hear.

—*What do you think of me, Annat?*

—*Don't know. I thought you'd be like* Zaide.

—If I were like him, I wouldn't have run away.

Annat shrugged. She had not missed him because she had not known him. *Zaide* had supplied the place of a father, though he had always been a little distant and awesome, preoccupied with his faith and his work.

—I can't believe you're my kind. You were nothing when I left. You could barely sit up.

"Can I have some more?" said Annat aloud, blocking his thoughts.

"You can finish mine."

"Why don't you want it?"

—I don't each much when I'm on the road. I get the fear and it makes me queasy.

—You don't seem scared.

—There's nothing to be scared of—yet. Have you ever seen anyone attacked by a shaman? They can get internal burns. If they're lucky, they'll die in a few minutes, screaming in agony. There's no time to help them, you're too busy fighting. No sane shaman would make an attack like that, but Soul Men aren't sane. If one of them gets the driver, the whole train is dead. They'll kill children, animals, everyone.

—You've seen it, haven't you?

Annat glimpsed the image in his mind of the scene that had haunted him since he was a young man: bodies sprawled by the track in the cold daylight, fallen in the twisted shapes of the poisoned; and the faces, black with the dried blood that had spilled from eyes, nose and mouth.

—I wasn't a guard then, just a healer. Part of a team that was sent to look for survivors. The train was a burnt-out shell.

—Why do they do it?

—One Soul Man isn't so bad. He's just a shaman whose mind has gone. But some of them wander out into the wild, and they're drawn together. They become a gestalt—one sick mass mind. They may have a leader; not mad, but someone with no moral restraints, no feelings. He'll control the others, stop them killing each other. Yuda lit a cigarette and drew on it between sips of *chai.—Yuste will kill me if I let anything happen to you,* he added.

—We're old enough to look after ourselves.

—Not Malchik. Zaide has made him fit for nothing but scholarship. You've got potential. The Scorpion looked you over, and she thinks you'll be powerful some day.

"What do you mean? How does she know?" said Annat aloud.

—She's one of us. A shaman so strong she can hide it from the others. She could look into your mind without you knowing. It's a dangerous power, though she doesn't abuse it.

—Why's she got a gun?

—We don't use our powers unless we have to. Not even on bandits. The other guards can deal with them. You don't keep a dog and bark.

—Malchik doesn't like you.

Annat found the thought forming in her mind before she could stop it. Her father made a small, wry gesture with his hand.

—I haven't given him much cause to like me.

—What do you mean?

—That's between him and me.

He shut her out adroitly. Annat watched him stub out his cigarette in one of the canteen's polished metal ashtrays.

"Thanks, Rosa," he said to the cook, and Annat saw her half-hidden look, soft and dog-like. It suggested an unconditional and unrecognised devotion which Annat did not understand. She had seen nothing in him that could deserve it.

She followed him back down the train in thoughtful mood. She had not been forced to wonder about any of the adults who surrounded her before. At home, there had been secrets and strange emotions, but they had all been familiar. Yuda was turning out to be a mystery, a map on which a few clear landmarks only emphasized the tracts of unexplored territory. Annat wanted to find out why the cook had looked at him so strangely. The woman wore a coif covering her hair, which meant she must be married. A married woman should not look at anyone but her husband. Rosa must know that there was no hope of Yuda noticing her when he was so open about being a . . . *divko.*

Yuda turned back to her, mischief in his eyes. He had overheard her thoughts.

—You're thirteen, and Yuste hasn't told you? All shamans are alike. You too. We can choose men and women.

—Not me. It's a sin.

"Sweet thirteen and never been kissed," he mocked her.

"Shut up."

"Show some respect to your father."

Annat jumped the gap towards him in a temper, almost missing her footing, and had the breath knocked out of her as he caught her. They were back on the leading coach where Scorpion, Lyude and Pyotr lounged, smoking and passing the cigarette between them. They ignored Annat's ungainly arrival.

"Put me down!"

Scorpion glanced up at them, and shook her head.

"It's not fair. I can't hear what you're thinking unless you let me," said Annat.

"You'll have to learn how to shut him out, *kind*. You don't want your father eavesdropping on everything you think."

"I can hardly avoid it," said Yuda. "She's so quiet she might as well be shouting into a loud-hailer."

"I'm glad he can't hear my thoughts," said Pyotr with a lewd grin.

"You don't have any thoughts," said Scorpion.

"Food and sex," said Lyude.

"That's not thinking. A pig has more intellect," said Scorpion.

Yuda sat down amongst them and dipped in his pocket to bring out a handful of jacks.

"You playing?" he asked Annat, who was still standing with folded arms, buffeted by the head-wind.

"No."

He grinned, and took the shared cigarette from Pyotr.

"Let me know if you change your mind."

Annat sat down cross-legged with her back to them. She could not stop herself thinking, and she could not figure out how to keep her thoughts private. She glowered at the scenery, the smooth blue skin of the Kron river and the water meadows, dull green, where the track meandered. Villages swept past, and ruined castles; herds of horned cattle with brown pelts grazed in the fields; Doxan shrines with images of the Mother dotted the trackside. The rhythm of the train was a rocking cradle, and Annat let her mind wander into dreams.

A world of snow. The sky was shimmering white, but sealed like a lid; the opalescent ground stretched into the distance, yet Annat sensed that the horizon was nearer than it seemed. The whole place could have been tucked into a cupboard drawer, or stored inside a child's music-box. And yet, at the same time, it was infinite, its boundaries stretching beyond time. Annat shivered as its chill drew in upon her, curling around her limbs like fingers of mist. Her own breath misted in slow clouds before her face, and she kept utterly still, knowing that the Genius of the place was poring over her as if she were a book, searching for the secret words that would spill out her weakness . . .

Annat's head jerked up.

"Sleep well?" asked Yuda.

It was dusk. Small hurricane lamps were alight down the length of the train's roof, giving out a pale, glow-worm light.

"I had a shaman's dream," said Annat.

"Tell it to me later. We're coming into Axar. When we stop, I want you to find Malchik and tell him to go to the guards' van. I'll meet you back at the engine in half an hour."

"Okay, Mister," said Annat, subdued by the dream.

"Don't let it worry you," said Yuda. "I've stopped bothering about my dark dreams. The future isn't fixed."

"It saw me," said Annat. He took her forlorn hand.

"As long as you've got me, girl, I won't let anything happen to you."

"That's quite a promise," said Scorpion.

The train was pulling into the dark streets of Axar. Spires and domes loomed blue against the tinted sky like shadows on a rose window. The locomotive blew a column of sparks and steam as it barged between the crooked houses. Metal magic, it rolled easily on the dim quicksilver of the tracks, its pistons pounding like the valves of a huge heart. There was a rhythm in the beat, a rhythm you could dance to, stamping your feet. They passed under the shadow of the Dom where the Doxoi worshipped, its pinnacles carved from solid night. Scents drifted in, of sewers and incense and baking. Then the station engulfed them with its white arc lights, and the pounding of the train became a hollow throbbing that echoed from the vaults. The locomotive braked smoothly in an expulsion of white steam, and the carriages bumped gently together as their brakes cut in.

"Half an hour," Yuda said to Annat, and sprang lightly down to the platform, landing in a crouch. As he headed for the rear of the train, Annat slipped over the edge and let herself drop to the ground. There were lamps lit inside the carriages. The dismounting travellers jostled her as they unloaded their bags. Annat wandered along the train, peering in through the yellow-lighted windows. Faces looked out at her, wan as corpses in the pale light. *Half an hour*, she repeated to herself. Malchik might be hidden on the other side of the train, packed into the corridor. She did not want to go in there and wriggle through that hot, stuffy space crammed with *tabak* smoke and bodies. She stood on tiptoe, peering through the panes at the lucky ones who had found a seat in the compartments, until she glimpsed her brother's face pressed against a carriage door. Seeing her, he opened it and all but fell out on to the platform.

"*Tate* says you're to go to the guards' van," she said.

"Why?"

"Because it's safer in there. I expect it would be more comfortable too."

"That's very thoughtful of him."

"He's worried, Malchik, I can tell. And it's quite nice in there, the food's good, only there aren't any windows."

"Okay. It's awful in the carriage. I had to sit in the corridor, and people tread on you all the time. Someone tried to give me a sausage."

"I suppose they meant to be kind," said Annat, swallowing a giggle.

"I had to hide it in my pocket. I dropped it down the privy when no one was looking."

"You ought to come up on top."

"No thanks. I'll see you later. Wait—I'll give you some of the food."

"Keep it," said Annat, who was still full of lentils.

When she climbed back on to the first wagon, it was deserted. She wandered up to the front and looked down on to the tender and the driver's cab. She could see the glow of the firebox and the shadows that must be Shaka and the firer. Another, smaller train was stationed on the track alongside, separated by a deep trench of darkness. Annat heard voices coming from the trench, whispered and insistent. There were two figures down there, half-hidden by the shadows. Annat lay down on her stomach and peered over the edge of the roof, trying to see what they were doing. It was a man and a woman, pinned close together, leaning against the wheels, their faces interlocked. Annat saw the white of bare flesh, a naked leg, and the strange writhing of the two bodies joined together. She shrank back.

They were doing that! In the open, where anyone could see them. Annat moved to the far side of the roof and sat on the edge, putting her fingers in her ears so as not to hear the hot sounds, gasps and whispers, that seemed loud over the noise of the station. She swallowed saliva, feeling a little queasy. She did not want to know what she had seen, and she felt dirty with the thought of it. She would never do anything like that, not with anyone. Men were so horrible, big and dirty and rough, and they all wanted to do it to you. Doxoi men. *Zaide* wasn't like that, or Malchik. Wanderers were different.

Then Yuda sat down beside her, lighting a cigarette. Annat glanced at him. She had not heard him approach, but that was not surprising as her ears had been blocked. He did not comment on that, but said, "Back already?" as if he had not been expecting to see her. Annat's heart began to pound. She kept the thought locked inside her, where he could not find it. He had been the man, and the woman was Rosa, the cook.

"What's up? Did you find the boy?"

Annat could not turn to face him. She nodded, and her stomach felt sick and tight. This time, his voice was gentle.

"You saw us, didn't you? Me and Rosa."

Annat shrank up tight into a fist.

"Never mind. You'll get used to it. When I was a *kind*, I couldn't imagine my parents doing it. They can't have done it very much, or Yuste and I would have had more brothers and sisters."

"Shut up, shut up," said Annat. She did not want to hear him talking about *Bubbe* and *Zaide* like that.

"You really mind, don't you? I suppose Yuste explained the mechanics. Or your *Mame*."

"Go away."

"I like Rosa. She likes me. It's a warm, friendly thing to do when two people are lonely and scared."

"What about Shaka?"

"He knows about me and Rosa. I like women, but he's the one. Come down now and talk to him."

"No."

"Someone frightened you, didn't they? Someone told you it was a horrible thing that men do to women."

"Please leave me alone."

"Listen, Natka. I didn't mean you to see, but you've seen, and you have to take me as I am. I'm not a saint like *Zaide*. If I want a woman, and she wants me, I'll have her. You're not a little *kind*, you're a young woman, and you can't stay with your doll for ever. I don't want you to be afraid like your *Mame* was."

Annat uncurled a little and looked at him over her arm. "You shouldn't be like them. The Doxoi. Wanderers are good. They respect women."

"Listen, *kind*. *Zaide* is a good man, a holy man, but we can't all live like that. I'll tell you a story. When I was eighteen, I got your mother pregnant. No one taught me how to be careful because I was a Wanderer, a good boy, and they don't know of such things. Her father found out and threatened to kill me unless I married her. So we went to the Doxoi priest who said some words, and there we were, eighteen and married. The same age that Malchik is now. Your *Mame* had to live with us because her parents disowned her. When Malchik was born, her father tried to take him away, to raise him in the true faith, but I was a little older then, and not so scared of him, and I told him to get lost. But your *Mame* used to take Malchik to the temple, and their priest put the Wheel on him in secret. As far as she was concerned, Malchik was hers, and I was an irrelevance. She tried to forget what we'd done. She believed it was a sin, and the Mother was punishing her for it, so she wouldn't let me near her."

He paused, staring into space, and Annat scrutinised him more closely than she had done before. The set of his face was hard and wild, but it was a mask over sadness. Even though she could read his mind, she realised that this was not going to enable her to know him deeply in a short time. There were hidden layers and silences that kept her out. She leaned towards him with mingled curiosity and prurience.

"You didn't—you didn't make her do it?"

Yuda cracked a smile. "You mean, am I a rapist? No. But I was not kind to her. I didn't know that some women go funny after their first baby. I was eighteen. I didn't know anything. She didn't want any more *kinder*, either, she was besotted with Malchik. But I think her priest must have told her to obey her husband, or some such shit. Maybe she really changed her mind. She let me back into her bed for a while, but it didn't last. After you were born, she shut me out again, and this time it was for good. I stuck it for a few months, because I wanted to be a good husband and father like *Zaide*, but something snapped. I had to run away before I hurt her—or Malchik. I wanted to take you with me, but Yuste had become too attached to you, so I left one night without saying goodbye. I thought of coming back when Aude—your *Mame*—died, but I couldn't face that house again. I'm a coward, you see. I had to wait until you were both old enough to make up your own minds."

He seemed to have finished, and Annat felt the shadow of his pain. "Were you sorry when *Mame* died?" she asked.

"No. She hurt Malchik worse than I ever did, though he doesn't know it. I need to talk to him, but I don't know how."

Annat thought of her brother's face, with its obstinate, vulnerable look. "He's odd. I don't feel I know him," she said.

"That's the thing. Shamans can't hide as much as people with no powers. You're like a book, Annat, and Malchik is a wall."

The guards were returning. Yuda stood up, stretched, and took out a cigarette. He snapped his fingers to make a small flame.

"Come on, Natka. I'm on duty in the cab, and I want you with me."

"Will you tell Shaka about Rosa?"

"He knows."

She clambered after him, down into the tender, which was full of splintery wood chips. Though the driver's cab was quite large, four people filled it.

"Hallo, Annat," said Shaka. His red overalls were smeared with soot. Annat blushed and could not answer.

"She caught me screwing Rosa," said Yuda. The firer grinned, white teeth in a soot-masked face, and smacked her gloved hands together. Her hair was tucked into a blue cap like the one that Shaka wore.

"He's a lecherous little Mother, isn't he, Shaka?"

Yuda approached Shaka and touched his arm. "Are you sore at me, Mister?"

"Nah. But you could be more careful. Someone might tell Rosa's husband."

"I won't be seeing her after this trip."

"I won't be seeing you either," said Shaka, with a wry smile.

"It's only for six months. You can stop over at Gard Ademar. See Govorin. Kill two birds with one stone."

The driver threw back his head and laughed. Annat was mystified. Govorin was a Sklav name, like her father's, not Franj. So were the guards Pyotr and Lyude. None of the people she had met on the train so far seemed to be Franj. She knew that some Sklav migrants had settled in Masalyar, fleeing south from the Great Cold, but most had crossed the sea to Morea. There could not be more than a few thousand living in the city, but they seemed to run the Railway. She wondered if the Franj resented that.

The whistle sounded from the platform, and Shaka let off the brakes. When he opened the regulator Annat felt the loco-motive surge forward and heard the hiss of steam as the pistons began to work. She tucked herself into a corner of the tender, out of the way, feeling the glowing heat from the fire-box on her face. The front of the cab was a mass of levers, valves and gauges that Annat did not understand. She admired Shaka's calm mastery of his engine. Her father stood in the cab doorway, staring out into the darkness, his black hair blown wildly about as the train got up speed. She sensed the beginnings of fear in him. He knew the danger which they were approaching; something shapeless and nameless, that could attack from any direction. Annat felt his mind searching, probing the night which his sight could not penetrate, seeking the trace of other, hostile minds. Soul Men.

Annat was not yet afraid. They had left Axar hours ago, and nothing had happened. The train was travelling too fast for anyone to attack it, even on horseback. The only times when she became a little uneasy were the night stops, when a few lamps or a cluster of torches by the line signalled the presence of a remote station. The station master would come to the engine, his face glowing like a night ghost's as he opened his dark lantern, and would give Shaka the staff showing that the next section of line was clear. Once, too, a group of men waving storm lanterns had brought them to a halt at a level crossing where a traction engine was passing with a load of charcoal. The woman in charge of the crossing was Franj; she came to exchange greetings with the driver while the load traversed the crossing.

"Seen any trouble, Mister?" she asked. She wore a uniform peaked cap with her workday clothes, a thick felt coat over a long skirt.

"None yet, Missis, thank the Son," said Shaka.

"May his blessing go with you, Mister. I've brought some eggs. They're from the duck, so mind you cook 'em well." •

The firer, whose name Annat had learned was Nami, took the eggs and put them in her food box.

"I reckon we could fry 'em on the boiler right now, Missis," she said.

Annat felt Yuda's tense and watchful presence. His mind was awake, alert, searching the shadows all the time they were at the crossing. When Shaka pulled on the cord and the whistle

gave a mournful blast to signal that they were off, he seemed
to relax a little. He leaned over the edge of the tender to look
at Annat.

"Trouble is, the passengers get out if we stop too long. Then
we have to wait while someone goes to fetch 'em. If I had my
way, we'd leave the bastards."

"Why do they get out?"

"To stretch their legs, go for a piss, talk to the lineside men.
Some of them even head off to the nearest farm to buy brews
and tucker. They get bored, see, and a lot of 'em are city folk
who don't know about danger."

Annat scrambled out of the tender, brushing wood chips
from her coat. She stood beside him in the doorway and let her
mind empty. The black shadows of trees racketed past like pictures on a zoetrope. She shut her eyes and looked beyond the
darkness, probing for the faint sparks that were human minds.
Here and there, a cluster of distant flames would flicker across
her inner vision, but they did not have the pulsing brightness
of a shaman mind. Beside her, Yuda was reaching much further into the empty landscape, sending out a ray of thought
that swept the inner dark like a lighthouse beam.

Annat opened her eyes and steadied herself in the doorway.
A fear crept over her of the unseen world she had just touched.
There was a risk in laying your mind open like this. She was
not trained as Yuda had been to protect himself while he made
his search. She saw the rushing mist that the train ripped
through, flying back in shapeless clouds. The night seemed to
watch her with hidden, glittering eyes. She returned to her safe
but uncomfortable place in the tender, pierced through with
sudden cold. The image of the dead from Yuda's mind was still
in hers, those helpless faces, some already flyblown, the skin
shiny and tight.

She woke, her head jerking up, not knowing that she had
been asleep. The eastern sky had a tinge of lustrous, watery
jade. Mist welled up from beside the track, dulling the hiss of
steam from the stalled train. Shaka was leaning out of the cab
watching the line ahead, while Nami stamped her feet to keep
warm. Yuda had gone. Annat raised herself stiffly, stretching
her arms and legs. Once the sun rose it would be Kingsday.

"Why have we stopped?" she asked Nami.

"Sheep on the track. Shepherd's trying to drive them off now."

Annat peered out of the cab to see sheep skittering over the ballast, their bleating making a thin, reedy sound. She was tempted to climb down to help the shepherd, for she knew a little about herding sheep, but when she stepped out on to the footplate, Shaka caught her sleeve.

"You stay here, Missis," he said. "We don't want anyone wandering off."

"Where's *Tate*?"

"He went back to talk to Scorpion."

They had a long wait while the shepherd and his dogs drove the sheep down from the permanent way, but at last the track ahead was empty and the shepherd hollered his thanks.

"We're running late," said Shaka. "Better hope the crossings are open from here to Gard Ademar."

He gave a short blast on the whistle, a sound that startled a flock of dark birds from a nearby coppice. For a few moments the air was full of sudden wings and rattling pinions. Annat gave a little shiver, wondering whether they were rooks, or crows. Their harsh voices seemed to reverberate through the mist. Unflustered, Shaka opened the regulator to give the engine its head, but as they began to move off there was a shout from the carriages behind. Nami pulled on the brake lever and the train stopped with a jolt.

"Shit," said the driver. "What now?"

Lyude appeared at the front of the leading coach.

"Sorry, Chief," he called, "passenger gone AWOL."

"How do they know?" Shaka muttered to himself.

"Pyotr's gone to get him back," Lyude went on. "It's that Vasilyevich *kind*, the boy. Went off to look at the trees."

Shaka uttered several expletives that Annat did not recognise.

"Sheep, bloody birds and bloody wandering boys," he exclaimed. "This isn't a bloody school-house picnic."

Annat yelled. It came out of her suddenly, in a reflex vomiting of fear. *They were coming.* A bitter taste was in her mouth, chaos in her mind. An utter panic urged her to run out into the cool mist, away from the scalding, searing touch of concentrated evil. Then she felt the impact of a huge blast of power, stronger than any she had ever known.

"Malchik," she said, and jumped down on to the ballast. She ran towards the source of the power. Someone was screaming in the mist, with terrible, howling sobs. Yuda was ahead of her; she felt the heat of him concentrated into a white-hot core. Behind her, Scorpion yelled a battle cry. Annat ran down the embankment, anger hurling her forward. The mist split, and she saw them: dressed in rags, four men and a woman bending over a prone figure that writhed on the ground. It was, it had been, Pyotr. The sum of their joint power was a pulsating mass, a living, separate creature that stank of cruelty and unbounded wildness.

Yuda stopped, dropped on one knee and stretched out his right arm, sending a surge of power into the group. Annat felt the impact from where she stood, but it seemed to have no effect on the five. Their heads turned towards Yuda with one slick, mechanical movement, and Annat saw that their eyes were white. She ran towards her father, carried by panic and rage, and sent her own small, hopeless flame searing towards them. Scorpion fired her gun over Yuda's head, in a blue jet of charged ozone that struck one of the men under the chin, spinning him backwards. For an instant the group wavered, then Annat felt them gathering force for their counter attack, which would shrivel and burn the soft parts of her body. There was nothing the eye could see, but she felt a tearing pain that wrenched her from her feet. As she fell, she saw Yuda on his feet, his arms spread to make a wall. The blast was deflected, fracturing into splinters that pierced the mist, sending up jets of superheated steam. As Scorpion flung down her gun and sent a bolt of lightning from her cupped right hand, Yuda ran in close and caught the foremost man in the belly with his knife. Annat saw the blue-tinted entrails slither from the gash; the dying man caught Yuda by the shoulders, trying to raze his mind with the gaze of those milky eyes.

The mass of inhuman power quavered, rent by Scorpion's fire, but the three survivors gathered the strength of their dying companions. They seemed to merge into a hydra-cloud, sucking power into their depths from everything that surrounded them. Forced to his knees, Yuda still managed to gather his strength for another blast; white lightning roared from his hands and caught in the toils of the power-cloud, tearing great holes in it. He was bleeding from head and chest; Annat could smell Scorpion's burns.

Annat tried to get up, but her arms and legs seemed to be made of hollow plaster. Scorpion stooped for her gun and fired another jet at the Soul Men. This time, they fed on her power, absorbing it into their overcharged bodies. Their faces were burnt black and red, and skin was dripping from their hands. Fighting nausea, Annat struggled to her knees, trying to draw together enough force to reach them. It was Yuda who attacked first, hurling himself into the middle of them so that the chain was broken and they were thrown apart. He knelt astride the one in the centre, plunging his knife into the face and body so that blood siphoned over his face and hands. Annat felt the gestalt collapse, tearing into shreds of ruin; the screams of the last two were eerie and distant, and beyond them, in the distance, she thought she heard the laughter of the crows. The smell of evil dwindled and drifted away, dispersing with the mist.

Yuda staggered to his feet, wiping blood from his eyes. Annat stayed on her hands and knees, howling tears as the fear caught up with her.

"Mother," said Scorpion. "They nearly had us. You okay, Vasilyevich?"

"Go fuck yourself."

Scorpion bent over Annat and helped her up, wincing as she tried to use her burnt hands.

"He's pissed off," she said.

A figure, tall and thin, emerged from the mist near the lake. Malchik's face was almost as white as the clouds, and he was visibly shaking. He went up to Yuda and touched him on the sleeve. Yuda lashed out with his arm, catching Malchik across the face and knocking him headlong.

"What the fuck were you doing, boy? One of my men is dead because of you."

Malchik lay on the ground, shielding his head with his hands. "I don't know," he stammered. "I went to look at the birds . . ."

"Never seen crows before?" said Yuda, wiping his bleeding face.

"I'm sorry, I don't know why I did it . . ."

Yuda kicked him. "Get up!"

"Leave him alone," cried Annat, pulling away from Scorpion. "He didn't know."

"Get back to the train, you. I'll deal with you later."

"Come on, *kind*," said Scorpion. "He'll calm down in a bit."

"But he's hurting Malchik."

"I don't reckon he'll hurt him much, seeing what he went through to rescue him."

Scorpion put her arm under Annat's shoulders and helped her back to the train, where a flustered, motherly Rosa took charge of her. Annat sat on a stool in the guards' van while Rosa dabbed her cuts and grazes with hot, clean water.

"I told that boy not to go," she said, lifting Annat's hair to wipe her face.

In a corner, Scorpion had stripped to her vest and was attending to her own injuries with lint and ointment, holding the safety pins in her teeth. Annat was still crying. She could not forget the burnt faces of the Soul Men, or their white eyes.

"He couldn't help it," she sobbed. "He didn't know about the danger."

Rosa gave her a hug, full of white linen and lavender-scented bosom.

"I don't expect he'll do that again in a hurry," said Scorpion.

"Where is he?" said Rosa.

"I think Vasilyevich took him to the engine. Shaka won't let the others near him. I expect they're quite keen to murder him just now."

The van door flew open, and Yuda stepped inside. His face and most of his body were daubed with blood. He stripped off his jacket and dropped it on the floor, snarling, "Get me some water, woman," to Rosa. As she hurried away, he slumped down on the floor next to Scorpion.

"Not a pretty sight," she said.

"What about your burns?"

"I've seen worse."

"Pity we can't heal ourselves, eh?"

"How badly are you hurt, Vasilyevich?"

"Pretty badly," he said, and fainted.

Chapter 4

It was Kingsday. Annat sat on the roof of the train, chanting her prayers silently in time to the rhythm of the wheels. Her right arm was in a sling; she had burnt her hand using her power against the Soul Men. She had just been to visit Malchik in the driver's cab; there were bruises on his face, and he was still pale with rage and fright. Annat sighed inwardly. Yuda should not have hit him, but she could understand why he had. They had brought Pyotr's body to the guards' van where it lay, covered by a blanket. The face was a blur of melted flesh. Now there was a brooding silence amongst the men and women on top of the train, as if they were remembering their dead comrade and hoarding their anger. Yuda had sent Malchik to the engine so that Shaka could protect him. Only the Scorpion, stretched out full length on the roof, wrapped in her woollen cloak, emitted no feelings of anger and loss. Lyude sat by himself at the rear of the carriage, fiddling with his gun, his legs dangling over the edge. He had smiled at Annat when she returned, but it was a smile stretched over grief.

Annat watched the sun of Kingsday rise above the eastern hills. This day was dedicated to the One, it was his bride. At home, the women in the house would take turns to play the part of the holy bride, wearing a silvered crown from sunrise to sunset. The Wanderers would do no work today; they would sit in their houses, reading the Holy Books, while the men would go to the House of Teaching to pray. The Wanderers did not have temples; there had been only one true Temple, in Zyon, and that was destroyed.

Annat wished that she were at home with Yuste and her grandparents. *Bubbe* made special poppy-seed cakes on the eve of Kingsday, and Annat helped her, listening to her grandmother's stories of magic. But *Bubbe* had not been the only one to tell stories. In *Mame*'s bedroom, sitting on the bed as *Mame*'s fingers worked over the soft wool that she liked to knit, while Malchik lay curled up against his mother's arm, thumb in mouth, his pale eyes warning Annat to stay back, she had listened to Aude's whispered tales of a great forest, green and dark. *Mame* had been born in the Forest of Ademar, which had a whispering voice, like the sea. Half the year it slept under snow; half the year it quivered alive with a tapestry of animals: deer, foxes, badgers and even wolves. Cut off during the time of the Great Cold, the forest had endured the long winter that imprisoned the northern lands for five hundred years. Only in the lifetime of Annat's grandparents had the Thaw begun, peeling back the layers of snow to reveal villages, towns and whole tracts of country lost in time.

The hills in the east grew closer, losing their blue tinge. Soon Annat could see the shapes of the trees; tall black pines, conical firs, and the spreading yellow of oak leaves. Scattered birches stood on the slopes, ankle-deep in bracken. It was as if the woods had sent out spies to watch the intruding iron road. The breeze brought in a faint scent of amber. Annat stood up to try to see the extent of the forest, but the hills were in the way.

With a flick of its tail, the snake-track turned a corner, and Annat saw a little station ahead. As the train began to brake, she felt a quickening of excitement and fear. But there was no one to share her mood: Scorpion lounged, half-asleep, her mind closed, and Lyude's back was turned. Annat wanted to shout aloud, to let them know that this was her important day, her journey. Instead she watched as the stone houses with their red-tiled roofs grew large, before the locomotive misted them with great gouts of steam from its brakes.

The train stopped, and passengers began to emerge like maggots from a great carcass, prolific with new life. Annat perched on the edge of the roof, watching them. Yuda had not told her what to do when they arrived. When she saw Lyude swing over the side and move off into the crowd, she began to feel nervous with uncertainty, as if she had come to a strange place alone.

"Go on, jump," said Scorpion's voice, lazy and warm. "Unless you want to come on to the depot with me."

Annat sprang down to the platform, landing asprawl on her hands and knees. At once, she felt the casual stares of the people in the station as they noticed her Wanderer's black. They wore the customary Doxan colors of grey, blue and dull green. Annat picked herself up, trying to be proud under those stares only to find that she was no longer the subject of their attention. She heard the people babbling and shouting in Franj like the villagers at home, but with a different accent that she found hard to understand. And she was alone.

Someone was watching her. A broad-backed, stocky Darkman with massive shoulders and a muscular neck. He smiled as Annat met his gaze, and approached her, greeting her in Sklav.

"You must be Annat."

His head was covered in fine, tight curls of black hair, and a thick beard grew on his chin; he wore blue overalls, which hardly seemed to contain his muscled body. He was far darker than Sival, with a big nose and high-boned cheeks; Annat decided that he must be one of the Darkmen of Morea, like Shaka.

"Who are you?" she said.

"Govorin, Sheriff of Gard Ademar. Pleased to meet you," he said, extending a hand the size of a small island. Annat examined it, unsure of what she was meant to do next. She wanted to point out that a Darkman could not have a Sklav name, but she did not want to look stupid. Govorin shook her good hand, engulfing but not crushing her small fingers. "Yuda's *kind*," he said, half to himself. "You have such a look of him. An echo. He's my oldest friend, and yet there's this hidden side of him—you, your brother and the mother I never knew. How did you hurt your hand?"

"We fought the Soul Men. I didn't know they were so strong." Cold welled up inside Annat, blocking her mouth. She stared at him intensely, wishing she could speed her thoughts into his mind. He gave her a small, embarrassed smile, as if he understood her wish and pitied her helplessness.

"Yuda often used to say he wished I was a shaman," he said. "Sometimes I've thought it strange that neither Shaka nor I have the power. And we're both Darkmen."

Annat found the question spilling out of her mouth. It came out wrong. "But you're Sklavan, Mister Govorin. How can you be a Darkman?"

She was relieved to see the smile deepen into a grin. "Do you know, your father asked me the same question when we first met? He was new to Masalyar, all dressed up in Wanderer's black, with a long coat, big hat and a beard. Of course he couldn't know, but I thought he was trying to insult me. I was about to leave him there in the road, alone in the midst of the City—and you've seen how big the City is—when he said, in that quiet way he has, "Come back, Mister Govorin. Except for Sival, you're the only one who has spoken to me as a man, not as a Wanderer. I think we could be friends." That stopped me in my tracks. I went back, and told him my history, and he told me his. And we both had ancestors that had lived in Sklava for generations—his were Wanderers, mine were black. His people had lived in the Shtetl, mine at the court of the Staryetz. I suppose that's the beginning of an answer."

Shyly, Annat returned his smile. Govorin patted her shoulder. "Your father and I have been friends almost as long as you've been alive," he said. "Blood brothers too. But where is he? I thought he'd be bringing you to meet me, not lurking on the train."

She did not have time to tell him, for Shaka shouldered his way through the crowd and clasped Govorin's wrist in an exuberant handshake.

"Sergey Gavrilovich! I see the new wife has grown a beard on you."

Govorin grasped Shaka's wrist firmly, staring into his face with the complete ease of an old acquaintance.

"I hear you had an interesting journey."

"Not without incident." Shaka smiled grimly. "Pyotr's dead, and Vasilyevich is bleeding all over the guards' van. And Rosa, I imagine."

"Pyotr dead? He was an old Railway hand. He'll be missed longer than any of us. How did it happen?"

"Yuda's boy went looking for crows—and found Soul Men instead. He's not popular on the train. Not very happy himself, either. Yuda whacked him."

"That's rough justice," said Govorin. "How bad is Yuda?"

"Scorpion healed him, more or less. I expect he'll walk out of there once he's finished saying goodbye to Rosa. Or I might go and throw him out."

"Who's Rosa?"

"His bit of skin. You know Yuda. He can't stay one side of the track."

Govorin thumped Shaka on the arm. "He can't help it. It's a shaman thing."

"He knows if he went after other men I'd break his bloody neck."

As he spoke, Annat saw Yuda emerge from the guards' van, looking dishevelled and bloodstained. He gave them a shaky wave.

"I'll go and help him with the bags," said Shaka. "You'd better fetch the boy. He's hiding in the cab, like I told him to. I didn't want another murder today."

As Govorin strode off towards the engine, Annat stood, poised in indecision, before running after Shaka. Yuda was leaning against the guards' van, lighting a cigarette.

"Hallo, my little almond biscuit," he said, as she arrived. His face was paper white. Shaka gripped him by the shoulders.

"What am I going to do with you, you little Mother?" he said, and glanced at Annat. Yuda smiled sweetly at him. "I don't want to lose you. Not to a woman, and not to Death." Yuda said nothing, but stroked Shaka's cheek. "You could at least lie to me. Give me some false hope."

Yuda blew smoke up high, away from Shaka's face. "You

deserve better than that, Mister," he said. Shaka released him, and rested both his hands on the wall of the van, on either side of Yuda's head. Their faces were very close, but Shaka did not look into Yuda's eyes.

"I'm not sure that I'm strong enough," he said. Annat did not understand, for he seemed to be the very picture of strength beside Yuda's apparent frailty. She felt that Yuda was like a woman could be, he had that air of vulnerability masking resilience. His love for Shaka seemed clean and uncomplicated, like a smooth, round pebble.

"Yes you are. It's six months. We'll see each other," he said, gently. Shaka raised his eyes.

"You know that isn't what I meant."

Yuda stood on tiptoe and whispered into his ear. Shaka nodded.

"Yes," he said. "But I'm afraid. Something about this place. Remember what happened to Isabel."

Yuda gazed at him silently for a while. Then he said, "I'll be careful."

Shaka broke into a laugh. "You lying sod! When were you ever careful? Look at you now, half-dead and covered in blood."

He fetched Annat's pack and *vyel* from the van and escorted Yuda up the platform, the remaining bags dangling from his other fist. Annat kept pace with them, hugging her rucksack, with her thumb poked absent-mindedly into her mouth. Govorin and Malchik met them by the station entrance. Her brother's pale cheek bore the marks of separate fingers on it like a red brand.

Govorin shook her father's hand. "I can tell you had an eventful journey," he remarked drily.

"I've known quieter runs," said Yuda. "I hope you've brought the buggy, Mister, or you'll be carrying me up to the village."

"It's outside the station. We'll go back to my house, where you can wash and put on fresh clothes. My deputy has invited us to lunch at his house."

"The pleasure will be entirely his," said Shaka, slapping the Sheriff on the back.

"He's a good man, Sarl. Always hospitable to strangers," said Govorin, giving Shaka an odd look. Like a warning, Annat thought.

Yuda folded his arms. "I take it you didn't choose him, Sergey."

"He was elected to the post. Like me. A respected member of the community."

Shaka put his arm round Yuda's shoulders. "You know you don't fool us, Mister Govorin," he said.

Annat sensed that they were meaning much more than they said. Govorin in particular seemed to communicate with nervous movements of his hands and eyes. The three men knew each other very well and, though Yuda was the only shaman, they did not need to put into words what they wanted to convey.

"I'll be interested to meet him," said Yuda.

"I see you've already made an impression on your son."

Yuda glanced towards Malchik, who was staring at the ground.

"Yes, I've marked him up nicely. Sorry, boy," he said, with some regret.

"All right," said Malchik under his breath.

Govorin shook his head. "This is a different world," he said. "People remember. They bear grudges. They have a code of honour. They expect you to understand it without explanation. A misplaced word or a look can start a feud that lasts for generations. It's like walking on eggshells."

"Sounds like my family," said Yuda.

Govorin sighed. "I'm serious, Vasilyevich. Diplomacy isn't your middle name."

"He hasn't got a middle name," said Shaka.

"I'm a doctor now, Sergey. A doctor tries to heal people and goes to bed hoping that none of his patients dies. He doesn't bother about honour."

Govorin smacked his hands together. "You look terrible, Vasilyevich. Let met take you home. I shouldn't have kept you here talking like this."

"And I've got a train to take to the depot. I'll catch you

later, Sheriff. And you take care, Yudeleh," said Shaka, squeezing Yuda's arm.

"Yes, yes. I'll send for you when I need a grandmother."

Shaka held his arms wide in an expanded shrug. "I leave him in your care, Mister Govorin," he said. "Try to keep him alive."

Govorin gave him a small smile and raised his hands in farewell.

They took the eastern track into the hills to reach Gard Ademar. The journey took about half an hour in Govorin's horse-drawn buggy. The village itself stood on a rough eminence, perched on the hilltop above castellated walls of limestone which seemed to glow in the sun. And Annat saw the forest; a magnificent, thunderous shadow that crested the hills just to the east and crept down to the foot of the hill where the village stood.

—Zyon, I can feel it from here, Yuda thought in her mind.

Annat felt it too. The whole forest bore an imprint like a shaman mind, but vast and much more complex. She sensed it becoming aware of her. It was danger, but it was also dream and promise. In her hands, she felt the wooden body of the doll twist a fraction. Annat lifted it, startled, but the smooth features were unchanged.

The houses of the village were packed inside the walls like golden stones. The pony found a way between them, a narrow cobbled street between the blank walls. From the central square, where a fountain dribbled water out of a lion's mouth into a weathered trough, they had to make their way on foot up a stone stair to the Sheriff's house. It stood close to the Doxan temple, a square, stuccoed house with shuttered upper windows, three storeys high. The stucco was daubed with a faded rust pink the color of late apples.

"Will we live here?" asked Annat.

"No," said Govorin with a laugh. "I've found you an empty place close by. My wife, Casildis, has prepared it. We'll go there after we've eaten."

He opened the ironwork grille that covered the inner door, and they followed him into a narrow hall paved with marble. It had been swept clean, and the walls newly painted with lime wash, but the place had the chill of age. As Malchik closed the front door, there was a burst of laughter from the rear of the house, followed by running footsteps and a door slamming.

"That'll be my deputy's wife leaving now," said Govorin. "She's not allowed to meet strangers."

"Not allowed? Who says?" said Yuda.

"Her husband. Most of the local people are strict Doxans, and the women stay behind closed doors."

"It wasn't like that at home," said Malchik.

"It takes some getting used to," said Govorin. "They all say I'm much too lax with my wife. I'd like to meet the man who could keep her locked up."

As he spoke, a young woman came racing down the stairs and flung her arms round his neck. All Annat saw for a moment was a mass of golden hair unfastened, flying in all directions as if it were alive. The woman was a little taller than Govorin, with a strong, slender body; she wore baggy trousers of blue silk under a long silken tunic.

"There you are, my love," said Govorin, trying to tidy blonde hair out of his eyes. "I take it Mari got away safely?"

"Ssh! You're not supposed to know she was here. She wasn't here," said the woman excitedly, almost knocking him out with the wooden spoon in her right hand.

"Casildis, these are our guests."

Annat caught a glimpse of laughing blue eyes through the hair. Casildis covered her mouth with her hand.

"I'm sorry," she said. "I almost forgot you were there. You are very welcome. I've never met any Wanderers before. Are they all small people with dark eyes and big noses? Oh, and one tall one."

Her laughter had no meanness in it. Even Malchik did not seem offended by her bluntness, though like Yuda and Annat he could not help touching his nose.

"Not generally this big," said Yuda.

Casildis waved the spoon at them. Now Annat could see her face, she thought her very beautiful, though it was not a china symmetry. Casildis had a fine split in her upper lip, a hare-lip, which seemed to heighten rather than diminish her beauty.

"What is it they say about men with big noses?" she said

impishly. "I want the truth, husband, after you've had your bath."

"We're not bathing together! Are we?" said Malchik with profound dismay.

"It's one of our northern customs," said Casildis. "This house has a hot room. Annat and I will take our bath first, and then you men can make as much mess as you like."

"That's good," said Annat. "Of course, we ought to have had a bath before Kingsday came in, but we couldn't because we were on the train."

She followed Casildis upstairs into the scented heaven of her bedroom. The bed frame was massive, shaped like a stylized boat with prow and stern; all the linen was white, and so were the window-hangings and the walls. There was a faint smell of warm lavender.

Casildis stretched her arms skywards.

"I love this room," she said. "I made it myself. My room of freedom, where I sleep beside my lovely husband."

"It's very white," said Annat. "And it smells nice."

She put the doll down on the bed and started to take off her thick winter coat. Casildis glanced at the small wooden figure on the bed and moved with two swift strides to stare down at it, her hand outstretched to touch it, but hovering.

"Bright Lady," she said. "Where did you get that doll?"

Annat shrugged off the coat and stood holding it with formal stiffness.

"My *Mame* gave it me," she said, seized with sudden reticence.

Abandoning the spoon on the coverlet, Casildis knelt down and touched the doll's green kirtle with gentle reverence.

"She returns to us," she breathed. "What was your mother's name, Annat?"

"She was called Aude. Aude d'Iforas, I think."

Casildis shook her head. "How strange. I knew her. She was several years older than I. Her family left this . . . part of the country after my sister Huldis disappeared. Your mother was my sister's friend. A pretty girl, with such red hair. Her family had been keepers of the doll for centuries. And we thought it was lost."

"*Mame* gave me the doll before she killed herself. Or it may have been an accident. She drowned."

"Poor Aude," said Casildis, gazing up at Annat with heavy-lidded eyes. In the dusk of the white room, their blue was dark and cloudy. "Perhaps my sister's loss haunted her, though she was not to blame, and made you motherless."

"It's not exactly an ordinary doll, is it?" said Annat.

"No," said Casildis. "And you know that, which is why you carry her when you are too old for dolls."

They undressed with an odd solemnity, and Casildis gave Annat a large white towel to wrap herself in on the way to the hot room. She unwound the now dirty bandages from Annat's right hand and winced at the sight of the raw red skin and blisters.

"I will find you some ointment later," she said. "My mother had the best herb garden of any chatelaine this side of the mountains and I have inherited some of her skill with simples."

They ran across the stone landing, watched by stone foliate faces, into the hot room. There was no visible fire, but the room was steaming with heat, and they had to put on wooden sandals to keep the floor from burning their feet.

"There's a hypocaust under the floor," Casildis explained, "and a furnace in the kitchen. My maid helped me to stoke it early this morning. Some of these houses are very old. Parts of this one were built in the time of the Old Empire, in the days of the Kadagoi."

Annat had heard of the Kadagoi. Their empire had stretched across Neustria and Morea, and even as far as Zyon, and in latter days Doxa had been the state religion. She wanted to test Casildis, who must be Doxan, to see whether she shared their oldest and most infamous belief: that the Wanderers had betrayed the Son, that his own twin brother had sold him to the Kadagoi for a bag of silver and golden shekels.

"It was the Kadagoi who killed the Son, not the Wanderers," she said. "Everyone blames us for it."

Casildis sat on the wooden bench that ran round the walls of the hot room, rubbing her shoulders with her towel. "Some blame you. Not those who are wise."

"The Kadagoi expelled the Wanderers from Zyon," Annat continued. "*Mame* told me they broke the Son of the Wheel, as if he were a criminal."

"It's a cruel history," said Casildis. "But the Kadagoi also made strange and beautiful things—things that were destroyed by the Doxoi, so that we no longer know how to make them."

Annat folded up her knees and wrapped her arms round them. Her body was thin and dark-skinned, with almost no breasts. Casildis had a boyish figure herself, palely freckled, the color of almond blossom. Annat liked looking at her because she was strange and perfect.

The next room was cooler than the first, and a butt of cold water stood in the corner. Annat screamed with shock and delight as Casildis scooped the water out with a dipper and splashed it over her. Soon the room was awash as they poured the chill water over each other, chasing each other and laughing. When they were both soaked and dripping wet, Casildis led Annat to the last room, where they found fresh towels piled on a bench and small vials of scented oil to rub into their skins.

"Will the men do this as well?" asked Annat, when they were dressed in their dry towels.

"They will—though I'm not sure about the scented oils."

"Malchik will hate it. He's so self-conscious."

"Poor boy. And I'm sure your father and my husband will wander round naked without a thought."

"I wish we could eavesdrop," said Annat, vigorously towelling her hair.

"My rules are strict. Men and women bathe separately. Otherwise we'd have no secrets."

They hurried back to Casildis's bedroom, where Annat sat on the bed while Casildis chose herself some clean clothes.

"I've brought some new things for you from the laundry," she said, rummaging in the clothes press. "White and black, of course. Govorin told me that you would be small and slender. I think he heard something about you from Yuda."

Annat examined the garments that Casildis laid beside her on the bed: a smock of fine cotton and a black pinafore that would reach to her ankles, with an embroidered yoke.

"I like them," she said, fingering the soft fabric.

"I'm afraid you'll have to cover your legs to the ankle," said Casildis. "A girl of your age has to observe the same modesty as a woman. I should wear a veil, but I never bother in the house. Govorin hates all these restrictions, but I'm used to them. It's even stricter at home."

"Where do you come from?" said Annat.

"I was born in the Forest of Ademar," said Casildis, putting on a fine cotton shift. She shook out her wet hair and twisted it into a plait, wrapping it in a towel. There was a sound of voices from the landing outside, and some laughter. "There they go," said Casildis. "No peeping now," for Annat had started to sidle towards the door.

"My mother grew up in the Castle of Ademar," said Annat.

"Yes. Her father was the Seneschal."

"What's that?"

"The warden of the castle." Casildis sighed. "I have been much happier since I moved here with my brother and Mari, his wife. I'm not supposed to talk about our home. Even Govorin knows little more than what I've told you."

"My mother used to tell stories about the forest and the castle. I wish I could see it."

"They would kill you," said Casildis, standing very still, her petticoat in her hand. When serious, her face was like that of a painted statue in a Doxan temple.

Annat squeezed the edge of the towel she was wearing between her hands. "But I'm a *kind*," she said.

"You are a Wanderer, and an outsider. They would not consider your age. They burn infidels and shamans."

"Is that why you left?" asked Annat.

"I left because I felt trapped. Even so, I was only free to go because my brother went too. He is Govorin's deputy. It was his idea that we should come to live in Gard Ademar with the Railway People."

"So we're going to have lunch at your brother's house?"

Casildis smiled, stepping into her petticoat. "It was Zhan's suggestion. He wanted to meet all of you."

Annat dropped the towel on the floor and rummaged in her pack for some clean knickers and a vest. She began to dress in a hurry, for it was colder in this room than the heated ones they had just left. The pinafore and blouse that Casildis had chosen for her fitted quite well, though the skirt was a little too long.

"How do I look?" she said, stretching out her arms.

"Very pretty. I will dry your hair for you. Mine takes hours to dry, so I'll keep it covered. That will please my brother."

Casildis had put on a long green gown of woven wool. She slung a necklace of garnets round her neck and clipped tiny garnet studs into her ears. "Now I must paint my face," she said. "My brother hates that."

She sat down before the mahogany dressing table and began to unscrew some small jars, which stood amongst the brushes, tortoiseshell combs, silver hand-mirrors and glass perfume bottles. Annat was fascinated. Even her mother had never had such treasures. But before Casildis could show her the face paints and lip rouge, there was a knock at the door and Govorin's voice called, "I've got a man here who needs bandaging. Will you do it, Casildis?"

"Send him in. I have to see to Annat's hand, so I will be physician for the day."

The door opened and Yuda came in, wearing only his trousers—clean ones, not the bloodstained pair he had worn when they arrived. He kept his eyes averted from Annat and Casildis, as if he feared they might be naked.

"Come here, Yuda, and let me look at you," ordered Casildis.

Annat sat on the edge of the bed and watched while Casildis examined him. Yuda's chest and shoulders were criss-crossed with fine white scars, and there were two barely healed marks over his ribs, part burn, part wound. Casildis touched the injuries with careful fingers.

"The Soul Men did this?" she asked.

"I stopped a power blast. It's like throwing yourself through a window. One of the wounds was pretty bad, but my mate Scorpion healed them as best she could."

"I have some ointment that will stop wounds festering. Sit at my dressing table while I fetch it from the still room."

Yuda obeyed, looking strangely out of place next to the array of delicate objects that crowded Casildis's dressing table.

Annat stared at him as she towelled her hair, wondering how many fights he had been in to acquire so many scars. Whatever he was thinking, he was keeping it from her, though without much sign of conscious effort. He only looked up when Casildis returned with a stone jar, labelled in a neat italic hand.

"This ointment has tincture of comfrey in it," she said, unstoppering the jar. "You may find it a little cold."

Yuda grimaced as she smeared the ointment over his side. Casildis worked deftly, using only a small amount of the cream. She looked up to his face for the first time as she did so.

"I made it myself," she said. "There have been no doctors in this village until you came, so we have to provide our own medicine. My mother gave me the receipts for many of these ointments."

Yuda seemed to emerge from his thoughts. He gave her one of his sudden, brilliant smiles.

"Govorin knows how to choose a woman," he said.

Casildis averted her eyes, pursing her lips in mild amusement.

"I'm sure I'm not his first," she said, standing up and wiping her fingers on one of the discarded towels.

"You're not. But you're certainly the prettiest."

Casildis gave a short laugh. She opened one of the drawers in her dressing table and took out some rolls of bandage.

"I'm the one who married him. That's what matters to me," she said.

Yuda stood up to let her wind the bandages round his midriff, which she did quickly and skillfully, fastening them with a safety pin. She did not seem aware that he was watching her every movement with a strange absorption, smiling to himself.

"There," said Casildis, standing back to examine what she had done. "We'll change those tomorrow. I'll give Annat a jar of ointment and some bandages. It will be useful for her to learn."

"Nah, I'll do it myself. I doubt if she's got your steady hand."

Annat did not protest at his slighting of her. Almost holding her breath, she was observing the caution of his movements in Casildis's presence, as if he were afraid that too large a gesture might damage her. Casildis showed no such restraint; she was so easy with him that she might have seemed contemptuous, if she had not appeared incapable of such meanness. She showed herself to be entirely without awe of him, as if he were a small boy who had been brought to her for bandaging.

"From what I hear, we'll soon be coming to you for healing, Mister Vasilyevich."

"Yes, at last I'll be doing what my father wanted—settling down to practise as a doctor, though not quite as he had imagined. I think he still doesn't understand how the One came to visit such outlandish children upon him."

Casildis stood looking at him with clasped hands, sudden pain in her eyes.

"Where I come from, they burn shamans alive."

Yuda held her gaze. "Tell me where you come from so that I can avoid it."

"She comes from the Forest of Ademar," Annat interjected, aware of a weird, unspoken tension between them. She had never seen anything like it before: a dialogue of actions beneath the words. Yuda glanced at her rather sharply.

"That sounds uncomfortably close," he joked.

"You know that Govorin's tunnel cuts under part of the forest. People began to die since work started there."

"And what would that have to do with me, Casildis?" said Yuda, challenging her softly.

"Govorin said—"

"Govorin talks too much. I understand that we're going to have lunch with your brother?" he said, holding her gaze with a steely look. Annat watched the two of them, catching her breath. She wondered what it was that Yuda wanted to prevent Casildis from saying.

The woman lowered her gaze. "Zhan is eager to meet you," she said.

Yuda folded his arms across his chest. "Shaka has met him once or twice," he commented, lowering his eyes. Casildis studied him anxiously, with the look of one seeking to read another's mind from his expression or gesture. Annat too wished she could gain access to Yuda's hidden thoughts. She surmised that Shaka had not liked the Deputy.

"He speaks of Shaka with great respect," said Casildis, as if she were seeking to reassure Yuda. But it was not Yuda who seemed concerned. He was frowning to himself with a look of inward concentration that reminded Annat of Malchik.

"Does he?" he said.

Casildis seemed almost awkward. She had lost the air of calm superiority that had made her so at ease with him.

"He says he would like to try a turn with him, man to man."

Yuda's eyebrows quivered, as if he were meditating upon a dry retort to this—Annat was sure he was—but he said, "That's an interesting compliment."

"My brother is a warrior. He meant it kindly."

"I'm sure he did. I'll tell Shaka when I next see him."

—*And laugh*, Annat thought at him. He showed no sign that he had received her thought, but she knew he had. He was just on the edge of laughter now. Casildis gave a hopeless shrug.

"Our ways must seem quaint to you."

"I don't know *your* ways yet, Casildis. I like what I've seen."

"Good," said Casildis. She seemed to want to be rid of him.

"I'd better put my shirt on," said Yuda, as if he understood. "I don't want to put everyone off their food."

Casildis laughed tensely. "I doubt if you will do that," she said.

Yuda smiled, and left without answering. When he had gone, Casildis sat down at her dressing table and unwound the towel from her hair. She sat staring at her reflection for a while, and touched her cleft lip.

"What a strange man your father is," she said.

Annat could think of all sorts of answers to this: her father and Rosa; the fight; her father hitting Malchik. She did not believe that Casildis wanted a reply.

"I haven't known him long," she said.

Chapter 5

It was early afternoon when they approached the Deputy's house. Casildis had covered her hair, which hung almost to her knees, with a long white veil, held in place with a silver band; she wore a green velvet cloak over her gown. Beside her, Annat felt plain and shabby in the black coat that Yuste had made for her two winters ago. Casildis had fallen into step behind the men, leaving Annat to wonder whether all the women of Gard Ademar walked several paces behind their husbands. She noticed that many of the houses of the village stood open, with a forlorn and even sinister look; their windows were like sad, hollow eyes.

"This village was abandoned until the Railway People moved here," Casildis explained.

"Why was it abandoned?" asked Annat. She had to take two paces for each of Casildis's long strides.

"It was said to be haunted," said Casildis. She shook her head. "The forest has spread since the Great Cold. It lies much nearer to this village than it used to. The villagers were always superstitious about the forest, but twenty years ago, they came to believe that they were no longer safe even if they avoided it. They decided to leave."

"But the forest must have been there for longer than twenty years," said Annat.

"Something came out of the forest," said Casildis.

By now, they were walking in the sunlight down a narrow cobbled street, walled on either side by little houses whose stuccoed walls were stained brilliant colors, cobalt blue or rose or sunflower yellow. The colors seemed to glow in the sunlight, and though there was no one but themselves in the street, there was an atmosphere of quiet activity; smoke drifting from chimney pots, smells of baking, and the barking of unseen dogs. In this street, Casildis's ominous words seemed out of place.

"Do you believe it's haunted?" asked Annat.

"It's haunted by evil," said Casildis quietly. "But a battle is being fought every day, both here and in the forest."

They left the narrow street and climbed a flight of steps up to a small, sloping square, where a plane tree grew in the centre, surrounded by railings. Some of its leaves were scattered across the cobbles. The houses which surrounded the square were built of a golden limestone similar to that which Annat had seen at the station.

The five of them walked up the slope to the far side of the square, where a terrace of tall houses three storeys high peeped down from shuttered windows. The limestone blocks were smoothly dressed and fitted together with only the finest cracks between them. Govorin stepped up to an oaken door with an iron knocker gripped in the jaws of a hole-eyed mask. Before the Sheriff had time to knock, the door was opened by a dumpy woman who wore a spotless white apron over a grey dress; her hair was covered with a coif. Govorin gave her a smile that she did not return.

"Is my deputy home?" he asked, speaking Franj.

"Come inside. You're expected," said the woman.

They entered a long, panelled hall that smelled of beeswax. Silver sconces were fixed to the walls, holding unlit candles. Over the stair well, a deer's antlered skull hung on a plaque above a ferocious display of weapons: swords, pikes and muskets arranged in a sunburst. The woman, who seemed to be a servant, disappeared down a side passage, leaving them standing in the hall. Nobody knew what to do next, until a door on the left-hand side of the hall opened, and a man emerged. He was taller than Malchik and almost as broad as Govorin. His presence seemed to fill the hall, as he bowed courteously, placing his hand on his breast. He wore ordinary clothes—grey trousers, and a blue checked shirt beneath a blue corduroy waistcoat—but his fingers were heavy with gold and jewelled rings of a simple yet rich design. Casildis was the first to approach him; she kissed him lightly on both cheeks.

"The Mother's peace to you, Zhan," she said.

Govorin stepped forward with an air of eager diffidence, and clasped the man's hand in his huge palm.

"Good day to you, Mister," he said. "This is Yuda Vasilyevich, and his children Annat and Malchik."

Annat felt that she ought to curtsey, but did not know how. She watched Yuda clasp the ringed hand; the man dwarfed him. Sarl had a broad, handsome face, with prominent cheekbones, a square jaw, and large, pale blue eyes. His hair, like Casildis's, was corn-fair, and clipped close to his head in ram's curls; he sported a pair of tawny sideburns.

"You are welcome to this house," he said.

"Thank you," said Malchik, who was the only one tall enough to look him in the eye. He seemed like a reed beside Sarl's muscled form.

The Deputy ushered them into a room furnished with the same massive grandeur as his rings. The chairs were hewn from oak and the table was a single polished board. Two huge grey dogs lay before a fire of logs, and a tabby cat was curled on the hearth stone. Woven hangings patterned with leaves trembled in the draught from the fire, and there was a heady scent of cinnamon and cloves. When Annat saw the dining table, she was inclined to gasp; the wine goblets were made from rose-colored crystal, the plates were gold, and a silver salt cellar towered in the centre of the table.

Sarl poured wine from a dusty bottle into one of the goblets, and pledged them in turn, before passing the cup to Govorin. Govorin seemed to know what he was expected to do, for he pledged Sarl in return, took a mouthful of wine and handed the goblet to Yuda. Yuda took it in his right hand, but instead of repeating the process, said a blessing over it, smiled and drank. When he gave it to Malchik, the young man seemed to suffer a moment of indecision before he repeated the blessing, sipped the wine and then waved it uncertainly at Sarl, who took it from him with a small inclination of the head. He did not offer it to Casildis or Annat. When the men had shared the cup of wine, the maid returned to take their outdoor clothes.

"Beautiful dogs," said Yuda, wandering over to scratch one behind the ears. It lifted its head and looked at him with soul-ful eyes.

"A pair of wolfhounds," said Sarl. "They come from a fine stock."

"Do you hunt wolves?" asked Yuda. He went on fondling the dog's neck.

"Wolves, deer, wild boar; the forest is full of game," said Sarl.

"Sarl is a good marksman. He can use a bow or a gun," said Govorin.

"I will show you my stable," said Sarl. "You can pick any mount you wish."

"I can't ride," said Yuda, standing up. He grimaced slightly, having forgotten his wounds.

"I think Vasilyevich needs a chair," said Govorin amiably. "He was wounded today fighting the Soul Men."

"Where was he wounded?" said Sarl.

Annat thought this an odd question.

"Too near the kidneys," said Yuda, easing himself into a chair. He felt his right side, disproving what he had just said. Sarl began to smile, as if a joke had been made that he would not admit he did not understand.

"Don't let him fool you, Sarl," said Govorin. "He's one of the Railway's best fighters. The guards would follow him into hell and back."

"What is your weapon, Mister Vasilyevich?" asked Sarl.

"I am," said Yuda. "But I can use a knife if I have to."

"And is your son a warrior too?" asked Sarl, thumping Malchik on the shoulder.

"No, I'm not," said Malchik firmly.

Annat saw Yuda's face. He would have preferred a son who was a shaman, and who shared some of his daring. He was dis-appointed and ashamed that he could not even hope to train

Malchik to follow him. Annat wished her father could be satisfied with her talents, but she feared that he would not find the same satisfaction in teaching a daughter, however powerful. She could not help thinking that Sarl had somehow perceived this and deliberately drawn attention to it, though he seemed so amicable.

The meal was delicious. There were no Unclean meats to offend a Wanderer: pigeon pies cooked with wild mushrooms, a salad of endives, and pears stewed in wine. It was only when Annat finished eating and began to listen to the conversation that she became aware of an unease, like an itch in her mind. Somehow, she could not like Sarl, though his smile was effulgent and his eyes seemed friendly. Govorin was so different. For all his bulk there was a delicacy about him; he handled the fragile glasses lightly, with precision. He could be both strong and gentle. Annat puzzled herself over what characteristics of Sarl's repelled her. Nothing that she summoned up seemed fair or sensible. His eyes were too blue; his hair too yellow; his smile too brilliant. Annat reproved herself for taking a dislike to him. She could not help noticing, however, that Yuda was giving off a similar emotion. Though he did not let it show in his conduct, he was not enjoying himself.

"How is Madame your wife?" said Govorin, politely.

"She is well, thank you. The women may go up to see her, if they wish. Then we can talk freely without fear of offending them. I am not used to this southern custom where the women take meat with the men."

"I suppose it must seem strange to you, but it seems very ordinary to us," said Govorin and, with just a touch of irony, "What do you want to do, Casildis?"

"Have no fear. I know Zhan wants us gone so he can talk of hunting, fighting and other male pleasures."

Casildis rose from her chair with a silvery rustle of cotton and silk. "Go on, Zhan. I know you're itching to ask Mister Vasilyevich about the fight."

"Do I have to go too?" said Annat, indignant that Malchik should be privileged to stay, though the conversation promised sounded infinitely dull. Casildis took her hand in a cool, firm grip.

"Mari Reine wants to meet you. I know she is upstairs with nothing but her loom for company. Besides, Zhan won't be happy unless we both leave."

The men had to stand up as they left the table, though both Malchik and Yuda hesitated as if they were worshippers attending the wrong ceremony. Yuda gave Annat a small ironic wave. She was sure he would have preferred women's gossip to Sarl's oratory. Malchik looked dismayed, as if faced with another communal bath.

Casildis led Annat up the stairs at the end of the hall, beneath the stag's head. Higher up were more animal heads, some bone, some stuffed. As Annat noticed a handsome armorial shield, bearing a design of four black birds on a red ground, something stirred in her mind, and she paused to look at it, before hurrying after Casildis. On the first landing hung a huge tapestry which depicted men in green tunics and leggings spearing a black boar. A glass case housed a collection of reliquaries, fashioned from silver and beaten gold, which bore labels in an italic hand describing in faded ink the fragments of saint and martyr that each contained. Annat scuttled past the relics; she did not understand the pleasure the Doxoi took in preserving and venerating the corpses of their holy people. To the Wanderers only their books, given them by the One, were sacred.

On the next floor, everything was different. It was not just the perfume, with hints of cloves and musk; the wall-hanging showed a lovely woman greeting a unicorn and showing it its reflection in a mirror. The background was spangled with stylized flowers.

"Mari made these tapestries as part of her dowry," said Casildis. "She has become a mistress of her art. I can only weave patterns myself."

She opened one of the doors off the landing. Annat entered a room that was empty except for a big loom and cushions and bolsters strewn across the floor over a rich woven rug. A veiled woman was sitting at the loom, working the shuttles with deft fingers. She looked up as Casildis opened the door and Annat saw that her right eye was bruised and swollen.

"Bright Lady!" Casildis crossed the room in a few strides. "What has he done to you now!"

"It's nothing," said Mari Reine, tugging the veil forward to obscure her face. "He was angry that I stayed so long at your house."

"Leave him, Mari."

"Sarl is my husband."

"And have you become so good a Doxan that you will stay with him however he abuses you?"

"You know that I am not Doxan in my heart, Casildis."

Annat leaned on the door, uncertain whether or not she should be listening. The women were speaking Franj, and several of the words they used were unfamiliar to her. Mari Reine seemed to notice the shape of her silence for the first time, for she stretched out her hand to draw Annat closer. Annat approached the loom almost on tiptoe, as if she were in the presence of a religious. The room had a strange quiet, a stillness, and the slanting light from the windows seemed to fall crisp and cool on the white of the walls and the bare wood of the loom. It was like walking into a shrine, or the room where *Zaide* studied, in which Annat had often stood in silence watching the movement of her grandfather's head as he rocked to and fro over the Holy Books.

Mari Reine took Annat's hand in her cool, dry fingers. Her face was smooth and flawless with golden skin like the painted face of the Mother's statue in the temples. Her uninjured eye was brown and sad. Annat felt that she was looking into a whirlpool of knowledge and time: the knowledge of many centuries of women who had worked at a loom like this, even in the time of the Kadagoi, even in the Year of the Son. If she held Mari's hand for long, she would be sucked into that whirlpool.

"Who are you, Missis?" she asked. As she spoke, she felt that something had been snatched from her, a glimpse of a cold world. But Mari Reine was only the gateway to that world, and she was not stained or chilled by it.

"Just as your mother had her doll, we have our secrets," said Casildis.

Annat stared at the half-finished design on the loom. A myriad star-like flowers bloomed around the feet of a woman and the hooves of a unicorn. She reached out to touch the web with its many knots of color.

"I don't know what you mean," she said, thinking aloud.

Casildis rested her hand gently on Mari's shoulder, as if to comfort her. "There is so little that we can tell you, beyond rumours. Stories that our mothers whispered to us."

Annat pretended not to hear. She felt her gaze drawn to Mari's sad eikon-face.

"Let me examine your eye," she said, without shyness. Small healings were easy, even to someone like herself, with no training.

Casildis drew back, and Annat took Mari's face between her hands, turning it carefully to the light. The sun turned the woman's open eye a rich, light-filled bronze.

"I am far from my mother's house," said Mari, and Annat saw water welling at the edge of her lids and spilling from the bruised eye. Annat bit her lip. The pain of the other woman seemed to become her pain. She thought of coolness, and raised her right hand until it skimmed the swollen and shiny skin of Mari's eyelid. The power trickled out of her fingertips in a chill stream very different from the harsh fighting blasts of yesterday, which had burned her.

"Where does she live?" she heard herself say.

As she watched, the swelling began to dwindle, and the cruel redness faded. Mari made a small, choked sound in her throat. Casildis's reply seemed to reach Annat from a distance, the words drifting through the air like motes of dust.

"Our mothers were born of the forest, and they remembered how it was once told that women worshipped there without men to rule them."

Annat blinked. The tips of her fingers were itching. She bent close to Mari's eye, and inspected it, the long dark lashes, the honey skin, and the clear, undamaged lens. The eye itself was not a window that looked out at her, but a living stone glistening on the bed of a stream.

"You should keep it covered for a few hours," she said, in *Zaide*'s doctor-voice. "To let the healing settle."

Mari raised her hand to her face, and felt her eye with cautious fingers. "It is healed," she said, turning to her friend with a smile. Annat drew back, gathering her hands together at her waist. She felt ashamed at the women's wonder, when she had only performed a simple healing, far more rudimentary than the complex work she knew her father could perform. Casildis was inspecting Mari's eye like a watchmaker who studies a precious gem.

"It's flawless," she said, straightening to smile at Annat as if she wanted not only to praise, but also to share her pride in Annat's success. Annat was not used to such quick rewards for her work; though Yuste had been pleased, she had seldom showed it. The new emotion was like a sudden draught of warm wine, strong and sweet.

"It wasn't very much," she said, awkwardly.

Casildis took her by the shoulders and kissed her on both cheeks, her lips lightly brushing Annat's skin.

"Perhaps soon, the time of the stories will return," she said.

Annat could not make much sense of this talk. Her religion spoke only of the One, who was remote and indivisible, and yet as close and ready to hand as a wooden cup.

"I don't know what you're talking about," she said, drawing back.

Casildis gazed at her, smiling, and fingering the beads of her garnet necklace. "When I have known you longer, there will be things I can tell you, Annat," she said. "But for now, like Mari, I must keep silence."

They were probably talking about knitting, Malchik thought. He did not know which was worse. He had never suspected that there was so much to say about venison. And when Sarl had finished talking about the hunt, he began to question Yuda about his battles. It had been very different when he and Yuda were alone with Govorin. The Sheriff was a cultured man and, as he talked of City times with Yuda, Malchik caught some of the excitement of Masalyar with its wide boulevards, markets and dockside bars. Sitting at Sarl's table, Govorin did not show any sign of boredom, but Malchik's face was stiff with trying not to yawn. The rich, thick dessert wine beckoned him towards sleep; he felt his eyelids begin to waver.

"Is your wife ill?" Malchik heard his father say. He sat up. Sarl was toying with an empty goblet.

"It is not the custom among our people for a married woman to come amongst strangers."

A word formed on Govorin's lips and his brow creased into an exclamation mark of annoyance.

"You mean she doesn't go out?" said Yuda.

"Should not. She forgets herself, sometimes."

Malchik thought of his aunt and what she would have to say about this situation. In his home, women had been the strong force; *Zaide* kept to his room and his studies. He stared at Sarl's face, trying to detect a hint of irony. Though he knew his father would be laughing behind Sarl's back, something about the Deputy's assurance angered him.

"How do you justify that?" he burst out. *Zaide* had encouraged such scholarly disputation, which had sometimes degenerated into squabbling.

Sarl's blue eyes met his, but with no flash of anger or surprise. Malchik had not spoken until now; he was not a warrior, not a hunter, and there had been nothing he could say.

"Justify?" The Deputy was honestly puzzled. Malchik felt the heat of embarrassment in his cheeks, but pressed on, though he feared that his question might offend against local custom.

"Why do you keep her indoors?"

"Men are weak." Sarl shrugged at the obvious. "The sight of a woman's beauty might tempt them. And a woman who loses her honour is nothing. So it is best for all if the women keep indoors. The Sheriff knows that I think he gives Casildis too large a rein."

"What happens when you find that your wife has been out?" said Yuda, puckering his mouth with his fingers.

"I punish her," said Sarl. "I am her lord, she is my vassal. She owes me obedience."

"It doesn't quite work like that where we come from," said Govorin, leaning back in his chair to steal a glance at Yuda.

"I know. I have seen the City women. I do not understand it. The City must be a decadent place where men show women no respect."

"But I understand that you were friends with Isabel Guerreres," said Yuda.

Sarl thought for a while before answering. "Isabel had the mind and spirit of a man. She was wedded to her sword, like one of the Mother's sacred virgins. She was not as other women are."

"I'll say she wasn't," muttered Yuda.

"I have nothing but sorrow for her death," said Sarl. "But you knew her?"

Yuda thumped his chest with his fist. "In here," he said. "She used to be my sword-partner."

"Who was she?" said Malchik. The wine had fired him up inside, and he felt none of his usual shyness.

"The Railway People engaged her to investigate the trouble," said Govorin. "She was murdered. It must have been someone she knew, for there were no signs of a forced entry, but her throat had been cut."

"Isabel could have defended herself. Unless it was another shaman," said Yuda.

"There were no other shamans in Gard Ademar then," said Govorin.

"It could have been a cloaked shaman. Someone so powerful that they could hide their powers."

"Maybe." Govorin peered into the bottom of his glass.

"Do you seek revenge?" Sarl asked Yuda.

"Me? I'd like to see his face. Or hers, if it was a woman."

"Justice is more important," said Govorin.

Malchik swigged from his glass and wiped his mouth, seeking more courage. The lamps looked a little brighter now. The three men were haloed. He thought about revenge, wondering if he felt more than a dull hate towards his father. The difference in their physical strength was too great. He could never stand up against Yuda and strike him down. The thought was overwhelming and frightening, transforming the warmth of the drink into hollow fear.

"Revenge is good," he heard himself say, with a thick tongue.

"What do you know about revenge?" said Yuda, turning towards him with friendly mockery.

Malchik got the words out. Underneath surged fright, but the heat of bravado kept it down.

"You hit my mother once," he said, in a voice that was slow and dull as clay.

Yuda said nothing. There was a strange look on his face, as if he had been slapped and was too shocked for an instant to feel anger.

"You remember all that," he said.

"All of it," said Malchik, unaware of anyone else in the room.

"Malchik—" Govorin began.

"No, Sergey. I want to hear him talk," said Yuda, stretching out his hand.

"That's it," said Malchik, feeling a surge of relief tinged with nausea. The wine ebbed and flowed in his skull like a golden wave.

"I remember too," said Yuda. His gaze pleaded with Malchik. "All those years, from when you were a little *kind*. I had to run away." He swung round to look at Sarl. "Tell me the secret of it, Mister. How you forgive yourself. How you learn to say it doesn't matter."

Sarl looked sidelong at Govorin, as if trying to bring in his sympathy with a smile, but the Sheriff had covered his eyes with his hands.

"I don't think I understand you, Mister Vasilyevich."

"We treat our women with respect," said Yuda, raggedly. "Too much respect. They creep like worms into our hearts. We can't hit the bitches. You've got the right idea, Mister Sarl. Don't let 'em go out."

"Enough, Vasilyevich," said Govorin in a voice low as distant thunder.

The crystal glass cracked into beaded fragments in Yuda's hand. "She took my son away from me," he said.

Malchik felt the overwhelming nausea wash over him. He gripped the table, swallowing bile. The room had become the deck of a ship, pitching and yawing. He gazed at his father through tears of sickness and felt an unknown, jagged emotion tear at him. *A worm in the heart.* He understood his father's rage and hurt. The same emotions gripped him, tossing him

over the drunken waves of the wine. Someone had taken his
father's son from him. *Alone on the clifftop his mother cradled
him in arms that gave no warmth or safety.* He bit his tongue.

"I didn't want you to go," he said, spitting the words out of
his chest like a sob.

Yuda was staring at his cut hand in astonishment. "Zyon!"
he said. The sudden pain had sobered him. Sarl stood up.

"I will send the maid to fetch water," he said.

"No. We should leave. I've drunk too much. And so has
Malchik."

"Listen to me!" Malchik shouted. "I didn't want you to go."

Yuda looked at him with quiet eyes. "I know that, Malchku.
But I had no choice."

Someone staggered towards him across the swaying floor.
Malchik collapsed on the floor at his feet and hid his face in
his father's lap. Cool smell of laundered cloth. Darkness. He
had crossed the distance of the void, torn and racked by that
strange new emotion. His tears fell from a stranger's eyes. He
felt the touch on his head, light as a bird's wing brushing his
hair.

"We've got a long way to go, you and I," said Yuda's voice,
his speech broken by uneven breaths.

Govorin's arms lifted Malchik easily to his feet. The Sheriff
held him steady like a place of anchor in a storm. Yuda stood
up, hands in his jacket pockets.

"I'm sorry," he said to Sarl.

The Deputy's mighty form towered across the room, like a
golden statue.

"I have no sons," he said.

"I'm sorry," said Yuda again. He turned to Govorin, and
their eyes met.

"Someone had better call the women," said the Sheriff.

"We can't go upstairs, Mister," said Malchik, thumping him
on the shoulders.

"You certainly can't. We'll go on ahead. It's not dark yet."
Malchik heard Govorin sigh.

"I will accompany them. They should not be out alone,"
said Sarl.

"She's your sister, Sarl. You square it with her," said the Sheriff.

They staggered back through the twilit streets, with Malchik unevenly supported between Yuda and Govorin. Malchik's legs seemed to want to go the opposite way to his body; he kept trying to count them, and was uneasy to find that he sometimes numbered more than two. After the anguish of the last minutes, he felt light-headed and happy. If he got any lighter, he would take off over the rooftops, dragging his companions with him. Govorin was his oldest friend and he felt he had to tell him everything.

"I didn't like him. You see."

Govorin grunted. He had one of Malchik's arms wound round his neck and was trying to stop it from strangling him. On the other side, Yuda was too short to provide much assistance.

"I think he means me," Yuda commented.

"He was so tall," Malchik mused. There was someone much smaller than him, small and thin. He tried to remember who it was.

"I had to protect her. The falcon and the tower. When my true father came for me."

Yuda's hand gripped his shirt. Malchik tried to focus on the pied features, seeing a mess of eyebrows, nose and mouth.

"What do you mean, your *true father*?"

"*Mame* told me. That he would rescue us. From the evil one."

"Let him go, Yuda. It's the wine talking."

"Tell me the truth, Malchik. Are you mine? Tell me!"

"She said—" Malchik broke off. "I'm afraid of him," he said to no one.

Yuda tore away from him and kicked a stone. "She'd do that," he swore bitterly, "tell the *kind* he wasn't mine. Fill his head with shit."

"I knew all along," Malchik confided, breathing warmly over Govorin's neck. He burped, and a bubble burst in his mind, letting him see with clarity. "It didn't matter," he congratulated himself.

Yuda sat down in the road. "I can't take this," he said. "You take him home, Sergey. Take him away from me."

"He was my father," Malchik concluded.

"Tell me his name, then. Get it over with," said Yuda, running his hands through his hair.

Malchik looked at the little man in the road, shrunken and blackened, without enchantment. He felt a little surprised.

"Who's that?" he asked Govorin.

"Come on, Malchik. You need to lie down," said the Sheriff.

"I'll remember who he was in the morning," Malchik agreed.

The road was hard. Long, warm shadows made flabby lines across the cobbles. Malchik stumbled along, his weight dragging against the strength that upheld him. The moment of clarity had left his mind and he did not understand what he had known. From somewhere behind him came a cry like the voice of a beast.

Govorin stopped and drew the Circle on his brow. "Mother," he said.

Malchik stared up at the sloping tawny roofs. The sound of madness chilled him to sobriety. His father's quick shape appeared beside him. "Boy? Did you hear that?"

"Yes," said Malchik, soberly. He reached out to touch the man's shoulders. "I thought it was you."

"You scared us, Yuda," said the Sheriff.

"Even I don't scream that loud," said Yuda, his cheeks puckering.

"Then what the hell was it?" said Govorin.

Yuda snapped a flame from his fingers. "I'd give a lot to know," he said, shielding the flame to light his cigarette. "I'm almost glad Sarl is seeing the women home, though he may yet bore them to death."

Malchik felt he moment of knowledge and pity slipping away from him. He caught his father's sleeve, almost roughly, and for an instant saw an unguarded look from Yuda, one which did not quite conceal his sadness. "I can't say it yet," said Malchik, struggling against his heart. "Don't you see? It doesn't matter what *Mame* said. Even if someone else was my father. He never did come to rescue us. That was just her dream, a princess in a castle with a knight coming to save her. Because my real father was a Wanderer."

"I see," said Yuda. "Thanks, boy. It can't be easy for you to say that. I know you have no love for me."

"I wish—"

"What?"

Malchik looked at his father. He wanted to squeeze him tightly, to feel the pressure of his slender bones. He laughed at himself. There were certain things that a man or a boy was not allowed to say; a rule as rigid and ridiculous as Sarl's strictures concerning women. His spectacles were askew and Yuda appeared slightly blurred. Malchik had never been able to see him right.

Yuda turned away. "This is a dangerous place," he said.

"I knew things wouldn't be peaceful once you arrived," said Govorin.

They made it home without any further mishap. In the kitchen of the Sheriff's house, Govorin lit the lamps and brewed strong coffee. They sat in silence until Annat and Casildis arrived, laughing.

"He saw us all the way home," said Casildis, doffing her cloak.

"He hits his wife," said Annat, gravely.

Malchik stared at his little sister. He wished he could forget what he had been saying, but somehow it was etched into his mind. Annat was so much the image of their father, with her swart brows and brilliant eyes. She never had any difficulty in saying what she thought; the words came from her mind into her mouth. Or, if she wanted, she could use *sprechen* in silence. He could not tell Yuda something very simple, that hatred and anger in him co-existed with a painful, long-forgotten love.

"Bad man," said Yuda, wryly, giving Malchik a look.

Casildis stared at them. "What happened to you three?" she asked.

"Ask Govorin in bed," said Yuda.

"We all had a little too much to drink. That's all," said Govorin.

Annat gave her father a quizzical glance. He shook his head.

Malchik wondered what had passed between them. He envied their easy communication. With the best words he could not say enough. He watched his sister's neat form draw out a chair next to Yuda's and sit down beside him, saying nothing. Malchik could tell from the little movements they made that they were conversing.

"Zhan intimated that there had been some heated discussion," said Casildis. "I don't think he could tell what was going on."

"I doubt if he's met anyone like Vasilyevich before. Or Malchik. They don't know his code and he certainly doesn't know theirs."

"Mari's face was bruised again."

"I wish I could do something, but I have no jurisdiction."

"You could speak to him, Sergey. He respects you. He won't listen to me."

"I don't think he would understand—or tolerate—any attempt to interfere with his rights. Mari belongs to him."

"Thank the Mother that I married you."

Malchik listened shyly. He hoped Casildis would not notice him staring at her. Her face was perfect oval, and the crack of her split lip, which gave her voice a slight sibilance, did not mar her appearance. Whereas Sarl seemed cast in bronze or gold, she was mobile and soft, like a bough of blossom quivering in the wind. Except for his mother, whose face he scarcely recalled, all the women that Malchik had known had been plain and strong-featured. He glanced at his sister to make a secret comparison, but he knew her face too well. Instead, a sudden and urgent nausea rose from his belly, reminding him that he had drunk too much tonight. He stumbled to the sink and was violently, thankfully sick.

Chapter 6

Malchik was so ill that they had had to leave him at the Sheriff's house, and Govorin brought Annat and her father to their new house alone. And she had her own bedroom! While Govorin and Yuda were talking in the kitchen, she ran from room to room, opening up cupboards and peering under beds. The house was one of the small, brightly painted dwellings that they had passed earlier that day. Downstairs were the kitchen and the room that Yuda was to use as his surgery; on the first floor were two neat, whitewashed bedrooms; and a ladder led from the landing up to the loft, which Annat claimed as her own. The signature of Casildis's lavender floated from closets and between sheets pressed flat as the leaves of a book. Annat flung herself down on the narrow bed, though she was too elated to be tired. At home, she had always shared a room with Malchik, though it was divided by a curtain to give them privacy. Here there was a dormer window in each side of the roof, one overlooking the street and the other the dark garden behind the house. She lay looking at the rafters in the light of her oil lamp, her mind racing as she tried to remember what Casildis had hinted to her.

Annat felt a little snaky shiver go down her back. Picking up the doll, she crossed the room to gaze into the mirror that hung by the door. She saw a thin, sallow-faced girl about whose head shadows leapt and danced. A grey mist of age bloomed across the surface of the gilt-framed glass, so that her reflection seemed to peer at her out of a distant watery darkness. Annat breathed a mist on to the surface. If she stood here too long, the warmth of her blood would draw something out of the depths, something cold and hungry. Annat hugged the doll against her thin chest. She felt a faint, unseen fire that coiled under her hand. *Mame* had given her the doll as if it were a toy, telling her nothing of its name or secrets. But now she knew that, in its helplessness, the doll protected Annat from the hungry, hollow eyes that lay beneath the surface of the mirror.

She lay down on the bed again, and the bed became a boat that carried her off down an unknown river. The light woke her, lying on top of the covers, still dressed in her new clothes. She jumped out of bed and ran to the window that overlooked the street, throwing open the shutters. Outside, a silvery dawn was rising over the misty streets. And a queue of people was waiting outside their front door. Annat leaned perilously out of the window.

"Hallo," she shouted, "have you come to see the Doctor?"

She was used to similar scenes from *Zaide*'s house. The waiting patients looked up at her in surprise. At this hour, the streets were chill, and they were muffled up in coats and thick scarves. Annat could not quite hear what they were trying to tell her, but she called out, "Wait there. I'll go and wake him."

She burst into Yuda's room to find that he was still a hump under the covers. Annat shook him vigorously, and was nearly knocked out for her pains. Yuda surfaced, blinking furiously.

"Never do that again, *kind*," he warned. "I might have killed you."

Annat was unquelled. "You've got patients downstairs waiting for you."

Yuda swung his legs over the side of the bed, using the sheet to protect his modesty. "Great," he said. "I was hoping to enjoy my hangover a little longer."

Annat grinned at him. "I'll get you some water," she said. "And I'll go down and let them in."

"Next time you burst into my bedroom, please knock first. I might have had company."

"I don't mind."

"But I do. Get out of here while I put some clothes on," he added, giving her a playful shove.

Annat bounded down the stairs to open the front door. She looked up into the face of an elderly man with rime-touched eyebrows. The kitchen was warm from the heat of the wood stove, and she let in all the patients, who stood about, dripping on to the floor. Instead of using a pump in the rear yard, Annat found that she could get water out of a metal tap over a sturdy white sink that stood next to the stove. Back home, she would have had to put on her coat and boots and go to the pump outside the back door, to crank it by hand until the bucket was full of water, flakes of rust and drowned spiders. She searched for a kettle to brew hot water for *chai*, which Sklavs preferred to coffee. When she counted the patients, she found that there were five, including a mother with a small boy who was so tightly wrapped that his arms and legs stood out stiffly. Leaving the kettle heating on the stove, Annat hurried up the stairs, slopping water in all directions. She found Yuda dressed, trying to comb his hair and shave at the same time.

"I'll make you some breakfast," she said.

"No food. Just *chai*. Zyon, what time is it?"

"Just after dawn."

"What time do these people get up?"

"We always rise at dawn at home."

"I hate the countryside," he grunted, wiping his chin with a towel. "What's that noise?"

Annat stood still. The faint hubbub of voices from downstairs had changed to a clamour of shouts and heavy feet.

"I'll go down and look," she began.

"No, you wait here. I don't like the sound of that."

Belting on his knife, Yuda hurried from the room. Annat sat down on the bed, listening to his light footsteps go down the stair. She wished that she could go with him, to be like Scorpion, a shaman-warrior who could fight at her father's side. She was beginning to feel cold in her thin blouse and smock. She rummaged through his pack, but Yuda was not the sort of person who bothered to carry thick sweaters. Annat had to return to her own room, where she struggled to pull on woollen tights and one of the ungainly pullovers that Yuste had knitted for her. Suddenly, Yuda was standing in the door. The sense of his shock was like a blow in the face.

"Come now," he commanded, and Annat followed him without question. Halfway down the stairs, he took her hand in a thin, hard grip. "Do you faint at the sight of blood?"

"I don't faint," said Annat.

In the new surgery, a man lay on the plain white table, half his throat torn out, his breath faint and rattling. The room was full of sweating, frightened men, earth grained into their hands. Yuda, small, separate, quiet, touched the fluttering pulse in the unsevered vein. His eyes met Annat's. Bile tasted thin and sour in her mouth, but she must not fail him. He had brought her down to confirm his opinion, that there was nothing to be done. She shook her head.

"We can't save him," said Yuda. "Where did you find him?"

"He was on guard at the tunnel mouth. We always have someone there since—"

The one speaking was a tall boy with blue eyes and a shock of dark hair. He looked as if anger were keeping his tears in. Yuda put his hand over the dying man's eyes. The faint pulse stilled.

"A wild animal might have done this," he said. "What was his name?" His pale face had no color in it, like newly bleached paper.

"Zarras, sir. He's the seventh one, not counting Missis Isabel and the ones who've disappeared. They were all found near the tunnel," said the tall youth.

"I'm sorry," said Yuda. "Did they all die this way?"

The men glanced at Annat, who stood with her back to the wall, still staring at the sad, ruined body on the table. It was the first death she had witnessed.

"Some was worse," said the youth. "And some hadn't a mark on them. But their faces! They died of fright."

"You'd better tell the Sheriff. Let him know that I want to see him."

"Yes, sir," they said, hesitantly stepping forward to pick up the body.

"The name's Vasilyevich," he said.

When they had gone, he stumbled into the kitchen where the first patients still waited, subdued and silent, and began to wash his hands in the sink. Annat followed him.

—*You helped him to die,* she thought.

—*All I could do.*

He leaned over the sink, trying to calm himself with lung-fuls of air. A death under his hands; he had nursed the last spark of life into nothingness.

—*I'm sorry.*

—*To be sorry isn't enough; you have to die with them.*

—*I don't understand.*

Yuda turned and rested his wet hand on her shoulder.

—*I hope it's a long time before you do understand.*

When he had dealt with the other patients, with Annat's help, she accompanied him to the Sheriff's house, where they found Malchik installed in the kitchen, eating a considerable breakfast that Govorin had cooked for them both. The smell of fried eggs made Annat's stomach turn, but her brother seemed to have suffered no after-effects from last night. Casildis had already gone out.

Govorin came to greet them with a frying pan in his hand. There were some strange-looking fritters in it, sizzling in olive oil.

"I hope you'll join us," he said.

Yuda shook his head. "Cigarettes and *chai* will do me," he said. "Natka can have some if she wants. You heard the news about Mister Zarras?"

Govorin flipped two of the fritters on to Malchik's plate. "I heard," he said. "That makes seven deaths—no, eight. Not counting the ones killed in accidents." He served himself, sat down and began to eat. "There's *chai* in the samovar. Casildis can't work out how to use it."

Annat sat down at the table, staring as the Sheriff consumed large mouthfuls of food. She could not understand how little he seemed to mind that one of his men had just died a horrible death. She watched Yuda turn the tap on the brass samovar and fill four mugs with *chai*.

"What about the ones who disappeared?" asked Yuda, placing a mug of steaming brew before the Sheriff. For some reason, Annat found herself recalling his exchange of yesterday with Casildis. He had interrupted the woman when she was trying to tell him what he seemed keen to ask Govorin now.

"Accoring to the locals, that was why they abandoned the village in the first place. People started to wander off into the forest, and never came back." He waved a fork, chewing. "But since our people settle here, there have been deaths as well as disappearances."

"It must have occurred to you that someone is trying to drive out the Railway People," said Yuda.

"It's certainly occurred to me," said Govorin. "But who? The villagers are as scared as us."

Annat smelled blood. Suddenly the room grew small, distantly focused. She felt the faint heartbeats against her own pulse, and breathed the fear with its stench of shit and piss. A warm tide rolled up over her head, and she saw their distant startled faces rise, turning into the ceiling.

She woke up lying on a couch in a blue-draped room. Yuda was kneeling beside her holding her wrist.

"What happened?" she asked, sitting up.

"You tell me."

He let go of her wrist with a professional frown.

"Where am I?"

"Some room belonging to Casildis. Why did you faint now?"

"I don't know."

Yuda stood up and turned his back on her. "Nothing like it before?" he asked, touching one of the iris-blue hangings.

"It was the blood."

Annat found it difficult to explain what had happened to her.

"You'll have to get used to that," Yuda said, brusquely.

Annat struggled to find the right words. She wished she could think straight into his mind, but he had sealed it to her.

"It was *my* blood," she said.

Yuda sat down beside her on the couch. As if thinking

aloud, he began, "In the mines, the men keep a bird in a cage.
It's the first to die if there's poison gas in the air, and they
know that they have to escape. You could be like that bird,
sensing the danger before the others can. Let's go."

"Where?" asked Annat, who was still dizzy and confused.

"To the tunnel."

Silver rails wound between new embankments, still rough-cut
and thick with fireweed. A long autumn shadow danced from
Annat's feet as she ran ahead of Yuda and Govorin. The thick,
sickly dread she had felt in the house was dispelled like rags of
mist from a breeze, and she forgot the dead man's face with its
rictus of terror. Still, the tunnel was an awesome place, gaping
like the mouth of an earth-god. Higher than the steeple of a
Doxan temple, the arch swarmed with men and women in blue
overalls who pushed spoil carts. The first few hundred yards
were already lined with courses of new brick; beyond stood
the massive wooden frames where the masons worked, lining
the vaults with stone; and at the end, the work face, was the
great metal frame built of sections of bolted steel, where the
gangers worked with mattocks, carving out solid rock. It was
too noisy to speak or think; by the wavering light of oil lamps,
Annat watched the striving shadows. There was a smell of
fresh sweat and raw earth. She felt small and unsafe, and
shrank close to Yuda. A fat woman strode past with a basket of
soil on her shoulder, nodding to Govorin as she passed. Her
face was a mask of grime.

When they returned to the tunnel entrance, Govorin showed
them where the gangers had found the dead man. The foreman,
a Franj called Lesol, had marked the spot with a cairn of peb-
bles, but there was no need. Gouts of blood lay on the grass,
and the ground was trampled and scarred.

"How did they find him?" Yuda asked Lesol.

"The guard was changed at mid of the night. They left
Zarras with a lamp and a gun. Just before dawn, some of the
gangers in the camp heard screams. They found him lying
here, his throat torn. The gun had vanished."

"So the animal that killed him took the gun," said Yuda,
with a dark smile. Govorin snorted.

"It wasn't an animal, Mister," said Lesol. He was a short brown man, whose curly hair was thinning on top. He wore a dirty-grey singlet and baggy blue trousers. Yuda offered him a cigarette, which he took with cautious pleasure.

"Did he fire the gun?" Yuda asked him.

"We heard two shots. And then the screaming, as if a man's soul was being torn out."

Yuda made a flame between his thumb and finger, and enjoyed the foreman's look of surprise. Lesol drew a circle on his brow, the sign of the Wheel.

"He's a shaman, Lesol," said Govorin.

"Thank you, Mister," said the foreman, doubtfully, and lit his cigarette from the flame as if he expected it to explode in his face.

"So who was the first at the scene?" Yuda asked.

"They fetched me. The boy, Philippe, and one of the strangers. Philippe helped to bring him to your house."

"You're a local man, Mister Lesol?"

The foreman turned to Govorin. His hands and his shrug expressed suspicion.

"Who is he, Mister Sheriff?"

Govorin put his hand on Yuda's shoulder. "My friend and a friend of Zhan Sarl's. He has come here to be our doctor."

Lesol fingered his chin, letting his glance drift towards Yuda and then Annat. "You know nothing, you Railway People," he said. "You don't know what we've suffered. This was a good place once. Do you think you can come here and make it right with your science and steam? Some things are too dark."

"You're right, Lesol," said Govorin. "We don't understand what's going on. And we're suffering with you. The girl Isabel was murdered, and seven more of the strangers, as you call us, have been killed here. You have to help us."

Lesol made a cutting gesture with his hand. "No. My wife needs a husband, my children need a father. I have already said too much."

Yuda caught Lesol by the straps of his singlet and, without much sign of effort, lifted him off the ground. Since Lesol was a little taller than Yuda, and plaqued with muscle, this was a surprising feat.

"Listen," he said. "The Sheriff is a reasonable man. I'm not. Isabel was my friend, and I'm going to find out who killed her, at the least."

Govorin tried to get between them, but Yuda had taken such a ferocious grip on Lesol that the Sheriff's efforts were in vain.

"By the Mother, Yuda, let him go!" he exclaimed.

Yuda dropped Lesol on the ground.

"I'm sorry, Mister. I'm short-tempered," he said, smiling a dog's smile. It was a threat, not an apology.

Lesol picked himself up and spat on to the ground, close to Yuda's feet.

"Enough," shouted Govorin, smiting his fist into his hand. "A man lies dead, and you quarrel like boys. Shake hands, or I'll smack your empty heads together."

Yuda took Lesol's grudgingly proffered hand without rancour. Deceptive, those long, slender fingers, thought Annat. Difficult to resist, the power and warmth of that smile. She saw Lesol thaw under its influence.

"We are all afraid, Mister. Fear is a cruel mistress," he said.

"Fear betrays its servants," said Yuda.

They followed the path of the sun back to the gangers' camp. Govorin had his own tent there. Before he became Sheriff, he had been both an engineer and a ganger; he was still the chief foreman. Inside the tent, he sank into a canvas chair.

"Mother, Yuda, you'll have to watch your temper. These people have long memories."

"You keep the peace, Sergey, that's your job. It's not mine. I think someone has got you sewn up in a bag."

Yuda paced to the tent opening and looked out into the midday sunlight. Govorin watched him with tiredness in his face.

"Do you think so?" he said at last.

A thrush trilled in the stillness and the sounds of the site were muted. Annat could hear the faint rattle of pots and pans. She hoped that one of the two men would remember lunch soon. She was sitting on the low camp bed at the rear of the tent with her knees drawn up to her chin. It seemed to her, though she did not say it, that Yuda was showing more than mere curiosity about the deaths and disappearances. When Govorin had told Lesol that her father was the village doctor, it had sounded incongruous. Yuda was not acting like *Zaide* nor like any other doctor she could imagine. He was asking questions that had nothing to do with his work.

"I'm going to find out," said Yuda. "That man, Lesol, is he a local?"

"Yes. He's a native of Gard Ademar. The villagers work alongside us. Only Sarl and Casildis came from outside."

Yuda turned to look at him, listening intently, and Annat broke in, "Casildis said that Gard Ademar is haunted by evil."

"Evil doesn't take a man's gun," said Yuda.

"You think it's some human agency?" said Govorin.

"Let's rule out the obvious first. I'd like to know what Isabel thought."

"Her notebooks were stolen."

"It's pretty plain that she did find something out, and that's why she was killed."

"Of course. You heard what Lesol said: 'I have already said too much.' "

Yuda sat down on the ground cross-legged, and his head sank low.

"You're right, as always, Sergey. I can't charge in here and expect them to trust me. I'm a Wanderer, a shaman, a *divko*."

"You'll find a way, Yuda."

Annat listened to them without speaking, her hands folded in her lap. A question had begun to form in her mind, but she was not ready to ask Yuda yet.

After a hasty lunch at the works canteen, where men and women sat at separate tables, Yuda and Annat walked back to the settlement alone. Annat was becoming more fluent in communicating with her father without having to spell out her thoughts as if she were speaking aloud. They walked under the shadow of the forest. And the forest was a third mind, vast, with fine and complex tendrils down which thoughts that Annat could not translate travelled. Yuda felt it too, and often he turned his head towards the trees as if expecting to hear a voice.

"What do you think killed Mister Zarras?" she asked him, as they came in sight of the track that led away from the new line up to Gard Ademar.

"The wounds could have been made by an animal. But there's the matter of the missing gun. I need to read the records of the other deaths. I think we can discount Isabel. She was the only one whose body wasn't found near the tunnel."

He stopped speaking suddenly, and Annat felt the image of his friend snatched quickly from his mind. Isabel had been the only woman he loved and trusted as a friend, after he lost Yuste. Annat was embarrassed to acquire this piece of personal information. She had no such secrets.

When Yuda opened the door of the Blue House, the scent met them at once; not blood, the perfume of death, but lavender, strong and antiseptic. Annat sneezed.

"*Gesundheit*," said Yuda, stepping into the kitchen. "That woman's been here."

The table was thick with packages, some neatly wrapped in gingham, others spilling their contents like a cornucopia: roots to which clods of earth still clung, green leaves so dark they were almost black, and red, bosomy tomatoes.

"*That woman* is still here," said Casildis, emerging from the surgery room, a wet rag in her hand. Her hair was piled up on top of her head in an extraordinary crown, and wrapped in white cloth as if she were a woman of Morea; she wore a dusty pinafore, patterned with old stains, and a pair of baggy blue jeans that she must have borrowed from Govorin. Yuda stopped, and Annat, moving to inspect the table with its burden, wondered how it was that Casildis managed to appear still more beautiful in her skivvying clothes. Annat had never met anyone else who could give pleasure simply by their appearance. She did not need to look at Yuda to sense his admiration.

Casildis shook the cloth at them. "I knew you'd be too busy to clean up," she said. "And laying out the dead is women's work here. I came to do my part."

"That poor sod," said Yuda, referring to Zarras. He gestured to the table. "What's all this? Did you dig up your garden?"

Casildis laughed. "I share an allotment with Mari Reine. She wanted to give Annat something in return for the healing."

"What healing?" Yuda demanded. Annat looked up at him

timidly. He seemed annoyed, as if he would have expected her to ask his permission before daring to use her powers.

"Sarl bashed her eye. I fixed it."

"Zyon!" Yuda glanced down at the table, and picked up a calico bundle. "She must have thought it was worth a lot of vegetables."

Casildis moved nearer to point out some of the other items on the tabletop. "Zarras's mother left a jar of honey for you. And Zhan Sarl asked me to pass on a bottle of his wine. This is how you will be paid, in kind. We use very little coin in the village."

"That's pretty much how they used to pay my father, though he tended to refuse the pigs they offered him. Kindly-meant pigs," he added, glancing at Annat. "But we could feed a whole train crew with this lot."

"You'll need to store some of it for winter," said Casildis.

Weighing the package in his hand, Yuda fixed her with his stare. "And do you always leave the scent of lavender wherever you go?" he said, in an accusatory tone. The question took both Annat and Casildis by surprise.

"It has many virtues," said Casildis, looking him in the eye. Annat found herself thinking how small and insignificant she and her father seemed in the presence of this tall, queenly woman. Then she corrected herself; Yuda could never be insignificant.

"So do you," he said, roughly. "I'd never have envisaged you scrubbing floors."

"I do what needs to be done," said Casildis.

"No *kinder* yet, hmm?"

Annat could tell the woman was discomforted. She made a quick movement as Casildis said, "What is '*kinder*'?"

"Kids. Children."

Annat rounded on her father. "*Tante* says we shouldn't make personal remarks," she said.

"Who asked you to speak?" said Yuda, raising his eyebrows.

"We have no children yet," said Casildis.

Yuda turned away, fishing in his pocket for cigarettes. Annat was puzzled by the signals of emotion he was sending out; his thoughts were closed to her.

"I left my wife when I was twenty-three," he said, hunching over the cigarette. "In the villages, girls get pregnant as young as fourteen. My Aude was eighteen. And you must be twenty-seven."

"No one would marry me because of my hare-lip," said Casildis with precise, clipped words. "Until I met Sergey."

Yuda blew smoke. "They couldn't see you because of a hare-lip," he said, scornfully. "And it took someone like Sergey to see you as you are."

"Sergey is a good man."

"Bugger that! He's a very lucky man."

Suddenly he laughed, and Casildis caught his laughter. Annat was utterly confused.

"You love him very much, don't you?" said Casildis. The tension of the last few minutes was gone, dispelled with the smoke.

"We're blood brothers. That's about as close as men get—except for Shaka, of course. But I knew Govorin before I met Shaka." He shrugged, putting down the packet amongst its fellows, and added with a touch of mischief, "I don't suppose you cook too?" As Casildis opened her mouth to retort, he went on, "We'll manage. I can teach Annat a few tricks. And the boy . . . where the hell is he, by the way?"

"I sent him to Zhan Sarl to ask for work. I believe he is gardening. Weeding the cemetery."

"I suppose he might get some pleasure from that. I've been racking my brains over what he could do. My father was training him up for a scribe or a *Rashim*, which means he's good for nothing else. And he likes watching birds."

"I must go," said Casildis, starting to unfasten her pinny. "I promised to do a shift at the laundry this afternoon. I have left a note by the sink listing your house calls. He seems a nice boy, if rather shy," she added, lifting the pinny over her head.

"I'm not sure I'd call him nice," said Yuda slowly. "He put me though it last night. We heard a scream on the way back—Zyon, perhaps that was Mister Zarras meeting his Maker."

"We must have still been indoors at the time," said Casildis.

"I keep wondering what killed the man. Down by the tunnel, late at night, alone. I wouldn't fancy it myself."

Casildis gazed at him, the pinny folded in her hands. "The tunnel should not be there," she said.

"What?"

"I told Isabel. Now she is dead, and I don't know why. It is better for me to keep silent."

She pulled on her long coat and started to make for the door, but Yuda barred her way.

"Wait. Missis Govorin, have you any idea who killed Isabel?"

"No," she said simply. "Mari and I were close friends of hers. Zhan Sarl too. She sometimes spoke of you. Once, she said you were like a fire that cannot be put out." She reached past him for the door handle. Then, hesitating, she said, "I begin to see what she meant."

Yuda stepped aside to let her go, and shut the door behind her. He stood for a few moments with his face towards the wooden panels, then turned back to Annat.

"You've got no idea, have you, what all that was about," he said.

Left alone with him, Annat felt suddenly shy and constrained. She thought she recognised the strange heat, like another perfume in the room, as the one that had followed his encounter with Rosa. But there was something subtler in its makeup, a note that she could not recognise or wholly distinguish. She was not sure she wanted to share her knowledge with him. He might be displeased to find her picking up his private emotions.

"Go on, spit it out," he said, impatiently.

Annat bent to examine the cabbage leaves on the table, wondering what she could make with them. She thought she had seen some fennel spilling from another bag. It was better not to say anything until Yuda chose to admit to her what he was feeling.

"Do you want me to come with you on your rounds?" she said.

"You little cuss! You learn fast," said Yuda, with admiration. "Sure you can come. How else am I going to teach you anything?"

Annat beamed at him. It did not make her feel superior to

know that he was drawn to Casildis; she was sure that he knew it himself. But she was pleased that she had started to learn how to stop him eavesdropping on her thoughts. It made them more equal.

The home visits occupied the rest of the afternoon. Yuda carried with him a leather bag bulging with instruments and medicines, though he rarely needed to use the former. The worst case he had to deal with was a tubercular lung; he spent a long time in talk with the sick man's wife, writing notes and addresses for her on a scrap of paper. What astonished Annat was his manner; he was candid, sometimes blunt, but unfailingly kind; when he wanted to swear, he did so some way from the patient's house. He allowed Annat to watch all the examinations except one, where he explained he would be "looking up a woman's snatch" (a technical term that was new to Annat), and he encouraged her to ask questions. However, he did not permit her to carry out the simplest healing, not even to deal with a megrim, which she had often done for Yuste at home.

"These people asked for a doctor," he said. "If I'd let you do anything, we'd be seen as a wonder-working circus act, not a consultation. I'm in this business as a healer, not a bloody miracle-worker."

And with that Annat had to be satisfied, remembering the unnerving awe that Mari Reine had shown after her one experiment last night. She decided that now was not the time to ask him whether Govorin had truly taken him on only to practise as a doctor.

Both were tired and tetchy when they got home, and Yuda was not amused to find Malchik sitting at the kitchen table, reading next to an untouched pile of vegetables. He snatched the book from his son's hands.

"I'm not a paid servant, boy, and nor is your sister. We've worked hard today, and I didn't expect to find you lounging in the kitchen, waiting for us to make your supper."

"I've been working in the cemetery all afternoon," said Malchik resentfully, flushing so that the finger-marks stood out on his cheek.

Yuda snapped the book shut. "All afternoon," he snarled.

"My heart bleeds for you. Do something useful and help your sister sort this out while I clean up and say my evening prayers."

As Yuda went upstairs, Malchik began to examine the table's contents in a desultory manner, muttering under his breath. Annat watched him for a few moments, and then took charge.

"We'll have braised fennel," she said. "You can find the fennel for me, and some garlic and herbs, while I sort out this lot."

"I thought I'd made up with him last night," Malchik grumbled.

"Don't be such a baby, Malchku," said Annat, imitating her aunt's brisk manner. "Somebody died here this morning, and *Tate* has been hard at work ever since."

Her brother poked out his tongue, but reluctantly began to search for the fennel, while Annat set to work ascertaining what the bundles contained, and storing them accordingly. She was already calculating in her mind what could be pickled and set side for the long winter, and what needed to be eaten fresh. They had been given enough food for several feasts: a medley of vegetables, dry goods, fruits, nuts and grain, but no meat. Casildis had thoughtfully provided a bread crock and two long flute loaves, together with a pat of fresh butter wrapped in a damp cloth.

Having assured herself that Malchik was cleaning the fennel, Annat began her preparations, pouring pale olive oil into a skillet and sprinkling in some of her favorite herbs.

"I have to say my evening prayers too, you know," her brother grunted.

"Lazy bum! Off you go then, I can cook better when you're not in the way."

As she prepared the meal, Annat wished she could stop thinking about Yuste. At home, they had often performed such tasks together, sometimes with *Bubbe* supervising. Annat hoped that her aunt would write her a letter, but once the Railway closed for winter, there would be no news until next year, after the thaw. She thought of her grandmother too, wondering how she must feel, alone in the house with *Zaide*, who was not a man of many words. Her grandmother was clever and quick-witted, like a young woman inhabiting the body of an elderly one.

Once the fennel was simmering on the hob—Malchik had at least replenished the wood in the stove—Annat herself went off to wash and recite her own prayers. Women's prayers were not as long as those for men, and she found Yuda and Malchik still performing their orisons in the back garden when she went out to join them. Each man had covered his head with a prayer shawl, and was facing east, towards Zyon, holding a small book of prayers in his right hand. They rocked to and fro as they prayed, Malchik more energetically than Yuda, who was addressing his benedictions to the Almighty with a cigarette dangling from his left hand. Annat covered her face, muttered the blessings quickly to herself, and thought again of Yuste. Her aunt could read *ebreu*, the ancient script of the Wanderers, which Annat had never learned. She had memorized the prayers rote-fashion, and only understood a few of the words. She could not help noticing that Yuda was reciting the phrases as if he were in the midst of a conversation. She remembered what Casildis had told her about the women who once worshipped in the forest, and wondered if she should mention it to him.

They ate in silence, largely because Malchik had decided to sulk. As Yuda appeared not to have noticed his son's pointed lack of conversation, Annat found it difficult not to giggle. She was pleased with the flavor of her fennel stew, which Malchik seemed to be enjoying whenever he forgot that he was in a bad mood. Yuda ate little, and drank only one glass of rough red wine, which was not taken from the impressive, dusty bottle Sarl had sent from his cellar. He seemed abstracted, and Annat made no attempt to probe his thoughts. Instead, she busied herself in teasing her brother, kicking him under the table and trying to steal his food.

"Will you two simmer down," said Yuda irritably, stubbing out another cigarette with nervous fingers. "I'm doing my best to think."

They sat fidgeting in front of their clean plates, watching him and making faces at each other sidelong. After a few minutes, they realised that Yuda was watching them with a thoughtful expression, and they subsided into stillness.

"I'm beginning to wish I hadn't brought you," he said. As Annat opened her mouth to protest, he held up his hand. "It's nothing to do with you, though I must say you're enough to drive a man mad. No, it's this place. Whatever is going on here, it's much worse than I had expected. The causes are darker, and they run deeper."

"What do you mean, sir?" said Malchik, his pale eyes rounding into worried O's.

"Zyon, boy, don't call me 'sir'—we're not in the militias. Call me Vasilyevich, or Mister, or anything you please—no, not 'frog-face'," he added, glowering at Annat, who had let her thought slip out, and was forced to stifle a giggle.

"She calls me that too, sir, Mister," said Malchik, indignantly.

Yuda rolled up his eyes. "I'm trying to talk seriously to you. I promised Yuste I'd try to keep you out of trouble, though so far you both seem to be lodestones for danger—you especially, boy. Common sense isn't among your virtues, and you have all the survival instincts of a snail in a frying pan. I can trust Natka—up to a point," he said, swiftly, fixing her with a warning glance, "because her powers make her sensitive to danger." He steepled his fingers. "As for you, Malchku, I just don't know."

Annat saw her brother blink, and knew that he was affected more by the use of his diminutive name rather than by their father's ominous words.

"I'll try to be careful, Vasilyevich," he said, leaning forwards and gazing earnestly through his spectacles.

"It isn't that, boy," said Yuda, with an unhappy smile. "It's your judgement. You don't know when to be careful. That can be an instinct you're born with, or it can be something you learn—either way, you don't have it."

"I'm sorry, sir."

Yuda folded his arms. "Don't apologise to me, boy," he said. "You're not to blame. But it will get you into danger—it already has—and others too. Old Pyotr was killed going after you, and though he wasn't my favorite guard, I expect he had a few more good years in him, to drink and whore. But that wasn't why I whacked you—I was scared shitless. I thought I'd lost you."

"I'm really sorry," said Malchik, with what Annat could now see to be true and troubled sincerity.

"But can I trust you?" said Yuda, softly.

"I—I don't know," said Malchik, lowering his eyes.

"Nor do I. And I'm wondering if you'd be better off returning to Masalyar, to be near Yuste. I wanted you to know what I was thinking, and to understand that it wasn't meant as punishment, or to humiliate you."

"But I've only just got here," Malchik stammered.

"You can blame me if you want, Malchku. I'm the one who misjudged the situation. I think we're up against something worse than a few unexplained deaths. When I looked into Zarras's dying mind, all I could see was fear. Nothing of his life, no memories; that poor bastard had been rubbed clean, like a chalkboard. Erased by fear." He bit his nails, and Annat sensed his concern. Like Malchik, she watched him in silence, sobered. "Do you begin to understand, Malchku?" Yuda said, after a pause. "Whatever caused his death wasn't animal, wasn't human. In that kind of situation, Natka or I would have stood a fighting chance, but not you. You've got just enough shaman in you to make you vulnerable."

"Please don't send me back, Mister," said Malchik. "I feel it's a chance—one I won't get otherwise. *Zaide* wants me to become a *Rashim* or a scholar, and I don't—don't believe . . ." He trailed off, and Annat saw his fearful gaze fixed on Yuda's bleak face.

"You don't believe," said Yuda, flatly. "That's a matter for you, and no business of mine. But your safety is my business. You were at the cemetery today? Outside the village walls, right up by the forest edge. I'll bet you saw no harm in that."

"Zhan Sarl told me to go there."

"I suppose we have to trust his judgement—he's lived in the forest all his life. And you seem to have survived—so far," he added, cracking a grim smile.

"I don't know—there was something odd," said Malchik, wrinkling his forehead.

Yuda leaned back in his chair, giving Malchik a pensive look. "What was that, boy?" he said, fiddling with the ring on his wedding finger. Malchik's eyes seemed to turn inward, as if he were viewing the scene in his memory.

"It was a quiet place, very overgrown. And peaceful. Not eerie at all," he went on, raising his glance to meet Yuda's. "Most of the graves were untended, and a lot were new. I think Sarl wanted me to make the place look tidy in readiness for Zarras's burial. Some of the graves had flowers on them, and there was a big bunch of white roses by the headstone of the woman you used to know—Isabel Guerreres. I went to look at it, and as I reached out to touch the roses, I pricked my finger. And then it went dark." He paused to examine his hand.

"And you fell asleep for a hundred years and were rescued by a handsome prince?" said Yuda, raising an eyebrow.

Malchik gave his father a crooked smile. "I could have been, Mister," he said. "I can't remember. I woke up kneeling by the tomb, and my finger was bleeding—but I had lost a bit of time. Just as if I'd fainted."

"Aren't you the pair," said Yuda, glancing at Annat, "fainting away like a couple of maiden aunts." He gave a shrug that was like a shiver. "You did right to tell me, boy. Let's hope it was nothing, eh? But I'd better have a word with Sarl tomorrow—I'd prefer it if you kept within the village walls, for now."

"I liked it at the cemetery. It was quiet, and I could think."

"We'll see," said Yuda. "I haven't decided yet whether to keep you in Gard Ademar. I need you to show me that I can trust you—that you won't go wandering off after birds or some such. Is that settled?"

"Yes, sir, Yuda."

"And make up your mind what you're going to call me," Yuda added. He stood up, pushing back his chair. "No more lectures tonight. I'm going out. There are no bars in this place, but Govorin told me that the Railway workers are running a shebeen down at their encampment. So I'll be back late. And drunk, I hope," he added, patting his pockets.

After he was gone, Annat and Malchik behaved as they would have done at home, clearing up the dishes and arguing.

They were accustomed to entertaining themselves, and they spent the evening playing cards, making music with harp and *vyel*, and talking inconsequentially. Annat noticed what a luxury it was to be left alone with her brother, untroubled by adult strictures. She had to admit that she enjoyed his company and the old jokes he told with a clown's mournful face. She would have liked to go out with him and walk the village's dark streets, but Yuda's warning had put a chill into her soul, and she was glad to sit near the warmth of the stove, sharing with Malchik some cobnuts that they had found amongst their store of food. She was relieved that Malchik did not try to discuss their father with her; she wanted to make believe that they were back home in Sankt-Eglis, but without adults to pester them. She wished they could play one of their childhood games, making an upturned table into a boat, or a tent from sheets and pillows. But Malchik was too old for that, and so was she. She had not forgotten what Yuda said to Casildis about the village girls who bore children at fourteen. Her own body was changing, whether she wanted it or not; her breasts had begun to bud, making small, soft pouches under her dress, and dark hair was gathering between her legs like bees on sugar. She hunched in on herself, laughing too raucously at her brother's jokes, and wishing she could cling to this moment before it slipped away from her.

Malchik went to bed early, as he would have done at home. Annat stayed up alone, feeding the stove with profligate wood, and day-dreaming, not of a handsome prince or a white-flanked charger, but of winged creatures, floating castles and maidens with emerald-green eyes. At last, admitting she was tired, she trailed upstairs after a perfunctory wash, to find the doll lying, stark and vigilant, on her pillow. It never slept.

Chapter 7

Remembering how early the first patients had arrived yesterday, Annat was up before dawn and dressing in the eerie silence that came after the birds had finished their song. She donned a black pullover, a white blouse and one of the her old skirts, still scented with a trace of the soap Yuste had used to wash them. Creeping downstairs in her stockinged feet, she began to bank up the fire in the stove, which she had damped down before going to bed last night. She crouched close to the door and let the warmth of the flames within caress her face like cats' tongues. She fed the fire patiently with lumps of wood, until she was satisfied that it would give a steady flame. It made her think of Nami the firer, shovelling wood into the engine's firebox to feed its bottomless hunger. Perhaps somewhere in this same dawn, Nami and Shaka were drawing smoke from the locomotive, huddling in the cold morning beneath its pillar of cloud. Latching the oven door, Annat went to fill the kettle from the tap over the sink, marvelling at the unclouded stream that issued from its spout. She heaved the heavy iron kettle on to the hob, which was barely warm to the touch. At the back of her mind were the remnants of a half-forgotten dream, drifting like rags of cloud across the sky. Though it had left some sense of anxiety, affecting her mood as she sat alone in the unlit kitchen, waiting for the water to boil, she could not remember any details. When the sun rose, she went out into the back garden to offer a blessing, and stayed to watch the shadow roofs of Gard Ademar changing color as the light touched them, bringing out subtle shades of terracotta and faded pink. She returned to the kitchen to open the windows and unfasten the shutters, letting in the first silvery daylight.

The kettle on the hob began to rattle and steam, and Annat wondered if Malchik would emerge to claim all the hot water for his daily bath. She had not yet worked out how and when she would have a chance to bathe; she did not intend to sit in the kitchen, as Malchik was content to do, and she would once have done at home. But her brother failed to appear, and since a packet of roasted *kava* beans had lain amongst the gifts that Mari Reine had brought yesterday, Annat decided to brew a pot, so she could pretend to herself that she was still staying at the *Shkola* with Sival and her aunt. She searched through the cupboard for a *moule* to grind the swart beans, and sat at the table inhaling their pungent, reviving scent.

She had not heard Yuda return last night, and she wondered how late he had come back. If the patients arrived as early today as they had done yesterday, she suspected that she would have to waken him. As she poured boiling water into the *kava* pot, she decided that she would ask him today whether he had come to Gard Ademar simply because the settlement needed a healer, or whether there were other reasons he had chosen to keep from her. While waiting for the *kava* to brew, she fetched three bowls from the cupboard and placed them in a row on the table, looking at the blue glazes that had been laid over the fired red clay beneath. She knew that Sklavs drank *chai*, while the Franj preferred *kava*; it had been her mother who introduced the seductive and bitter taste of that fulvous brew into their household. Having poured herself a bowl, she set the pot on the top of the stove to keep warm and sat down at the table, breathing in the fumes of the *kava*. She savored the liquid on her tongue, wondering whether the queue of patients had started to form outside yet. And then the world turned over . . .

*   *   *

Malchik lay in bed, his eyes open on the dark, listening to the voices in his head. At first, they had seemed to be arguing at a distance, but now they were speaking to him, beckoning him towards an unknown destination. Yuda's warning lay in his gut like bread sown with ergot. He blinked hard, trying to pretend that the voices—or the Voice—were a dream. It seemed to come from a great distance, but it whispered to him intimately, like a mother, leaving no trace of the words it had spoken. He must not listen to it, or like the night demons of his childhood it would fill his mind with troubled dreams.

He turned restively, leaning his cheek on his fist, and stared at the place where the door stood. If he were to go out into the dark, he would be betraying his father, who had offered Malchik the gift of trust. If he stayed here, with the Voice pouring its sweetness into his mind, by the morning it would have provoked a madness in which he could no longer distinguish its murmurings from his own thoughts. He sat up, swinging his legs over the side of the bed. The summons had come for him, and he had to go, to find out what it was offering with its half-heard, enticing words. He pulled the night-shirt over his head and stood naked in the dark, listening, until the Voice spoke to him again.

Malchik lit the oil lamp on the nightstand by his bed, and picked up his spectacles to polish the lenses. Gold reflections glinted off the bevelled glass, disappearing when he pressed the frame over his nose. Around him, the house was asleep, its stertorous breathing enclosing him as he dressed hurriedly. He pulled on his grey-green duffel coat over his clothes and, as an afterthought, seized the harp from its place by the foot of the bed, and slung it across his back. Something in him sensed that he was going on a long journey, and the harp's pressure against his backbone felt like a friendly hand.

He opened the door and cast a cautious glance along the landing towards Yuda's door, to see that it stood wide open. His father was not at home. Pushing his bedroom door to, Malchik made his way downstairs to the kitchen, and unlatched the kitchen door, feeling the cold air grasp at his face as he stepped outside. The Voice seemed to wrap him in a cocoon of warmth, drawing him along the cobbled street towards a distant lamp, past the shuttered and blind houses. Malchik let it guide him. He walked purposefully, though he could if he had wished have drifted along to the rhythm of the Voice, letting its embalming perfume engulf him. But he was not yet ready to surrender to the power of its intoxication; bitter and hard inside him, Yuda's warning bruised against his ribs, keeping him alert when the Voice itself would have sung him to sleep. The Voice urged him onwards, cajoling him when he hesitated, and promising vague marvels to seduce his imagination. He told himself that it was too late to turn back now; his father would be waiting, angry and disappointed. Yuda's anger seemed to swell in his mind to a giant, menacing shadow that he dared not face.

When he came to the village gate, it stood open, and there was no watchman in sight. Without pausing to wonder why, Malchik stepped through into the cool, earthen darkness beyond, and began to descend the steep path that led down from the village towards the Railway line. He found his way down the track with its loose, uneven stones, as if he knew his footing in the dark. A golden light hovered on the edge of his vision, out of which the Voice called him yearningly, begging him to respond to her cry; she was so lonely, so hungry, down the long years. Malchik could not help wondering who was calling him; he wanted to ask her but the question seemed to freeze in his mind, leaving him caught in a narcoleptic stupor: Though he was a little afraid to imagine what kind of being could exert such power over him, her longing remained persuasive, as did the images of pleasure and fulfilment that she fed him to gratify his senses.

The night was cool with the misty breath of autumn; around him the trees and bushes sighed, exhaling into the air that had been warm by day. Malchik found that he was following the silent Railway lines, a silver road that pointed like a spear into the blackness ahead. His feet crunched on the ballast, keeping up a regular rhythm; the harp nudged his back as if it were trying to remind him, even now, of the promise he had made to Yuda. When he saw the tunnel mouth ahead, Malchik felt his heart quicken. Though the Voice urged him on, he felt a moment of disappointment, wondering why he had been brought to a hole in a hill. The ominous height of the great archway failed to impress him and he had no sense of danger alone in the face of the deserted workings where others had died. He paused in the tunnel entrance, feeling breathless from his forced march, as the golden song of the Voice swirled triumphantly round him, beckoning him into the tunnel.

For the first time, Malchik resisted, seeking more than the blandishments which seemed to offer whatever he wished. At once, the shining threads that bound and shielded him seemed to fray, as if a knife had cut through the web of a loom, and out of the fissure she came screaming at him: an eyeless crow with claws bent to raze his face. Malchik crouched down, shielding his head as she swooped over him, and shivered in the cruel cold that her wings shed. Ahead of him, the dark was alive, torn open by a silver rent out of which snow and light plucked at him with tearing fingers. He struggled to resist, but he had come too far; the Goddess had planted her seed in his soul, and now she swept her black wing-cloak round him with a cry of triumph, forcing him through into the pale light of the world beyond.

Annat opened her eyes. For an instant, she had no idea where she was, or what had happened to her. She was lying on hard ground, with someone supporting her head and shoulders, and her fingertips brushed cold, polished stone. She moved her head, to find herself looking into Yuda's face. He grinned.

"Hallo, my little canary," he said. "You've done it again."

Annat tried to move, but her limbs would not answer her commands. "Did I spill the *kava*?" she said weakly.

"All over the floor," he said, cheerfully. "Do you want to tell me where you went this time?"

"Malchik," she said.

"D'you want your brother? I can go and fetch him . . ."

"He's gone, *Tate*. The Cold One has taken him."

Tears began to well in her eyes; very gently, Yuda wiped them away with his thumb.

"Let's take this slowly, shall we?" he said. "One step at a time. You say Malchik has gone? We can check that out right now." Scooping Annat up in his arms, for she was still too weak to stand, he headed for the stairs, and climbed to the landing where his room lay, next to Malchik's. When he pushed open the door to the boy's room, they both saw at a glance in the dim light from the shuttered window the empty bed with its pale, disordered sheets. Just as she had seen it last night, Malchik had taken his harp and walked out into the darkness.

"She stole him, from us, *Tate*."

Yuda looked into her face. He was not bothering to use *sprechen*. "You'd better tell me what happened," he said, softly. He carried her down the stairs and settled her in one of the kitchen chairs, before pouring two fresh bowls of *kava*, one for each of them. "Why did you faint?" he said, as he set the new bowl in front of Annat. "I'm pretty sure you do it for a good reason." Noticing her hands trembling as she tried to lift the bowl, he picked it up and held it to her lips, allowing her to take a few sips before she answered. Annat wiped her mouth on the back of her hand, and looked up at him. She felt calmer, but she knew she had to communicate the gravity of what she had seen. It would be no good if he thought her dream no more than the nightmare of a little girl, a *kind*. Wringing her hands to stop them shaking, she began to tell her father how the Voice had cajoled Malchik to leave the house, lured him to the tunnel, and there swept him through the gate to an unseen world.

"A shaman world," said Yuda softly, when she had finished. In stillness, he seemed like a coiled spring.

"What is that?"

He lowered his eyes. "We have the power, as shamans, to enter other dimensions, other worlds."

"Have you done that?" Annat whispered. "Travelled in shaman worlds?"

"Yes," said Yuda. "And so will you."

"Then you do believe me?" she said.

Yuda regarded her thoughtfully, his thoughts clear on the surface of his mind. He was making no attempt to shut her out. "I believe you," he said, quietly. "But the sooner you and I talk to Govorin, the better. We need to check out whether the Sheriff knows anything before we start searching for the boy."

"He is in danger," said Annat, clenching her hands so that her nails cut into her palms.

Yuda reached inside his coat to check the knife at his belt. "If Malchik's gone into a shaman world, we'll need to follow him as swiftly as possible," he said. "Are you ready to come with me?"

Annat looked into his eyes. She felt a chill slip down the skin over her spine. "Yes," she said. In a way, she was surprised that Yuda had not mocked her story. It had sounded so incredible when she was repeating it to him that she had begun to doubt herself. She felt a little frightened that he seemed to trust her implicitly. She would not have expected him to ask her for her company on a shaman's journey.

When she had put on her coat and boots, they left the house to find a forlorn queue waiting by the front door. There was a little sigh of hope as the patients saw Yuda, and they began to pick up their bags, ready to go inside.

"No surgery this morning, *mes amis*," said Yuda quickly. "My son has gone missing, and I need to see the Sheriff. Come back at mid of the day, and I'll see what I can do."

The queue began to disperse, with murmurings of resigned disappointment, and a few of the people approached Yuda to share their regrets and make offers of help, which he declined. Annat remembered witnessing similar scenes at home, amongst the villagers who came to consult *Zaide*. When Yuda rejoined her, he had an apple in his hand, which he held out to her saying, "Offerings to appease the witch doctor."

"What do you mean?" she asked, taking the apple and biting into it as they began to walk down the street.

"They're afraid of me. Of shamans," said Yuda, grimly.

At Govorin's house, a young maid opened the door and bobbed a curtsey. She was not much older than Annat, and her head was ineffectively covered by a pretty lace coif, from which wisps and tendrils of brown hair escaped. Rubbing nervous hands on her apron, she showed them into the kitchen, where Govorin and Casildis were seated at the table, in animated conversation over a platter of freshly broken bread. The Sheriff rose to his feet, almost knocking over his chair, and strode to meet Yuda with a delighted smile.

"Yudeleh," he said, pumping Yuda's hand. "*Miching* from surgery already? Come and join us!"

"I need to know if you've had word of Malchik," said Yuda.

"What's the matter? I thought you'd left him at home in bed," said the Sheriff.

Yuda shook his head. "He wasn't in his bed this morning," he said. "He's gone. And Natka thinks she knows where."

"The Cold One has taken him," Annat repeated.

"What was that?" said Govorin, and Casildis gasped.

"You'd better tell 'em what you saw, Natka," said Yuda, pulling out a chair.

They sat in silence while Annat recounted her dream. When she had finished, Govorin gave a whistle. Casildis took her husband's hand in an absent-minded grip.

"So you think Annat's dream was real, Yuda?" said the Sheriff.

"I see no reason not to believe it. I'm less sure what it means."

"There were stories—" Casildis began, and broke off, leaving her sentence unfinished. Yuda leaned forward across the table, unsmiling.

"I need more than stories now, Missis Govorin," he said. Casildis shook herself, as if shrugging off a chill hand.

"You've heard the tales of people—villagers and others—disappearing," she said. She stopped again, looking from Yuda to Annat and back. Yuda gave her a faint smile.

"Never mind that now," he said. "Annat has to know the true reason I'm here. This isn't the time to keep it from her."

"What do you mean?" said Annat, sitting up.

"Yuda's posting. His mission," said Govorin. "We did need a healer, but I chose Yuda because he has—other skills. I needed someone to take Isabel's place. An investigator."

"Why didn't you tell me?"

Yuda looked at her for a while before answering. "Yuste and I agreed to keep the true reason from you. And to begin with, I thought we'd done the right thing. But since I've come to know you, I'm not so sure. Never mind. You have to know now. And Casildis can speak freely," he added, with a dark smile.

Casildis sighed. "I had an older sister called Huldis," she said. "When I was four years old, she disappeared. It was only then that people began to go missing, until the villagers left Gard Ademar. The Railway People found the village abandoned."

Govorin toyed with a piece of bread. "But our people have been dying in this place," he said to Yuda.

The two men gazed at each other in silence for a while; they might have been two shamans, conversing in silence, and once more Annat observed how long friendship had given them ways of communicating that did not need words. When Yuda spoke again, he was talking only to Govorin, excluding the rest of them.

"It seems our coming changed something, Mister. Made it worse. When the chiefs sent Isabel to find out why, she was beginning to uncover the truth before she died. Not only is there a mystery, but someone wants to stop us solving it. Now my son has gone, the son of the new investigator."

"But why take Malchik? He's no threat to anyone," said Govorin.

"I've been thinking. He told me something odd yesterday, though I didn't take much notice at the time. Some story about blacking out while he was at the cemetery. I wonder if that was when he became—infected. Do you get what I'm saying, Mister?"

Govorin folded his broad arms across his chest. "I can see it, Yuda—but I can't imagine how."

"He said he had pricked his finger on the roses from Isabel's grave. It was that which caused him to lose consciousness. Though it hardly seems important, I think it is. But who would leave flowers there?"

"We all have, Yuda," said Casildis quickly. "Though my brother, Zhan Sarl, was especially grieved by her death. He often takes flowers there from his garden."

"Sarl's roses," said Yuda, shaking his head. "It makes no sense."

"I find it hard even to believe that the boy was dragged into another world. What's my tunnel got to do with it?" said Govorin.

"It looks as if the tunnel forms a gateway to the shaman world. Perhaps that's why the deaths started after we came. As if we disturbed something." He stood up. "No more talk. I want to see if I can find this portal." He sat down cross-legged on the stone flags, resting his hands on his knees. Catching Annat's thought, he added, "It's dangerous, *kind*, but you can follow me if you want."

Govorin and Casildis watched as Annat knelt beside him on the floor and sat back on her heels. She tugged her skirt into place and looked at Yuda, waiting for him to give a lead.

"You ready?" he said. Annat nodded. She reached out to take his hand; her fingers were icy, his warm. Yuda regarded her seriously. "Are you sure you want to do this, Missis?"

"Yes, *Tate*."

It felt like diving into a dark sea. They sank down slowly, and a chain of bright bubbles streamed from them up to the surface. On Annat's right, Yuda was a silver-blue fire; she sensed herself as a red flame, dimmer than he was. The sensation of drifting downwards continued for a long time, until at last her feet touched ground. She almost drew her hand from his, for here there were dark, exciting shapes, and pinpoints of light like great pearls in open shells. Yuda held her fast. He stretched out his right arm in a shimmering trail of stars and luminescence. Drawing Annat forward into the watery gloom, he sent out a long probe of light from his free hand. Annat saw illuminated a glittering world of jewels and bones and skulls. Keeping utterly still, she watched as the light skimmed the landscape. Though she did not understand what she saw, Yuda seemed to know what he was looking for, and he drew the beam slowly across the darkness, letting it linger on gnarled rocks and vein-like trees.

—*Ach, there it is.*

Annat did not know what he had seen, but he kept the light shaft steady, allowing it to play over a vent in the ground, from which jets of boiling water seemed to shoot upwards. A red glow issued from the mouth of the vent, coloring the streams many hues, from vivid orange to a dull sanguine.

—*It looks like a volcano*, Annat thought.

—That's a gateway. A big one, too. It's not far away, but to see if it lies athwart the tunnel we need to change levels.

Gripping her fast, he kicked off from the seabed and they began to rise, much more swiftly, in a fog of luminous blue bubbles. Though the water sang shrilly in Annat's ears she felt no fear, only exhilaration, as they surged up through the deep like dolphins. She would have liked to linger there in the water, but Yuda swept on. They broke the surface in a burst of spray, as if on the crest of a whale's spout, and soared upwards into the air.

When they came to rest, they were floating over a high ridge, close to the larks and the sky, which looked a darker blue than Annat had ever seen it in daylight. Below them rose a wall of rock through which the wind had cut a round, rough-edged opening, revealing the landscape spread out below. Annat saw the brightly painted fields and green-tinged valleys through a haze, the mist of an autumn morning.

—Is this a real place?

—It's part of a range of hills that overlooks the forest.

Yuda pointed out to her the roofs of Gard Ademar, pale in the distance, and the rich, sombre green of the forest's cloak, dappled here and there with sprays of emerald or gold. When he showed her the place where the tunnel lay, in a velvety fold of cypress green, Annat could see tiny ants swarming round the glinting toy machinery and a faint smudge of smoke from the funnel of an unseen engine. Down by the station, a long train gave off tinny glints from its eel's body. It was such a bright, fresh morning that Annat wished she were standing here in the flesh to breathe the sweet air and gaze across the plain to the blue smear of the Kron river.

—Zyon, Yuda thought. He pointed to the slope above the tunnel, and Annat saw what he had seen: a clustering, multifoliate darkness that brooded over the scurrying ants below, which were oblivious to its presence. Annat felt a shiver in her soul as Yuda scryed the map of the trees, studying the patch of shadow that seemed to change shape before their eyes.

—I can see the gateway; but there's something else there, too. Shit!

He swung back, dragging Annat with him, as a shiver went

over the surface of the forest, and she saw the ripple of movement tracing out a shape on the textured green, like the outline of a woman. It went coursing across the bending treetops, searching, like a wave rising out of the deep.

—*I reckon she's looking for us,* said Yuda.—*Time to go.*

They plunged over the edge and fell, plummeting like falcons in a dive. As they neared the forest roof, the ripple swept towards them, and Annat felt the breath of the cold wind that drove it, bending the tops of the trees. Great hands were stretching out to seize them as they fell, but Yuda was too quick; with a salmon-like twist, he pulled them from the sky, to sweep down, hard, into their own bodies. It felt as if they had truly fallen from air to earth; Annat gasped for breath, winded by the speed of their descent. When she lifted her hand, she found that Yuda had gripped her so hard that his nails had left crescent shapes on her palm. Yuda sat back, uncrossing his legs, and wiped the perspiration from his brow with the back of his hand.

"What did you see?" said Govorin, bending over him.

Annat shivered. She felt as if she had swum in the sea naked, and stepped out into freezing air. She was surprised and grateful when Casildis draped a shawl, warm and deliciously soft, about her shoulders.

Yuda leaned forward, breathing like a runner at the end of a race. He bent his head over his knees, letting his hair hide his face. Annat could see that he was shaking.

"The shadow of a Goddess," he muttered, "the shadow of a Goddess."

As soon as Yuda and Annat had recovered, the four of them began to discuss what to do; Yuda was quiet and subdued.

"I don't think there's any choice," he said. "Annat and I must go through the tunnel tonight."

"Just the two of you?" said Govorin.

"I can't ask anyone else to follow me. This is my private business, and the fewer that go, the better."

"That's not how I see it," said Govorin. "You can't go alone, just you and the *kind*. It would be easy for me to leave Sarl in charge of the workings and go with you."

"It's a kind offer, Sergey, but what if we don't come back? What will happen to the tunnel and all your plans?"

Govorin gave a belly laugh. "The Railway People will have to find a replacement for me, won't they!"

"I'd be grateful for your company," said Yuda. "But we know nothing about this world that we plan to enter. You're no shaman, Mister."

"I think the world you are speaking of has a name," said Casildis. "The forest people call it La Souterraine, because it lies at the roots of the forest."

"You knew of it?" said Yuda, sharply.

"There has long been a legend concerning such a place, but it remained a legend. People repeat these stories without knowing who invented them, and whether they carry any truth."

"La Souterraine means 'the underground place' in Franj," said Govorin. He folded his fingers together. "I wish we'd known this before we started to dig. The last thing I'd have wanted to do is disturb any holy sites."

"You could not have known, Sergey," said Casildis. "By the time we came out of the forest to join you, the tunnel was begun."

"And surveyors don't trouble with local legends," said Govorin, glancing at his wife. "No matter. I'm going with you, Yudeleh. I can't let you and Natka face this alone."

"If Sergey goes, I go too," said Casildis.

"Not you, Missis," said Yuda. "I need troops, not passengers. I don't want someone along that I'll have to protect."

"Is that how poorly you think of me?" said Casildis, softly. "That I would only be a burden to you? I would not offer to come if I could not bear my part. I can ride a horse and shoot a bow, and I am hardy and strong. Govorin will vouch for me, if you will not take my word."

"It's true, Yuda," said Govorin. "Casildis may not be a trained fighter like Isabel, but she's tougher than she looks. And I'd be happier with her by my side. She's not the sort of wife a man leaves behind to snivel into her hanky."

Yuda looked from one to the other, his face set. "You don't understand," he said. "Neither of you has ever entered a shaman world. To someone who isn't a shaman, they can seem deceptively like this world. But Govorin at least has warrior training. I can rely on him to fend for himself in any situation—and to watch my back."

Casildis leaned forward. "Please trust me, Yuda," she said. "I am the only one of us who knows the legends of the forest. It may be that my knowledge will prove useful. You are all southerners, who do not know what it has been like to live in these parts since the trouble started. You will not regret taking me."

Yuda studied her intently. "I can't promise to protect you, Missis," he said. "You have to understand that, if you're going to come. And Govorin can't promise it either. We travel as equal partners in this enterprise, or not at all."

Casildis smiled at him. "I will go with you, Yuda, on those terms."

He nodded. "That's settled, then," he said. "Natka and I will meet you at the tunnel mouth an hour after the sun goes down. Tell no one but Sarl where we're going."

Chapter 8

Annat felt as if there were a cloud over the streets as she walked back with Yuda to their house. She kept glancing up at the sky, half-afraid that she might see the Goddess's vast shape darkening the horizon as it stooped down to them. Yuda's silence gave her little comfort; she had seen his hands still trembling when he struggled to light a cigarette. There was nothing to do now but wait; Yuda had decided to hold his surgery as if it were a normal day. They would pack what little they could carry after the last of the patients had gone.

Annat felt strangely cold inside, as if there were no warmth in the sun that washed over the cobbled street. She wished that Yuda would open his thoughts to her, so she need not feel so small and alone. It was not that she was afraid of the journey; she dreaded the moment when they would have to enter the tunnel itself. Haunted by the thought of her brother, trapped in that strange world, she folded her thin arms against her chest, wishing she could reach out to Malchik along the faint thread that barely told her he was still alive.

"You all right?" said Yuda, glancing down at her, with the rough tenderness she was beginning to recognise.

"No."

He did not reply, but his hand reached out to rest against the small of her back, as if to remind her that she was not alone; Yuda was there to share her worries and her fear.

When they reached the blue-walled house where they had slept only two nights, it seemed like the most comforting and familiar place in the world. While Yuda tidied the surgery ready for his consultations, Annat wiped away the *kava* she had spilled on the kitchen floor, and swept up the fragments of the shattered bowl. She would have to sit with her father while he saw his patients, and she wondered how she would be able to endure listening to their complaints. When she looked in on Yuda, he was working quietly and methodically as if he had nothing else on his mind. She went up to her room and began to assemble her meagre possessions. There was no question in her mind about taking the doll; it had been the sole relic of Aude's former life that she had given Annat, apart from her stories.

Annat carefully wrapped the doll and placed it in her rucksack. Though she had always called Aude *Mame*, it was Yuste who had been a mother to her, for as far back as she could remember. It might have been different for Malchik, since Aude had clung to him possessively; but Annat believed that for him too Yuste had taken their mother's place. She could not recall grieving when her mother had died, because Aude had never shown her either love or interest; her presence in the house in Sankt-Eglis had been like that of her doll, beautiful and remote.

The day passed more swiftly than Annat had expected. After sharing a hasty supper of wurst and rye bread with her, Yuda finished his packing and rejoined her in the kitchen. Annat was surprised to see that he carried his *vyel* strapped to his back; all his other possessions filled the small leather knapsack slung over his shoulder. She wondered how he would manage with so little. He looked quizzically at her bulging rucksack, and took it out of her hands, emptying it on to the kitchen table.

"You've got too much in there. Get rid of some things."

"I can't," Annat protested.

"One change of clothes is enough. You'll have to get by. We

need to travel light, and there will be other stuff to carry. Govorin and Casildis are bringing it."

Unwillingly, Annat discarded several tightly rolled skirts and blouses, retaining only a short skirt of thick material and the trews Yuda had given her for the train journey. She was determined to keep several pairs of clean knickers, and a toothbrush and tooth powder were essential. She found Yuda struggling not to smile as she bundled the remaining items into the sack.

"You're taking a *vyel!*" she accused him.

"Music has power," he said, his eyes glinting.

The streets outside were cool and misty. Yuda whistled as he walked, as if they were preparing to go on a short and pleasant hike through the countryside. If he were feeling any apprehension, he had tucked it away inside where Annat could not sense it. She was caught between excitement and trepidation as they walked between the shuttered houses over cobbles that gleamed with dew. When Yuda paused to light the lantern he was carrying, Annat bent over the flame that lit her father's face and hands. She was shivering a little with the cold, but also with nerves. They were the only ones walking the streets; the inhabitants had shut their doors on the dark. Annat was leaving them behind, to go on a journey she could not begin to imagine. She glanced up at Yuda's face, wondering how many times he had set out into the night with only a dim idea of where he was going, and no certainty as to when he would return. He was the master and she was the pupil; in the old times, shamans had learned their craft in this way, before migrants like Sival set up their schools and colleges.

The Sheriff had given Yuda a pass to let him leave the village after sundown. The gate stood on the village's northern edge, a sturdy bolted door in the crumbling walls. Waiting while Yuda showed his pass to the watchman, Annat gazed at the piled stones with their loose mortar and weathered surfaces. At the top, where the remains of crenellations could still be seen, bushes had taken root amongst the blocks. The watchman's floodlight outlined them against the sky, like a fantastic garden growing just out of reach. She found herself wondering why there had been no watchman on the gate when Malchik left last night, and resolved to ask her father.

When the door was locked and bolted behind them, they stood on the edge of the hill, staring outwards into the dark landscape. Shamans had good night vision, and Annat could distinguish both the precipitous slope below them, the pale stony track they had to follow, and the cypress trees growing blue out of the ground like witch-smoke. Yuda began to descend the path, moving quick and sure-footed over the uneven stones, and she followed him more slowly, looking about her at the shimmering layers of the night: the valley, soaked with mist, that separated the outcrop where the village stood from the forest; the deep shadow that marked the forest's bulk, climbing blackly to the top of the next hill; and, as she rounded the corner, the pale streak of the Railway tracks like a snail's path drawn across the darkness.

Annat hurried after Yuda, her gaze fixed on the dancing lantern that dangled from his right hand. It made a round globe of yellow light that cast a glimmer about his feet, and sometimes caught on his sleek hair. He did not look back to see whether she were keeping up with him. She knew that this was a message of trust; he did not think of her as a little girl whose footsteps needed to be watched, but as a shaman whose powers could guard his back. Fleetingly, she wondered about the dead Isabel, who had been his fighting partner; he would have trusted Isabel to walk behind him and keep a watch in many dangerous places. Annat doubted whether Yuda would ever show the same faith in her. She was too inexperienced and, because she was his daughter, he would always believe that he must shield her from danger.

When they reached the level of the Railway line, Yuda paused to look at her. She saw his face for an instant before he doused the flame and placed the darkened lantern down on the ballast. He had a cigarette in his free hand, and the tiny red glow burned like a firefly nursed in his palm.

"*Tate,*" she said, in the snatched moment before they hurried on, "why didn't the watchman stop Malchik from leaving last night? Where was he?"

Yuda did not answer her at once. When he spoke, he did not

look at her. "Someone invited the watchman to visit the shebeen. There was a group of us."

Annat paused before her hand darted out to touch his sleeve.

"It's not your fault, Mister."

"I'd say it was. There was no other way to guarantee that we
got back into the village after the gate should have been
closed. So the boy was able to slip through unmarked. But it's
no good me dwelling on it. He's gone; now we have to get him
back."

They walked together down the middle of the track, which
seemed itself to be an eerie, shining pathway that led towards
the stars. Yuda had stopped whistling, but he let Annat share
the keen edge of his excitement. Though he had spoken of his
dread of fighting when they were on the train, she understood
that a part of him relished the danger. The night ahead was
black, except for the faint glow of the sky with its powder of
stars, and they were heading towards the blackness, with their
backs to the fires of the village.

On their way to the tunnel, they passed the marshalling
yards, where two trains stood silent and dead, their bulk like
vast lumps of unlit coal, while a third, smaller engine throbbed
in the darkness, sending up a column of flame-tinged steam.

"Is Shaka there?" Annat whispered.

"Not him. He'll be back down south." He gave a shrug.
"The man is used to me disappearing. Govorin will leave a
message to let him know where we've gone."

"If you love him, why do you sleep with women?" said
Annat, without pausing to think.

Yuda caught his breath. Aloud, he said, "Who knows? But
the fact is that I do love him. I only sleep with women because
I enjoy it, and I don't promise them anything else. Though I
think some would ask for more, if I let them."

"What about Isabel?"

Yuda gave a rueful chuckle. "I never slept with her. We were
too close. She was a friend, the same way Govorin is a friend.
And Shaka too . . . I don't think you can understand, yet."

"I don't have any friends," said Annat, looking down at the
sleepers and the piles of ballast between them.

"Nor did I, when I lived in Sankt-Eglis. Until I met your

mother. She was brave and clever and pretty—" He broke off. "And talking about it won't mend matters."

With a skip of the heart, Annat saw looming ahead the burning oil lamps that marked out the site. Yuda glanced at her. "This is the hard part," he said. "But we'll go down to the tunnel, and we'll meet Govorin and Casildis, and the rest will soon be over."

Annat nodded, but she felt as if her heart were swooping inside her ribs, diving down to resurface, only to dive again. She stared straight ahead, watching the dim golden lights like holes pricked in the darkness, and feeling her palms turn clammy. They were only about a hundred yards from the tunnel mouth, and in her imagination she saw Zarras, a sad ghost, waiting for them with his torn throat, amongst a crowd of other, shadowy figures. She blinked. Someone *was* standing beside the track, close to the tunnel's entrance, but it was not Govorin's stocky shape, or the slender form of Casildis. Without knowing why, Annat felt an instant pure, unreasoning fear, as she recognised the man by his stature and the glints on his yellow curls. It was Sarl, the Deputy.

Sarl came striding to meet them, the lights reflected from his eyes and the steel at his waist. Annat saw with a small shock that he was wearing a sword slung from his belt. She moved closer to Yuda, who put his arm round her shoulders. The Deputy stopped a few feet away from them, standing with his feet planted apart. His handsome face was sculpted by the shadows.

"Good evening," he said, bowing.

"And good evening to you, Mister Sarl," said Yuda softly. The question was in his voice before he asked it: "And what brings you here tonight?"

"My sister told me of your journey."

"I see you remembered to bring your poker," Yuda said, gesturing towards the sword. Nevertheless, Annat felt the relief go through him; for a moment, like her, he had been wondering if Sarl had other intentions.

Sarl did not seem to understand the reference, though he did move his hand on his sword hilt. Apart from the display at the Deputy's house, Annat had only seen swords once before, in the house of her *Mame*'s father, where they had hung on the chimney breast above the mantel.

"Are the Sheriff and his wife here yet?" Yuda asked.

"The Sheriff asked me to tell you that he would be late, so he sent me ahead to make sure that you were safe. He was detained by an important message."

"Very gracious of you," said Yuda tersely. Annat knew at once that he was suspicious; she too could not imagine why Govorin and Casildis would suddenly change their plans, or what could be so pressing that Govorin could not ask Sarl to deal with it himself.

"I have brought some companions," said Sarl, gesturing to the shadows to the right of the tunnel. "This is not the place to be alone at night."

"I was hoping to go without a leaving party, but no doubt you're right," said Yuda. "Seven deaths are enough to make a man pause."

Without answering, Sarl stepped out of their way, and began to walk beside them along the track towards the tunnel's arched opening. Annat felt once more the cold breath that issued from it, as if the tunnel itself were the throat of a giant. A terror came over her, that they would be swallowed up, lost and destroyed inside the darkness. She wished that Yuda had kept the lantern. Her father's thoughts were quite clear, and they spoke his distrust of the Deputy's motives. He wanted to keep Sarl talking until it was plain why he had come. She kept close to her father's footsteps, wishing her heart were not so loud.

At the edge of the tunnel, Yuda paused and turned towards Sarl. "It's not like Govorin to be late," he said, rubbing his hands together. "Must have been a very important message."

"I believe that the news came in from Masalyar on the evening train," said Sarl.

"Anything I should know?" said Yuda, staring up at him. "Or was it for the Sheriff's notice only?"

"I did not read it myself," said Sarl.

"In your place I'd be curious," said Yuda, with a faint smile.

"I had my instructions from the Sheriff," said Sarl, without humour.

"No doubt he'll tell us when he comes," said Yuda.

Annat started. Through the leather of her rucksack, she had felt the doll stir and twist in its wrappings as if it were coming alive. Suddenly, Sarl looked at her in a strange way, and she knew he had sensed it too. The shock of the knowledge was so great that she could scarcely believe Yuda had not noticed something himself. It could mean only one thing: that Sarl was a shaman, but a shaman so powerful that, like Scorpion, he could hide it. She caught her father's wrist.

"What?" he said, irritably.

"We can't go," said Annat, her voice thin with fear.

"What are you talking about, girl?"

Annat stared up at Sarl. She seemed unable to take her eyes away from his. He was watching her with an intensity that seemed to devour her, as if his gaze could strip the flesh from her bones. She realised that he was able to stop her from saying what she knew. At once, the truth was clear to her; they would never return, not because they had been lost entering La Souterraine, but because Sarl and his unseen companions had killed them there, in the darkness. And their bodies would never be found.

Yuda glanced in bewilderment from the man to his daughter. "What's the matter?" he said softly, gripping her shoulder. His touch somehow released her from Sarl's power, and the thought flew from her mind to Yuda's. Quicker than that, so swiftly that Annat did not see him move, Yuda crouched down on one knee and sent a silver-blue streak of lightning at Sarl. The Deputy staggered ·back, momentarily blinded, his hand reaching for his sword.

"Run," said Yuda to Annat, but before they could plunge into the night's concealing gloom, a swarm of black figures scattered into the light, the yellow glow reflected from their steel-edged weapons. Yuda backed against the tunnel wall just inside the entrance to the left, dragging Annat with him, as Sarl wiped the dazzle from his streaming eyes.

"Don't try to use your powers," Yuda hissed in her ear. "Leave it to me."

A semicircle of men was closing in upon them, brandishing the shapes of swords and axes. Annat could only see the light reflected from their eyes. She pressed herself against Yuda, wishing she could hide behind him. Sarl loomed above the ranks of his followers, the blade now drawn in his hand, and shouldered his way through to tower over Yuda and Annat like a great pine dwarfing a birch tree.

"What do you want?" said Yuda, keeping his arm folded across Annat to hold her tight.

"The girl knows what I want," said the Deputy, showing white teeth.

"Don't waste my time. Do you mean to kill us?"

"I am going to kill you, Wanderer, as slowly as I want to. But I can be merciful. The girl's death will be quick."

—*Zyon, he's crazy*, Yuda thought. Feeling Annat tremble, he added, —*Steady*.

"Any reason?" he said aloud.

"I have my reasons," said Sarl. "But I see no cause to tell you them. When I am finished with you, I shall cut out your heart and feed it to my dogs."

"Don't make promises you may not keep," said Yuda, showing his teeth. —*Keep him talking. Gain time*. "I don't see what you've got against me, Mister. I've barely been here three days."

"You don't know, do you, Wanderer? Perhaps you're not as clever as you claim to be. If you are such a powerful shaman, prove it. Tell me my thoughts."

Yuda swayed on his feet, blinking, and Annat felt the edges of a searing psychic attack, like the wind from a fire blowing in her face. She saw her father's face twist with a look of scorn and disgust.

"So, it's like that, is it?" he said. "I know your thoughts better than you do, Sarl." He pushed Annat roughly back against the brick wall and stood in front of her, saying, "Your quarrel is with me, not the *kind*. Let her go. What harm has she done to you?"

Sarl lifted the sword so its point rested against Yuda's breast. Annat felt her father stiffen. The blade was not an elegant, silvery weapon, but a murderous hunk of raw steel, meant for piercing and chopping limbs. She felt the power fluxing wildly in her hands, searching a way to leap out and

sting Sarl's face. She fought to control it, thrusting her hands
into her armpits. If she struck the Deputy now, it would only
serve to enrage him, but she itched to burn that smiling, wide-
eyed face. Her panic was mingling with anger, like ink in
water; but there was no fear left in Yuda.

"Go on, you daft bastard," he said, scornfully. "Skewer us
now, and I'll take you with me. D'you think I can't do it?"

He took a grip on the sword and pulled it against him, cutting his hand on the sharp edges. Sarl reacted as Yuda had
hoped, taking a pace back in momentary surprise. And Yuda
went after him, the power blossoming from his hands. At the
same time, there was a scream in the night: a long, shrieking
call that echoed from the tunnel's curved walls. It did not stop,
and Annat clapped her hands to her ears. From the darkness, a
black, throbbing mass with a grey mane of smoke came storm-
ing, scattering Sarl's followers as they leapt out of its path.
The Deputy fell back over the rails, losing his footing in his attempt to avoid the monster's wrath. Annat cowered, frightened
by the huge bulk of metal and wheels, which for a moment she
could not identify. It screamed like a horse in agony as it came
to a halt, and Yuda was sweeping her up in his arms and running towards it, so that she struggled against him in her fear.
He threw her into its belly, and she landed, hard, on a hot
metal floor, while her father came scrambling through the door
behind her. She heard a familiar voice shouting, and a cool
hand touched her face, before the engine juddered into reverse,
its screeching voice filling the darkness, and began to back
away from the tunnel, heading back towards the marshalling
yards. Yuda crouched down beside Annat, panting, and bleeding from his hand and his chest. He glanced over his shoulder
as a wild face with gaping eyes appeared at the door. The skin
was liverish, like a corpse's, and the eyes were gelid. Yuda
crouched over Annat to shield her, and she saw Casildis, her
blond hair swirling about her, stride to the opening and thrust
back the attacker with a long-handled shovel. Govorin was
working the engine's controls, sending it speeding backwards
up the line.

"Sergey," Yuda panted. "We have to return to the tunnel."

"We need to get you away from here, Mister!"

"Drive her into the tunnel. It's our last chance. If we don't get through tonight, d'you think Sarl will let any of us live? We'll take the engine with us into La Souterraine."

Govorin tugged on the brake lever, and wound the reversing handle hard so that the engine jolted to a halt, its metal wheels shrieking on the tracks.

"You want me to drive straight at the wall," he said, wiping soot from his face with his sleeve.

"You have to do what he says, Sergey," said Casildis, straightening from her work at the firebox. "You saw what Zhan was going to do. Do you think he will leave a stone of your tunnel standing after tonight? We have to risk it."

"We are going to die, you know that," said Govorin drily.

"D'you think I would ask you to kill yourself, my daughter and your wife? Zyon, man, there's a shaman gate down there as big as a barn door. Fire her up!" Yuda shouted, staggering to his feet.

Govorin paused for a moment, then, his face grim, he turned the reversing handle and pulled on the regulator, letting out a great jet of steam. The engine surged forwards, beating down the line like an iron dragon, and Annat saw the tunnel hurtling towards them, a mouth gaping wide to engulf them in its throat. The small figures rushed towards the train, and she saw Sarl again, waving his sword as he ran out of the shadows. He might as well have been holding a bodkin; the train swept past him and Annat saw his yelling face for an instant, before they plunged into the dark. She struggled to her feet, feeling the hot air and soot blasting against her face; her mind was filled with the crash of the wheels and the pounding of the engine. It gathered speed as it went on, and she saw the unfinished wall of blank rock rushing towards them, girded by the steel gantries of the drilling frame. She bent double, shielding her head with her hands, as the engine threw itself against the rock. There was a wailing sound, the roar of steam and the screech of metal, before the darkness ripped apart in front of them and the engine leapt the gap, burning its way through into a cold light.

Chapter 9

The pale daylight seemed to sear Annat's eyes, and she blinked back tears of fright, rubbing her lids. She did not understand why the train was gliding along, as if the tracks continued on the other side of the gateway to La Souterraine. Govorin applied the brakes again, more smoothly this time, and the engine grunted to a halt, sitting furled in the whispering and piping coils of its own steam. Annat heard Casildis coughing; she herself lunged at Yuda and threw her arms around him, clinging to him as she would once have clung to Yuste. Yuda held her tight.

"You were brave enough, Missis," he said, stroking her hair. "I've seen Death a few times, but this time he came so near I could smell his dirty breath. What kept you so long, Mister Govorin?"

Govorin stood splay-footed, bent half-double and fighting for breath. "By the Mother, Yuda," he gasped. "That was a lucky thing. Cas and I *were* late because Sarl brought me messages from Masalyar, but when I'd glanced at them and seen how trivial they were, something made me suspicious. We left the house and hurried all the way here. As soon as we arrived, we saw which way the wind was blowing, so I ran to the marshalling yards, commandeered this train and drove to the tunnel at full speed. Now I'm going to take her on down the line. No sense in waiting until Sarl comes through to join us."

"What line?" Yuda exclaimed.

"Seems as if someone kept laying the tracks this side of the tunnel."

Yuda, Annat and Casildis crowded to Govorin's side, where they could peer through the engineer's window. The tracks ran straight into the distance, steel-grey across a blank and snow-whitened plain.

Yuda wiped his face with the back of his hand. "It'll give us a start on Sarl," he said. "But I'd be happier if I could see where it was going—and know who laid the plates. They might lead us straight over a cliff."

"Only one way to find out," said Govorin with a grim smile. He turned to the controls once more, and pulled on the regulator so that the train began to draw away from the tunnel, gaining speed as it moved across the gleaming plain. The sky was a pearl-white dome that stretched from horizon to horizon without a flaw. Annat thought it must feel like this to find oneself inside a hen's egg, looking up at the pale canopy of the shell. On either side of the track, the flat land swept into the distance, capped with a crystalline deposit of snow. She stepped back from Yuda and said, "You're bleeding."

"You can fix that, Natka," said Yuda. "It's simple cut-work. If Sarl had gone any deeper, we'd be reassembling my insides."

"He was going to kill you, wasn't he?" said Casildis sadly. "I couldn't believe it. I don't understand what has changed him so much."

"He was going to kill us both," said Yuda quietly. "I'm sorry, Missis," he added, as Casildis turned away, burying her face in her hands.

"It doesn't matter, Yuda. Not now. You're hurt; let me carry on with the firing while Annat heals you."

Yuda watched the woman with a troubled expression, as he held out his hand to Annat. The sword had cut two deep grooves in his palm, which were shedding copious amounts of blood.

"I can't do that, Mister," she said, anxiously.

"Yes you can," he said, frowning and smiling at her at the same time. "It's time I started to show you what to do. I was healing much bigger wounds by the time I was your age—but then I had Sival to teach me."

Leaving the Sheriff and his wife in the cab, Yuda clambered back over the tender filled with logs, to sit at the rear of the locomotive on top of the water tank. He held up his right hand, examining the cuts across his palm with an expert eye, while Annat crouched beside him, oblivious for now to the landscape through which they were passing. When he stretched out his hand to her, she took it gently between her own.

"There's three things to look for," said Yuda. "Tissue, blood vessels and skin. Don't bother about the nerves for now. Close your eyes and see through your fingertips."

Annat obeyed and was lost at once in a jostling world of nuclei, cells and plasma. Using her power, she tried to put them back into the patterns from which they had been broken, but they bobbed this way and that, sliding away from her.

"It's like sewing," said Yuda. "I'll guide you."

He put his left hand over hers and steered her power, making it the needle's point that moved amongst the colored cells, slowly threading them together. Under Annat's touch the fibres of muscle began to divide and regroup, closing the gash that had severed them. She gave a breathless laugh.

"Work slowly," he said, squeezing the back of her hand. "You just—have—to nudge them."

Annat moved her fingertips steadily along the line of the fissure; she kept her eyes screwed tightly shut so that against her lids she could see the thin filaments of muscle, the bobbing globes of corpuscles and the fragile blood vessels that clung together like tiny organ-pipes. Amongst them, Yuda's nerve-endings were wisps of fiery blue that sparked and sputtered.

She was surprised how soon she reached the end of the crevasse that formed the first wound in Yuda's palm. Her eyes opened and she smiled into his face.

"Not bad at all, for a beginner," said Yuda, showing her the rough red scar that the healing had left behind. "A suture like this should settle after a few hours, leaving a faint mark. Now it should be easier for you to do the other one."

The second groove was shallower, severing only the skin, and Annat found it easier to fuse the two sides without needing to close her eyes and see through her fingertips. She drew the flaps of skin together and moulded them into one, letting the tissue flow together beneath her touch. When she had finished, Yuda lifted and flexed his hand, turning it from side to side.

"I needn't tell you that this is my knife hand," he said, drily. "I hope I'll be able to use it again."

"Have I done something wrong?" she said, worriedly.

"Nah. But you've got a lot to learn. As well as telling the cells to divide, you've got to tell them when to stop." He grinned. "I've done that. I didn't want to grow a pair of gloves."

Annat shuddered. His words brought back to her the horror and bottomless fear of those moments in the tunnel when Sarl had taunted them. "How could you not be afraid when Sarl . . . ?"

"You noticed that. Funny thing, fear. I'm going to take over the firing now, and I'd advise you to sleep. Must be getting late."

Annat sensed that he was hiding his true emotions from her with a show of indifference. "How about the wound in your chest?" she said.

Yuda smiled. "That isn't a wound," he said. "That's a scratch," and he climbed down from the water tank into the tender, on his way to relieve Casildis.

Annat did not feel remotely sleepy. She stood up on the tender roof to let the head-wind beat against her and fling back her hair. From where she stood, she could see Casildis shovelling wood into the open, glaring firebox, and Govorin with his hand steady on the regulator, turning his head from time to time to check the array of dials and gauges on the back plate of the engine. This was not a massive locomotive like the one that Shaka drove; the boiler was shorter and more compact, and it had both a long, flared smoke-stack and a brass dome. The engine was painted with a glossy black livery that gleamed in the pale light of the sky and the reflections from the white ground; the exhaust issued from its funnel in a long plume of cloud-grey that blew over Annat's head, shedding cinders and a tarry smell.

The cold air snagged in Annat's hair as it raced past, and she stretched her arms wide to embrace it. If this land were La Souterraine, just now it belonged to her alone. There were no footprints in the snow, no tracks of birds or traces of sub-merged trees to disturb its surface: only the dark lines of the Railway track that seemed to merge at the horizon. Annat turned on the spot, the wind buffeting the back of her neck, to look back the way they had come. She could just make out the dark smudge that marked the tunnel from which they had emerged; and then she saw the horses. She turned towards the cab, preparing to call out to her father and show him what she had seen, but she decided against it. The horsemen were so far behind that she could hardly distinguish their colors. This train was not slow-moving like the one she had ridden from Masal-yar to Gard Ademar; it was travelling swiftly enough over the plain to leave the riders behind—for now.

She studied Casildis, who had curled up in the tender in an attempt to get some sleep. Annat felt frustrated that the woman was dozing when she wanted someone to share her excitement at the strangeness of this world, which looked as if it had been newly formed to receive them. There was a smoothness about the landscape that suggested it had indeed hatched from an egg, and had not yet hardened. She sat down on the cold roof, clasping her knee with both hands, and let her thoughts empty until there was nothing left except the perfect whiteness and stillness of La Souterraine.

Suddenly, the engine careered to a halt. The wheels shrieked against the brake shoes, sparking and grinding, and steam rushed from the piston exhausts, swaddling the engine in mist. Govorin was leaning out of the left-hand side of the cab, with Yuda craning over his shoulder. From her vantage point, Annat saw the figure in the distance, stumbling towards them down the centre of the track, with bent head, as if oblivious to the train's approach.

"By the Mother, it's Malchik!" Govorin exclaimed.

Annat saw her father jump from the cab and vanish for a moment before he reappeared on the track ahead, striding towards her oblivious brother. She went after Yuda, leaping down into the tender, to stumble through the unstable logs as Casildis sat up, rubbing her eyes, to ask why they had stopped. Annat didn't answer; her heart was beating faster than it should, and a weird emotion welled up within her, almost choking her as she clambered down from the cab.

Before Yuda reached the boy, Malchik came to a halt, stooping as if under an impossible burden, and raised his head. He stood like a figure of molten wax, as if he were about to deliquesce and seep away into the snow-covered ballast. With a pang of dismay, Annat wondered if this were truly her brother, or an illusion sent to trap them. She saw Yuda put his hands on Malchik's shoulders, but the boy slumped down at his feet, clinging to Yuda as if he did not know who he was. A surge of anguish went through Annat; she knew that she was sharing her father's response. She had to stop, clutching at her midriff as if she had a stitch.

It was very still, except for the hissing of the train behind her. She heard Yuda say, "Malchku," under his breath, and then, "What's happened to you?" Her brother did not answer, or move. Her father bent over him, gripping him by the upper arms to help him to stand. "Come on, *kind*. Be a man," he said, gently, his face almost touching Malchik's bent head. Annat hesitated at a distance, feeling that her presence was not required. She watched Yuda coax Malchik to his feet, murmuring encouragement to the boy as he might have done to a small child. Malchik drooped against his father, scarcely able to stand upright, and Annat hurried to his side, seeing that Yuda was struggling to support his son's tall form. She took her brother's left arm and wound it round her shoulders, and Malchik said, "Hallo, Annat," in a muzzy but pleased way, and Yuda said, "Thanks, *kind*. I thought we were both about to bite the dust."

"Are we going home?" said Malchik, blinking at the train, which he seemed to see for the first time.

Once again, Annat felt Yuda's sadness. "Not just yet, boy," he said. "We're going to see Mister Govorin, and you can lie down on some nice, knobbly wood."

Malchik made a hissing sound that was plainly meant to be

a laugh. He leaned heavily on Yuda and Annat in turn, swaying from side to side as they helped him along the track. Incredibly, he was still carrying the harp slung from his back, and several times it swung against Annat, bruising her arm. When they were a short distance from the engine, Govorin came striding to meet them and took Annat's place, all but carrying Malchik the last few yards by himself. He deposited the boy in the tender, having first disentangled him from the harp, and Casildis took off her jacket and folded it under Malchik's head. Malchik peered at her shortsightedly; her face was grimy with soot, which made the blue of her eyes seem more intense.

"Well, boy," said Yuda, leaning on the tender door. "Now we've found you, what are we going to do with you?"

"Can't escape," said Malchik; it seemed an effort to force the words out.

Yuda sat down on the mound of logs beside his son. "You'd better tell us everything, Malchku," he said, taking the boy's hand in his.

Malchik sniffed, and pinched the end of his nose. "I didn't know where I was. Lost." He paused, shutting his eyes, and gave a wide yawn. "So tired," he said, sleepily.

"Go on, *kind*. We'll let you sleep in a while."

"I came through, but I couldn't go back," Malchik said, spacing the words with effort. He thumped his chest. "Seed, seed of ice. Inside me. Growing. Like Sarl. Mustn't be like Sarl."

"But how could Sarl—?" Casildis exclaimed. Yuda stretched out his free hand to stop her, shaking his head.

"What's this about a seed of ice, boy?" he said. "We're listening."

"She made me go through. And she put the seed of ice in me. To make me her servant." He stared straight ahead, a look of horror on his features. "The Cold One. I had to follow her. Mustn't disobey. I'm sorry, *Tate*, I'm so sorry . . ." and he rolled over on to his side, tears spilling from his closed lids. Yuda squeezed Malchik's hand.

"Don't apologize to *me*, boy," he said softly. "Like I said, you've got just enough shaman in you to make you vulnerable.

But do you know what's up ahead? Have you seen anyone else?"

Malchik gazed at him piteously. "No one else, *Tate*. Only snow, endless snow. I was alone."

"That's enough for now, boy," said Yuda. "You sleep. Sleep!" and he passed his hand over Malchik's forehead, letting it linger for a while until the boy's eyelids drifted shut, and his body relaxed. Yuda sat back amongst the logs and gazed at Govorin with a grim face. "You heard that, Mister?" he said. "We've got ourselves a one-way ticket to hell, with Sarl on our heels."

"But now we've got Malchik, why can't we go home?" said Annat. "We could fight Sarl!"

Yuda gazed at her for a while before answering. "It's not that simple, Natka. Something *has* infected Malchik—the seed of ice. He said himself that he couldn't escape. If we try to leave this world now, it may kill him. We have to find out more about the Cold One, and why she brought him here. We can't turn back."

"What troubles me is why Sarl is following us," said Govorin. "He's got rid of us all at a stroke. He doesn't need to kill us."

"He wants me dead," said Yuda. "But you're right, Sergey. That can't be his only reason for plunging into an unknown world and chasing us on horseback, when he must know we can outrun him."

Casildis wiped her face, smearing the coal smuts. "I can't believe that my brother could be so murderous," she said. "He's always been a hard man, a harsh man—but not evil. It's true that he has changed much in the last few years. He never used to beat Mari . . ."

Annat felt her father's pity for Casildis, but inside the pity was a kernel of something else, a small glowing spark whose meaning Yuda kept to himself. It was subtler yet more intense than the rough passion he had felt for Rosa: a new thing.

While Yuda returned to the firing, Casildis and Annat moved Malchik further into the tender, so that he would not be in the way of the shovel. Since Casildis hesitated to climb on the roof of the water tank, they settled themselves at the rear of

the wood-pile, trying to make themselves comfortable
amongst the logs. Casildis persuaded Annat to lean against her,
and they sat in silence for a time, watching the dreamlike landscape drift by. It never grew dull; the light seemed to change,
casting strange and beautiful reflections off the wastes of ice,
and making the snow shimmer with transient blue shadows.
Casildis stroked Annat's hair, and the soothing touch of her
fingers helped Annat to drift in and out of sleep, despite the
roar of the fire on the grate and the clanking of the engine.

Annat hugged her pack against her chest, feeling the awkward shape of the doll through the leather. It had not moved
since the moment outside the tunnel when it stirred like a living thing. In her mind, Annat pictured the three of them, like a
carving: Casildis with Annat's head resting on her knees, and
herself with the doll cradled in her arms, wrapped like an ancient mummy in cloth and skins. Just below the place where
her feet rested, Malchik was snoring with his mouth open. Beyond him, in the cab, her father tirelessly shovelled wood, his
jacket off and his sleeves rolled up. The glow of the firebox
flickered on his pale face and hands whenever he stopped to
speak to Govorin. The Sheriff's dark, shiny skin turned to red-
hued bronze in the same light, and his white teeth gleamed like
porcelain. From time to time, as the noise died down for a second, she caught the edge of Govorin's laughter. But she could
not stop her thoughts returning to Sarl and his calm, handsome
face as he menaced Yuda. If Yuda had learned anything from
the Deputy in their moment of *sprechen*, he had not chosen to
confide in her.

Annat frowned. She wondered what would have happened if
they had chosen to turn back and confront their pursuers.
Surely they could have backed up the line and slipped past
Sarl before he was able to stop them? Then, just as before,
they could have jumped the shaman gate to the upper world,
and driven away to safety . . . Annat fingered the thongs that
fastened her rucksack, letting her gaze drift from the glow of
the driver's cab to the pearly textures of the landscape and
back. Everything around her was moving: the two men in the
cab, struggling to rein in the engine, and feeding its ever-
hungry maw; and the land flowing backwards out of sight,

changing like a kaleidoscope before her eyes, but always white. Her father must be right. Though they had found Malchik, they could not risk the Cold One's anger by trying to wrench him free of the place in which she had immured him. They must go on until they could discover the way to cure him.

Night came so suddenly that Annat gasped and sat up. The pale, glimmering clouds rolled back to reveal a deep, majestic well of midnight blue, across which phantasmal lights rippled and shuddered in curtains of violet, indigo and mauve. There were stars, thicker and clearer than she had ever seen, cold and close, and great pock-marked moons that glowed on the horizon. Govorin applied the brakes, more smoothly this time, and the engine juddered to a halt, the smoke from its cowl radiant with sparks. The two men stood in the cab door, gazing up at the sky; Annat saw Yuda shiver.

"Zyon, it's beautiful!" he said. "'Blessed be the One who brings the nightfall.'"

"Blessed be His name," Annat murmured.

Govorin laid his mighty hand on Yuda's back. "A good prayer, my friend," he boomed. "We're going to need it."

Chapter 10

They made camp for the night by the side of the line. In preparation for their journey, Govorin and Casildis had brought two packs filled with bedrolls, blankets, provisions and water-bottles. Leaving Malchik to sleep undisturbed, Govorin roughly divided his estimate of the dark time into four watches, suggesting that the three who were not on watch should share the bedrolls, while the guard should keep the fire alight. Yuda elected to take the first watch, and the last thing Annat saw before she fell asleep, comfortably squeezed between Govorin and Casildis, was her father's umbered face on the far side of the flames, sipping from a bottle of *schnapps*.

She was woken by the sound of voices. She tried to sit up, but was pinned tight like a swaddled baby, and it took her some effort to wriggle free without disturbing Govorin or Casildis. There was a man sitting by the fire next to Yuda: a man with long grey hair who wore nothing but leather trews and a waistcoat of skins. Annat watched his gnarled hands gesturing as he spoke; there were several bright rings on his fingers. She wondered who he was and where he could have come from. Yuda seemed to be listening without any trace of worry; as she watched, he offered the uncorked bottle of *schnapps* to the stranger, who took it and swigged deeply.

Annat stood up. She lifted her coat from the pile and put it on, for the night was profoundly cold. Overhead, the astonishing sky glittered with pure brightness; the great moons were high above, and a red-skinned planet hung in the deep, striped with yellow bars that seemed to move slowly across its face. Annat walked round the fire, hearing the men's soft voices murmuring in the stillness of La Souterraine. Behind her, the engine rumbled in its sleep; Govorin had damped down the furnace, making sure that it would not go out before the morning, and a steady pillar of smoke drifted upwards from the chimney, smearing the sky with grey.

Annat approached the two men, her feet crunching on the snow, and the stranger turned his head to see her. He had a lined brown face, and his skin was tanned like tobacco leaves with age and weather. His dark eyes gleamed at her, and he rose, showing her a smile that revealed broken teeth. He was not much taller than Yuda, and his hair was snarled into rat's tails, but the smile was warm and friendly.

"Greetings, pretty one, my name is Santos," he said, pressing his hand flat on his hairless chest. He spoke Franj, but with an accent that Annat did not recognise. She did not know what to say. No one had ever called her pretty before. While she hesitated, he went on, "What is your name?"

Annat looked across the fire at Yuda, who was watching her with an inscrutable face, his chin on his hand. She thought she saw the vestiges of a smile on his lips.

"I'm Annat and that's my father," she said, quickly.

"Come and sit down with us," said Santos. "I was telling your father that you must be our guests tonight. We can give you food and warm beds beside a glowing fire. In La Souterraine, it is never wise to be outdoors after dark."

Yuda had lit a cigarette, and was blowing wisps of smoke from his lips. He seemed to be waiting to hear what Annat would say.

"Where do you come from?" she said. "I haven't seen any houses."

"If it were daylight, you could see our house. I live with my brothers inside a hill, the Bald Hill. Our home has no roof, and no walls; only the earth covers us from the sky."

Annat hesitated. She wished that Yuda would say something, or send her a thought; then she realized that he was relying on her instinct for danger, the reason that he sometimes called her his "little canary." He did not want to influence her response by letting her know his own judgement. Silently, she told him that she could find no reason to distrust Santos; she was not aware of any strangeness.

"I am hungry," she admitted. Their supper had been meagre, for they needed to eke out rations, not knowing how long it would be before they found food.

Yuda spoke. "My daughter always has an empty belly, Mister Santos," he said.

"Then it is time to wake your chief and ask him. Do not sleep outside under the cold stars and the face of Rogastron, the bitter planet. Come back to the hill and be our guests, and wake tomorrow fresh for your journey."

Yuda stood up easily, and stretched like a cat before it leaves the hearth. "I'll see what he has to say, but I for one would prefer not to sleep on the snow, when there's a better offer," he said. Santos remained by the fire, rubbing his hands as if to warm them, and Annat watched her father approach the sleeping bundles that were Govorin and Casildis. The Sheriff sat up abruptly when Yuda touched his shoulder, and Casildis began to stir. Having listened to some whispered words from Yuda, Govorin came striding over to the fire, struggling into his overcoat, and looked Santos up and down with a critical eye.

"Welcome, friend, and driver of the iron beast," said Santos, bowing to Govorin. "My brothers have sent me to bring you to our dwelling, where you will find safety from the chill of the night."

"I'd like nothing better," said Govorin. "But I can't accept your hospitality. Someone has to stay behind to watch the train—the iron beast. I can see no reason why my friends shouldn't return with you, if they wish." He glanced at Yuda, who nodded. Govorin went on, "I'll sleep in the cab where I can keep an eye on the boy. It seems a shame to wake him just to move him. That's if you agree, Yuda."

"He's better off where he is," said Yuda. "I've put him into a deep sleep, and he won't wake until daylight."

Once Casildis had joined them, they carried the bedding

over to the engine, and left Govorin to make himself comfortable inside the cab. They covered the fire as best they could, hoping that it would last till morning, while Santos watched them, moving from foot to foot as if he were eager to be gone. When they were ready, he cupped his hand, and a glowing blue orb appeared in his palm, twisting and shimmering like a soap bubble. Casildis gasped, and Annat went closer to peer at the luminous ball, which cast a sapphire radiance around Santos, lighting up the snow.

"A simple trick, but one that will light our way," said Santos.

"Are you a shaman?" Annat asked.

"I am only a magician, but one who knows a few such sleights of hand. Follow me," and holding up the orb, he set off into the darkness, heading away from the Railway line. Yuda, Casildis and Annat followed him, the two women huddled together; Casildis wrapped Annat in a fold of her cloak, and Annat clutched the doll's hard body against her, as if it too needed to be kept warm.

"Do you think this man can be trusted, Mister Vasilyevich?" whispered Casildis.

"He seemed friendly enough when we were talking by the fire," said Yuda. "Natka hasn't picked up any bad signals from him, and her instincts are pretty reliable."

"Santos is a strange name," said Casildis. "It isn't Franj, and I've never heard one like it."

Yuda nodded, gazing at their host's retreating back. "His speech reminds me of Isabel, and the accents of Hi Bresil," he said, pensively.

The Bald Hill was about the size of a house two storeys high, and thick with snow. There was only one entrance, a narrow opening covered by a woven blanket, and in front of this Santos stood aside to let them enter. Inside was a low room like a cave, and Annat drew breath at the luxurious warmth. A fire burnt in the centre of the chamber, directly beneath a smoke-hole, and two men who were seated by the hearth rose to their feet. They might indeed have been Santos's brothers, for they looked much like him; but one had a flowing handle-

bar moustache, and the other a pair of lopsided pince-nez
perched on the bridge of his nose.

"These are my brothers, Dios and Muerte," said Santos, as
Pince-nez and Moustache bowed in turn.

"Welcome to our hearth," said the one Santos had named
Muerte. He had sun-lined skin and blue-grey eyes that smiled
at Annat as he approached; his voice was unexpectedly high-
pitched.

"We are honoured to have guests," said Dios, pushing his
pince-nez further up his nose. "Very few come to visit us, so
far out in the wastes."

Casildis assumed the demeanour of the courtly woman she
was, and swept forward, extending her hand. The brothers almost jostled each other in their eagerness to stoop over the
outstretched hand, and Dios guided Casildis to the fireside,
placing a large cushion on the ground for her. While the three
men were dancing attendance on Casildis, Annat took a hasty
glance round the room. The walls were lined with animal pelts
and woven blankets; tanned hides covered the floor; and from
the ceiling hung numerous bunches of dried herbs, salted fish
as stiff as boards, and the stuffed, withered carcasses of lizards
and small animals. There was a smell, not altogether pleasant,
of cinnamon and cloves masking something ranker that Annat
could not identify.

Then Muerte took her hand, saying, "Come to the fire and
warm yourself," in that high, nasal tone that did not fit his
avuncular face. Annat let him lead her to the fire, though with
her long coat she was beginning to feel too hot. Yuda followed
her, his hands in his jacket pockets, and sat down on the
ground without waiting for anyone to fetch him a cushion. As
Annat started to take off her coat, she set the doll down on the
ground beside her father, and was startled to see Muerte recoil
from it, as if it were a burning brand. Annat stared at him, and
saw his glance meet that of Dios. When Dios saw the doll, he
too backed away from it, making sure that the fire lay between
them. Only Santos seemed untroubled. "We have food for you,
and then you will sleep," he said, gesturing towards a small
black stove at the back edge of the chamber, where a large pot
simmered.

"You must find it hard to obtain supplies," said Casildis, politely.

"Alas, we must eat what we find and kill," said Dios. "Our diet is chiefly of fish, as you will find if you travel much further in this land." He seemed to have recovered his nerve, though Annat thought that from time to time he cast doubtful glances in the direction of the doll. She was tempted to laugh at this extraordinary behaviour, but it also made her wary. Why should these strangers be frightened of her doll?

"We hope you will share our repast of salt-fish and herbs," added Muerte, as he approached the stove. He lifted down the cauldron, while Santos ascended a ladder to the unseen upper room, returning with a ladle and an armful of wooden platters. Annat felt her stomach roll as she watched Muerte spooning the stew from the pot on to the dishes. She was not forced to wait, for Dios swiftly brought two plates to her and Casildis, bowing as he handed them over. He did not linger, but stepped back hastily. Annat waited to be given a spoon, and was startled when she received a hunk of black bread. She noticed that Casildis accepted the bread with a gracious smile, and began to eat at once, using morsels of the loaf to mop up the stew with her fingers. Yuda watched the woman eat, and once again Annat perceived that faint spark of amusement and approval in him. It was interesting that he liked to observe Casildis so much, though there was nothing intrusive about his stare.

Annat turned her attention to the stew. The bread was moist and crumbly, and tasted slightly of malt; the stew had several flavours, and the salt was not too strong. She picked at the flakes of fish, extracting a few large bones, and began to eat with relish. Yuste and *Bubbe* had often prepared fish at home: fried in crumbs, poached in milk, or served in its own jelly. She noticed that Yuda was once more picking at his food, and wondered if he would let her eat what he left.

Squinting with annoyance, she realised that she had almost swallowed another bone, and hastily pulled it from her mouth, hoping that no one had noticed. As she slipped it on to her plate with the others, something about its shape caught her eye. It was not a fish-bone at all, but a large nailparing. Annat gagged. To think she had nearly eaten that! She was about to complain, when her eyes fell on Santos and his brothers, eating their portions of stew. From time to time, one would pause, to steal a glance at Casildis, Yuda or herself, watching them as they ate. As if they were waiting to see what would happen.

—*Tate! Be careful. There's something in the food.*

She saw him wince.

—*I thought you'd learned not to shout.*

—*I found a nail in my stew. I think they're trying to harm us.*

—*I doubt it, kind. Probably just careless cooks.*

He smiled to himself. Annat took a fearful glance at Casildis. The woman was wiping her plate with the last piece of bread. If there had been anything in her share of the meal, she had swallowed it. Annat could not quell her suspicions. Her fingers strayed to the doll, lying on the ground beside her. Sure enough, it stirred under her touch, as if it were coming to life.

—*You've got to listen to me . . . Yuda. There's something wrong. These men are afraid of my doll. And I felt it move. It only moves when there is danger.*

Yuda rolled his eyes at her, but she saw that he was taking more care over his food. He ate with deliberate mouthfuls, and after a short time, without his making any outward sign or gesture, she heard him think: —*Zyon. You're right, kind.*

He wiped his mouth on his sleeve, and Annat was sure that he had rid himself of the encumbrance. He put down his almost-empty platter and flashed a smile at their hosts.

"An excellent supper," he said.

Casildis stood up, stretching. "I am so sleepy," she said, yawning. "I could sleep for a year."

"There are beds in the upper chamber," said Dios, rising, "where the beautiful lady can sleep like a princess."

"Reckon I'll turn in too," said Yuda, rising to his feet. "What better companion than a beautiful lady?"

Annat expected Casildis to make some retort, but instead she smiled dreamily, as if she had not heard what he said.

—*You too, Annat,* Yuda thought. —*I'm not leaving you alone with this bunch.*

—*Can't you tell there's something wrong with Casildis?*

—*That's plain enough.*

The three men were chuckling at Yuda's pleasantry, which he emphasised by taking Casildis's elbow and shepherding her towards the ladder. Careful not to be too quick in her movements, Annat too stood up, yawned and stretched. She picked up the doll and cradled it against her. Casildis was sagging against Yuda, already half-asleep. He turned to beckon Annat with an ironic gesture.

"Come on, little one. It's past your bedtime."

Annat went to him, her arms folded across her chest, trying not to see the brothers' gap-toothed grins.

"Up the ladder with you," said Yuda.

Heeding the warning in his voice, she began to clamber up the rungs that led to the upper room. There were three pallets, piled with quilts and pillows; and a pungent scent like incense filled the room, mingled with wood-smoke from the fire below. Annat took off her coat but kept her boots on, and lay down on the mattress furthest from the ladder. Though the bed was covered with a clean, if much-mended, linen sheet, when Annat lay down she experienced a strong unease and distress, as if she were touching something tainted. She was glad that very little of her skin had to come in contact with the sheet.

Casildis emerged slowly through the hatch, her head drooping, and slumped on to the middle bed, where she seemed at once to slip into a deep slumber. Yuda followed her, sat down on the third pallet and lifted his finger to his lips.

—*What are they going to do?* Annat thought. He shook his head, pointing to the chamber below, and she understood that he wanted her to avoid using even *sprechen*. There was silence for some time before they heard Muerte speak.

"It is long since we have had such a catch, my brothers."

"Perhaps we could keep the little one. She has great power," said Dios.

"No, my brothers," said Santos. "We must pay our tribute to the Cold One. She will let us leave if we give her the heart of a shaman."

"What else shall we harvest tonight?" said Muerte, humming a little tune between his teeth.

"I have need of a head," said Dios. "I will take the man's head."

"That is good," said Muerte. "Brother Santos and I will divide the women between us. It is a while since we have tasted female flesh. I can use the eyes, the lips and the secret parts in many ways." He gave a long sigh. "We will see far, and fly, and share great power. We might even return to our homes."

"Ah, Brother Muerte," said Santos. "Even you could not fly so high. The Goddess will not let us leave. You know the tribute she requires for trespassing on her lands. But we will have new servants the old ones are almost dry."

"Let me do the killing this time," said Dios. "I want to cut the head while it is still fresh."

—*I might have something to say about that,* Yuda thought with dark humour. His eyes met Annat's, and he sent her, like a touch, a feeling of comfort.

—*What can we do?* Annat thought. She scrunched her hands together over the coverlet to stop them shaking.

—*Wait. And listen.*

"The Prince of Ademar is coming," said Santos. "I looked upon his face in my scrying glass."

"Perhaps we should invite him to the feast," said Muerte, chuckling.

"He does not eat man-flesh. But he may speak for us to the Goddess when we show him the skulls of his enemies."

"Perhaps," said Santos. "We do not know the one he is seeking. There are two not in our power. Perhaps it is the maid-child. She carries the doll."

"Do not speak of it," said Dios, in a low voice. "We must find a way to dispose of it."

"We shall leave that task to you, my brother," said Santos, mockingly. "By now, they will all be asleep. And when you have it, we can ask young Ademar for his counsel. We would be foolish to destroy his quarry without first seeking his leave."

Yuda sat very still, listening, but the talk below had ceased. He took the knife from its sheath at his belt and began to clean his fingernails with it, as if there were nothing to trouble him. A few instants later, as Annat saw a head emerging through the hatch, her father lashed out with the strength and sped of a viper. The knife took the man in the back of the neck, below the brain-pan, and with a sound like a sigh, he released the poles of the ladder and dropped out of sight. Yuda was on his feet.

—Wake Casildis and follow me.

Annat felt the force of the command, like a whiplash. She threw herself on Casildis and began to shake her, trying to reach into her mind. It was near impossible. Unlike a shaman mind, Casildis's thoughts were enciphered in an insoluble code, and they were woven shut too with blue fibres of enchantment, wisps of power that clung like leeches. Annat, frantic with fear, began to drag the tall woman's body out of the bed, across the floor towards the entrance. But how would she be able to lower Casildis through the opening without hurting her?

Suddenly, the woman stirred, rubbing her eyes.

"Annat, what are you doing?" she said. "I was having such lovely dreams—let me sleep . . ." and she rolled over, covering her ear with her hand. Annat shook her again.

"No, Casildis, you have to stay awake!" she cried. She was scarcely aware of what was happening below, but as she tried to pull Casildis to her feet, a terrible head appeared slowly through the open hatch and moved from side to side. There were no eyes, only empty red cavities, and the lips had been cut away, revealing the teeth in a fixed grin. The skin of the face was red and shrivelled. Annat gave an involuntary cry of fear, letting Casildis fall, as the thing began to lift itself through the opening, seeking her with its blind muzzle. While Casildis began to raise herself, complaining weakly through the haze of magic, Annat let fly with her powers, with little more accuracy than she had shown during the attack on the Masalyar train. But the force of her fire unbalanced the creature, which fell back across the floor, and in those few moments Annat was able to bundle Casildis on to the ladder, half-lowering her and half-dropping her, praying that she would be conscious enough to grip the rungs. Annat pressed herself on top of Casildis, clinging to her back like a baby monkey out of a picture book, and gripped the rails on either side of her, hoping that Casildis would support her own weight. Casildis slipped rather than climbed to the ground, and

Annat let herself slide down the ladder poles, skinning her palms as she went, and twisting before she reached the foot of the steps so that she faces outwards into the room.

Yuda was at bay, locked in a duel of magic with Santos and Muerte, whose spells wove about him in blue and orange threads, like a many-colored spider's web. He had no magic with which to oppose them, only the multi-formed tool of his powers, which he was using to sever the clinging fibres of their web, scything rainbow slashes through the net winding in upon him. With Casildis drooping against her, Annat snapped her fingers, and briefly distracted the two men, who spun to see where the sound had come from. The power sang joyfully in Annat's ears as she spread her right hand and let it flow out of her in a glorious stream whose colors lit up the room. It was not like Yuda's sapphire lightning, honed and precise, but a diffuse wave of fire that swept over the witches, shrivelling the skeins of their power. Set free, Yuda sprang towards her and plucked Casildis from her arms, heaving the woman's form across his shoulders like a sack of wheat. Shouting, "Follow me!" he ran for the door, and Annat, trying to shake off the wonder of her moment of triumph, flew after him, bumping into him as he stooped to negotiate the narrow entrance.

Outside in the dark, her father hunted from side to side before running away to the right with Casildis bobbing across his back in an ungainly fashion. Annat saw the three mutilated shapes that came moving across the night, and sped to keep pace with Yuda, who was gasping for breath as he staggered along. Casildis's hair had come loose and was winding itself round his face and neck as if it were alive. Annat glimpsed the blue-grey shadow of a hideous handless figure running alongside them. She was a husk drained of power; that one flowering had taken all her reserves, and she needed her strength to run.

"Yuda! They're overtaking us!"

—*Save your breath. I can see 'em.*

Suddenly, with a gasp of pain, he let Casildis tumble over his bent head on to the snow, and stood astride her body. As Annat reached him, the three creatures were closing in, moving with the slow steps of automata. Yuda caught her by the wrist, tugging her against him, and bared his teeth in a war-snarl. As the first creature lunged towards him, the blue lightning soared from his fingers, staining the night. While the *mutilé*, as Annat thought of it, staggered backwards, the other two closed in, making no sound, and pounced suddenly like dogs, trying to overwhelm Yuda with their strength. He lashed out with knife and kicked, but he was encumbered with Annat and Casildis. Annat slipped out from under his arm and dashed into the dark. As she had hoped, one of the creatures broke away from her father and lumbered after her. Annat felt laughter as well as fear as she led the clumsy thing further and further from Yuda. But the laughter faded when the *mutilé* began to move faster, and she heard its feet pounding in the snow as it drew level with her.

Out of the night came a long, haunting cry like the call of a bird echoing across the wilderness. Annat turned on her heel and dodged past the blunt, bone-thin arms that reached out to grab her. She made for the blue beacon of Yuda's power, speeding light-footed over the hard snow, and saw him slash at the cords that held a withered head on its neck.

"Govorin is coming! The train is coming!" she shouted as she ran. She saw Yuda shove the staggering figure away from him, and stoop to gather Casildis up in his arms. Once more, her height nearly defeated him, but he swung her limp form across his back and came lurching towards Annat, bent almost double. Annat could hear the footsteps of the other *mutilé* behind her, while the third closed in upon Yuda from the rear. But the ground was throbbing now with the beat of the engine's approach, and Annat saw its fiery cloud streaming into the air as it flew towards them. It began to brake as Govorin sighted them by the trackside in the blue flare of Yuda's power, and Annat sprang up to the ballast, running alongside it to seize the running bar and pull herself up into the cab. Yuda was close behind her, letting Casildis slump to the metal floor. For a heart-stopping moment, the train stood still, as Govorin let off the brakes and pulled on the regulator. The two remaining *mutilés* were closing in, and Annat saw their hideous faces over Yuda's shoulder as he stood in the doorway. Slowly the engine edged forward in a cacophony of sound, gouts of steam erupting from its funnel, but the two deformed figures continued to keep pace with it, and it was not until the locomotive began to draw away from them that Yuda snatched up the shovel and began to feed the furnace, stepping over the recumbent body of Casildis.

It was left to Annat to haul the woman out of his way into the tender, where Malchik still slept amongst the blankets and bedrolls. Casildis, who seemed unaware of the rough handling she had received, turned over and curled up amongst the wood chips, sinking back into her enchanted slumber. Annat sat beside her, exhausted but too wrought up to rest, her hand tingling with the power that flowed through it. She stroked Casildis's hair, wondering how they would be able to destroy the spell, which might have effects more harmful than mere sleep.

The train was thundering through the night, lit by the light of Rogastron and its three strange moons. Annat lay back and stared at the unknown constellations, huddled up against Casildis to keep warm. In the cab, the two men seemed to work tirelessly, and as time drifted past and they drew further away from the Bald Hill, the brothers seemed to fade in Annat's mind like the inhabitants of a dream. She began to doze, and was only wakened when the engine once more slid to a halt, unfurling silver flags of steam that hid the stars from her. Annat sat up in the tender to see Yuda leaning on the shovel, his head bent, while Govorin set the brakes and checked the water gauge. Annat's face must have caught his eye, for he turned to her and beckoned, saying, "Your father's spent, Natka, and I could use a rest. We seem to be coming into different country, and we may as well stop here. We've put a good few miles between us and those horrors."

Annat stood up and climbed out into the cab. Her short nap had left her feeling more refreshed. "Where are you going to sleep, Mister Govorin?" she said.

"I'll spread a pallet on the floor here, and Yuda will find a space in the tender."

"Have to see to Casildis," said Yuda, who was almost asleep on his feet.

"By the Mother, man, can't it wait till morning? You're dead beat."

"Can't wait," said Yuda, letting the shovel fall with a clang that wakened neither of the sleepers. Annat offered him her arm to lean on, and helped him into the tender, where he stood over Casildis, swaying on his feet.

"Maybe he's right, *Tate*," she whispered.

"Must get out the nail," said Yuda, without looking at her. He stooped over Casildis and began to shake her firmly, muttering her name, until she stirred and her eyes opened. Yuda knelt down beside her. Her stroked her head. "I'm sorry for this," he said, "but I'm going to make you sick . . ." and he stuck his finger down her throat. Casildis came up, gagging, and Yuda thumped her on the back, guiding her to the side of the train, where she vomited over the edge. The sound made Annat's stomach turn, but Yuda stayed with Casildis, rubbing her shoulders, until she had finished. She sat back on her heels, wiping her mouth in disgust.

"Bright Lady! Yuda, why did you do that?"

"Do you feel sleepy now?" he said, with a smile in his eyes.

"Sleepy? Goddess, no—how could I be sleepy?"

Yuda dragged himself to the top of the wood-pile where Malchik lay, and spread out a blanket, making himself a nest. "That's very good," he said, and slumped down on his knobbly bed, turning until he was comfortable.

"Yuda!" Casildis exclaimed. Govorin touched her shoulder.

"Let him rest, my love," he said. "We will have to wait for the morning for the story. I have some water for you to drink."

Casildis shivered, and the Sheriff put his arms round her, drawing her down to the pallet on the engine floor, where one cloak could cover them both. Annat discovered the other pallet, which Yuda had disregarded, lying half-unrolled in a corner of the wood-box. She spread it out and lay down, wishing they had more blankets. She edged close to Yuda, but he was lying curled up, his face in the crook of his arm, and she hesitated to disturb him. The thought came to her that, as she was wide awake, she should keep watch while the others slept. She made her way up to the roof of the water-tank and sat there cross-legged, gazing around her at the scenery.

On her left, away towards the northern horizon—if it was
the north—a range of white-coated hills rose up against the
sky, arching like the backbones of whales. The plain ran
smoothly towards them, glittering like mica dust, in which
every grain seemed to reflect facets of a star. The stillness was
vast, perfect and not unfriendly; the gaunt shapes of the hills
carried dark lodes that marked the ascent of trees, and a frozen
river meandered towards them across the waste, a river of stars
waiting to ascend into the sky. Annat stayed motionless,
wrapped in the loud sounds of her breath and heartbeat. She
did not want to disturb the silence that was revealing itself to
her alone.

She wondered if the river had a name, and whether tomorrow the Railway track would bring them closer to those hills.
The plain itself might have been the footprint of a giant, left
behind as he bestrode the world, or a footstep of the Goddess
herself. Perhaps next day they would see whether a sun rose,
burning off the cloud that had masked the sky by day. Annat
lay back on the cold metal roof and gazed at the three moons,
which glowed so intensely that they gave off a blue aura. A
distant galaxy filled one corner of the sky with its milky spiral,
caught in a cloud of stars that hovered round it like bees.

Annat wished she could ask someone what the galaxy was
called, and the identities of the constellations that decked the
stellar field, hanging so close she felt she could have touched
them, or gathered them like flowers out of a meadow. She tried
to imagine whether the One saw all the lights in the universe at
once, like a great map, or whether He moved amongst them,
endlessly studying their beauty and strangeness. The Goddess
would flame like a comet across the heavens, but the One
would stretch boundlessly, holding the worlds and galaxies
and universes as if they were bright toys of which He was the
maker.

Suddenly, Annat heard a faint, hollow cry like the call of a
night bird. She sat up eagerly, hoping that she might catch
sight of it. Instead, an incredible sight met her eyes. Striding
across the plain out of the west came a group of spindly figures, impossibly tall, who waded over the ground as if it were
soft underfoot. Annat's heart raced as she watched them; they

were approaching, but their direction of travel lay towards the far-off hills. With a shock that made her laugh, she realised that the figures were ordinary men and women, balancing easily on huge stilts that enabled them to bestride the marshy ground. There were about fifty of them, and they moved in a slow, graceful flock like wading birds, trailing faint shadows behind them in the moons' light. Annat wondered if they could see the train and herself sitting high on the roof. On an impulse, she stood up, stretching her arm high to wave. She saw a ripple pass through the group as they strode along, and then she realised that they were waving back at her, without turning from their course. Annat laughed silently to herself, glad that she was the only one awake to see this strange sight. The ground over which the stilt-walkers strode must be marshy under the snow, instead of the firm surface that she had encountered further back up the line. She watched them for a long time, seeing their shapes seem to dwindle in size as they travelled away northwards towards the hills, just as if they were cranes picking their way across a seaboard mud-flat. Annat felt a sense of longing to follow them, to find out who they were and where they were going in the emptiness of the night. There had been nothing menacing about them; they were following some strange errand or pilgrimage of their own, migrating across the plains like a skein of geese flying south at the beginning of winter. She doubted whether she would see them again; the Railway line was likely to skim the foot of the distant hills, without climbing into their interior, where gradients would be too steep for an engine. She watched the figures dwindle until she could no longer make out their forms against the striated hills. She sat down with a sigh. She did not know yet whether she would tell her companions of what she had seen. It seemed to belong to her alone, during her vigil, when she was the only one awake.

Chapter 11

No one was in a good mood at breakfast. All they had to eat was pemmican and dry biscuit, and there was only water to drink. There was not enough to wash with, or clean one's teeth; but Yuda insisted on shaving, since, as he pointed out, with a night's growth of beard he resembled a desperado. They sat in a forlorn circle on the snow, on blankets spread out round a small fire that Govorin had managed to light. Their only consolation was the pallid, misty blue of the sky above; strangely, though there was sunlight, they could not see the sun.

"Bloody marvellous place for a picnic," said Yuda, who was smoking; he seemed to have filled most of his pack with tobacco.

"I can't eat this stuff," said Casildis, spitting out a mouthful of pemmican.

"You shouldn't waste it, my love," said Govorin.

"Don't 'my love' me, Sergey! I know that."

"There's no need to shout, Casildis," said Govorin in a low voice.

"Please don't argue, I've got a splitting headache," said Malchik, pressing his hands to his forehead.

"Annat, see to your brother's head," said Yuda, curtly.

"I can't. My hand is still sore after last night."

"You two don't know what hardship is," said Yuda in disgust. He stood up and stalked away from the fire, his shoulders hunched under his jacket. Govorin sighed.

"Some of us should try to find wood for the engine," he said. Nobody seemed to want to be the first to answer. The Sheriff went on, "We've all had a rough night. The least we could do is to be civil to each other."

Annat folded her arms across her chest, and stared at the blanket on which she was sitting. She resented Malchik's complaining of a megrim when he had slept through all the troubles. She did not see why Yuda could not attend to her brother's headache himself.

"Do I have to spell it out for you?" shouted Yuda, rounding on her. He had heard her thought.

"Yuda," said Govorin, gruffly. "I need your help. Some of us must stay with the engine while the others forage for wood and food. Water's easy enough; we can melt some of the snow."

"I feel so dirty," Casildis lamented.

Yuda gave a shrug, as if trying to shake off his bad temper. Grinding the cigarette into the snow with his foot, he walked up to Malchik and hunkered down behind him, laying his hands on the boy's temples.

"I'm easy, to tell the truth," he said, slowly massaging his hands over Malchik's scalp. "What about you, boy?"

"I don't know," said Malchik, shutting his eyes as his father's touch eased off his pain. "I've been walking for so long. I thought it would never end."

"Never mind that now," said Yuda, his eyes moving to meet Annat's. Today they had an opaque, flinty look, and his thoughts were locked tightly shut. Annat glanced away from him, still hurt that he had yelled at her in front of everyone.

"Perhaps Annat and I can go alone. Casildis looks worn out, and Malchik should rest a while longer," said Govorin.

"What about me?" Annat burst out. "I was working hard last night. I had to run from the *mutilés*!"

"We were all working hard last night, little Natka," said Govorin, gently. "No one has forgotten what you did. But you and I will stand a walk better than the others would. I reckon

the track runs close to those hills, and we should find timber
there, if nothing else. Casildis packed some hooks and lines, so
we could make an ice hole and fish for minnows." He grinned
in his beard. "I bet they taste better than pemmican."

"Anything would taste better than pemmican," said Casildis,
with a shudder.

They covered the fire with snow and folded up the blankets
before making their way in silence to the locomotive. Once in
the cab, Yuda picked up the fireman's shovel with a grimace,
rubbing the small of his back; Annat guessed that he had
strained it last night, carrying Casildis and shovelling wood.
She walked up behind him and laid her hand on his spine, to
see whether she had any reserves of healing left with which to
ease him. Yuda straightened in surprise and glanced over his
shoulder at her.

"Changed your mind, did you?" he said.

"I won't do it if you don't want."

The man gave a shrug, and winced. "You'd better carry on,"
he said. Annat was tempted to tell him he could put up with
the pain, but she persisted, letting little wavelets of power
trickle over the muscles that girded the spine. When she had
finished, Yuda bent over and then stretched to his full height,
standing on his toes. "That's better," he said. "I feel more like
a man and less like a hedgehog."

"Can the man shovel wood, or must I ask my wife?" said
Govorin with a mischievous look.

"Let her rest," said Yuda.

The Sheriff drove the train slowly down the line to a place
where, as he had predicted, the hills with their dark freight of
trees grew closer. Soon the track was running alongside the
frozen river, which lay between them and the steep slopes clad
in sombre pines. As soon as the engine came to a standstill,
Annat sprang lightly into the driver's cab, where the heat from
the firebox was such that Yuda was working in his shirtsleeves.

"I wouldn't do this for a living if they paid me," he said, examining the blisters on his palms.

"I'll bet Shaka would laugh if he could see us now," said
Govorin.

"If he did laugh, I'd punch his bloody nose," said Yuda with feeling.

They noticed Annat watching them, and her father promptly said, "What are you staring at?"

"You," Annat retorted.

Govorin flicked open the steam-cocks, which let out a great rush and sigh of vapour. "Natka, d'you reckon the three of us could safely leave Malchik and Casildis to mind the train?"

"Don't know," said Annat, shoving her hands into her coat pockets.

"What my daughter means, Mister Govorin, is that she can't sense any danger, but she can't be bothered to tell us," said Yuda. Annat scowled at him, and he answered with a horrible grin.

"I'm going to take a risk," said Govorin. "I don't reckon Sarl could ride hard all day and all night without killing his horses. Two or three hours' halt should be safe enough. Casildis and I packed some rope, and a couple of hooks and lines for you—we can take those, and some rations."

While the Sheriff fetched his overcoat from the tender, where he paused to exchange a few words with Casildis, Yuda slipped on his jacket and began to unfasten the fireman's axe from its fittings on the side of the cab. He hefted the axe in his hand, testing its balance, before slipping it through his belt. Govorin returned carrying one of the rucksacks that he and Casildis had brought, together with Yuda and Annat's own smaller packs.

"I took the liberty of emptying out your kit," he said, with a mollifying smile. "Casildis has agreed to sort through our stuff and divide it more evenly. Though I wasn't expecting the harp and the *vyel*!"

"Wherever I go, the *vyel* goes too," said Yuda. "And the boy wasn't so stupid. Music has power in a place like this."

"Has he said anything more about what happened to him?"

Yuda glanced at Annat. "Not to me," he said. "But there are traces of the intruder in his mind. I picked that up when I was fixing his headache."

"Does he pose any threat to us?" said the Sheriff, wrinkling his brow.

"Not yet. Malchik is still in charge, for now. But we'll have to watch him."

Annat felt a twinge of regret for resenting her father; like a shadow, she glimpsed the different Yuda within the shell that so often seemed harsh and uncaring. Even though he had not unfettered his thoughts, she sensed how troubled he was about her brother. She realised that a link had developed between Yuda's emotions and hers; she could often sense what he was feeling whether or not he revealed it to her, and she wondered if he experienced the same empathy. The knowledge frightened her a little; Yuda's mind was so intense and powerful that sometimes what he felt seemed to overwhelm her. She decided that, when she had the chance, she would ask him what it meant.

Govorin glanced towards Malchik, now sitting in the tender.

"Have you any idea yet why the Cold One picked him?"

"Only guesses," said Yuda. "But we learnt some things eavesdropping on the brothers last night. They mentioned a Prince of Ademar."

"And they were afraid of the doll," said Annat.

As Govorin gave her a startled look, Yuda nodded. "They were indeed," he said to the Sheriff. "They were planning to destroy it. I'd like to know why they thought it was so important."

"We're riding on blind, Vasilyevich," said Govorin, pulling the rucksack straps over his shoulders. "Our enemies know the rules and hold all the cards. We don't even know where the line is headed, or who built it."

"I guess we'll find out if we keep following it," said Yuda, grimly.

Annat thought of the doll and wondered whether she should take it with her. Instinct prompted her to leave it with Malchik and Casildis, for she believed that it might protect them, like a talisman. She hurried to take it from its wrappings and ran to Casildis, pressing it into her hands.

"Please guard it for me," she said. "I think it would be better to leave it here."

Casildis smiled. "I will keep her safe," she said.

Annat felt a surge of eagerness as they climbed down from

the engine. The high hills with their arched backs seemed to beckon, and the deep ravines shadowed with pines invited her to enter them and explore. She hoped that the ground by the river was not boggy like the plain over which the stilt-walkers had waded last night. She hurried to keep pace with Govorin and her father; in spite of his bulk, the Sheriff was a quick walker, and he strode over the snow as if its surface were firm beneath his feet. Yuda's small figure kept pace with him, cigarette dangling as ever from his hand. They were black shapes against the unyielding pallor of the landscape, harder and firmer than shadows, and their feet left deep prints in the white ground. Annat scuttled after them, forgetting her tiredness; she was pleased that the Sheriff had chosen her as a companion, instead of leaving her to languish on the train with the invalids.

Casildis was dozing. Malchik tried to work out how long Annat and the others had been away. With no means of telling the time, he could only think that it must be about an hour. The sky above remained blank, with no journeying sun to give him a clue as to the time of day. He had already consumed his lunchtime rations: rye bread, cheese and a slice of pickled gherkin to protect against scurvy. Casildis could not eat anything; she had sustained herself with sips of water from the canteen that Govorin had left.

Malchik sat with the harp unwrapped on his knees, letting his fingers steal over the strings. He had lost the power to play tunes, but the soft ripples of sound consoled him, and kept him from thinking of the cancer in his thoughts, a black shadow like an insect that seemed to gnaw him from within. Through it Malchik could perceive Sarl and his band of horsemen riding across the plains back to the west. He suspected that Sarl was able to see him in the same way, if he chose to; Malchik could smell in his thoughts the rank sweat of that sharp, broken mind. When Yuda and Govorin returned, he must tell them what he knew—if he was able to do so. The black beetle in his skull held him tight with its claws, and he was not sure whether it would let him speak. Though Yuda had cured his headache, his brain still seemed to throb to the beat of an extra pulse, as if something were growing under the skin.

If only he could remember a tune! Music would give him some relief. Malchik plucked random patterns from the harp, picking out scales and arpeggios, which at least had a pattern. And then, incredibly, someone came to him: a gentle ghost whom Malchik could not see. He felt her presence beside him, and the cool touch of her fingers against his brow.

"Who are you?" he whispered under his breath, so as not to wake Casildis.

—*Sing, Malchik. Sing for me.*

"I can't sing, my friend," he said, feeling tears in his eyes.

—*I shall be sad if you don't remember my song . . .*

He felt her laughing gently at him, like the breath of the wind stirring in his ear, or the voice of a shell echoing his blood.

"How can I remember your song when I don't know who you are?" he said, wretchedly.

He felt her touch on the crown of his head. —*They can destroy many things, but they can't take music from us. Life, but not music. I have sung this song so often for your father . . .*

"Isabel?" he said, feeling his breath catch in his throat. He felt that, if he shut his eyes so he could just peep through his lashes, he might be able to see her.

—*Sarl stole my voice, so you have to sing for me. Sing, Malchik!*

His fingers moved over the harp strings, and the chords began to emerge, softly at first. He felt the beginnings of a smile move his mouth as the tune grew under his fingers, and Isabel whispered the words in his ear.

"A red ship goes sailing out on the shining sea
She flies on the dawn wind that comes in the night . . ."

Malchik felt the sadness of the words as he sang, with their longing for lost friendship and their sadness at parting. Once he had them by heart, he sang with pleasure, and the music took all other thoughts from his mind. Beside him, the ghost of Isabel Guerreres whispered the words she had written, and he felt he shape of her presence: a small, neat woman with cropped amber hair, rocking in time to the tune, just out of sight. For a few moments, he was free of the Goddess and her devouring stare.

"I stood on the shoreline with a lantern in my hand
And the flame of the candle burning bright."

He could almost see Isabel beside him now, as if the song were giving body to her form, and summoning her into being. But if he turned his head to look at her directly, there was nothing there. He concentrated on singing the verses that she gave to him, feeling a sureness in his hands as he plucked the strings. He could see that Casildis had woken up and was listening to him sing, with her chin resting on her hand, her long fair hair following the sinuous line of her body. It seemed to him that at the touch of the notes, the air was coming alive; a soft breeze played round him, and the whisper of Isabel's voice echoed his words.

When he finished, Casildis clapped her hands. Malchik smiled at her, and turned to look for Isabel, but she was gone. The breeze had turned to a cold, cruel wind, which pushed at him like a kitten teasing a mouse before the kill. He clung to the harp, trying to hold in his mind the gentle sadness of Isabel's presence, but the air's tongue rasped at him, claiming him greedily. Out of the sky came ragged shapes like crows, which circled his head, beating at him with their wings. Malchik threw up his arms to shield his head, and heard Casildis scream in fear. The dark birds tore at him with beaks and claws that he could not see; he staggered to his feet, dropping the harp, and tried to beat them off with hands that were beginning to bleed.

Casildis stumbled towards him; she pulled off her cloak, flapping it like a great wing to drive off Malchik's assailants, but the cloth was ripped from her hands and borne up into the air, twisting in the violent eddies of the vortex. She staggered forwards, trying to embrace Malchik and shield him with her body, and her yellow hair was swept wildly around them both, tangled with ice and hail and black crows. They stood at the

centre of a whirlwind, clinging together, unable to hear each
other's voices above the shrieking of the wind and the birds. It
seemed to Malchik that the only safety and warmth lay in the
space enclosed by their bodies; he shut his eyes and hid his
face against Casildis's shoulder, wondering if the torment
would ever end.

They were walking along the bottom of a deep valley, sheltered by the snow-laden branches of fir trees. They had already
stopped to make a hole in the ice covering the frozen stream
that lay at the bottom of the dale; baiting their hooks with
bread, they had waited, still and silent, crouching round the
opening, to see if any fish took the bait. Yuda had caught a pair
of silvery trout, and Govorin a young pike, which he had
grabbed with his hands out of the icy water and brought up,
flailing and threshing. Annat squatted with her forlorn line
dangling through the ice, and caught nothing. They had
wrapped the fish and placed them in Yuda's pack, before going
on along the course of the stream up the valley, wading
through the virgin snow.

Suddenly, the sloping dale split open into a canyon, its walls
glistening with ice, and the stream spread out into a wide and
opaque pool. Annat gasped. Ahead of them was a pinnacled
barbican of glass, a frozen waterfall that cast a shining gate
across the rocks ahead, rising sheer to an insurmountable
height. The stalactites and icicles hung down like silent wind-
chimes, petrified in the moment of ringing.

"I don't reckon we'll get any further up this valley," said
Govorin laconically. "Maybe it's time for us to turn back and
cut some wood."

The three of them walked out on the surface of the glassy
pool, and stood gazing from its depths up to the silver spires of
the cascade.

"I wonder if anyone else has ever seen this?" said Annat
aloud.

Yuda walked up to the edge of the ice-wall and peered
round it, slipping his hand into the crevice.

"Zyon, you won't believe this," he said. "There's a cave behind here, and I reckon we could squeeze through. Even you, Mister Govorin."

"Even I?" said Govorin, setting his hands on his hips. "And why should I want to squeeze through into that cave, Mister Vasilyevich?"

Yuda leaned on the slippery rock, his face puckered with dimples and his eyes bright with mischief. "Why don't you come and look, Chief?"

"Ten to one there's a deep, muddy hole, and I'll end up in it," said Govorin to Annat, in a stage whisper. But they both crowded up to Yuda, and peered round the edge of the ice-fall. Inside was a deep cave whose amber and saffron walls were veined with coppery green; steam hung in the air, issuing from a wide pool that stretched into the rear of the cave, and poured its contents in a smooth, liquid skein over a rock ledge down to invisible depths.

"That water's hot!" said Govorin, withdrawing his head and staring at Yuda.

"I suggest we leave the fish outside," said Yuda.

"What about the *kind*?" said Govorin, peering at Annat and almost laughing.

"Zyon, this is no time for modesty. We're three dirty people who need a bath. Unless you want to send her back to fetch Casildis, et cetera."

"Do you think it's safe, *Tate*?" said Annat uncertainly. Their encounter with the brothers had left her wary and less confident of the power of her protective instincts.

Squeezing her shoulder, Yuda said, "You and I should pick up on any danger before it comes too close. This place has a good feeling, I'd say. What do you reckon, my little canary?"

"Ye-es," said Annat hesitantly. "There's nothing bad. But how do you know you can trust me? I got it wrong last night."

Yuda smiled at her with his eyes. "I'd trust you above anything, Natka," he said. "You weren't the one who was fooled last night. I let myself be persuaded because Santos seemed such an amiable fellow when he was drinking with me by the fire."

With Yuda in the lead, they placed their packs together at the entrance, and squeezed through the narrow gap between

the ice and the rocks of the cave-mouth. Inside, there was a
strange twilight, mingled with the silvery light that penetrated
through the frozen cataract, and the reflected glimmer of the
pool, whose walls gleamed with the ambery deposits of iron
oxide. A wide shelf, smooth underfoot, led along the wall of
the cave to its interior, where they found the source of the hot
spring that bubbled up from the ground. Yuda went down on
one knee and dipped his cupped hand into the water to taste it.
He grimaced.

"Tastes of rust," he observed.

"Hot and cold running water, just like a bath-house," said
Govorin.

"And a bath is what I need," said Yuda, sitting down on the
rock shelf and unlacing his boots.

"Are you actually going to take your clothes off?" said
Annat, who had not quite been able to believe that they would
go so far.

"I'm not jumping in fully clad for your benefit, Missis. Either you can wait just outside and preserve your modesty, or
you can strip down to your vest and knickers. I can promise
you that the body of a thirteen-year-old girl will excite neither
the Sheriff nor me. We like stronger meat."

Annat felt herself go red. Yuda had assessed her fears cor-
rectly, but she wished that he would not discuss them in front
of Govorin, of whom she was a little in awe. The Sheriff ran
his hand back over his mossy hair.

"It's not a problem that I was expecting," he said. "There
must be some fold in the rock you could use to get changed.
But it doesn't seem right, somehow."

"Don't be an old woman, Seriozha," said Yuda, taking his
jacket off. "If Annat is unhappy, she can wait outside until
we're finished, and then take a dive later, by herself."

Annat wished that she could stop blushing. However, she
decided to take Govorin's advice, and found herself a small,
hollow place at the back of the cave, where she hurriedly
pulled off all her clothes except her underpants, folded her
arms across her small and inadequate breasts, and took a running jump straight into the water. She was too busy spluttering
and coughing at the heat to take much notice of what Yuda and

Govorin were doing, or whether they were looking at her, but a few moments later, there were two bigger splashes, and two sets of heads and shoulders appeared in the water beside her. Govorin's skin was a luscious, chocolatey brown, and Yuda was comically pale in comparison, like a skinned lizard.

"Whoa! This is hot!" said Yuda, and sneezed. Govorin struck out across the pool, splashing him, and revealing a pair of buttocks like two brown boulders. Annat suddenly started to giggle for no reason, and stuffed her fingers into her mouth. The only man she had ever seen naked was her brother, and she at once realized that he was far from typical.

"What's the matter with you?" said Yuda, indignantly.

"The Sheriff is brown all over!" Annat exclaimed.

Govorin flipped over on to his back, and sat in the water on the other side of the pool. "Am I missing something here, Yuda?" he said.

"I don't think there were many Darkmen in Sankt-Eglis," said Yuda. "And they must have kept their trousers on."

Annat guiltily stifled her laughter. She could not help wondering whether the Sheriff's penis was brown too, and what it must look like. She was tempted to swim underwater for a closer look, but decided that this would be unfair when Govorin had been eager not to embarrass her. She did observe that Yuda had very little hair on his chest, except a thin tuft of long black hairs below the collarbone, and that his shoulders and arms were muscular, though nothing like the giant sinews of Govorin's breast and back. She began to swim across the pond, thinking to herself how strange men's bodies were. Their skin had a hard look, like cardboard, their feet and hands were too big, and their shape was straight where it should be curved.

Annat shut her eyes and dipped her head under the water to wet her hair. Having grown up near the sea, she found this warm, fresh water a luxury to which she was not accustomed. She flipped over to float on her back, then almost sank as she remembered that she had to cover her chest. Turning over on to her front, she observed Govorin and Yuda swimming to and fro. Yuda swam with grace, moving easily through the water like a seal, but Govorin splashed and thwacked, making ripples that rocked the surface. Annat recognised with relief that they were not even slightly interested in her or her adolescent body. She was as safe as if she had still been a little girl, smooth and flat as a peeled wand. She dived down to the bottom of the pool, opening her eyes to inspect the rich deposits of iron gilding the rocks below. There were waving weeds, long and subtle as hair, and the water itself had a greenish tinge, so that in the depths it was almost opaque.

When she surfaced, Govorin and Yuda were larking like two boys, ducking each other and splashing wildly with their feet. Annat watched them with a tinge of contempt, wondering how they could be so silly. She climbed out of the pool—

—and came face to face with a strange man who had appeared from nowhere, naked except for a bearskin loincloth. Before she could call for help, he had knelt down at her feet and touched the ground before her with his forehead. Folding her arms tightly across her breasts, Annat wondered what she should do. The man sat back on his heels and addressed her from that position. "Welcome, nymph, servant of the Great Goddess Artemyas!" By this time, Yuda was out of the water and striding towards them. He stood beside Annat, naked and dripping, and demanded, "Who the hell are you?"

The man, whose grey eyes seemed slightly unfocused, lifted both his hands palms uppermost, and intoned, "The Bear People have sent me to welcome you, O servants of the Goddess! We have seen her in your company, riding in her chariot of steel and fire, and we knew her by her tall stature and the radiance of her wheaten hair!"

"Oh, shit," said Yuda under his breath. They were joined by Govorin, who, unlike Yuda, covered his privates with his hand.

"Who is this fellow?" he demanded, speaking Sklav to prevent the stranger from understanding.

"He seems to think your wife is the Great Goddess Artemyas," said Yuda. "Not sure what that makes us."

The three of them inspected the stranger, who in turn regarded them with awe. He was tall, light-skinned, with dark hair and a blue tattoo like a bear's paw on his shoulder.

"I beg you to enter our halls, O Great Ones," said the man, bowing his head. "Some of my people have been sent from

Arrun, our chief, to conduct the Goddess and her minstrel
thither. We have set guard to watch the magic chariot, to see
that none dares to lay sacrilegious hands upon it. I crave that
you follow me, as honoured guests."

"The last time someone said that, I nearly ended up in the
stew," Yuda said. He glanced at Annat, who was shivering. The
air in the cave was far from warm, compared to the water in
the pool. "What do you say, my little canary?"

"What is a nymph?" Annat asked the man, speaking Franj.
She felt a little sorry for him, and thought it was rude of them
to keep him on his knees while they made jokes at his expense.
To her surprise, the man smiled, and his eyes seemed to become less wild and distant.

"You are a nymph, maiden, a chaste follower of the virtuous
goddess," he said.

Annat returned his smile. There was no obvious scent of
danger about him, though she did reflect that things might not
go so well if he and his people discovered that Casildis was
not a Goddess.

"Please tell me your name, Mister," she said.

"I am Teress, of the House of Arrun," he said. "I beg you to
follow me, Great Ones, so that my people may honour you."

—*He's okay,* Tate. *Just a bit confused. I think there will only
be trouble if we try to run away.*

—*We haven't got much choice, for now. I just hope they
don't keep us too long. We don't want Sarl to find the iron
chariot and smash it to bits.* He laid his hand on his chest, and
bowed to Teress, saying, "I am Yuda of the House of Vasilyevich, and this is the mighty Chief Govorin, of the House of
Gavril"—Govorin gave a snort—"and we would be very
happy to follow you, O Teress, once we have put on our
clothes."

"I for one am freezing," Govorin added, stamping up and
down on the spot.

"Our handmaidens will bring you fresh clothing, and take
your old raiment to be cleansed," said Teress.

The handmaidens proved to be four women and two young
girls. They wore long skirts and richly embroidered blouses
beneath the handsome leather jackets edged with fur. Like Ter-

ess, they had dark hair and eyes that were grey or a startling, wintry blue—but none of them were fair. The women presented Yuda and Govorin each with a towel and retreated to a modest distance while they dried themselves. The girls did the same for Annat, and she was a little upset by their fearful demeanour and downcast eyes. She wanted to shout at them and tell them that she was not a nymph, or companion of the Goddess, or anything like that; but instead she wrapped herself in the towel and began to dry herself hurriedly, for her skin was cold and her feet were frozen. Govorin and Yuda were talking in low voices as they got dry; Yuda had seized his knife and belt from his pile of clothes before anyone could take them away.

When they were almost ready, the handmaidens departed, only to return in a hurry with three piles of garments. The Bear People plainly thought their own clothing too simple for the servants of their Goddess. The girls presented her with a white shift, a grey over-tunic, and an apron embroidered with red thread. To keep her warm, they provided a cloak woven from reddish wool, fastened at the shoulder with a golden pin. When Annat saw what Govorin and Yuda were wearing, she had to smile, it was so different to their usual garb. Govorin wore a splendid long robe of wool dyed red, decorated with gold thread, a bearskin waistcoat and a yellow cloak; Yuda had on grey trews, a blue shirt and a black waistcoat with silver and mirrors sewn on to the surface. He had insisted on belting on his knife over the top, but this did not look as incongruous as Annat might have expected. They had given him a grey cloak, and Annat wondered whether they kept such garments in different sizes or whether Yuda just happened to fit those that they had chosen for him. For some reason, she found the fact that all their clothes fitted so well a little disturbing. There was no way in which the Bear People could have known that they were coming, unless they had some unusually accurate soothsayers.

Once they were all dressed, Teress led them towards a narrow crevice at the back of the cave, from which he and the handmaidens had emerged. When they approached the entrance, it proved to be wider than it seemed, and they were able to pass through without difficulty. A passageway led up through the rock, interspersed with flights of stone steps. The walls were moist with running water, and veined with vivid ores. Annat, who was walking at the front, behind Teress and the women, drew her hands over the oily surface. The light of the torches that burned in the tunnel caught on vivid greens, which shaded into blues as rich as the waters of the Middle Sea.

It was a long climb, but at last they emerged into the daylight. They found themselves in a forest clearing, whose low stockade walls were surrounded by high trees with lush fronds almost bare of snow. The ground had been swept clear and strewn with pine needles, and a small flock of sheep, white and rufous and black, stood huddled against the wall of the stockade to their left, munching on piles of needles and herbs which had been piled high round them for fodder. The inner walls were hung with massive bearskins, tanned whole, and one or two still had the bear's skull attached to them.

"This is our dwelling-place, in Bear Forest," said Teress, simply. "The Bear is our guardian, our friend—and our enemy. We hunt him, but we may not eat of his sacred flesh, which is offered up to the Goddess, the She-Bear."

Within the stockade stood many round huts of differing sizes, their walls built of solid mud and their roofs made from branches thickly plaited with reeds. Teress led them along a narrow way that passed between these rondavels, some of which were brightly painted with stylised shapes that Annat would have liked to pause and examine more closely. She followed Teress with Yuda and Govorin on her heels, and the six handmaidens bringing up the rear. At the centre of the village was a round meeting-place, where the whole tribe seemed to be gathered in a great ring, waiting for them. In the middle of the circle stood a tall man with a noble face, leaning on a staff; but the most impressive thing about him was the complete bearskin that he wore draped over his head and hanging down his back. When he saw Teress approaching, he stepped forward and struck his staff on the ground three times, crying, "Welcome, Great Ones, companions of the Goddess! I am Arrun, Chieftain of the People of the Bear."

Govorin, Yuda and Annat stopped in a row, uncertain what to say as the assembled people shouted in acclamation. After some hesitation and conferring between the two men, Govorin stepped forward and made a bow.

"Greetings, noble Arrun," he said. "I am Govorin of Masalyar, consort of the Goddess, and this is my friend and blood-brother, the mighty Yuda son of Mordechai." Before he could say anything more, a strange sigh went through the crowd, and all except Arrun dropped to their knees. "Oh dear," said Govorin, under his breath, "what have I said?"

"You've certainly made an impression," said Yuda.

Arrun bowed low before them, pressing his hand to his breast. "Then this is a thrice-blessed day for us, O Great Ones, that you come to honour our halls in this way. Follow me, and I will conduct you into the presence of the Goddess."

Lowering his staff, he set off at a diagonal across the circle, and the crowd parted to let him pass. Having hesitated a few moments, Annat realised that she was supposed to follow Arrun, and scuttled after him with a lack of dignity that did not quite befit a nymph and chaste companion of the Goddess. The Chief was making for a large, high-roofed rondavel that stood at the edge of the circle, to the right of the clearing. For some reason, the entrance was less than half a man's height, and even Annat was forced to duck to go through. She found herself inside a shadowy circular room with a high-vaulted roof, in which the only source of light came from a series of pine torches fixed to the walls of wattle-and-daub. There was a small dais on the opposite side of the space, with a chair set upon it, and Casildis was enthroned on the dais, her face clean and her hair brushed out straight, dressed in flowing white robes adorned with gold. The doll lay in her lap. Malchik sat uncomfortably at her feet, the harp balanced on his knees, and Annat noticed at once the new scratches on his face and neck. She started towards him, before recollecting that she was supposed to be playing a part. Managing a wobbly curtsey before Casildis, she intoned:

"All hail, Great Goddess Artemyas, Mistress of the

Nymphs." The woman's eyes met hers, sharing mingled amusement and apprehension.

"Greetings unto you, Annat my faithful servant," said Casildis, raising her hand in a royal gesture. "I bid you to stand behind my throne and minister to me, as you have done so often in paradise."

—*That's right,* Yuda thought. —*We've got to take our cue from Casildis—and hope she knows what she's doing!*

"It is ever a pleasure to perform your commands, Most Gracious One," said Annat, who was beginning to enjoy acting out the role that had been foisted upon her. Taking care not to hurry this time, she swept across the room, letting her hand brush Malchik's shoulder as she passed, and took up a position on the dais behind the throne, where she had a good view of what was happening in the hut. Casildis now rose to her feet in stately fashion, and lifted her arms, bent at the elbow, palms outwards.

"Most noble husband and spouse," she said, smiling at Govorin, "I am right happy to see you once again, after the perils that have befallen us. For my sister, the envious Nyssa, sent her birds of evil to harry my servant Malchik, and he scarce escaped with his life."

Malchik nodded energetically, pointing to the scratches on his face. Govorin stepped forward and, addressing Casildis, said, "Noble Lady, is the Goddess Nyssa known amongst mortal men as the Cold One?"

"Yea, my husband, and she seeks ever to destroy my people." She threw back her head and lifted her arms high above her, shouting, "Set me free, free me, I beg you. For without me, my sister grows evil, and I weaken. I prophesy that, when the day comes, without the five all will be lost." Having finished, Casildis suddenly went limp, and collapsed gently to the floor of the dais, like a wilting rose. Arrun cried out in alarm, and Annat and Govorin both rushed forward to pick up the fallen woman.

—*That was a good performance—if it was a performance . . .* Yuda thought in Annat's mind.

Casildis opened her eyes and smiled dreamily up at Govorin. "She came upon me—the Bright Lady came upon me," she murmured. "It has been such along time . . ."

Govorin looked startled by these words, but all he said was, "Unfortunately, she spoke in riddles, my love," discreetly using the Sklav language.

Together, Govorin and Annat helped Casildis back on to her chair, and Annat tidied her wild hair, which had once more started to go astray. She picked up the doll and returned it to Casildis with a smile that only they shared. Arrun seemed to think that he should have a greater part in the proceedings, for he strode to the foot of the dais and struck the floor with his staff three times.

"It is a marvellous chance, most Holy Incarnate Goddess, that brought you here to consecrate our hearth with your presence, bringing with you your spouse and his brother," he said. "For now, through your union, the earth will be made fruitful and blossom, and the sun of spring will warm the sky that has been winter for three years gone."

"Union?" said Govorin.

Arrun, who seemed to be enjoying his moment of glory as both Chief and High Priest, went on, "For you must first mate with one who is your husband's brother, to bid farewell to the old year. And then, at your gracious pleasure, unite with your mighty consort to usher in the birth of the new year."

There was a rather intent silence, before Govorin straightened up and said, "What?" and Casildis hastily interposed, "Nay, noble Arrun, it is not so. I will lie with my true spouse tonight, and all shall be well."

"No, Most High. You yourself have set it down in your teachings that you must lie with your bridegroom of the old year, before you can renew your pleasure with your own true spouse, who is your King and consort."

"Now wait a minute—" Govorin began, but Arrun continued, "If it is not rightly done, according to custom, the power of the Cold One will not be broken, and the winter will continue. My people begin to grow stunted and sickly, and few little ones are born to us. There would be great anger if they knew that their own dear Goddess had failed to keep her promise."

Govorin and Yuda looked at each other. Govorin made a movement like a shrug, and Yuda shook his head.

"So must it be," said Arrun concluded triumphantly, though Annat detected a note of anxiety in his voice. He had not expected anyone to disagree with him.

"So must it be," said Govorin, squeezing his wife's shoulder. Casildis glanced up at him with a look of dismay.

"See, Goddess, how your noble husband submits to the law," said Arrun, quickly. "We have waited so long for your coming, we were certain that you knew of our need when we learned that you had brought both your husband and his brother amongst us. Indeed, it must be so."

"It is so," said Casildis, rising to her feet. "But, like any wife, my heart stirs to my spouse, and his to mine. For mortal and divine hold consort in my breast in equal measure. My loving is to my husband, but I shall not forget my duty to my people, who have waited so long and so patiently for my coming."

"All praise to the Great and Beloved Goddess, who sees all things true in her wisdom, "Arrun declaimed. "I shall convey your words to the people, so that they may spend the night of your espousals in feasting and rejoicing."

As soon as he had left the chamber, the five of them gathered together.

"What were you thinking of, Sergey?" Casildis demanded. "I can't go through with this."

"You've let them call you their Goddess, Missis. Now we have to keep up the pretence."

"I am not making love to Casildis," said Yuda, folding his arms across his chest.

"I don't think you have much choice, Yuda," said Govorin. "Our necks may depend on it."

Swiftly, they rearranged themselves as Arrun ducked through the door. He was smiling, and he looked so genuinely happy that Annat felt a pang of pity for him.

"Your people have sent me to convey their thanks, Great Goddess," he said. "And my thanks too, for I have seen my own dear people consumed and wasting away. The place is being prepared, and when it is ready, we will conduct you to it.

But before that, as the hungers of mortal flesh must be satisfied, I beg you to grace our feast with your presence."

Casildis rose to her feet, and offered her hand to Govorin, without looking at him. As he led her from the dais, she stretched out her other hand to Yuda, and a look passed between them that mingled fear with another emotion Annat was beginning to think she recognised.

Chapter 12

All the way through the feast, Annat could not keep her eyes off Yuda, Govorin and Casildis. The three of them sat at a separate table that was raised above the level of the others, where they were in plain view of the gathering. Annat watched them smiling, joking and talking together as if they had nothing to worry them beyond the pleasure of the meal; but she noticed that Govorin was draining the goblets of wine poured for him as if he were drinking lemonade, and Casildis almost matched him, cup for cup. Yuda, by contrast, was taking his time, making sure that the server refilled his goblet before it was empty. When he was not talking to his friends, Anna saw his eyes studying the crowd as if he were planning his escape, and assessing the dangers and chances of each exit. Though Casildis sat between him and Govorin, he seldom looked at her at all, examining what lay on his plate and stirring it with his knife as if he found it fascinating. Even at a distance, Annat could read the strong emotion that he was not troubling to hide from her, and which she did not fully understand. It was something like fear, but it possessed a vector that fear lacked. He rolled it round his mind as if it were a tasty morsel on his tongue, savouring it, tasting it, before gulping it down as if he dreaded the pleasure that it gave him.

Annat had been given a table to herself on the women's

side, but close enough to the High Table to give her a good
view of what was going on. The food was served in several
courses, and seemed to consist of lamb, mutton and other deli-
cacies taken from sheep. She was fairly sure that during one
course, all the men present were served a plate of ram's testi-
cles, while the women were given small wheaten biscuits
baked in a ring. Malchik, who had been given a chair at the
foot of the High Table, surreptitiously let the fried balls slip off
his plate on to the grass, almost causing Annat to choke on her
biscuit. Casildis and the two men seemed to be swapping
bawdy comments, and Annat imagined, from the woman's expression, that she was capable of saying things that shocked
even Yuda. When Casildis poked her finger through the hole in
the biscuit, Annat belatedly realised that it represented a
vagina, and was seized with a sudden wish that she had thrown
hers under the table, like Malchik.

Fortunately for all of them, they were not served sausages,
corn cobs or other phallic food, which was as well given the
laughter the biscuit had provoked on the High Table. Annat
could not see why they found it so funny; she thought it was
creepy and slightly disgusting. She was relieved when the final
course proved to be ewe's cheese, which even Malchik could
eat without blushing. When the repast had finished, Arrun
made a long, boring speech like the ones the Mayor of Sankt-
Eglis used to make at the annual village festival. She was a little surprised when Teress, walking past her table, gave her a
sudden and mischievous wink. In an attempt to return the
wink, Annat shut both eyes. Once the speech was over, Arrun
called on Malchik to play to the company. A look of panic
crossed her brother's face; but he stood with the harp on his
knee and struck up a song she had never heard him play before, hesitantly at first, before his voice grew stronger and his
playing more certain. She saw Yuda lean forward across the
table with an astonished expression; he seemed to be drinking
in every word. The song had no significance for Annat; it was
something about a red ship. But she did see, for a few moments, the shape of the small woman who stood at Yuda's
shoulder, smiling at him. As soon as the song was over, the

woman vanished; Yuda did not seem to have noticed that she was there.

When Malchik had finished, to enthusiastic applause, the sudden night had come. Overhead, Annat saw the planet Rogastron and its three moons. She gave a little shiver, and drew her cloak about her. She wondered who the woman was that she had seen standing behind Yuda. There was to be no chance for her to ask him, because Arrun clapped his hands together and announced that it was time for them to conduct the Goddess and her bridegroom to their bed. Casildis staggered to her feet, smiling tipsily; Govorin drained another cup of wine. Only Yuda seemed calm, but he did not look happy. Annat was summoned to support Casildis, and Arrun led them through the village to a small hut that lay beyond the edge of the stockade. A crowd of women waited outside, and as Annat and Casildis approached, they began to sing a pretty song about a dove flying to her nest. Casildis paused.

"I can't do it, Annat," she said. "I can't betray my husband."

"You don't have to," said Annat in surprise. "Just tell them you did it in the morning."

"But you don't understand. The Bright Lady . . ." Casildis trailed off. "Come inside and help me to prepare," she said, in a clearer voice.

The Bear People had certainly made a cosy nest inside the hut; it was hung with bearskins, and the floor was covered with carpets and woven blankets in rich shades of red and blue. Casildis took the doll, which she had kept with her all this time, and laid it on one of the pillows, regarding it with a grave face. The bed was soft, and Annat thought that it must be filled with bracken or heather. She bounced on it a couple of times until she saw Casildis's expression. She helped the woman divest herself of her heavy outer robes, and began to brush her long golden hair with measured strokes. Casildis stood upright and still, gazing out of the door at the torch-lit crowed waiting outside.

"How can I make love to a man that I don't love?" she said. Annat chose not to answer; she suspected that Casildis was thinking aloud. She walked round the woman, who had stripped down to her shift, reflecting that in the twilight

Casildis could have been mistaken for a Goddess. She offered the hairbrush to her, and Casildis seemed to focus on her for the first time, as if she had only just become aware of Annat's presence.

"Wish me luck, Natka," she said, stooping to kiss her on the cheek. "Pray for me to your God that I do the right thing."

"Okay," said Annat, standing on tiptoe to return the kiss. She hesitated before adding, "A lot of ladies seem to think *Tate* is very nice."

Casildis threw back her head and laughed till she wept. She touched Annat with a soft hand. "Oh, you silly goose, don't you see that that's the problem?" she said, without unkindness. "A woman can love only one man, but that does not mean she cannot—notice the value of others." She sighed, cradling the hairbrush against her breast. "Tomorrow, we will know the outcome," she said, speaking to herself once again.

When Annat stepped outside into the cool night air, a rustle went through the assembled crowd, as Yuda stepped forward. He faced Annat across a small space, gazing at the hut behind her. There was no sign of Govorin. Yuda walked up to Annat, and laid his hand on her shoulder. He was not even slightly tipsy.

"Let this be a lesson, to you, *kind*," he said. "One: don't eat the stew. Two: don't meddle with the religion."

Annat gazed up at him. That emotion he gave off was so strong that it was like a smell: the fumes of wine, or honey on a warm day. Annat found its presence disturbing and alien to her, though it was not unpleasant in itself. She was tempted to ask him what it meant, but shyness kept her silent.

"Good luck, *Tate*," she said, solemnly.

Yuda grinned. "I'm not going to be executed, Natka," he said. "Just to spend a night trying not to sleep with my best friend's wife." And he walked into the hut and drew the door curtain.

A sigh went through the crowd, and they began to drift away. Annat found Malchik standing alone at the edge, a strange expression on his face. Like anger.

"Are you all right, Malchku?" she asked, timidly.

"How can he go through with that?" he burst out.

"I don't think he has much choice," Annat replied. She tugged at his sleeve and led him back within the walls of the stockade, where the gates were closed behind them. "What was that song you sang?" she asked. "I've never heard it before."

Malchik gazed at her, his brown eyes large behind his spectacles. "You'd never believe me if I told you," he said, without resentment.

"I might," said Annat, trying to smile.

Malchik sighed. "I learned it from Isabel Guerreres. From her ghost." Annat nodded. "You do believe me?" he said, in astonishment.

"I think I saw her standing behind Yuda when you played tonight. Just for a few moments."

"Even she couldn't help me," said Malchik slowly. "The crows drove her away."

He turned and strode off through the dusk towards the centre of the village. Annat made to follow him, with an odd suspicion that somehow he was jealous of Yuda, when someone seized her arm. It was Teress.

"Have no fear, maiden, I have not come to threaten your virtue," he said, kindly. "Though no doubt there will be many couplings tonight. Hurry back to the virgins' house before some silly youth tries to claim you as his bride. But I came to warn you: when Arrun understands, as he must do tomorrow, that your goddess is false—if a true priestess of mortal flesh—you will not be without friends. We follow the old ways, but not all our eyes are covered with blinkers."

"Thank you, Teress," said Annat, as he released her. "I will remember—but where is the virgins' house?"

Teress chuckled and pointed her to a lodge that lay just on the other side of the village meeting hall. Annat hastened there and was startled to be given a friendly reception by the other girls, who treated her as one of themselves. They kept her up late, asking questions and giggling, especially when she told them about Casildis and the biscuit. They seemed much pleasanter than the village girls in Sankt-Eglis, and it was strange for Annat to be welcomed and treated as an equal by those her own age. At last, however, she lay down on her narrow pallet

to go to sleep. Although it was cold outdoors, under the quilts
and blankets Annat felt unbearably hot. She threw them off
and lay on her bed, tossing from side to side, troubled with an
itch in her mind that she could not scratch. At last she stood up
and crept to the door, pushing it ajar so that she could peer outside. The moonlit night seemed to be full of soft moaning and
sighing, like the breath of the waves on the shore. Scattered
here and there were little lights, between the houses and under
the trees, like the glimmering of glow-worms. Annat rubbed
the goose-flesh on her bare arms. *His hands touching my bare
skin . . . the soft feel of her flesh . . .* Annat blinked. The feeling
was like draining a goblet of wine slowly, languorously, to the
dregs, and then licking up each grain of sugar with her tongue.
*One grain at a time, until there were so many grains, and each
was impossibly sweet. Then bitterness. The perfect taste of bitter amongst the sweet . . .* Annat clapped her hands to her
head, wishing that the strange, overpowering sensations would
leave her alone. She had no idea where they were coming
from, but they were too strong for her. Her mouth felt dry and
her palms clammy. *Together. We link two hands, plaiting the
fingers together, finger over finger, each finger penetrating the
softness of the other hand, weaving together again and
again . . .* Annat felt dizzy and sick. She sat down on the
ground with her head between her knees, assailed by waves of
wine.

"Please stop," she whispered. But instead, a volcano erupted
in her head. Annat slumped forward, assailed by flakes of hot
ash and clouds of stinging, singing bees, and each sting was so
unbearably sweet, like lips caressed with honey. Her throat
was parched, and she longed for a glass of pure, still water.
She opened her mouth and yelled with all her might, blasting
the sweetness into a million fragments that showered down
upon her like the ash from the volcano, burying her gently, en-
tombing her with perfect, sensual fingers . . .

One of the other girls was stooping over her, dabbing at her
forehead with a damp cloth.

"Don't worry," she whispered, "it's only a hot dream. We all
get them, especially on nights like tonight."

Annat sat up. She was sure that it had not been a dream. She felt vague and dreamy, like a milk-fed baby replete on its mother's breast.

"I think it was my father and Casildis," she heard herself say. She let the other girl assist her to stand up, and went back inside to slump down on her own bed, her thoughts heavy and confused.

After a good night's sleep, she was woken with the other girls at dawn. As they were getting dressed, she was tempted to question them about the contents of her dream, but something made her hold her tongue. Wearing their cloaks, all of them went out together to greet the Goddess and her bridegroom. It was a sharp morning, and even the chill did nothing to dampen the spirits of the girls; there was even a hint of blue from the frozen sky, and a glimpse of the elusive sun rising beyond the forest. They walked along, gossiping and laughing like a flock of bright birds, and for once Annat was one of them, her arm linked with that of the girl who had come to help her last night. As they drew near to the gate of the stockade, the girls began to sing, an open-throated, sweet-sour song like the one Annat had heard last night. The tune sounded fresh in the still morning, as if spring were on its way in spite of the weather. Annat could not imitate the soaring voices of the other girls, but she swung along in step with them, enfolded by the music.

The gate of the stockade stood open, but apart from a couple of warriors and the ubiquitous Arrun, they were the first to arrive to greet the Goddess. There was no sign of Malchik or Govorin, both of whom must have spent last night sleeping in the men's side. When they were all assembled, Arrun smote the earth three times with his staff and proclaimed in a loud voice: "Greetings unto you, great Goddess, our saviour and bringer of the spring."

There was a short pause, before Yuda and Casildis emerged from their hut, both looking refreshed and awake. They held each other's hands, and Annat observed that Casildis wore only her shift, and Yuda his new shirt and trews. As they smiled at the assembled flock of girls, Annat realised with a shock that they had indeed slept together the previous night, and she remembered the significance of her dream. The link between her mind and Yuda's had grown so strong that she shared his feelings, his pleasure or pain. Though the idea could have revolted her, somehow it did not. The thought came to her that this would be terrible for Govorin, and she wondered whether Casildis and Yuda would let him know the truth. It was fortunate that he was not here to see them at this hour, when it was simply obvious that they were happy together, not like two people who had done a guilty thing. It made Annat recall the fragmentary words Casildis had uttered, as if she had indeed been possessed . . .

"My greetings to you on this fair morning, Holy Goddess," said Arrun, stepping forward. "I trust that it was a most prosperous and successful union."

Casildis laughed, not remotely embarrassed by this silly question. "Most prosperous and successful, noble Arrun," she said, her eyes full of laughter, and Yuda suddenly kissed her, full on the mouth. She stooped to him, and Annat thought what a strange couple they made. Casildis's hair fell about him, cloaking him in gold. Suddenly, Annat broke away from her new friend, and ran across to them.

"You did it," she said, neither pleased nor reproachful. "You did do it."

They turned to her, and Casildis said, softly, "We must lie to my husband. For now. He could not bear it, though I took Yuda to me to fulfil the wish of the Bright Lady. I don't know why she wished it, but it was not wrong."

"And a good morning to you too, Missis," said Yuda, smiling at Annat, as she stared in astonishment at Casildis, wondering what she meant. Annat looked back at him seriously, for in spite of last night's dream, the desire of full-grown men and women was alien to her. Yuda touched her shoulder. "Don't let it worry you," he said gently. "In your own time."

"And now," Arrun intoned, "it is time for the sacrifice."

They turned to face the Chieftain, to find him looking at them expectantly. There was no sign of any hapless beast in tow.

"What sacrifice is that, most noble Arrun?" Casildis asked.

"You, Great Goddess, with your own hand, will now take

the life of your bridegroom, and shed his blood upon the barren earth."

"Whoops," said Yuda, and started to laugh in a manner not suitable to the dignity of the occasion. Annat glanced back at her companions, to see the looks of dismay and horror on their faces. The guards looked stolid and uninterested, as if doctrinal matters did not concern them.

"No I shall not," said Casildis, firmly. "The Bright Lady does not ask for blood sacrifice. There is no lore that the bridegroom must die."

"Then you are no true Goddess," Arrun retorted. "Time out of time this has been done. But the sacrifice will be made and you too, faithless woman, will die for your sacrilege."

Teress came walking out from the stockade, as if he had been waiting there, listening, all this time. "Listen to me, Arrun the old fool, Arrun the blind," he said. There was a gasp from the assembled girls. "I call you fool, my father, because you have deceived yourself, who was once called Arrun the Wise. It is plain and has been plain to all that this is a mortal woman, and a priestess, for she spoke words of prophecy to you. For a while, I too thought I saw the Goddess in her. And that is the truth. The Goddess may dwell in her, but she herself is not the Goddess. The Goddess does not eat nor drink, nor lie with mortal men."

Arrun clutched his staff, trembling with rage, but Annat saw tears in his eyes. When he spoke, there was a note of pleading in his voice. "How can you, my own son, speak to me thus before the people?" he said.

"Because I want to stop you from doing wrong, noble father. I owe you all honour and duty, but not in the killing of an innocent man. They have done the deed as you wished and, in time, spring will return. The Cold One cannot reign for ever, and the coming of these strangers amongst us must presage that. The priestess has brought us a prophecy. Of that itself you should be glad."

"No doubt a false prophecy," said Arrun, the tears spilling from his eyes. He struck the ground once more, but he knew that he had lost.

"I have spoken with the warriors of the men's side, and they are of my mind," said Teress, firmly. "I am sorry to have grieved you, but there will be no sacrifice. We will thank the strangers for their kindness, and send them safely on their way. For, like gods, they cannot abide with us, but must continue their journey."

"Thank you, Teress," said Casildis. "I am the priestess of Artemyas, and she does speak through me. I hope, when we find what we are seeking, that you will get back your spring."

Annat gasped. Casildis had spoken so simply, as if what she said was of little moment. She must know that the words changed everything; she had affirmed to Yuda and Annat that she was the acolyte of a goddess she had called the Cold One's sister.

Teress put his hand on Arrun's shoulder. "Do not blame him, lady," he said. "He only cares for the good of his people. Perhaps, before my time, the Goddess's bridegroom was put to death. But these are new times."

Suddenly, released from their fear, the girls rushed forward, crowding Annat, Yuda and Casildis. Some of them had tears in their eyes, as Arrun did.

"Please don't go, lady," said one. "Stay with us and be our priestess."

"We don't have any flowers to give you," said another. "There have been none for so long. We can barely grow the wheat to make our bread."

"Can Annat stay behind?" said a third.

"We can't stay," said Casildis, sadly. "And I must return to my husband, who is waiting for me."

The girls pleaded and cajoled a little longer, but at last they were content to accompany Casildis and Yuda back into the stockade. Teress remained behind for a while, speaking gently to Arrun, but it was clear that he had quietly assumed the chieftainship. At the centre of the village, they found Govorin and Malchik waiting, in front of a crowd of villagers. The Sheriff's face was grey with exhaustion and his eyes were bloodshot. Casildis went to him at once and kissed him on the cheek, then whispered in his ear. He tried to smile at her, stroking her hair, but he did not look much happier. Malchik had a sullen face, and Annat wondered what could have made him discontented. It was so strange to think that he too might have been nurturing a liking for Casildis. She noticed that Yuda was hanging back, as if he hesitated to approach Govorin. Annat could not imagine how either he or Casildis would be able to keep the truth from the Sheriff for long. Govorin was an astute man, and he would surely notice both the change in their demeanour when they were together, and Yuda's reticence towards himself.

"You're no fool, little Annat," said Yuda softly. "I wish we'd never seen this place."

"I know you wanted to lie with Casildis," she said.

"Yes," he said slowly, "yes, I did. If only that were all."

There was no longer any question between them about his feelings for Casildis; beyond the shape of desire, he had come to love the woman.

When the time came for them to leave, they learned that Arrun had ordered their old clothes to be burnt. Since the ceremonial garments they had put on were not suitable for travelling, Teress offered to provide replacements. At Casildis's suggestion, she and Annat, like the men, dressed in shirts, baggy trews, waistcoats and long cloaks. Annat was delighted when she was permitted to keep the mantle of soft red wool that she had been given at the beginning. Teress also provided them with weapons: a bow and a quiver of arrows for Casildis, a short club for Govorin and a small knife for Annat. Both Yuda and Malchik declined the offer of arrows and spears, though Yuda accepted a small axe to replace the one from the driver's cab he had left behind at the pool. Casildis seemed particularly pleased with her bow, which she said she could use for hunting. Annat was relieved to see that she had not forgotten the doll, having brought it from the hut where she had spent the night with Yuda. Fortunately, Teress had recovered their three packs, which he gave to Annat, Govorin and Yuda in haste before they left.

Though Teress was eager to provide them with provisions and wood, the thought of Sarl was in all their minds by the time they descended from the wooded hills to see the train standing forlornly by the river bank, with neither steam nor smoke issuing from its chimney. After they had said goodbye to their hosts, they stood in a row, anxiously surveying their only means of escape.

"It'll take us a while to fire her up," said Govorin, the first words he had spoken to anyone other than Casildis.

"He could be close on our heels by now," said Yuda. No one needed to ask whom he meant. It was disheartening to find the engine cold, and the fire grey and dead. Govorin and Yuda at once set to clearing out the ash and clinker from the firebox, but though they worked together comfortably, Annat observed that there was a silence between them, as if neither dared to speak his mind. She took up a position on the roof of the water-tank, looking back down the line to watch for any sign of the riders. Casildis and Malchik joined her. Annat would have liked to discuss with Casildis the significance of the night's events, but Malchik's presence imposed a constraint. She was not sure that he would be sympathetic if he learned the truth; he did seem to take the possibility that Casildis might have lain with Yuda as an affront to himself, and Annat was afraid to broach the subject with him. She watched the line's black forks converging in the middle distance with an uneasy sensation of anticipation. She strained her eyes to see if she could make out any movement at the horizon line, but nothing was visible except the monochrome geometry of the tracks, curving subtly across the plain to the west.

"How long will it take to fire up the engine?" said Casildis, shifting her weight from foot to foot. She was carrying the quiver of arrows slung from her back, and the bow across her shoulder. The clothes she had chosen were the color of pale sand, which blended well against the shimmering snow. Annat had opted for shades of grey for the same reason, but Malchik was defiantly resplendent in speedwell blue, which, as Yuda had commented, made him a perfect target for any archers.

"I don't know," said Annat, truthfully. She glanced back towards the cab, where the two men had succeeded in lighting a fire on the grate, and the chimney was emitting wisps of dark smoke. "They have to heat the water in the boiler until it boils, and then there has to be steam. Enough steam to move the pistons."

"That sounds like a long time," said Casildis, fingering the string of her bow.

"What we need are long poles to fend off the riders," said Malchik. "I wish I had taken a spear."

"They'd only grab it and pull you off the engine," said Annat. "Or use it to spit you."

"They won't hurt me," said Malchik, with grim certainty. "Sarl thinks I'm a servant of the Cold One."

"How do you know?" said Annat, in surprise. Until the last few days, her brother had shown no signs of shamanic ability.

"I can sense him. In my head," said Malchik, fixing her with a glance that was more steel than brown.

"Do you know why he pursues us, Malchik? And why he wants to kill Yuda?" said Casildis.

Malchik hunkered down, touching the cold metal of the tank with his fingertips. "If I told you that I had an idea why, would you promise not to ask any more about it?" he said.

"I don't know what you mean, Malchku," said Annat, and Casildis looked puzzled.

"I mean that you really don't want to know the reason," said Malchik, glancing up at them with an unhappy face.

"But now you have made us curious," said Casildis, trying to encourage him to smile.

"Well, I'd like to know what happened between you and my father last night, but I'm not going to ask because I don't want to know," said Malchik, with a bluntness that was almost cruel.

"That's horrible," said Annat, vehemently. "How could you speak to Missis Govorin like that?"

"Because it's the truth," said Malchik.

"Malchik is right," said Casildis. "It is between my husband and myself. But there are other things that I have to tell you; I owe you an explanation."

They fell silent, and Annat wondered whether Casildis was aware of the questions she wanted to ask, above all concerning the Bright Lady. She gazed once more into the blank horizon with its snowy mirages of cold against the frail blue of the early morning sky, trying to distinguish forms from the shapeless haze that slipped and twisted on the extremity of her vision. She was beginning to hope that, rather than enduring this fretful waiting, she would see a movement, and the forms of horsemen would coalesce out of the mist. Casildis shaded her eyes to scan the horizon, which was bitterly bright. Malchik stood up, and turned on his heel as if to walk back to the engine, but he stopped in mid step, and suddenly shouted a warning, pointing to the left.

Casildis spun round, stringing an arrow to her bow, and Annat followed her. There were riders to the south of the train, approaching at a gallop across the plain. They had drawn near enough for Annat to make out the colors of their mounts: smudge of roan, a chestnut and a grey. The rest were blurs of movement fanned out over the snow, riding tall above their shimmering reflections.

Yuda came clambering up to the roof of the tank, and stood beside Annat, watching the charge. He rubbed the finger and thumb of his right hand together to make a small flame, and lit a cigarette. His hands were shaking.

—*Can you throw your power?* he asked her.

—*I think so.*

The riders were dissolving into distinct shapes. At their head, astride the white horse, rode Sarl. To his right, a man brandishing an axe sat his mount without holding the reins. A swirl of green cloak marked out another to his left; a third was aiming for the side of the train with a couched lance. Annat felt her breathing go out of control, lifting her chest in shallow, quick gasps. Yuda gripped her right arm to calm her. He was standing with his feet planted wide apart, and twirling the cigarette between his fingers. Malchik had crouched down and was shading his eyes.

"What are we going to do?" he said, abruptly.

They could hear the thrum of the hoofs on the hard snow. The light flashed from the sword in Sarl's right hand. He was leaning forward on his mount, teeth bared in a white grin. Casildis took aim, but did not loose her arrow from the string.

"Why doesn't she shoot?" said Malchik, his voice cracking with panic.

"Steady, boy," said Yuda.

Although their horses' legs seemed to flow in a miasma of

movement, the horsemen seemed to come no nearer. The only sound was the steady drubbing of their iron-shod feet. War-cries stretched the men's faces into distorted masks. Swallowing to moisten her dry throat, Annat made herself count them. Three in front, including Sarl; four at the back, their steeds slowly gaining color and shape.

"It's time," said Yuda. "Get down low. Except Casildis."

Annat was glad to make herself small, huddled on the metal roof. Beside her, Yuda balanced on his toes, drawing coolly on his cigarette. She could hear the men's shouts, and see their lips move, and the froth on their horses' bits.

"Now," said Yuda.

Casildis aimed high. She drew back the bowstring, and then the arrow cleaved the air with a rattle like pigeons' wings, as it soared upwards in an arc. As soon as it was loosed, Casildis drew another from the quiver, notched it to the bow, and drew back the string, pointing at the sky. From Annat's right came a shout, and a clattering of metal. She saw the green cloak go down, and the horse rolling on its side, hoofs in the air. Spots of blood on the snow. Having loosed her second barb, Casildis knelt down, already reaching for a third shaft. The riders were upon them.

Sarl rode straight at them, standing high in his stirrups, and brandishing the sword over his head. The sword swept high, close to their feet, cutting the air like silver foil, but Yuda was quicker. The blue lightning flew from his palm, glancing off the blade, and a second bolt caught Sarl amid-ships, throwing him back in the saddle. While he wheeled away, the others closed in, and one crossed the rails, making for the far side of the train.

"Annat," said Yuda, without looking at her.

Annat crawled across the roof, keeping the man in her sights. Behind her, she heard the twang as Casildis loosed another arrow. The man, who sat astride a chestnut gelding, had seen her; suddenly he rode in towards her with spear levelled, and she saw his eyes, hooded beneath his helmet. She lay flat on her stomach, but the spear-head seemed to follow her. The horse grew large, and she saw its rolling eye. When the lance was too close, she rolled on to her side and flung the power

down her arm, dredging all her reserves. She saw the lightning
strike the spear's leaf-blade and travel down the haft. It struck
the man's hand where he held the lance in rest, and the spear
flew up like a lightning rod, fizzing with electricity. The man
jerked in the saddle, falling backwards; the horse wheeled and
cantered away, dragging its rider dangling from the stirrups.
Annat put her face down on the cold alloy and sobbed.

There was no time for her to waste. Dragging herself to her
knees, she turned back to the fight. Yuda was grappling with a
helmeted figure that had leapt on to the train. Malchik had
somehow got hold of a spear and was waving it dangerously,
yelling like a madman. Between them, Casildis aimed a precious arrow at the four remaining riders, who were regrouping
to attack again. Annat saw Yuda's knife-hand draw back and
plunge itself once, twice, into the man's mailed throat. He
clawed at the wound and toppled from the roof, as his helmet
slipped from his head.

"Govorin," Yuda shouted, "when is this fucking train going
somewhere?"

"I need you, man! I can't fire it and drive."

"I'll go," said Casildis, swiftly. She slipped the bow over
her head across her breast, and sprang down into the tender. It
was only then that Annat saw the lazy blood truckling down
from Yuda's left hand to puddle on the metal. Glancing at her
brother, she saw a red rent in his sleeve, and another across his
shoulder; his nose was bleeding too.

"You're hurt," she cried.

"No time," said Yuda, lightly.

The knights were charging again. This time, three bran-
dished swords and the fourth an axe. Their cold cries cut Annat
to the bone. She stood between her brother and her father,
shaking so much she thought she would fall. The horses
moved like great machines, blasting the snow with their hoofs.

"Aim for Sarl," said Yuda, speaking low. "Aim for their
leader."

A long, shrieking call came from the engine as Govorin
pulled on the whistle. Glancing towards the locomotive, Annat
saw the grey steam issuing from its chimney. If they could
hold out just a little longer . . .

"Down," said Yuda. The horsemen rode in, slashing high with their swords. Yuda blasted them with both hands, letting loose a fireball that ripped through the snow between them. At once, the horses were rearing and shrieking as their riders clutched at the reins. Sarl calmed his mount before the rest. As the train began to draw away, slowly at first, he galloped alongside, and Annat saw his livid face from above. He stood up in the stirrups and, before they could stop him, caught the trailing edge of Malchik's cloak, dragging him bodily from the roof. With a thrill of horror, Annat heard her brother cry out as he lost his footing and slipped over the edge. As the train was drawing away, she saw Sarl catch him and throw him across his saddle-bow. Yuda made to leap down from the train, but Annat caught his sleeve. The train was moving too fast, and they were drawing away from the horseman. Sarl's horse caricoled, and she saw him stick spurs into its flanks and ride away, heading back the way he had come. Yuda dropped to his knees.

"The boy. I've lost the boy . . ." he whispered.

Chapter 13

It was Annat who stripped off Yuda's bloody shirt and waist-coat, while Casildis went to help Govorin in the cab. When she had wiped away the blood, she found that Yuda had two deep wounds, a thrust into his left side, and a slash to his upper left arm.

"Can you heal this, Annat?" he asked, in a quiet voice. Annat shook her head.

"I can scan you to see what the damage is, but it's too much for me to heal," she said. "I used up most of my strength in the fight."

"Then scan," said Yuda. "If nothing else, you can bind these wounds to staunch the bleeding."

Biting her lip, Annat passed her hand over the gaping wound in Yuda's side. It had been a glancing blow, which had missed the lungs and the heart but cut through one of the many big veins that passed through the torso. She would have to try to mend that, if nothing else. Grimacing, her mouth watering as if she were about to vomit, she slipped her fingers into the wound and shut her eyes to focus on the vein. She told herself to pretend that it was a bicycle tyre that she was mending with a puncture kit. There was none of the slow fascination of working to mend the cuts in Yuda's hands; if she got this wrong, he would bleed to death, and she would be helpless.

She scraped at her reserves of power, and with a tiny flame weaker than a blow-torch, she worked to thread the walls of the vein together. With satisfaction, she saw them coalesce, and the hole grew smaller and smaller until it fused, leaving a tiny scar. Shuddering, Annat withdrew her hand, and wiped her bloody fingers on her trews. She was about to speak to Yuda, but he had passed out.

Annat washed the wounds with water from the newly filled canteen, and tore one of Yuda's spare shirts into strips to bind the two gashes. Carefully, she moved her father on to one of the pallets, and covered him with blankets to keep him warm. She stayed where she was, gripping Yuda's hand, for she knew that shock could kill as easily as wounds. She kept going over in her mind the last awful moments when Sarl pulled Malchik from the train; she heard again his helpless cry, and saw him plummet over the edge, and there was nothing she could do.

After a time, the rhythm of the train began to soothe her. She watched Casildis in the cab speaking to her husband, who listened to her without turning his head. From time to time, Govorin would ask her to check a gauge—the water level in the boiler, or the steam pressure. Casildis stood beside him, her hair blowing wildly in the wind. Annat thought she could understand why Yuda loved the woman so much; it was not just her looks, but a strength and serenity about her that made her beautiful whether her face was laughing or in repose.

She could sense Yuda dreaming in his unconscious state. His eyes moved under closed lids, and sometimes he twitched, like a cat. Annat hoped that they would soon find a place to halt, a town or a village where the inhabitants were friendly. If they were attacked, without Yuda to defend them, it would be a disaster. She held his wrist to take his pulse, and found it slower than she would have liked. If too much blood had been lost, his heart would fail. Once again, she scraped together her reserves of power, and passed her hands over his body, letting the energy wash through him, to strengthen him. It might help the blood cells to divide and multiply, though she had never been taught how to make that happen. But the warmth and nourishment of a general healing should be enough to keep him from slipping away.

Yuda's eyes opened. At once, the pain was turned on inside her, like a rasping saw.

"Hallo, little Natka," he said. "I really messed up this time, eh?"

"You've lost a lot of blood," said Annat.

"But you fixed the bleeding? Clever girl."

"You shouldn't talk," she said, as his eyes closed and she felt the echo of his pain.

"Nah. Better if I stay awake now."

"It's not your fault that Sarl got Malchik," she said, fiercely, for she felt the shadow of the thought in his mind.

"Isn't it? I should have known that Malchik was the one Sarl was after. Instead, I flattered myself that he was out to get me." He stopped, grimacing.

"I think Malchik knew, but he had only just told us . . ."

"The curse is, Natkeleh, I don't know how we'll get him back."

"We have to get you healed first. I fixed what I could, but I can't replace lost blood. And you've lost so much blood . . ." She heard her voice tremble.

"Where's Casildis?" he said, as if he had not heard her.

"She's helping Govorin."

"Good woman. I could be in love with her."

He moved his uninjured arm, and scratched his chest above the bandages.

"I know that, Yuda. But there's going to be trouble."

"Can't help it," said Yuda, drowsily. "She got inside me, here." He tapped his chest. "Under the skin. Different to Shaka, see. Known him so long. Brother, friend, lover. Couldn't live without him around somewhere. Not like this; it burns. I didn't know I could do that. Love two people."

Annat found herself looking at Govorin's back and Casildis where she stood with her face turned away from them. "What are you going to do?" she said.

"Don't know. Best friend's wife. Can't do anything." He sank back, his hand resting on his breast, and gazed silently at the sky overhead, which rushed away from them. Annat felt helpless almost to despair; she could sense in him a wish to slip away and give up the struggle of making sense out of things that were too harsh to understand. She saw his eyes drift shut and his head slip sideways; snatching his wrist, she felt the pulse stammering beneath her fingers.

—*Yuda!* she cried, and felt the force of the cry go through her, reaching out to him, to call him back. But the beat in the vein beneath her fingers seemed to grow slack, as if he were letting death take him easily, drifting out of sight on the sunken river of his blood.

"Yuda," she sobbed. And in that moment, someone came to sit beside her, a small, neat woman in a short, flower-patterned dress, who wore a red scarf tied round her neck and throat.

—*We can't have this,* said Isabel, and she leaned over Yuda to shake him gently, with arms and hands that passed through his body. Annat sat back, her mouth open. The ghost smiled at her, the brown freckles clear on her pale skin. —*You're not afraid of me, Annat?* Annat was too shocked to answer, for an instant. Then her common sense came back, and she said, quickly, "Help me, Isabel. He is dying."

—*He wants to die. It isn't the same thing.* The small woman bent over Yuda and whispered into his ear. Once more, Annat seized the slack wrist, and felt the pulse still limping beneath her touch.

"Isabel?" said Yuda, under his breath. Isabel stroked his hair with fingers that slipped through the black strands and the forehead beneath. "Isabel!" His eyes opened and he sat up, but in the same moment, the phantom was gone, dissipated like shreds of cloud before the breeze. Annat caught his shoulders and forced him to lie down, but his grip was suddenly strong, and she felt the blood beating hard and fast in him, like a small animal stirred to the fight.

"Lie still, Mister," she said.

Yuda looked at her with uncomprehending eyes, and said, "I thought Isabel was here. She spoke to me."

"Perhaps you were dreaming," she said.

"Stay with me, Natka." He gripped her forearm in a firm, and living, grasp.

"I will if you don't leave me, *Tate.*"

Yuda gazed at her, but said nothing. His thoughts too were silent, but he did not let go of her wrist. Annat sat beside him,

hoping and willing that they would soon come to a place that
was not hostile, where there might be doctors, or even healers.
Conscious only of his grip on her, she gazed out into the terrain through which they were passing. They were running between the tall hills now, along a winding valley. The stands of
trees looked down on them, racing down the hillsides to catch
the river and the speeding train as it swept past them. Annat
recognised a few of them from the rocky hillsides near her
home; others she had seen only in picture books. Black cy-
presses like furled umbrellas, strewn across the hills; crowds
of blue spruce, like a flock of birds caught and turned to wood
and leaves; tall pines with their ragged spindle of branches;
and firs, neatly bearing their burden of snow like the cape of a
maiden aunt. The cold wind of the train's passage blew
through her hair. Though it moved, she was caught in a moment of stasis, alone with this man who had once been her father only in name. Annat did not know whether he had become
a father; to her the word meant home and stability: *Zaide*
studying the holy texts in the kitchen while *Bubbe* worked, or
reading the stories aloud, chuckling in his beard and pausing to
expound a joke or a piece of wisdom to her while she sat
awake in bed. Yuda might have carried her in his arms when
she was a baby, but she had no memory of him, no ghostly
face that had haunted her while she was a child. But now his
grip on her arm was urgent, as if she were the only thing that
anchored him in the world.

It seemed to her that the moment lasted for hours. Slowly,
the hills began to bow their heads, and spread out into lower
countryside, more thickly wooded. On either side of the track,
they crowded up to the rails, exhaling their myrrh-like scent in
spite of the cold. Yuda lay with his eyes shut, his breathing
quiet, but from time to time Annat would glance at him with a
qualm of fear, afraid that he might have slipped away when
her attention was elsewhere. If only they could find a settlement or a village where they could stop! She wanted to tell
Govorin to go faster, and Casildis to shovel wood until she
broke her back. She sat still, blinking the tears out of her eyes
and hoping that her father would not notice.

The valley was broadening and opening as the hills and the

woods drew away from them. Once more, the blue and empty sky loomed ahead. Only the river kept its constant, sinuous rhythm beside the track, sometimes disappearing to meander amongst its snowy banks, sometimes returning like an old friend to echo the path of the line.

"How is he?" said Casildis, softly. She had left her place in the cab and come to stand at the edge of the tender.

Annat opened her mouth, but a sob came out instead of words. "I thought he was going to die," she said.

"No," said Yuda, in a firm voice. "No chance."

"Annat, if you want to rest, I'll sit with him," said Casildis. "Govorin can spare me for a few minutes."

"I can't leave him!"

Yuda opened his eyes, and she saw the trace of a smile there. "You go, Missis," he whispered, squeezing her wrist. "I promise I won't slip off while you're gone."

Annat did not want to leave him, but she guessed without much difficulty that he wanted to be alone with Casildis. For a moment, she was overmastered by a powerful jealousy. She wanted to keep him for herself, to preserve the bond she had woven, which had kept him alive. But she reminded herself sternly that it was Isabel who had called him back when she had failed. She looked into Casildis's eyes, afraid that her hate might show; it was worse that Casildis might see it and yet understand and forgive her. Yuda released her arm, and she stood up, noticing the marks his fingers had made on her skin. Annat stood over him, buffeted by the wind, rubbing her wrist to ease the discomfort. Fear still fluttered inside her, like a bird caged in her ribs, as she saw the drained smile with which he greeted Casildis. He was still too weak, and all her efforts had not brought him nearer to life but merely sustained him in an equilibrium from which he could easily slip down again.

She climbed out into the cab, to stand in the doorway. Gazing out across the wide valley, she thought that, if spring ever came, this would be a beautiful place. Beside the river, bare, pollarded willows held their cracked fingers high in gestures of pleading. Annat studied their strange forms, wondering if they were dead, or whether inside, deep within the bark, a trace of sap lingered, waiting for the seasons to return. Then, as she gazed at them, the thought shook her that someone must have shaped the willows, cutting back their new growth so that they grew tall. If people had worked on the trees, there might be a dwelling or settlement not far away. Annat turned to speak to Govorin, to tell him what she had seen. The Sheriff smiled in his beard.

"Look through the window," he said.

At first, Annat could see nothing but the white curves of the valley ahead, and the long sweep of the line turning gently to her left. Then, as her heart skipped a beat, she made out other shapes, square blocks that became houses, walls and towers, which gleamed as the hidden sun caught their various hues. Annat caught Govorin's arm. All constraint towards him gone.

"It's a city, Mister Govorin!"

His hand steady on the reversing handle, Govorin shared a smile with her. It was a moment of joy, even though neither of them knew whether the tinted walls of the houses concealed citizens who were friendly or hostile. Suddenly, the Sheriff raised his hand and gave a great tug on the whistle-cord, and the train let out a shrill scream.

"Let 'em know we're coming," he said, showing Annat white teeth. She would have flung her arms round him, but she didn't want to distract him. Instead, she reached up her hand, and Govorin suddenly put his arms around her waist and lifted her up so that she too could pull the cord, letting out the long, haunted cry to echo across the valley. Annat put her arms round his neck, and kissed his whiskery face, feeling the softness of his unfamiliar skin, thicker than hers but not coarser. Govorin put his hand on the regulator, and began to wind the reversing handle to bring the train to a halt.

As the town drew nearer, Annat saw that it had no walls; it spread out across the valley, from the ramshackle shacks of the outer reaches, to the high, graceful buildings at its centre. It made a crooked shape on the snow, as if it had been dropped from the sky; the vivid colors of its painted stucco walls shouted against the white, and the coiled ironwork of balconies and fences, painted black, stood out like papercut silhouettes. Here and there, towards the outskirts, a building or two had been painted white, as if an attempt to seek camouflage against the brilliant snow; but the color beneath had leached through, so that the walls showed a faded pink, or a pale yellow, or azure blue.

Standing beside Govorin, Annat watched the little city coming towards them. Outside, she made out the shapes of figures swarming from amongst the buildings, hurrying across the frozen river to come to the line. It was almost as if they were running away from the city to meet the train, as if they had been hoping it would come.

"Looks like we've got a reception committee," said Govorin, giving the whistle another blast for good measure. He wound the reversing handle again, and reached down to pull on the brake lever. As the train bowled along the line, Annat ran to the door on the opposite side of the cab, eager to get a closer look at the people. She could make them out more clearly, and at a glance she took in the fact that almost every one of them was dressed in black, with touches of white here and there. As the train came gliding to a halt, Annat saw the faces, shocked and full of dread, gazing at her and the fabulous machine she rode in. The dark faces, pale skin and dark eyes, with a splash of golden-red hair garish amongst the black and brown. Wanderers!

The engine stopped, and blew out its welcoming cloud of steam, enveloping itself in bridal white. A Wanderers' train, clad in black with white tippets. Annat sprang out of the cab, forgetting what a strange figure she must present in her blood-stained grey trews and shirt, her hair wild and snarled. She stood with her back to the locomotive, gazing at the anxious faces of the diminutive people: the veiled mothers clutching small children by the hand, and the black-coated fathers with their wide-brimmed hats and dark beards, whose eyes seemed to stare at her across miles of loneliness and exile. And here and there amongst them, a splash of color: the amber beard and curls of a Red Wanderer, or a white-haired elder resplendent in a purple caftan, or a child in a brilliant dress, put on in defiance of Neustrian law. Annat's heart thumped in her chest as she faced them. Then she lifted her fist over her head, and shouted in *Ebreu*, the tongue of her people:

"There is One in Zyon!"

A ripple and a murmur went through those at the front of the crowd, faces turned towards each other, and some repeated her words. It was a young man with a black beard and smiling eyes who stepped forward and answered, "One, and One only." When he had spoken, other voices softly picked up the phrase, and it was repeated through the throng of people, some loudly, others only mouthing the ancient prayer and greeting. The young man stepped towards Annat.

"Then you are Wanderer," he said. "It is a miracle!" and he laughed to himself, plucked off the hat covering his dark curls and the skull-cap he wore beneath, and waved it over his head. Annat laughed too.

"What is this city?" she said. "What are you doing in La Souterraine?"

"We might ask you the same question, *kind,*" said the young man, breathlessly. "First the tracks came one night, and we wondered what they meant. Now here is the train!"

"You know about trains?" Annat exclaimed.

"We lived in Neustria until three years ago," he said, grinning. "But I must bring you and your friends to the *Rashim,* so that he can decide what to do about you. Are you all Wanderers?" he added, glancing up in awe at Govorin's black face.

"Three of us are Wanderers and two are *Dzuzukim,*" said Annat, using the word Wanderers shared amongst themselves when speaking of the Doxoi. "But they are Wanderer-friends, good people," she added hastily. "Mister, my father is badly hurt. Have you any physicians or shamans in your city? *Meine Tate* needs healing. There are evil *Dzuzukim* behind us, hunting us to death."

"*Oy vaz mir,*" the young man exclaimed. "The *Rashim* himself is a great healer. Wait here; I will ask some of my friends to get a stretcher for your father. The name of the city is Chorazin," he added, turning on his heel and pushing his way back into the crowd. When he had gone, Annat once more found herself confronting the crowd, and she noticed how wan and frightened many of the faces seemed. Then a young woman daringly leaned forward and touched Annat's sleeve, as if to see whether she was solid. She quickly withdrew her hand and smiled with downcast eyes. An older woman, who stood beside her, her hair covered with a silk bonnet, whispered some words of reproof. *They must think I look immodest*, thought Annat, belatedly remembering that she was wearing the shirt and trews given her by the Bear People.

When the young man returned, he was accompanied by two sturdy fellows who had stripped down to their waistcoats and shirtsleeves. One of them carried a folding stretcher over his shoulder.

"The *Rashim* sends word that you must bring the patient to his house," said the young man. "He would come out to greet you himself, but he is studying. Where is the injured man?"

Annat climbed back into the driver's cab, to show them where Yuda lay in the tender, awkwardly balanced amongst the logs. With surprising speed and handiness, the two men lifted the whole pallet and Yuda on to the stretcher, and carefully lowered him down from the cab to the trackside, while the people crowded round with words of dismay and pity. Annat felt a thrill of excitement, in spite of her anxiety about Yuda. It was wonderful to hear so many people speaking the language of the Wanderers at once, that strange argot made up of mingled Sklav, *Ebreu* and Alleman that her family had used at home. Having asked Casildis to hand her the doll, she followed the stretcher-bearers through the crowd, smiling at the staring, wondering faces, and after her came Govorin, hand in hand with his wife. It was the Sheriff's appearance that seemed to cause the most amazement, even exclamations of surprise and delight, for some people thought that it was good luck to see a *Schvartzer*. Annat supposed that most of them had never seen a Darkman before, let alone one as handsome and muscular as Govorin. The naïve adulation that he caused fortunately amused the Sheriff, who grinned and waved as if he were a prince greeting his people on a public holiday. Casildis's garments brought some shocked glances from the women, and many of the men turned away, shielding their eyes against such immodesty. Nobody seemed too concerned by Annat's garb, perhaps because they regarded her as a mere *kind*, who could not be blamed for her transgression.

They had to walk a short distance down from the line to cross the frozen river before they reached the outlying houses of the town. The crowd followed them, murmuring in soft voices, and Annat was once more aware of their anxiety. As they entered the city, she noticed that many people would run from house to house, without pausing to look at them, ducking down as if they feared to be seen from the sky above. She glanced up, and her heart skipped a beat as she saw high up a wheeling flock of black shapes patrolling above the houses: crows.

After the first moments of terror when Sarl dragged him from the roof of the train, Malchik had no time to think of anything but the discomfort of lying across a horse's back with his face close to its steaming flank. When he had seen horses from a distance, the power and grace of their movements had fascinated him. Pinned across the saddle, his head bouncing in time to the galloping feet, he felt nothing but fear of the sack of pounding muscle and bone. His spine jerked and the sinews of his neck cracked with pain. The stench of the animal filled his nostrils with rank sweat and fermented dung. The horse moved smoothly like a machine, but there was no doubt up close that it was a beast, one with hoofs that beat holes in the snow, tearing it open like weapons.

In his fall, Malchik had pissed himself, and now the cloud of odors and the motion of the steed made him dizzy and sick. His arms were free, but he could do nothing to steady himself; he had to endure the constant jolting that shook him like a boneless doll. He had no idea where he was going. All he could see was the swooping snow, and the horse's murderous hoofs striking out in a complex rhythm. If he could have lifted himself up, or somehow projected himself from the horse's back, he might have been able either to make himself comfortable or to attempt an escape, but he was too afraid of falling beneath those feet, and being trampled into a pulp. He tried to grab at the saddle, but his hands were slippery with sweat.

When Sarl suddenly pulled up his mount, drawing on the reins, the jolt shook Malchik from its back, and he slithered to the ground, to lie face down on the snow, his limbs and joints aching and a pulsing pain in his skull. He heard the snow crunch nearby him as Sarl dismounted, and the sound of the man's breathing as he stood over him.

"What do you think I've caught, *mes amis*? Sarl said. "Is it a fish, a fowl, or a boneless eel?"

In spite of the pain, Malchik struggled to roll over on to his back. He looked up into Sarl's face, flushed and smiling with the exertion of the ride and pleasure at his catch. Swiftly, Malchik decided that he must dissemble his true feelings as best he could; Sarl knew that their minds were linked, and that Malchik was in the power of the Cold One. He might believe that Malchik was pleased to have been captured by one of her servants.

Another of the riders came to stand beside Sarl. He wore a long shirt of mail links, with a coif that covered his head, and a steel-banded conical helmet with a nose-guard. His face was ruddy and smooth-skinned, the countenance of a middle-aged man, and he was thickset, a tall man diminished by Sarl's height.

"Looks like a fish to me, Mon Seigneur," he said. "What did you take him for? Better to slit his throat and save us the trouble."

"This is the one I wanted, De Boissac. The others can wait. They won't get past the Castle."

De Boissac gave a shrug that showed he thought his commander was wasting their time, and strode away. Sarl crouched down to that he was close to Malchik, who felt his mouth tremble.

"What are you going to do with me, Zhan Sarl?" he said in a whisper.

"That depends on you, Messieur Vasilyevich," said Sarl, folding his hands together into a knotted fist. "And on our mistress. I'm sure you know what I mean."

"The Cold One," said Malchik, rolling his head so that he did not have to look at Sarl. The icy snow burned his cheek.

"I can see you, and you can see me," said Sarl. "We are both her servants. And she has chosen you for a special purpose."

"What's that?" said Malchik, turning to look up at the Deputy. Sarl grinned at him.

"She's been watching you for some time. Before you ever

came to Gard Ademar, she marked you out. And she told me to make sure of you. Late in the year for roses, isn't it?"

"The flowers on Isabel's grave," said Malchik.

"I'm surprised your clever father didn't notice that. I thought you might. It was my only fear. But it seems everything went smoothly."

"But why?" said Malchik, feeling tears fill his lids.

Sarl stood up, and rested his hands at his belt. "I don't know how far I can trust you," he said amiably. "You're not wholly in the power of the Goddess, or you would have come to me of your own accord. But the seed is growing within you. The ice seed. To answer your question, I'm going to take you with me to the Castle of Ademar, which lies athwart the worlds. One way gives on to La Souterraine, and another on to the upper world. You can enter there as a prisoner, or as a guest; that's up to you."

Malchik struggled to sit up, groaning at the ache in his spine. "I will go with you," he said. Deep within his mind, he thought of Yuda, and knew that he owed it to his father both to stay alive and to fight the power of the Cold One from within.

Sarl laughed. "That is one matter in which you don't have any choice, little grub," he said, not unkindly. "You will indeed go with me to the Castle of Ademar. And when we are there, you will prove your loyalty to my noble father, the Doyen of Ademar."

"I will show that I am the Cold One's loyal servant," said Malchik. "I will become her loyal servant."

"We shall see," said Sarl, stooping to offer his hand to Malchik, to help him to his feet. From close to, Malchik observed that the Deputy—if he could still call him that—was wearing a long tunic of green cloth to the knee, a rich cloak fastened at the shoulder with a golden pin, and dark leggings beneath calfskin riding boots. Malchik was all too conscious of his own torn and stained clothing. He looked up at Sarl, wishing he felt less like a sapling beside a mighty oak. One blow from Sarl's fist would fell him. He wondered how much the deputy could hear of his thoughts, and hoped it was not much; Malchik was not a strong enough shaman for his mind to be open to another.

The knights were sanding by their horses, waiting for a signal from their leader. Sarl turned to his steed, which was waiting close by, and stroked its muzzle, whispering in its ear. Shivering with cold and shock, Malchik dreaded the moment when he would be once more pinned across its back, or required to ride it. As Sarl spoke to it, it lifted its long head and let out a fierce whinny. Sarl patted its neck, but instead of swinging himself up into the saddle, he took a hold of the reins and began to lead it towards the group of men, dragging Malchik after him with a handful of cloak. Malchik stumbled to keep pace with his long strides. As they approached the knights, De Boissac stepped forward and saluted Sarl with his sword.

"To the Castle, is it, Mon Seigneur?"

"To the Castle," said Sarl. "My noble father will be waiting for us. I have sent the crows to warn him of our coming."

"Not all of us will be riding back into his halls tonight," said De Boissac, sourly.

"You shall have vengeance for that, and more, *mon ami*," said Sarl. "Vengeance for all the wrongs done to our people."

Sarl and his men stood in a ring, their horses beside them. Sarl kept a hank of Malchik's cloak gripped tightly in his fist. Malchik wondered what they were going to do, and whether they were planning to offer up prayers to the Doxan Mother— or to the Cold One. Instead, as he watched, De Boissac stepped forward into the circle and began to draw a shape in the snow with the tip of his sword, like a child drawing patterns in the sand. As Malchik studied the growing shape, he began to make out the crude outline of a building with towers and crenellations, a gate and a portcullis. De Boissac was drawing a chateau.

When the knight had finished, he stepped back into the circle and took up his horse's reins. Gazing at the roughly drawn image in the snow, Malchik was tempted to laugh hysterically. It seemed an absurd thing to do with such solemnity. He looked round the circle of faces, and saw them watching the picture intently, as if waiting for something to happen. The only sound was that of a horse stamping its feet, and the jingling of its harness. Malchik felt the silence beyond the circle pressing in on them. Suddenly, there was a rushing sound, as if a wind had swept in out of the desert of snow. A whirlwind sprang up beyond the edge of the circle, its eddies drawing clouds of powder from the ground. Slowly they were surrounded by a spiraling column of white, which grew until it seemed to touch the sky. It was then that De Boissac stepped forward into the centre of the circle, standing over the picture he had drawn, and vanished from sight. Malchik caught his breath. He glanced at Sarl, and saw him watching the place where De Boissac and his horse had stood, with a small smile on his features.

One by one, the knights took their place at the centre of the ring, leading their docile mounts, and each disappeared in turn, as if the vortex had suddenly swept him up into the sky. At last, Sarl and Malchik were the only ones left. The Deputy glanced at Malchik, tugged on his cloak and dragged him forwards to stand on the remains of the trampled drawing, leading his horse with his free hand. Malchik shivered at the intense cold of the wind that blew outside the circle. Then there was a popping sound, and he felt himself jerked violently upwards. There was no sensation of flying through the air, but a moment of complete silence and vacuum, during which he seemed to be surrounded by the iridescence of a soap bubble. He could feel Sarl holding on to his cloak, and he wondered what would happen to him if the man let go. At that moment, the bubble seemed to burst soundlessly, and Malchik fell on his back on to hard, impacted snow, winded and bruised. The sky overhead seemed the same diaphanous blue, but overhead loomed the conical red turrets and drum-shaped white towers of a mighty chateau. He could hear the pennants on the flagpoles snapping in the breeze.

"Welcome to the Castle of Ademar, your new home," said Sarl.

At first, they trod the streets of mud, but as they came closer to the centre of Chorazin, uneven cobbles covered the ground and there were even gutters and drains for waste water. The houses stood tall, four or five storeys high, with roofs of grey slate and shuttered windows. They bore a thick coat of stucco that caught the winter sunlight, so that on every corner their new or faded hues flashed at Annat; cornflower blue, mimosa yellow or rose clay. They leaned together crookedly, as if some mighty earthquake had shaken them loose, and there were many long cracks seaming their facades. The shutters hung awry, dangling from the window frames, and Annat kept expecting the buildings to crumble and collapse before her eyes. Ornate iron grilles shielded the windows on the lower floors, and several times Annat glimpsed wan and frightened faces peeping out at her through shattered glass.

The *Beit* or House of Prayer stood at the heart of the town, a long, low building with a sloping roof, whose main window, protected by a gilded screen, overlooked the central square. Built near its walls was a narrow street of houses whose jutting gables almost touched the roof of the *Beit*. The young man led them into this dark chasm, and paused before a massive door studded with many bolts, where he rang the bell. Annat glanced down at Yuda's face; though his eyes were sunken and he looked pale as paper, he was conscious, and seemed as interested as she in the strange place to which they had come.

There was a sound of footsteps from within the house, and a few moments later a young woman in a long, narrow-waisted dress of dark stuff, whose black hair was pinned back in a chignon, opened the street door. Seeing the young man on the doorstep, she lowered her eyes and smiled.

"Are these the visitors, Natan? My father will see them now, upstairs in his chambers. He has asked Hadass and me to prepare water and wound-dressings."

"It must be a day of miracle, Dalit, if this is the second time he has sent you to speak to me."

The girl made an angry face. "Hush, Natan, you will get me an evil reputation," she said. "Tell them to bring the wounded man straight upstairs. And the strangers must come in, the Ya-Udi and the *Dzuzukim*. But not you, Natan ben Schmuel!"

Holding the door open to admit the stretcher-bearers, she flashed a shy smile at Annat, and flew back upstairs in a rustle of skirts, leaving the spurned young man grinning merrily on the doorstep. The two men bore Yuda up the steep stairs, and Annat clambered behind them, feeling the ancient smoothness of the banister beneath her palm, and noticing how the passage of many feet had worn hollows into the stone steps. She saw a wisp of dark grey skirt vanish through a doorway on the second floor, before the door was banged shut. As she passed the landing, she could hear the sound of smothered laughter.

The *Rashim*'s chambers were on the second floor, and as she followed the men with the stretcher through the open door, Annat inhaled with pleasure the familiar scent of dust, candle-snuff and old books that reminded her of *Zaide*'s study. In one corner of the room stood a magnificent four-poster bed, draped funereally in purple and black; the polished floor was covered with rich Turkmen rugs, some so frayed that only the bare weft remained in patches; and a massive mahogany bureau stood by the window, on which vast books and scrolls were piled in heaps, marked with the black needle-and-hook script of the Ya-Udi. Next to the desk, an old man sat in a gilded chair, his white hair covered by a rust-red kippa, and his small frame draped in a fur-lined caftan of purple silk, thick with golden embroidery.

As they entered the room, the *Rashim* rose to his feet, slipping the prayer shawl from his shoulders, and pulled the small pair of black pince-nez from his nose. Although his white locks gave him an air of venerability, he strode across the room as the two men set the stretcher down on the floor, and Annat realized that, like *Zaide*, he could not be more than sixty. She approached him, hesitated, plaiting her fingers behind her back, and wished she were wearing more seemly clothing.

"Is this the man?" the *Rashim* snapped, to no one in particular.

"There is One in Zyon," said Yuda hoarsely. With difficulty, the *Rashim* bent over the stretcher and went down on one knee, inspecting Yuda with one eye shut.

"One, and One only," he said, absent-mindedly. "What is your name, young man?"

"Yuda ben Mordechai, known as Vasilyevich."

The *Rashim* tutted in his beard. "Such a long time, and still they give us these absurd *Dzuzuk* names," he muttered. "And someone says you need a healer?"

"I've lost much blood, *Zaide*."

Wincing, the old man lowered himself so that he was kneeling on the floor. "These dressings seem well-soaked," he said. "Who healed you?"

Yuda gestured weakly with his right hand. "My *kindeleh*, Annat bat Yuda," he said, managing a crooked smile. "We are both shamans."

"Shamans, hmm? The little one in the immodest dress? No matter." He peeled the bandages away and inspected the gashes to Yuda's chest and left arm, peering at them with his left eye shut. Then he ran his fingertips over the edges of the wounds, muttering to himself. "Tell me, *kind*, how you managed to get such injuries. They look like the work of a sword and a spear."

"That's because they are, *Zaide*," said Yuda, with a touch of mischief.

"So it seems. Natan ben Schmuel, that scoundrel and descendant of scoundrels, may he have a black year, told my daughter that you are pursued by evil *Dzuzukim*."

"By my enemy Zhan Sarl, and his men."

"Zyon," the old man exclaimed, opening both eyes wide. They were young, deep, and full of fire. He glanced at Annat, and then beckoned her. "Later, *kind*, you must tell me what brought you to the notice of the Prince of Ademar," he said to her. "I know him and his father of old. But now I must heal your father." Raising his head, he addressed the two stretchermen. "Yossi and Motke, take these folk down to the buttery and serve them with white bread and beer. There is no need to disturb Yosef. But you stay here with me, *kindeleh*," he added to Annat, who was wondering why he called Sarl Prince of Ademar.

When the two men had shown Govorin and Casildis out of the room, the *Rashim* stood up with difficulty and went to his desk, where he lifted a long-handled bell and shook it vigorously. After a few moments, Annat heard a heavy tread on the stair outside; then the door swung open, and a huge figure entered the room. Annat almost cried out; for the man's face was a blind mask of clay, and a letter of the Holy Name was carved into his forehead. A *Golem*!

"This is Yosef, my servant," said the *Rashim*, calmly. "In time of danger, he protects us from our enemies, but mostly he does menial tasks for me here and at the *Beit*, where he is one of the wardens. Yosef, take up the sick man and put him on the bed."

The huge creature lumbered across the room and bent to scoop Yuda up in his pottery hands, blankets, pallet and all. Cradling Yuda as lightly as a baby, he strode across to the four-poster bed and laid him down gently, straightening and turning his blind head back to his master for another command.

"Very good, Yosef," said the *Rashim*. "You may go."

Annat only realized how frightened she had been when the *Golem* left the room. She would not have liked to encounter it when the *Rashim* as absent. As soon as it had gone, the old man went to the bed and removed the remains of the soiled dressings. Then he went to the head of the stairs and called for his daughters, who quickly came, bringing hot water and fresh bandages. Annat recognised the girl Dalit she had met at the door. The younger sister, Hadass, was not much taller than Annat, with a head of lustrous red curls and eyes that were green as the sea. She flashed a smile at Annat as she went past, and whispered, "Our *Tate* has asked us to look out some clothes for you." Annat felt an unfamiliar pang as she stared back at the girl's softly freckled face. For a moment, she could not believe that she had ever seen anyone so lovely. Then the *Rashim* called to her impatiently. Having washed his hands, he was carefully swabbing the wounds, pausing from time to time to inspect them more closely. As he worked, he spoke to Annat. "I have used here a tincture of comfrey, that is the leaves of the herb macerated in alcohol, which are sovereign against infection. But thank the Holy One, Blessed be He, these are clean cuts." Having cleansed the wounds, he put the pieces of soiled cotton together in a basket on the floor, and bent over Yuda, passing his hands above the hole in his side. As he did so, the *Rashim* intoned a blessing in *Ebreu*. Annat knelt by the side of the bed and watched in fascination as the lips of the wound began to stir and creep towards each other. Yuda grimaced, but he did not move. Slowly, the two sides of the gash began to fuse, as if a tiny and invisible needle were pulling them together, until at last only an angry red scar remained on Yuda's side to show where the injury had been. The *Rashim* repeated the process with the fissure in Yuda's arm, and at no time did he touch it, letting his fingers hover a few inches from its surface. When he had finished, Yuda stirred restlessly, and lifted his hand as if to scratch at the scars.

"Lie still, young man," the *Rashim* commanded. "I have not yet concluded the healing." He rocked back on his heels, rubbing the small of his back, and addressed himself to Annat. "You see, *kind*, that is the easier part. Now I must stimulate the cells that make the blood. But your father will need to lie abed for a day or so while the blood is renewed."

"I don't know about that," said Yuda. Annat was relieved to see that he no longer looked so papery-pale.

"You are remarkably strong," said the *Rashim*, testily. "Such injuries would have killed a weaker man. And the work that your daughter did undoubtedly saved you, though it was clumsy and crude."

Annat was not sure whether to take this as praise or blame. She watched intently once more as the *Rashim* passed his hands over Yuda's limbs. Yuda too watched the old man working, and his eyes were alert and bright.

"I take it you know how to do this yourself, young man?" the *Rashim* said as he worked.

"I was taught how to do it," said Yuda. "I've never done it in the field."

"The power of the One flows through us, vastly and infinitely," the old man said in a dreamy voice. "We are like the smallest stars in his sky. Little lights that it is hard to extinguish. But you, my son, are a bright star, a small, shining sun. I was so in my youth. And so will your daughter be, for she has inherited your strength."

He raised his hands high and pressed them together, palm to palm. "It is done. Now we can only wait for the blood to replenish itself. I will send for Yosef to help you remove the rest of your stained garments, and he will wash you. In such things, he can be as gentle as a nursemaid. As for you, *kindeleh*, it is time for you to go downstairs to my daughters, who will find you some clothes and show you where to wash. Go on with you!" he added, as Annat hesitated.

She all but ran from the room, half-afraid that she might encounter the *Golem* alone on the stairs. She burst through the door of the first floor without knocking, to find herself in a shady room whose only light came from two tall windows. A walnut-wood table stood in the center, covered by a lace cloth, and six massive chairs were ranged round it. The walls were of lime-washed plaster, hung with faded pictures and religious texts in *Ebreu*, including a *Mizrach* on the eastern wall intended to help the inhabitants direct their prayers towards Zyon. The only patch of color came from a chaise-longue in the corner, which was draped with a red cloth embroidered in vivid colors and sewn with mirrors. On the chaise sat Dalit, reading a book; there was no sign of Hadass, whom Annat had hoped to see, but an inner door gave entrance to a room beyond.

Dalit gave a start as Annat rushed into the room, then smiled and rose from the couch, closing her book.

"Has my father sent you to us?" she said.

Annat nodded. "He said you would show me where to wash and find me some clothes."

Dalit placed the book down on the table, carefully marking her place in the text. "Hadass has agreed to give you some of her clothes, since you are nearer in height," she said. "And I commanded Yosef to fill a bath with water for you in our bedroom."

"Is he there now?" said Annat, fearfully.

Dalit gave a pleasant laugh. "You have nothing to fear from Yosef," she said. "So long as only we or our father give him commands, he will not do any mischief. His only trouble is that he does not know when to stop. But this is a strange house, which holds many wonders. You must not be surprised if you see or hear odd things, especially in the night. My father is a *Tzaddik*, a holy man, but also a great magician and master of illusion. Come, you must be eager to wash," she added, glancing curiously at the doll in Annat's arms.

Annat followed her into the inner room, which by contrast was filled with light. Two neat wooden beds with white pillows and flowery quilts stood against the far wall; to the left was a massy armoire made from pearwood, and its door hung open to reveal rows of gowns. Hadass was standing at the mirror behind the door, holding a long brocade dress with puffed sleeves against herself, and admiring her reflection. A pile of discarded robes lay strewn across a chair.

"Hadass, you little demon, I never gave you leave to try on my dresses!" Dalit exclaimed. She swept across the room and snatched the gown from her sister's hand, forcefully thrusting it back into the wardrobe. "What it is to have sisters! Though I should not say so, Annat."

"I'm thirteen, and I have only one brother," said Annat. "But he was captured by the evil *Dzuzukim*."

Hadass took her hand. "We will be your sisters, while you are here," she said, leading Annat to the chair with the piled dresses.

The next hour passed pleasantly for Annat, while she had a bath in a tin tub, and then tried on Hadass's gowns one by one. At last she chose a narrow-waisted gown of black taffeta with a white fichu. It would be no good for riding on the train, but she selected another, much plainer linen dress for that purpose. Dalit combed out her hair, which was growing quite long, and managed to scrape it up into a knot at the nape of Annat's neck, while Hadass watched enviously.

"You are so lucky to have long hair," she said. "Mine only stands up on end."

"But your hair is beautiful!" Annat exclaimed. "I had never seen any Red Wanderers till I came here. All my family are dark, except my brother."

Dalit put her hand on Hadass's shoulder. "We are in exile, here in La Souterraine," she said. "It seems so long since we saw spring or summer. But our *Tate* says that your coming means the time of waiting may soon be over."

"I hope so," said Annat. "But this man is chasing us, and he wants to kill us."

"The *Golem* will protect you while you are inside this house," said Dalit. "That was why our *Tate* made him. La Souterraine is a dangerous place."

"How did you come to be here, a city of Wanderers?" Annat asked.

"The *Rashim* plans to tell the whole story at supper," said Hadass. "But it concerns that man who pursues you, the Prince of Ademar, and his father the Doyen."

Chapter 14

Malchik picked himself up, rubbing his back. The castle rose above him, four-square and massive. Near the ground, the windows were narrow, arrow-shot thin, but higher up they opened into elegant panels of thick green glass that reflected the winter daylight. Behind the building rose the slopes of a white valley, which formed a natural amphitheater at its back; Malchik glimpsed slender trees that crowded the summit outlined against the sky.

Sarl took a firm grip on his upper arm. "Now is the time to choose," he said. "Will you enter the castle as a guest and a friend of Ademar, or as a prisoner and an enemy?"

"I don't have much choice, do I?" said Malchik, staring him in the face for the first time.

Sarl laughed. "The choice is yours. If you give me your *parole*, I will take it as your word of honor and use you accordingly. It is only a matter of time before your mind will be as mine, bent to the service of the Cold One. After that, there is no going back."

Malchik gazed at him. His instinct was to tell Sarl to go to hell, and live with the consequences; but once again he thought of Yuda, and knew his father would want him to stay alive. If it took lies and cunning, there was no fault in using such tools against a man like Sarl. He drew himself up, and said quietly, "I have always hated my father. I was anointed Doxan as a child, and that is my true faith."

"Is it so?" said Sarl, raising his eyebrows. Malchik had no idea whether he was deceived. "That news will please my noble father. He is a great lover of the true faith. But he will want to test your truth. Beware of trying to mislead him."

He led Malchik towards the great portal set into the castle wall. The other knights had dispersed, following De Boissac round to the rear of the building. As they drew nearer, Sarl raised a shout, and lifted his arm above his head. In response to his call, one of the mighty doors began to glide open, letting out the yellow light of tapers and flambeaux from within. A servant came running down the steps to greet them, and Sarl handed him the bridle of his horse without a second glance. He paused, putting his cloak of green wool back over his shoulders, to look Malchik up and down.

"There is no need for you to wear such clothes in my father's presence," he said. "I will send you to Cluny, my half-brother, who is about your height. He will find some better raiment for you."

Malchik followed him up the steps to the open door, scowling at his back. Inside, the doors gave access to a wide, draughty corridor, and Malchik glimpsed another, smaller entrance on the other side, which opened into a great crowded hall full of green-clad men. Sarl strode past the entrance, and led Malchik to a winding stair, set in one wall of a massive tower. "My brother's chambers are on the second floor," he said, adding, "It would not be wise of you to think of escape. Then I would cease to regard you as my friend and ally."

Malchik tried to look dismayed, unconvincingly, he felt. "Nothing was further from my thoughts, Mon Seigneur," he said, hoping that his voice did not reveal a hidden irony.

"Get you up to my brother," said Sarl, with a wry and not unfriendly smile, as if he knew Malchik's thought too well, and found it amusing.

Malchik began to mount the stairs, his head throbbing. His hand traced the stone of the tower wall, and he counted the steps that led him up to the first landing, trying to impose some order on his thoughts. There was a nail-studded door in one corner of the stair, and he paused before knocking. A quiet voice bade him to enter, and when Malchik stepped inside, he found himself in an unexpectedly airy semicircular room, lit with a mass of beeswax candles. There was a fire burning in a tall, cylindrical stove faced with clay tiles, close to one edge of the semicircle. Near the window was an easel, and a young man stood before it, painting. His rich brown hair was cropped above his ears, and he wore a long tunic of green wool over dull green leggings and slippers of kid leather. He turned his head as Malchik entered the room, and gave him a cautious smile. He brown eyes were dark and deep-set, and his skin honey-pale. Only the hauteur of his long nose gave a clue to the parentage that he shared with Sarl.

"I see the Heir has sent you to find me, Messieur," he said. "I am Cluny, Bastard of Ademar. My brother sent word that he was bringing home a captive; one would have thought he had chained some mighty warrior, rather than a stripling like myself."

"I am a stripling?" said Malchik. He felt suddenly dizzy, and sat down on the floor, which was strewn with rich rugs. There was only a single chair and a bed in the room, apart from the easel. Cluny put down his paintbrush and his palette.

"By the Mother," he exclaimed. "I am very sorry. You are wounded, and tired from your strange journey. Jean Sorel would not take much account of that."

Malchik stared up at him numbly. He could hardly bear the hope that this young man might prove to be some sort of ally, someone in the castle of his enemy whom he could trust. Cluny was right, he had noticed the small gashes in his arms smarting for the first time, and his body seemed to ache all over.

"What am I going to do?" he said, though it was a question addressed to himself rather than to his host.

Cluny gave him a penetrating stare. "You could sit in the chair, for one thing," he said. "And I will try to find some raiment that might fit you. Then we must talk."

As Cluny slipped into the garderobe, which shared the function of a wardrobe and a privy, Malchik hauled himself over to the chair, and sat in it. He leaned his elbow on the chair-arm

and his head on his hand. He found himself wondering what
had happened to the others, and where they had gone. He had
glimpsed the look of horror on their faces as Sarl dragged him
from the train. They might want to rescue him, but how long
would it take them to discover where he was, and how could
they ever enter the castle? When Cluny emerged, he was asking himself how far he dared to confide in the young man.

"I don't have many clothes," said Cluny, apologetically.
"This is one of my old tunics and a pair of hose." He held up a
long linen tunic, much mended, and a pair of darned blue leggings. "You may be threadbare, but you will find these garments more pleasing to my father than those which you are
wearing. You don't want to remind him that you have the
blood of the Wanderers in you."

"You know that I'm a Wanderer?" said Malchik, guardedly,
as he stripped off the shirt and waistcoat that the Bear People
had given him. Cluny approached, and examined his wounds
with a critical eye.

"They're not deep, but they should be cleansed," he said. "I
will send one of he servants for water." His gaze met
Malchik's. "Jean Sorel has sent us messages," he said, tersely.
"We knew that the folk he pursued included three Wanderers."

"My mother had me anointed a Doxan when I was a child,"
said Malchik again.

The young man raised his brows. "That is fortunate," he
said. "I suggest you mention it to my father when you are
brought into his presence. There remains a chance that he
might order you to be burnt."

Malchik stared back at him in horror, but Cluny turned
away, and went to the door to summon a servant. He had given
no sign whether he agreed or disagreed with the Doyen's view.
When the servant returned with a clean cloth and a bowl of hot
water, Cluny took it himself and began to swab Malchik's cuts
with a steady hand.

"My brother seemed to have especial care of you," he said,
without looking at Malchik. "He told us you were the one
most likely to be won to the cause of Ademar. The others are
as good as dead."

Malchik flinched, not because Cluny had hurt him, but because of his words. The young man paused, and said, "I am sorry. These must be kin of yours. But Jean Sorel had given us to understand you would care little for their fate."

Malchik hid his face in his hands. He was ashamed not only to be unable to hide his feelings from a stranger who might be Sarl's ally, but also that Cluny, who seemed a good person, should think him so heartless. "He might well say that," he said, bitterly. "He knows we are linked together—by the seed of ice the Cold One has placed in us both." He knew that it was reckless to admit so much to Cluny, but he had to take a chance. Cluny went on dabbing at the wounds, speaking as he worked.

"I know of this Goddess, and the evil that she sows in men. Need I tell you that the seed my brother Jean carries has grown until he is scarcely recognizable? The Doyen has accepted it, not I."

"What would you advise me to do, Cluny?" said Malchik. The hope in him had grown stronger that, by showing his true feelings to Cluny, he might have earned himself the chance of friendship.

Before he answered, the young man went to the garderobe and returned with an old shirt, which he tore into strips to bind Malchik's arm.

"Go before my father, as you must, and hope that he is merciful to you. After that, we can think."

As he spoke, there was a knock at the chamber door. Cluny went to open it, to admit Sarl, who strode into the room. Seeing Malchik still half-dressed in his old clothes, he ordered him to change at once. Malchik took refuge in the garderobe, where he was also able to relieve himself, and struggled into the unfamiliar garments. He felt a fool in the long tunic, which reminded him of a dress. When he shuffled out into the room, Sarl burst out laughing, and Cluny could not restrain a smile.

"I see you are a clown, boy," said Sarl. "You had better not try any japes before my father; he is not known for his humor."

Malchik struggled to straighten the tunic, and pull up the leggings, which were sagging about his knees. "The Doyen is ready for you," Sarl continued. "Do not keep him waiting."

* * *

The eve of Kingsday shared some of the holiness of the day it-self, and supper at the *Rashim*'s house was a festive occasion. Dalit and Hadass had spread the table with a white damask cloth, and placed silver knives and forks for each guest. There was a *challah*, and a flagon of red wine for the *Rashim* to bless before the meal. He sat at the head of the table, with Annat on his right and Govorin and Casildis on his left. The Sheriff and his wife had both put on fresh clothes: Govorin a black suit and white shirt like those of the Wanderer men, and Casildis a grey silk gown with a wide skirt that set off her fair-skinned beauty. Out of respect for custom, she had covered her long hair with a scarf. Dalit and Hadass served the repast, which consisted of vegetable broth, a carp cooked in its own juices, and an almond pudding. The formality and grandeur reminded Annat a little of their lunch at Sarl's house, but nothing could have been more different. There was little talk while they were eating, but once the *Rashim* had finished saying grace at the end of the meal, he began to tell stories and parables, many of which had a little joke hidden in them. It was Dalit who, as she finished clearing the table, prompted her father to recount the tale of their coming to La Souterraine. The *Rashim* clasped his hands and gazed round the table at each of the diners in turn, though he kept his eyes averted from Casildis's face.

"Yuda ben Mordechai told me how you are pursued by the Prince of Ademar, Zhan Sarl," he said.

"It's a long story, *Rashim*," said Govorin, "but there is a mystery at the heart of it. We don't yet know why, but he means to kill us all, except my wife, who is his sister. And now he has stolen the son of Yuda ben Mordechai."

"If I had known that you came from that house, Madame, I would not have given you shelter under my roof," said the old man, harshly. "No matter. The Wise say that not all who share the same name should be condemned. Perhaps when I have told you what I know, you will understand a little better the danger that we face. This town where we sit, Chorazin, once stood north of the Forest of Ademar, near the castle that houses the Seigneur of the Forest, the Doyen of Ademar. When I was still a young man studying at the *yeshiva*, the old Seigneur was an indolent man, who left us in peace—except for taxes. But when he died, his son came to our town to view his seigneury, and I saw in his face the blue eyes of a fanatic.

"The persecutions began slowly. At first, the taxes were put up, and up. Then the Doyen's men came to requisition our crops and our flocks, so that often the people starved. The Doyen borrowed money from us at interest, and called us accursed usurers. At least when the loans were out he did not send his men to steal our goods. But from time to time a group of knights would ride into the city and, if they found an unfortunate, they would shave off his beard and force him to eat dust, or unclean food. Sometimes they would kill him. Girls were defiled, houses burnt, children kidnapped and forced to become Doxoi. I was somewhat older than the Doyen, and I grew to manhood before he did. Like him, I married a wife and raised a family. Unlike him, I was blessed with many children. He had but three that were legitimate, his son and heir and two daughters. You, Madame, must be one of the daughters, and I wonder at the way you have grown to become a Wanderer-friend." He spoke with such sarcasm that Govorin almost protested, but Casildis answered, with downcast eyes, "My mother was never a Doxan, sir, and she raised her daughters to use all peoples justly. Indeed, I would not have married my husband if I had not known him for a man, and the best of men."

"A good answer," said the *Rashim*, stroking his beard. "I have little love for the *Dzuzukim*, and it amazed and distressed me to learn that Yuda ben Mordechai had chosen two as his companions. But you are my guests, the strangers within my gates.

"A little more than three years ago, the Doyen lost his wits. His elder daughter Huldis vanished, and he blamed us for her loss, swearing that we had stolen her away and put her to death on the Wheel, like the Son. His men surrounded the town, and he promised that he would burn us alive, each and every one, whether we converted to Doxa or not."

Casildis gasped. "I never knew that, sir. But I was only four years old when my sister disappeared." She paused and then added, "But it is twenty-three years since Huldis was lost—and you have been here but three?"

"It is a mystery," said the *Rashim* softly. "There is no doubt that our exile has lasted for three years only. Though there has been only winter, the famished light of the invisible sun has been enough for us to grow crops under glass. Had we been pent here longer, I fear we would all have perished."

Govorin turned to Casildis. "If only three years have passed in La Souterraine, but twenty-three years in our world, what does that mean for us? We have been here only a few days . . ."

"Then time in this world runs slowly," said Casildis, gravely. "We cannot tell how long we have been journeying. If we return, we may find that months or more have passed in our absence."

"What can we do?" asked Annat.

They looked at her in silence. There was nothing to be done; having embarked upon this journey, they must see it through to its end.

Casildis turned to the *Rashim*. "But what happened when my father attacked Chorazin? It seems that you survived."

The *Rashim* nodded. "All I could do was pray to the Holy One, Blessed be He, for deliverance," he said. "My revered father had died, and I had become *Rashim* in his place. The people looked to me for guidance. After evening prayers, I went to the empty *Beit* and stood alone before the tabernacle, watching the eternal flame. I could not despair, but I could not imagine why we should be saved when so many Wanderers before us had perished. In my heart, I questioned the wisdom of the Holy One, asking Him why this should be. I told Him that he was unjust, demanding so much of His People, yet giving them up to the wrath of their enemies. All night I strove with Him, raging and shedding tears like a child that defies its parent. And in the morning, when I left the House of Prayer, and made my way home, there was a strange silence in the streets. There was no camp of warriors outside our walls, and no walls to be seen. Instead of the bare August hills with their box and oak, there were white fields and a blue yet sunless sky. It seemed that the Holy One had indeed answered my prayer; He had cast us into exile in this strange land, and saved our lives. But alas, it was not long before we discovered that the evil we fled so eagerly was waiting for us here. A few miles distant, the Castle of Ademar stands, here as in the upper world. And though they have not sent their knights against us, we know it is only a matter of time; since not long after the town alighted here, flocks of crows have flown over the city like spies; the birds of the Cold One, sent out from Ademar."

"I saw them," said Annat, in a small voice.

"But do you mean that Sarl is in league with the Cold One?" said Govorin.

The *Rashim* shrugged. "How else would the Castle of Ademar be seen in this world, as well as in the upper forests?"

"But I grew up in the Castle of Ademar!" said Casildis. "I never knew of any entrance to La Souterraine."

"Perhaps they kept it from you," said the *Rashim*, folding his hands. "Or it may be that the gateway was opened in recent times."

Casildis took her head in her hands, and Govorin gently laid his arm across her back.

"This is news to me, *Rashim*," he said. "I knew that Sarl came from the forest, and that my wife was only too glad to leave her former home—but not that the man who worked as my deputy came from a line of tyrants. I doubt if Casildis knew it herself."

"Oh, I knew my father," said Casildis bitterly. "But I was a woman, and kept to the women's quarters, and knew my place."

"If the Prince of Ademar has taken Yuda's son, it is likely that he will convey him to the castle," said the *Rashim*.

"Not if I've got anything to do with it," said Yuda, swaying in the doorway. He was wearing only his bandages and a pair of pyjama bottoms, and his left arm was in a sling. The *Rashim* stood up, winced, and said, "Who gave you leave to get out of bed, my son? You are not yet well."

"*Golems* aren't much good at conversation," said Yuda, leaning on the doorpost and grinning. "It was either that or counting my new blood cells."

Govorin stood up also, strode across the room and put his arm round Yuda's shoulders.

"The *Rashim*'s right, Vasilyevich," he said. "If you can't

bear to be without us, we'll have to come up to you. You ought
to stay in bed."

"You might have sent Annat to amuse me," said Yuda cheerfully. "I could have taught her to do crossword puzzles in my
head. Or is it in her head? I forget."

"If you will not return to your chamber, at least sit down,"
said the *Rashim* testily. "There is an empty chair at the opposite end of the table. I will ask my daughters to make *kava* for
you and anyone else who wishes it. A rare commodity after
more than three years of exile, and so made with *chicorée*."

Govorin helped Yuda round the table to sit down, where he
promptly lit a cigarette. Somehow, his coming put an end to
the tension of the past hour. When Annat moved her chair to
sit close to him, Yuda raised an eyebrow at her. Apart from
being unsteady on his feet, he seemed to be completely recovered. He refrained from putting his feet on the table, but he appeared to be less in awe of the *Rashim* than the rest of them.

"So it was a miracle, *Rashim*," he said.

"It seemed to be a miracle. It came in answer to my
prayers." He clapped his hands to summon Dalit, who came
hurrying from the inner room. When the girl had gone down to
the kitchens to prepare the *chicorée*, the *Rashim* returned to
Yuda. "Do you then dispute that it was a miracle?" he said,
waggling his bushy brows. He seemed to have taken a liking
to Yuda, as if he were a prodigal son who could be forgiven
much.

"I was wondering if the Cold One brought you here. A little
joke on her part. Saving your lives and condemning you to
perpetual winter. I'm pretty sure she was the one who stole the
Doyen's daughter." He glanced at Casildis and added, in a
voice suddenly hard, "But you'd know more about that than
the rest of us, Missis Govorin. Seeing that you're the priestess
of the Bright Lady."

Casildis looked as if he had slapped her across the face, and
Annat was astonished by her father's harshness to the woman
she knew he loved well. She saw Govorin frown. Yuda went
on, "I've been wondering how much else you've been keeping
from us, Missis. I think it's time you told us the truth, don't
you?"

Casildis had gone white. "I have never lied to you, Yuda," she said, in a faint voice.

"Never lied to us, no. But you know a lot more about the Cold One than you've ever said. Things that might have been useful to us."

"Let her be, Yuda," said Govorin. "I've long known that there were things Casildis couldn't tell me. And I've trusted her."

"So you have," said Yuda. "But I want to hear what she knows."

Govorin started to get to his feet, but Casildis laid her hand on his arm. "It's all right, Sergey," she said, gently. "What Yuda says must be answered. But my sect has been persecuted for so long that we have learned habits of secrecy. As both of you are men, you would not customarily be told the mysteries of the Women."

Govorin gave a sigh, and sat down. "I think we'd all gathered that you are the priestess of the Bright Lady, my love," he said.

Casildis clenched her hands together. "This land was once ruled by twin goddesses," she said. "They ruled in harmony, darkness and light, warmth and cold. They balanced each other. All we—the Women—even priestesses—know is that, many years ago, the balance was upset and the goddesses severed. The Cold One haunts the forest, while all trace of the Bright Lady has been lost. Until those moments amongst the Bear People, when her spirit possessed me, the Goddess had not spoken for many years." She looked across the table at Yuda. "Do you understand that I have withheld nothing that could have harmed you?"

"I don't know, Missis," said Yuda. "We've been hunting blind—or running blind. And now Sarl has taken Malchik, and we don't know why. Instead we've been hearing about this Castle of Ademar, and that Sarl is some great lord's heir."

"It's not Missis Govorin's fault," said Annat, suddenly. "I knew there was a chateau in the forest. *Mame* came from there. But it didn't seem important until now."

"Maybe not," said Yuda. "All I know is that I've lost the boy, and I couldn't save him."

"My son," said the *Rashim*, "this shadow had enveloped us all, Wanderer and *Dzuzuk* alike. It is hard to know what to do for the best. The Holy One, Blessed be He, created many spirits, clean and unclean; there is the *Shkine*, his radiant presence, which is as a mother to us on this created world; but there is also the darkness, with its destructive power. Just as this young woman has spoken of the ones she calls goddesses, so we too can see shapes that take form under the aegis of the deity, though they should not be honoured in His stead," and he cast a frown in Casildis's direction. "But do not keep your anger and bitterness through the night. This is a house of peace."

Yuda leaned his head on his hand. "I'm sorry, Missis," he said gruffly. "There are some things that shouldn't be said."

"I am sorry too, Yuda," said Casildis. "But I thought, as a Wanderer, you would understand what it is to be persecuted, and live in fear."

They looked across at each other, and Annat saw the flicker of that invisible bond, that passed like a touch between them. She wondered if Govorin saw it too.

In turn, they bade the *Rashim* goodnight and retreated to their various rooms. Annat had been allotted a truckle bed between Dalit and Hadass; Govorin and Casildis were on the third floor; and Yuda returned to the solitary splendor of the four-poster in the *Rashim*'s chambers. It was not clear where the *Rashim* himself planned to sleep, or whether he would sleep at all. Annat found that, when all the lights were extinguished and the gossiping and whispering had ceased, she lay in the darkness wide awake, listening to the soft breathing of her two room-mates, and unable to close her eyes. A clock ticked somewhere in the house, and struck the hours and the quarters with a sonorous tone. Annat began to wait for its voice and the creaking of wheels that preceded each note, which only served to remind her how long she had lain awake since the last time it sounded. When one o'clock struck, she pulled back the blankets and slipped her feet over the side of the bed, feeling the rough surface of an old drugget under her soles. She crept out of the bedroom into the darkened parlour beyond, and out on to the stairs. Slowly, she ascended the cold stone steps, planning to enter the room where Yuda slept and wake him. Her mind was buzzing with wakeful thoughts and ideas, which she could not keep to herself.

There was a light burning in the *Rashim*'s chambers, and the *Tzaddik* himself sat at his desk, fast asleep, his head back and his mouth open, snoring gently. His white beard rose and fell like a cloud of dandelion fluff. Annat crept across the polished boards towards the antique bed, whose draperies hung in folds of lilac and black, like funeral flowers. It was when she reached the bed, with its curtains open, that she received her first surprise. Yuda was fast asleep, his hands folded on the coverlet, but he was not alone. On top of the covers, in a long white night-gown, Casildis lay wrapped in a skein of fair hair, still as a wax effigy, her left arm outstretched so that her hand rested close to Yuda's heart. Hardly daring to breathe, Annat stood by the swathes of purple damask and surveyed this strange sight. There was no question of her trying to wake Yuda now; she wondered whether he was aware of the woman's presence, Casildis lay so immobile.

Annat stole from the room, walking on tiptoe, but instead of returning to her bed, she began to mount the stair to the third floor. There were three doors leading off the landing, and she tried each in turn. In the second room stood a sturdy double bed, and Annat went in only little way before she saw Casildis once more, lying cosily against her husband, with her head in the crook of his shoulder. Annat stood gazing at them for a long time, and a small, cool shiver passed down her spine. If Casildis were asleep in her Govorin's arms, whom had she seen with Yuda in the room downstairs? She shut the door on the sleeping couple, and hesitantly approached the third door. There was a key in the lock that she had to turn before she could enter. The small room beyond was full of the lambent glow of many candles. A woman lay in the bed, her hands folded, her face frozen in death. She wore a white lace bonnet, and the white counterpane was embroidered with faded roses of lace; there was no smell of death in the room, only an odour of cedar and myrrh and embalming herbs, which hung in the air like a miasma, inviting her too to lie down and sleep. Annat backed away, her hand grasping the cold brass of the doorknob, scared by what she had seen. She was about to shut the door when something brushed against her shoulders, and she almost cried out in fear. It was Yosef, the *Golem*.

The mute face opened an awful crevice, and the *Golem* spoke to her. "My mistress is asleep," it said. "Do not wake her."

Annat glanced fearfully at the bed, half-afraid that the dark eyes would open and the figure sit up and stare at her. She backed away and the *Golem* advanced a step, repeating, "Do not wake her."

Annat released the doorknob and fled, her quick feet pattering on the stones, back to the safety of the floor below, where the *Rashim* slept. The *Golem* followed her with slow, lumbering steps, inexorable. But when she came to the *Rashim's* chambers, the light had been extinguished and his chair was empty. Annat stood on the edge of the black cavern that the room had become, afraid of what she might discover if she ventured into the dark.

"Yuda," she whispered, not daring to raise her voice, but no one answered. There was the sound of soft breathing, but she could not see where the bed stood, and she was afraid of groping her way across the room, in case she fell against something in the dark, or put out her hand to touch something—perhaps a face. She slipped through the door and the *Golem* was there on the landing, waiting for her.

"Do not wake her," it repeated in a monotone. Annat had no thought now but to return to her room and the safety of her bed. She remembered the doll, which she had left on her pillow, and wished that she had its wooden body to hug against her. Then the thought came to her that the doll itself was like a *Golem*, a wooden body that contained a spirit.

"By the Holy Name, leave me," she stammered. The *Golem* turned its back on her and continued to lumber down the stairs toward the cellars. Annat fled, her heart pounding, and regained the parlour door, pushing it wide open and almost slamming it shut behind her. Once inside, she came face to face with Hadass, holding a candle, and yawning.

"What's the matter, Annat?" she said, sleepily.

"Nothing. Nothing. Only I went to speak to *Tate*, and I disturbed the *Golem*."

"Don't worry about Yosef," said Hadass, taking Annat's arm in her warm grip. "He walks the house at night like a guard dog. But he wouldn't harm you. Look, you are shivering. You can share my bed if you want. Like Dalit said, this house is strange at night."

Annat was only too glad to climb into the warm bed and snuggle up against the girl's thin body. Hadass put her arms round Annat, and it was wonderfully soothing. She had not slept so close to anyone since she was a little child and had shared Yuste's bed. Slowly, little by little, she began to tell Hadass the truth: how she had seen what looked like Casildis in Yuda's bed, and of the dead woman in the room with the candles.

"That was my mother you saw," said Hadass softly. "For a long time, my father did not want to bury her body in the accursed earth of La Souterraine. He kept her embalmed in that room, as you saw. But one night, she came to him in a dream and asked him to bury her, in accordance with the Law of the Wanderers. She was interred the next day, and the room lies empty."

"I'm sorry, Hadass," said Annat. "I shouldn't have been so curious. And the *Golem* spoke to me. It told me to leave her in peace."

Hadass stroked her hair. "A *Golem* doesn't understand death," she said. "But perhaps you dreamed it. Yosef has never spoken, not even to my father."

"I don't think it was a dream," said Annat, trembling.

"Maybe not. At night, in this place, dreams and reality seem to blur, so that sometimes it can be hard to tell which is which. But you are here with me now, and Dalit is here too. Her courage would frighten off the fiercest dragon. Yosef obeys her, and she is the only one apart from *Tate* who can command him."

In spite of Hadass's words and her comforting arms, it took Annat some time to fall asleep; she kept seeing the face of the *Golem* and the waxen mask of the mother lying dead in the upper room. Together, these images seemed to form a message that she alone was meant to read, but she could not decipher it. Instead, it became an insoluble puzzle that kept her wakeful long after Hadass's breathing had grown soft and slow, and her grip on Annat had relaxed.

Malchik and Cluny followed Sarl down to the hall, where torches were alight, burning on iron sconces in the wall. The rafters were hung with ragged silk banners and decked with furze and green holly, which gave off a faint scent of amber. Evidence of a feast was being cleared away, and the nobles and commoners alike sat in rows at long trestle tables. There was not a single woman in the room; even the servants were male. Sarl marched Cluny and Malchik up the central aisle to the dais, where the Doyen sat enthroned, regarding them with a look of distant curiosity. His eyes were blue and hard as sapphires, set in a long, handsome face lined and tanned by the weather. His hair, which had faded to a wintry white, was cropped above his ears, and a band of gold ringed his brow. He was clad in an embroidered mantle of lilac wool over a long robe of pure white satin, belted at the waist with a long sword-belt. Massive gold rings set with many gems, onyx, ruby, emerald and amethyst, winked from his fingers as he moved his hands. He glowed like an *eikon* in a Doxan temple; a gold chain about his neck bore a massive pendant in the shape of the Wheel, set with diamonds, pearls and drops of garnet that resembled blood.

When Cluny reached the foot of the dais, he swept his father a low bow, and the Doyen inclined his head. Malchik, who had never bowed the knee to anyone in his life, managed a stiff obeisance from the waist up, which seemed to satisfy the Doyen, who beckoned him nearer. Malchik thought it prudent to kneel before the throne.

"So," the old man said, "a Doxan in a Wanderer's skin. Jean Sorel tells me you have come to add your name to our cause, renouncing your friends and kin."

"Yes, Mon Seigneur," said Malchik. "I was anointed in the true faith as a child. My mother—"

"We knew your mother," said the Doyen, cutting him short. "Was not her name Aude?"

"Yes," Malchik stammered. "Yes, Mon Seigneur."

The old man leaned forward, peering into Malchik's face. "So much of my Aude I see in you, and yet there is much of that accursed race also. She was one of my bastards, like Cluny here, though her father always thought her his own."

Malchik felt as if someone had struck him across the face.

"What a . . . great honour, Mon Seigneur," he gasped, imagining how Yuda would laugh if this news were divulged to him. *If Yuda were able to laugh*, Malchik reflected, with a shudder.

"In time, should you prove worthy, I will take you as one of my sons and acknowledge you," said the Doyen. "But first you must show your fastness in your faith and your adherence to Ademar. Did you know, boy, that I banished your mother and her family from his house, never to return upon pain of death?"

"I did not know, Mon Seigneur," said Malchik, gazing up into the winter-blue eyes like a rabbit entranced by a snake.

"You were not born when the offence occurred," said the Doyen, studying Malchik's features as if he were trying to read them like a book. "And yet it was a grievous offence, one that I could not pardon. My Huldis—" His voice cracked, and he sat back in his chair, raising his gaze to the rafters. "It was a bitter loss," he said. "Let others tell you the tale of woe. I have rehearsed it to myself many times, and still I do not know how she was taken, whether it was by the benighted Wanderers, or whether she was transported by some deed of darkness, as Aude confessed." He folded his hands in his lap. "But now the Heir has brought you to me, a child in recompense for the child I lost. Perhaps this is the time of the beginning of our victory."

He seemed to be waiting for Malchik to say something, but Malchik did not know what victory he was referring to. He looked up into the old man's face, and felt a sudden and unexpected pity for him. "I hope so, Mon Seigneur," he said, in a shaky voice.

The Doyen almost smiled at him. "You are one of the outsiders, the trespassers, and yet you have come to me," he said.

"Swear allegiance to me, and I will take you as my liege man and servant."

He held out his hands, with the palms parallel, a little distance apart. It was Cluny who hurried to Malchik's assistance, seizing his hands by the wrists and pressing them together as if Malchik were praying. He guided Malchik's folded hands until they lay between the Doyen's, and the old man clasped his fingers in a cold grip.

"Say after me, child: 'I do swear by the Mother and all Her saints that I take the Doyen of Ademar to be my liege lord, to serve him in good or ill, whatever may befall me, and unto my death.'"

Malchik slowly repeated the words in a faltering voice, never daring to take his gaze away from the Doyen's eyes, though he was sure the old man must see into his mind and perceive the doubts and rebellious thoughts within. When he had finished, the Doyen released him, and bent forward to plant a chill kiss on his brow.

"You are heartily welcome to us, my son," he said. "Now you are sworn to my service, just as are my sons, my noble Heir and Cluny the Bastard. I adjure you to remember that it is a mortal oath. Break it, and my wrath against you will be unswerving. And in days to come, you will see what my anger can do, when we seize upon those wretched creatures, your erstwhile companions, and bring them to the doom we have prepared for them."

Malchik gazed helplessly at the Doyen. "I am sure it is a doom richly deserved, Mon Seigneur," he said, feeling a traitor at every word.

The Doyen looked over his head, down into the body of the hall. "You do not know what you speak, child," he said. "But you must learn. For these are the first of the trespassers that have fallen within my grasp. My vengeance will be swift, and as exemplary as it is terrible."

Chapter 15

When the morning of Kingsday dawned, Dalit and Hadass were up and dressing in their white and silver gauze gowns, but Annat clung to her pillow and longed to stay in bed. Her mind was full of the dream-like events of the previous night, and when Hadass had roused her with the aid of a wet sponge, her first instinct was to seek out her father. Having adorned herself in borrowed finery, a satin petticoat and embroidered dress lent her by Hadass, she hurried to the *Rashim*'s chamber, half-afraid of what she might see there. Yuda was lying prone in the great four-poster, gazing up at the canopy, while the *Rashim*, resplendent in a purple caftan embroidered with gold thread, examined his wounds. Annat flew to the bedside, fearing that she would find Casildis, or a phantom of her, secreted in some corner, but the daylight had dispelled the ghosts.

"There you are, Natka," said her father, looking up at her. "All dressed to be the Kingsday Bride."

Annat smoothed her skirts absent-mindedly. "Will we leave as soon as Kingsday is out?" she said.

"Sooner, if I have my way," said Yuda, glancing at the *Rashim*, who straightened, rubbing his back.

"It is no sin to break Kingsday when a life is in peril," he said. "But it would be a sin for me as a healer to let your father stir from here today—and he knows it. This was a grave wound, deep and dangerous, and it needs time to settle. Moreover, not all the blood has yet replenished itself. If your son lives, Yuda ben Mordechai, you will not help him by going to his aid before you are well. Heed me as a father, if you will not listen to me as *Rashim*."

Yuda rolled his head towards the *Rashim* and smiled. "I was a very undutiful son to my own father," he said.

"That is between you and your conscience," said the *Rashim*, taking off his spectacles and polishing them on his handkerchief. "Perhaps you should practice the *mitzvah* of obedience for a change. It might do you some good."

Annat sat down on the edge of the bed and took her father's good hand. "We can stay here until tomorrow morning," she said. "I can sense that Malchik is alive. He told us that Sarl wouldn't harm him."

"It depends what you mean by harm, Natkeleh," said Yuda, gazing up at her out of fathomless eyes. "I don't imagine he'll kill the boy. But he will nurture the seed of cold that Malchik carries, to make Malchik as he is. And there's another thing, which the *Rashim* has been too kind to mention; our presence here brings danger to the city. If Sarl or the Doyen finds out that they have harboured us, they will suffer a swift retribution."

"It is so," said the *Rashim*, heavily. "The crows are watchers for Ademar."

"The birds of the Cold One," said Yuda. "They have been with us from the beginning. But don't you think it strange, *Rashim*, how the Cold One has not attacked us herself? We saw her over the forest, but we have not seen her in La Souterraine."

"I do not know the answer to that question, my son," said the *Rashim*. "But if Ademar could have called down the Evil One on our heads, he would have done so long since. Instead he has withheld his hand, but I know that he is only waiting, waiting for the hour when it will please him to strike."

Yuda sat up in bed, looking at Annat. "We will do all we can to prevent that, *Rashim*," he said. "Even if we have to confront the Cold One herself." He sighed. "And I will stay here like a good patient, until you give me leave to go."

Annat was amazed by the bustle of preparation and glitter for Kingsday, never having celebrated it with other Wanderers except her family. It was a day of rest, and they must do no work; breakfast had been set for them in the parlour last night. Though Govorin and Casildis joined the rest of them to eat, they would not be going to the service at the *Beit*, which was forbidden to *Dzuzukim*.

The three girls were the first to leave the house, hurrying up the street to the *Beit*, where they peeped into the empty men's . section before running upstairs to the women's gallery. A number of grand and dignified matrons were already filling the seats, and Dalit led them to a bench at the edge of the gallery, from which they could peer through the ornate screen on to the crowd of men that was beginning to assemble below. Many of the men paused to kiss their prayer-shawls before putting them on, and began to pray, rocking on their feet as they chanted the prayers from their little prayer-books, with a solemnity that made Annat guiltily want to giggle.

Silence only returned when the *Rashim* ascended the *Bima*, the tall dais ornamented with wood-carvings that stood before the tabernacle, ready for the service to begin. Women had little to do except follow the proceedings in their prayer-books and chant responses to the cantor, who now joined the *Rashim* and began the service by singing the opening prayer in a thrilling and sonorous voice. Annat did not take many pains to follow the service, but she did listen to the sad-sweet music of the cantor's voice, murmuring the words to herself when she recognised them, and even singing the responses. She was astonished and a little shocked when some of the men below began to dance, crooning the ancient prayers in melancholy voices. The most exciting moment came when the whole congregation stood to declaim the words that affirmed their faith: "There is only One in Zyon; One, and One only." For the first time, Annat felt that she was part of a community, not a small isolated cluster living amongst strangers. Her heart soared as she turned to Hadass and Hadass smiled at her, her green eyes reflecting the jewel-like lamps that lit the gallery.

The service lasted a long time, and it was hard to concentrate or to keep still. Some of the fashionable wives behind Annat shook out their silks and satins, and gossiped behind their prayer-books, admiring hats and censuring outlandish gowns. Annat would have preferred to be downstairs with the men, draping her head in a prayer-shawl and singing and dancing at the heart of things. Nevertheless, she began to long for the service to end, and could not stop thinking about her lunch as mid-of-the-day passed. After the concluding prayer, she was itching to run downstairs and into the street, but she had to wait with Dalit and Hadass while the matrons filed out in a stately line, followed by the younger women with their little children.

As they hurried back to the house, Annat caught once again the sense of panic as the people scurried home, without stopping outside the *Beit* to greet or gossip with one another. Hadass clutched her hand as they ran along and, glancing up at the sky, Annat caught the tail end of the circling crowd of crows, constantly on watch.

"You will have to be the Holy Bride today," whispered Hadass. "Normally Dalit and I take it in turns."

When they had returned to the house, Annat was enthroned and crowned with a crown of silver paper. She took charge and gave orders, while Govorin and Casildis brought in the midday meal they had prepared, since there was no law to prevent *Dzuzukim* from working. Annat had played the part of the Holy Bride before, so she knew what to do; it was her duty to see that the food was fairly distributed, that the eldest was served first and strangers did not go hungry. There was much unseemly laughter when Govorin suddenly remembered that he had forgotten to take Yuda his share, and was loudly rebuked by the latter.

After the meal was finished and the *Golem* had cleared away the dishes, Hadass and Dalit sat down to play cards, and invited the others to join them, while the *Rashim* retreated upstairs for a nap. Annat went to keep her father company, and found him sitting up in bed, reading a book in *Ebreu*. He closed it and looked up as she approached.

—*What is it, Missis?*

Annat smiled at the ease and pleasure of *sprechen*. She sat down on the edge of the bed, feeling a little awkward in her uncustomary white, and fingered the tassels on the massive coverlet.

—*What does it mean when you see the same person in two places at once?*

Yuda made a puzzled face.

—*I don't think I follow you, Missis.*

—*I came in here last night and saw Casildis lying on the bed. But when I went upstairs, she was asleep with Govorin.*

—*I think you must have dreamed it, Natka. Casildis was never here.*

Annat shook her head. —*I saw her.*

—*Then perhaps you should ask Casildis herself.*

Annat glanced towards the open door, through which she could hear the laughter of the card-players in the room below. She did not know when she would get the chance to speak to Casildis; she felt sneaky, trying to keep the matter secret from Govorin.

—*Perhaps you'd like me to do it,* thought Yuda, swinging his legs over the side of the bed and throwing back the coverlet.

"*Tate*, no!" she said, but he was already striding across the room towards the stair. Annat hurried after him, her skirts rustling, and caught at his arm, but he shook her off. She did not understand his sudden anger, which seemed to impel him to a reckless act.

Everyone in the room looked up in surprise as Yuda stopped in the doorway, suddenly swaying on his feet. He leaned on the door jamb, looking straight at Govorin, and said, "I want to speak to the Chief and his wife in private. Alone. Now."

Seeing his face, Dalit and Hadass did not pause to argue, but sprang to their feet, scattering playing-cards, and hurried into their bedroom. Yuda stepped into the room, turned without looking at Annat, and closed the door firmly, shutting her out on the landing.

When the Doyen dismissed him, Malchik hoped that he would be left to himself so that he could try to impose some order on his troubled thoughts. He could not understand why he did not

hate the old man as he should. He would have liked to talk to
Cluny, but instead a servant in green livery hurried him away
to the offices of the wardrobe, where he was measured and
draped in lengths of woollen cloth, both coarse and fine, as if
he were a bride making ready for her wedding. Great shears
sliced through the bolts of cloth, and silver needles flickered,
as the tailors set to work fashioning new robes for Malchik
more fitting to his status as the Doyen's grandson. He would
have been less uncomfortable if Sarl had not been there
throughout, watching in silence with a saturnine face as the
unfinished garments were pinned across Malchik's submissive
form. When the tailors were satisfied, Sarl conducted Malchik
to the armory to choose a weapon for him. Malchik looked in
dismay at the racks of gleaming swords and tall spears, and
wished he could have expressed his relief when Sarl furnished
him with a short dagger in a sheath. He could not help but notice the deference that everyone showed the Heir; Malchik received only cursory and curious stares from the men-at-arms
working on the armoury, and he heard their rough laughter as
Sarl led him away.

Rather than tiring of Malchik's company, the Heir pro-
ceeded to show him every corner of the castle, from the unclean darkness of the dungeons to the airy tower rooms where
the watchmen kept a vigil. Every one seemed to know Sarl,
and while some greeted him with open smiles and an untroubled countenance, others seemed wary and ill at ease, and
eager for him to leave. Malchik himself was more bored than
afraid; having understood that Sarl saw him as a convert rather
than a victim, he knew that his life was not in immediate danger. He forced himself to memorise the layout of the castle,
learning that Cluny's room was in the north-west tower, while
the Doyen had his apartments in the south-west. The question
he would have liked to ask, where the portal that gave entrance
to the upper world lay, he kept sealed in his mouth. He guessed
that it was the great door at the rear of the castle, which led out
to the stables and the servants' quarters. He noticed that this
door was more heavily guarded than the entrance, and that Sarl
did not take him outside. Malchik lingered on the threshold,
looking up at the pinnacles of the pines against the horizon

with an intense longing. Then he realised that, in La Souterraine, the high ramp of the natural amphitheater lay behind the
chateau, crowned with bare trees.

Malchik turned away from the open door, his heart full of
sadness. Even if the door had not been guarded, he did not
dare step outside. If he tried to leave La Souterraine against
the will of the Cold One, he knew that the seed of ice she had
buried in his mind would destroy him. He followed Sarl along
the carpeted corridor, feeling the cold air against his neck, and
knowing that he was turning away from the hope of freedom.

The Heir led Malchik back to Cluny's room, which Malchik
had observed to be much smaller than Sarl's own apartments
in the north-east tower. He wondered whether Cluny's illegiti-
macy explained the modesty of his lodgings, or whether there
was another reason. He had noticed that the main, if not the
only entrance to the dungeons lay at the base of the tower.

"Cluny's much younger than you, isn't he?" he said to Sarl
as they reached the landing on the spiral stair above Cluny's
chamber. Sarl looked startled, for it was the first time that
Malchik had ventured to speak other than in answer to a question.

"He's about the same age as you. An afterthought of my father's. The fruit of old loins," said Sarl, which was more information than Malchik cared to hear. He stared at Sarl,
wondering to himself why the Heir had no children. He wondered how far Sarl was aware that Malchik knew his secret.

"You will be as a son to me, in time," said Sarl, as if he had
partly understood what Malchik was thinking. "When I have
killed your father."

Malchik's gaze did not flinch. He felt as if the ice had
chilled him through. "You'll enjoy that, won't you, Sarl?" he
said.

Sarl's eyes seemed to focus on Malchik as if he had not
troubled to look at him before. He did not seem abashed by
Malchik's words, but he studied Malchik's face, as if seeking a
clue to his meaning. "You may watch, if you wish," he said.

Malchik shook his head. "No thanks," he said. "Though I
have no love for the man, I have no need to see him die." As
he spoke, he realised that he had found a weakness in Sarl, a

place where the corruption of the Goddess had made him vulnerable. However much her powers might change Malchik, they could not make him enjoy another's pain. He suspected that he would become as he felt now: stone cold and uncaring, as the Doyen could seem. He took a pace back, wondering if his revulsion showed in his expression.

Sarl folded his broad arms across his chest. He was not smiling, but he did not appear discomforted by what Malchik had said. "Don't you like the sight of blood, Vasilyevich?" he said.

Malchik felt a chill in the throat at the sound of his father's name. He wondered if Sarl was mocking him, trying to find his own weaknesses and soft places. But he was still in the grip of that all-pervading cold. He did not care whether Sarl thought him a coward. "It doesn't give me pleasure, no," he replied. "Now, if you'll excuse me, Mon Seigneur, I wish to lie down. No doubt we can continued this interview another time."

He felt that there was a touch of admiration in the look Sarl gave him, as if his cool manner had impressed the Heir. But the words Sarl spoke did not comfort him. "You have leave to go, boy. I can see that I was wrong to doubt you. The Goddess has chosen well."

Malchik closed the door of Cluny's chamber behind him and leaned against it, drawing in a deep breath. Although it was nearly dusk, he found Cluny standing once again at his easel, with a brush in his hand. Cluny glanced across at him and said, with a straight face, "Have you enjoyed your welcome to the Castle of Ademar?"

Malchik looked at him, pondering how to answer this question. He noticed that a truckle bed had been drawn out from beneath Cluny's bedstead, and made up with sheets and quilts.

"I didn't expect a welcome at all," he said.

"It was wise of you to tell my father of your birth. Now he looks on you as one of us," said Cluny, dabbing his brush in the blob of paint on his palette, and drawing it across the canvas.

"I never knew that my mother—" Malchik began. He stopped. "I doubt if she knew herself."

"Come and look at the painting," said Cluny, with a sudden,

warm smile. "I am beginning to think that it will turn out better than I expected."

Malchik went to stand at his shoulder, and gazed at the picture on the canvas. He was impressed by the image that he saw there, though it was not like anything he had seen before. It resembled the ornate background of an *eikon*, with stylised rocks and trees all limned with snow. Cluny glanced at his face. "I suppose it looks outlandish to you," he said with amusement.

"It looks—old," said Malchik hesitantly. "As if it were hundreds of years old, but only painted today."

Cluny put down his brush and palette, and turned to face Malchik. "You know that I have never left the forest," he said, simply. "My father forbids it. Our family has lived here for generations, since before the coming of the Great Cold."

"Now they are my family too. Isn't that strange?" said Malchik, wrinkling his forehead.

"It cannot continue. Strangers will come, sooner or later. My father believes that he can keep them out for ever."

"But he has accepted me. And I'm a stranger," said Malchik.

Cluny laid his hands lightly on Malchik's shoulders. "Are you truly going to stay here and serve him as your liege lord?" he said.

Malchik avoided his gaze. "You must know the answer to that, Cluny," he said.

"I want to hear it from you."

"No. Not in a thousand years. I have to get out of here as soon as possible."

Cluny turned away, and Malchik heard him draw breath. For a moment, he wondered if he had betrayed himself, until the young man said, "Thank the Mother. The Cold One has not mastered you yet. I couldn't bear to see someone else change as Jean has changed."

He swung back towards Malchik, his thin arms folded, hugging himself. "You do know that I am kept prisoner here," he said. Malchik shook his head. "My father does not refer to it, because of his shame. I told him to his face that I couldn't accept the pact that Jean has made with the Cold One, or my father's acquiescence in it. And yet it is only thanks to my brother's intervention that the Doyen did not have me imprisoned in the dungeons."

"So this tower is for prisoners," said Malchik.

"Prisoners of courtesy," said Cluny. "I may leave to take meat with the household, and to exercise once a day in the central court. Beyond that, I am pent up, and have no access either to La Souterraine or to the upper world."

"I am sorry," said Malchik. "And now you've had me foisted upon you."

Cluny stepped closer, his eyes bright. "It may be that I can do one good thing, one thing that could restore my family's proud name," he said.

"What do you mean?" said Malchik.

Cluny turned once again towards the canvas, where the latest layer of painting was drying. "I have my own secret magic," he said. "Something that neither my father nor Jean Sorel knows about. I can paint my image on to this canvas and escape for a while into La Souterraine. I must always return, for I painted the picture, but if I were to do so for you . . ."

"They brought me here by drawing a picture of the chateau in the snow," said Malchik.

"They use it when they need to travel swiftly, though they have only learned the means of returning to the castle. But if I sketched an image of you with my brush, you could be gone in a few moments."

Malchik studied the stylised landscape doubtfully. "Where would I be?" he said.

Cluny's smile deepened. "I am not sure where it is," he said. "It lies beyond the purlieus of the castle, but not far off. These trees that I have added here"—he pointed them out, at the edge of the scene—"form part of the wood that surrounds us."

"It might work," said Malchik. "But I am bound to Sarl by the seed of ice we both share. I'm sure he could follow. And somehow, I need to reach my family and friends. I don't know where they are. If I don't find them in time, they may come to the castle looking for me. They must guess that Sarl has brought me here."

"I understand," said Cluny. "Jean Sorel and my father will be waiting for them. Even if you should escape, the trap would still be baited unless you could warn them that you were free. Is there no way that you could discover where they are? You might even use the power of the Cold One."

Malchik bit his lip. "It doesn't work like that for me," he said. "I can't use her power. Not until I am wholly *in* her power. The only benefit so far has been my ability to sense what Sarl is thinking. I would rather be without that."

"We do not have much time," said Cluny. "Jean Sorel will try to work his will on you. I do not know what plans he has for you, but once he knows he can trust you, you are lost. Until then, you and I must try to think of a way to warn your people. If Sorel can use the crows to spy for him, there may be some way that we could use them to send a message."

"You will help me, then, Cluny?"

Cluny took Malchik's hand and held it. "By my mother's soul, I swear it," he said.

Annat stood on the landing, staring at the polished wood-grain of the door panels. After a few moments she heard raised voices, and turned away, stuffing her fingers in her ears. She sat down on the topmost step and curled herself into a ball, trying not to hear the angry sounds coming from the dining room. If only she knew where the *Rashim* had gone! She could go and fetch him, and he would stop them quarrelling. But that would mean disclosing to him what Yuda and Casildis had done, and she was sure he would condemn it; the Law of the Wanderers forbade adultery. She could not understand why Yuda had decided to confront the Sheriff and his wife together. It was as if the knowledge that Annat had seen Casildis with both men affronted him. She wondered what he was saying.

Suddenly, a small flame of anger ignited within her. It had been her dream or vision that prompted Yuda to demand an explanation, but he had shut her out of the room as if she were a little *kind*. She stood up, smoothing the skirt of her white dress. She was the Kingsday Bride, and he was not going to spoil the day by starting a quarrel. She looked at the door, feeling a chill beneath her breastbone at the thought of turning the handle and stepping into the room. One of her duties was to be a peacemaker, but she had always been the one who started the arguments at home. She wondered if she had the experience or commanded the respect to intervene in such a bitter dispute. Yuda might tell her it was none of her business and throw her out.

The door swung open, and Casildis stood before her. The woman was pale, except for two spots of high color on her cheekbones. Annat had never seen her so angry.

"Annat, where did you leave the doll?" she said, in a thin, controlled voice. Annat trembled.

"I left it on my pillow," she said.

"Please go to the bed where your father was sleeping and see whether or not it is there."

Puzzled, Annat was too frightened to argue. She hurried up to the *Rashim*'s study and turned over the covers of her father's bed. Sure enough, the doll lay there, as if Annat herself had placed it next to Yuda. She picked it up and stared at its painted features. She was certain that she had left it on her own pillow last night. She ran back down the stairs and held it out to Casildis without a word. The woman looked grim.

"I thought so," she said, without offering an explanation. She swept back into the dining room, and Annat darted after her before anyone could close the door. Yuda was standing by the window with his back to the room; Govorin was sitting at the table, resting his head on his hands. Casildis stopped at the end of the table, saying, "The doll was there, as I said. Do you believe me now?"

Govorin lowered his hands. His face was grey. "What does it matter whether or not I believe you?" he said. Yuda did not move.

Annat shrank into the corner, wishing already that she had not intruded where she did not belong. The pain in the room was tangible, like a scent or the presence of a third, unseen person. Casildis put the doll down on the table with a controlled movement, as if afraid she might throw it at someone. She glanced at Annat as if she hardly saw her.

"This cannot go on," she said, in a voice of iron.

"I understand your words, Casildis," said Govorin. "And that's all they are to me, words. I may not be like Sarl, for whom his wife is a chattel, but I can't take this story that somehow you love us both. It has no meaning for me."

Yuda turned round slowly. "That's where we're different, Mister," he said, looking at Govorin. "I've got no problem understanding what it is to love two people, only it cuts me to the bone. That's why I had to know what she was doing last night."

Casildis sat down at the table. "Then you know what it meant," she said. "Annat saw a shadow of me, not substance. The doll took my place, because you needed me. She has many strange powers, and she knew what was in my heart."

Yuda approached the table and leaned on it, looking straight at Govorin, as if he had not heard what Casildis said.

"What about you, Mister?" he said. "Can we go on, when you know how I feel? When there will always be something between us, like a mirror that doesn't reflect our faces?"

"I don't know," said Govorin. "I thought I knew you, Yuda. What hurts me, what destroys me, is that there's more than mere desire between you. That the two of you share something I can never share."

"Then kill me," said Yuda. "Get rid of me. I can't be the one to stand in your way."

He pulled the knife from his belt with his good hand, and offered it to Govorin. As the Sheriff took it from him, he pulled down the bandages that covered his heart.

Govorin weighed the knife in his hand. "No, Yuda," he said. "What makes you think I could kill you? I might as well cut my own throat." He threw the knife down on the table, where it landed between them. Yuda gazed into his face.

"Then I'm caught," he said. "Because I can't live without hurting you. Loving Casildis is like breathing to me, like bread or salt. And you know what you are to me."

"I know," said Govorin. "That's my problem. That you of all people should be the one. I'm not even man enough to hate you."

"I wish I could say sorry, Mister," said Yuda. "Sorry would never be enough. And in a way, I'm not sorry."

Govorin clenched his right hand into a fist. "That must be hard for you to say, Yuda," he said. "Harder for me to hear. But

I wanted the truth, not some mimsy half-felt apology. I expected as much from you, and you don't disappoint me. You
never have."

Yuda sat down at last at the table, leaning forward as if he
were about to faint. Casildis looked from one man to the other,
and said, "I am the one who broke my vows and betrayed a
trust. If Sarl knew, he would call me a whore. But I am the
priestess of the Bright Lady and not bound to any man, except
by choice. It was her will and my wish that I should lie with
Yuda. I am mortal and weak; she is a goddess. Though I cannot excuse what I have done, she gave her blessing to it."

Govorin reached across the table to take her hand. "I don't
know whether I can live with that, Missis," he said. "When I
take you in my arms, how will I know who you're thinking of?
You are the one thing I can't share. I want you for myself."

"I know," said Casildis. "For I could not share you with another woman. I would hate her with all my heart. I know how
you are torn. All I can plead is that, whether you believe me or
not, I have enough love for both of you. There is no corner of
my heart that loves you less, Sergey, because of Yuda. He is
different to you; so different."

"Well, here we are," said Govorin, stretching out his hands
to encompass the contents of the table: knife, doll and cards.
"We know where we stand. We each know what the other
thinks. Somehow, we have to carry on together."

Yuda looked towards Casildis, the fierce longing bare on his
face. "We have to go on as if nothing had happened," he said,
echoing Govorin. "As if we were free."

"You are free, Yuda," she said. He stood up, looking from
her to Govorin.

"No," he said, "I never was."

It was the evening of the day following Malchik's arrival at the
Castle of Ademar. The day had passed quietly, and he had received no further summons to the Doyen's presence. He had
supped with Cluny in their shared room, and spent a little time
wandering the chateau, trying to remember his way round. But
in the evening, he had grown strangely restless, and had wandered out into the central court, and from there to the great

door that opened on to La Souterraine. No one tried to stop him. At first, Malchik had been surprised and exhilarated as he made his escape, until he understood that an invisible thread was drawing him after Sarl, whose shadowy form he saw up ahead, moving on long skis across the empty grounds without looking back.

The night came suddenly, and the amber ball of Rogastron and its three moons filled the sky. The cold snapped shut on Malchik like a trap, reminding him that he was wearing only a tunic and hose. Though the thought of turning back came to him, he rejected it. He felt that he had gone too far. He staggered down the icy bed of a stream, following it between the shady, overhanging undergrowth towards the bottom of the hill. There was no sound here except his footsteps and his gasping breath; the trees watched him without eyes, and the snow seemed to have lost all trace of color, pallid as the skin of a corpse. Malchik looked neither to right nor to left, watching his feet as he sprang from step to step of the ice floe. The water beneath was thick and gelid, frozen into blue strands too shallow to sustain any life. Like the dark, empty vein in a dead man's throat, it was lifeless, a path that connected two nowheres.

He followed a blue ribbon of moonlight between the banks of shadow. He must have been walking for hours, and he did not want to struggle back up the steep slope. The sound of his heart seemed to have become dangerously loud. He went faster, slipping on the ice underfoot and disturbing lumps of snow from the banks as he skated from side to side. After what seemed much longer than a mile, the valley began to widen out, opening into a broad dell ringed with skeletal elms. Malchik waded across the perfect snow towards the far side, his feet making deep, clumsy holes through its surface. From time to time, he glanced up at the totem trees outlined against the phosphorescent sky. Then, when he was halfway across the dell, he looked up and felt his heart clench in his chest. A man's shape was standing outlined between the dead trees, his hands resting on the poles of skis. Malchik stopped where he was, gasping with terror. It was a few moments before he realised from the man's height and his bulk that it was Sarl himself.

The Prince of Ademar pushed off from the top of the slope and came gliding smoothly down to where Malchik stood, executing a twist that brought him to a halt close by.

"I knew you were going to follow me," he said, in a hot, meaningful voice. Malchik shuddered. He did not need to ask how Sarl knew when their minds were linked.

"What do you want with me?" he asked, rubbing his freezing hands together. He was not sure that he wanted to hear the answer.

Sarl threw back his head and laughed, a sound that echoed and re-echoed from the glacial shadows. "Still afraid?" he said, with a scornful kindness. "I have not brought you all this way to do you harm. I bear you no ill will. We are two of a kind, you and I. The Cold One dwells in each of us. The only difference is that I asked her to enter me, of my own free will. I knew what I was doing."

"You brought me all this way to tell me that?" said Malchik.

"We are closer to the Goddess out here. As close as we can be, in her own land. The Cold One is exiled from La Souterraine; a piece of old magic cast her out, and she roams the upper world, in exile."

"But I thought—"

"She drove you through, but she could not return herself. She haunts the Forest of Ademar, hungry and alone. Only one thing can bring her back: a sacrifice."

Malchik hugged himself. "And you want to bring her back," he said.

"It was the one price she asked of me. We made a bargain. I gave her my soul, and in return . . ." He paused, smiling at Malchik. "The time will come when I tell you what she has done for me—for Ademar. All you need to know is that she requires the death of a shaman, but not in just any place; the shaman must die within the Rotunda, at the heart of her *domaine*."

Malchik gazed at Sarl, guessing too well that he himself was a possible candidate for the sacrifice. He quelled an unsuitable desire to laugh, and answered, "I presume you intend to offer yourself?"

Sarl looked at him oddly, as if he could not tell whether Malchik was mocking him. "The victim has not yet been chosen," he said. "I am the Cold One's faithful servant, and she does not require my life. If you follow her as I have done, you need not fear that you will be chosen. See how my powers have increased. I was always a powerful shaman, but since I submitted to her, I have grown so strong that your father himself did not detect me—until it was too late. I have had to hide my powers in the castle, though my father knows that I serve—and am served by—the Goddess. You too could find strength that now you can only dream of, and have men fear you, and fear to cross you."

Malchik looked up at him. "I don't crave that sort of power, Sarl," he said. "Yes, I could grow strong in Ademar. I could become your father's most trusted adviser, and direct his policies. I could rule like the hand in his glove. But I would pass through the corridors like a shadow, and no one would bend the knee to me. I don't seek what you offer me, and I don't need to achieve it. I have my own pact with the Cold One—or I could have, if I chose to submit."

Sarl gazed at him for a while before speaking. "You always surprise me, little grub," he said. "You are wiser than you seem. To begin with, I wondered why the Goddess had chosen such a weakling—I thought she could only overcome you because you were weak. Yet twice today you have shown me another side. I doubt your simple father knows you are so subtle."

The thought of Yuda blazed like a beacon in Malchik's mind. "Oh, he knows me," he said. "He knows the darkness in me. And it was that which drew the Goddess to me, like a bee to sweet pollen. She loves the scent of darkness." He turned away, afraid his face would show his revulsion.

Sarl's voice came from behind him. "I think you are ready to join our cause," he said. "I shall tell my father what he needs to know of this meeting. It maybe that you will take the place of Cluny in his affection, when he sees what service you can give to us. Behold!"

There was a rattle of wings and Malchik turned, startled, to see a solitary black bird alight on Sarl's wrist, as if it were a hawk. The crow perched there with folded wings, and the one eye Malchik could see was a hole into darkness.

"The crows have reached Masalyar," he said. "The strangers do not know it yet, but they will come to regret the time they decided to trespass upon the lands of Ademar."

Chapter 16

When the time came for them to leave Chorazin, they gathered in the *Rashim*'s chambers in a mood of quiet foreboding. They had decided to make for the Castle of Ademar, to spy out the land and see whether they could discover Malchik's whereabouts. None of them was in any doubt that it was a hazardous errand, since they no longer knew whether Sarl was still behind them, or whether he had gone on ahead, taking Malchik with him, and was waiting for them to follow.

Annat had laid aside her silken frock from yesterday, and the cotton night-dress trimmed with lace that she had borrowed from Hadass, keeping only the plain linen gown that she knew would be serviceable. The others had asked to keep their new clothes, and Casildis was elegant in a dark satin that had belonged to the *Rashim*'s late wife, while Yuda and Govorin wore the black suits and white shirts of Wanderer men. Hadass had given Annat a black ribbon to tie back her hair, a luxury she had not previously enjoyed.

The *Rashim* greeted them solemnly, and motioned to them to sit. "You are going from here on a long journey," he said. "It may be that you will become our saviours, and free us from this netherworld to which we are now chained. I cannot see into the future, and so I shall not prophesy, but I do know that you go into danger, and face a darkness from which you may

not return. Therefore I give you each my blessing, and call
down upon your heads all the Blessings of the Almighty, who
knows the beginning and the end of every journey. I have a
few simple gifts for you, of which the simplest but the most
useful lies at my feet." He pointed to the floor beneath his
desk, and Annat saw that he was showing them a neat bundle
of skis, beautifully made from polished wood.

"Thank you, *Rashim*," said Govorin. "Those are going to be
more than useful."

"You will need them to reach the Castle of Ademar. It does
not lie close to the line; whoever built the track took pains to
avoid it. But apart from the skis, I have something to give to
each of you." He beckoned to Annat, who approached the desk
shyly. The *Rashim* stretched out his hand and let something
fall into her palm; he was careful not to touch her. She found
that he had given her a tiny circular box, wrought from silver
and mother-of-pearl. "Do not open the box until you need it,"
he said. "It contains some of the dust from the *Golem*'s brow.
It cannot give life, for only the One may do that, but it can
confer substance on that which is shadow, or make the inani-
mate move."

Annat found herself bobbing a curtsey; she slipped the
small, cold box inside the bodice of her dress. The *Rashim*
now turned to Casildis. "I have not forgotten you, Madame,"
he said. "I am sorry that I spoke to you as an enemy. This little
thing I made as a young man; it was my prentice-piece when I
worked as a jeweller in the outer world." Annat saw him drop
a tiny sphere into Casildis's hand. "It contains an unbreakable
thread that is as long as you need it to be," said the *Rashim*
with a faint smile, though he kept his eyes downcast. "It will
not carry the weight of a man, but is stronger than it looks, like
spider-thread. Perhaps there is a spider in there somewhere, at
the heart of things. It used to please my children when they
were small; perhaps in time, it will please your children also."

"I have never been afraid of spiders," said Casildis, smiling
back at him, and putting the ball into the pocket of her gown.

The *Rashim* called Yuda next. "My son," he said, taking
Yuda's hand. "I wish I could give you what you most need: a
wise heart. But the young seldom heed an old man's counsel.

Instead, all I have for you is a stone of little value that my father wore, and his father before him." He gave Yuda a plain latten ring with a black pebble set in the bezel. Yuda slipped it over his index finger, and held it up to the light.

"There's fire inside it, down in the depths," he said thoughtfully.

"Perhaps," said the *Rashim*. "It is the first time I have taken it off, since my father gave it to me. But I do not think my sons will miss it."

Govorin was the last. "But not the least," said the *Rashim*. "You are the first man descended from the burning lands that I have met. I wish that I had a better gift for you; your modesty and strength have impressed me, though you have said little. You may also be the first *Dzuzuk* who has spoken to me as a man, not a dog. Such things are greatly valued by the downtrodden, though it may seem a small matter to you. So to you I give this jewel, and the chain to wear it, because you already have that the price of which is above rubies." He handed Govorin a small locket on a gold chain, which the Sheriff put over his head and tucked inside his shirt.

"I'm speechless," said Govorin, beaming. "We ought to be giving you presents, *Rashim*, in gratitude for your hospitality. I'm afraid we haven't been the most comfortable guests."

"All strangers are welcome, Wanderers and *Dzuzukim* alike," said the *Rashim*. "But now I must send you away, for sadness has tired me. I trust in the One that He will bring you back to me, when all is finished."

"I doubt that we'll return, *Rashim*," said Yuda. "Even if we can rescue Malchik, we still lack the means to free him from the seed of ice that the Cold One has planted in him."

The *Rashim* passed his hand over his eyes. "Then you must seek the *domaine* of the Goddess," he said. "It lies to the east of here, I know not how far. But I do not doubt that the Railway line will lead you there. And I fear that indeed I will not see you again."

After they had said their farewells, they made their way through the streets to the train, and many passers-by stopped to say goodbye and to wish them well. They found that the tender had been filled with wood, and water poured into the tank, but no one had been foolhardy enough to light the fire on the grate. While Govorin and Yuda set to work to fire up the boiler, Annat and Casildis tidied through the debris of belongings, blankets, packs and cook-pans, trying to restore some order. Suddenly, Casildis said, "What is that the price of which is above rubies?"

"Hmm?" said Annat absently. "A woman of valour."

"A woman of *valour*?" Casildis repeated.

"Maybe it was virtue," said Annat, turning the harp over in her hands. "Why do you ask?"

"I don't know. Just a phrase I heard, that stayed in my mind," said Casildis, settling down in the space she had cleared and covered with a blanket amongst the logs.

Suddenly there was a shout from the other side of the river. Standing up to see who it was, Annat saw the small figure of Hadass crossing the ice, her hair flaming as she ran, slipping and sliding on the smooth surface. Annat scrambled out of the tender, jumped down from the engine and went to meet her. Breathless, Hadass flung her arms about Annat. "I couldn't let you go without saying goodbye," she said. "I wish you could stay with us longer. I was only just getting to know you."

Annat hugged the slim form against her. "I wish I could stay too, but I'm worried about Malchik," she said. Hadass slipped from her arms and stood facing her, panting.

"I would like to come with you," she said. "I have never ventured outside Chorazin."

Annat clasped her hands together. "It will be too dangerous," she said, aware that the engine at her back was getting up steam, ready to depart. "You don't have a shaman's powers, and we would have to protect you. But I wish you could come too. I think we could be friends."

"We are friends already," said Hadass, flashing a smile at her. "And I will be waiting for you when you get back from your journey. Perhaps by then Dalit will have persuaded our *Tate* to let her marry Natan ben Shmuel!"

They shared a laugh before Hadass darted forward to kiss Annat on the cheek. "May the One bless you, wherever you go," she said, fiercely.

"And you too," said Annat. She took Hadass's hand and

held it for a moment, before turning back to the train and climbing into the cab. She found that Yuda and Govorin had been watching her, but she turned her back on them and stood in the cab door, watching Hadass standing by the trackside as the train began slowly to pull away, wreathing itself in garlands of steam. Hadass began to wave, jumping up and down on the spot, and Annat waved back at her, with a heart full of strange emotions that seemed to include both laughter and tears. She carried on waving until the small black figure with fiery hair was no more than a speck in the distance. Then she went forlornly to sit beside Casildis in the tender, and was not very surprised when the woman put her arm round her. Annat leaned her head against Casildis's shoulder, thinking of the two kinds of loss: of Malchik stolen, locked up inside the castle; and of Hadass standing alone by the empty halt, watching the black train as it receded into the distance of danger. She picked up the doll out of their muddled heap of belongings, and hugged it to her chest, wishing that once more it would speak to her to let her know what she should do.

Malchik's dreams were full of the black wings of crows, circling overhead in the darkness. He kept seeing the streets of Masalyar, bright in the winter sunshine, until a shadow fell across them, the pattern of wheeling wings . . . He sat up in bed with a start, to see that the shutters stood ajar, letting light flood into the room. Cluny was up and dressed, already working at his easel, where he was trying to paint a steam train from Malchik's description; but the result looked more like a cross between a stove and a dragon, a fantastical monster that leaked spouts of steam from many orifices. Malchik climbed out of bed and padded across the floor in his bare feet to examine the picture, as Cluny stepped back to inspect his handiwork.

"What do you think, Malchik?" he said, with a note of pride in his voice.

"I think it looks like nothing on earth," said Malchik, picking up a slice of the manchet bread that had been brought for them to break their fast, and ignoring the wine.

Cluny gave him a playful punch, too light to hurt. "I have

been up since before dawn working on it, and listening to you snore," he said. "I find your lack of gratitude most disappointing."

Malchik choked on a morsel of dry bread and suffered a coughing fit, for Cluny had exactly mimicked the Doyen's voice and the manner of his speech. While he was swallowing a mouthful of the sour wine to clear his throat, there was a knock at the door.

"What now?" said Cluny to Malchik in a low voice.

"The Doyen requires the presence of Messieur Paul d'Iforas in his private chambers at once," said a man's loud voice from the landing outside.

"He will be with you presently," said Cluny, turning to look at Malchik in his night-shirt. The two of them scurried about the room, laughing as silently as they could; and while Malchik flung his night-shirt on the floor, snatching up his drawers and hose, Cluny threw him one of the newly made tunics and a fine cloak of red wool that the tailors had provided. At last, Malchik was dressed, and dragging his fingers through his hair, he opened the door to the green-liveried man-at-arms, who was waiting outside with every sign of impatience.

"My master does not like to be kept waiting," he said. Malchik adjusted the dagger on its belt round his waist, and hurried after the man, grateful that he did not have a sword and scabbard to stumble over. They hastened down the carpeted corridor of the passageway that connected the north-west to the south-west tower, and mounted the spiral stair to the next floor up, where the servant flung open the door and announced, "Messieur Paul d'Iforas," in a breathless voice. Malchik was having to become accustomed to using both his Franj names, since the Doyen had decreed that these were more suitable than his Sklavan ones. He hastily performed a low bow on the threshold, as Cluny had taught him, and waited to be invited to enter the room. As he straightened, he saw with surprise the millefleurs tapestries that decked the walls rippling in the breeze, as if the stone room were enclosed in a bank of glowing flowers. It was hard to associate the stark building and its austere lord with anything so delicate.

"Enter," said the Doyen in his harsh voice, and Malchik

stepped on to the polished parquet floor, where a single rug was spread before the hearth, and a liver-colored hound slept close to the embers.

The Doyen was not alone. Sarl stood behind his chair, with his back to the mullioned window, dressed in a long tunic of amber wool, a holly-green cloak and dark hose. He seemed completely relaxed, and the jewels at his hands and throat caught stars from the flickering fire. The Doyen was at ease in a fur-lined robe, worn over a long crimson gown with a golden belt. He beckoned Malchik to approach, and indicated that he should sit on a small stool by his feet. The room was sparsely furnished, except for a wooden buffet set against one wall, whose carved arches mimicked in dark oak the trefoils of the window.

Malchik settled himself on the stool and looked up uneasily at the Doyen's face. The old man seemed to be considering him with a faint smile on his thin lips.

"We are pleased with you, boy," he said. "My heir has told me of your readiness to serve the cause of Ademar, and to lend us your knowledge of matters that lie beyond these walls and this *domaine*."

"I am honoured, Mon Seigneur," said Malchik, studying the old man's face and trying not to see Sarl's behind his shoulder.

The Doyen nodded. "You should be so, for your birth was base, and I must strive to forget that you have blood of the Wanderers in you. But many such who have renounced their error and been anointed to the true faith have risen to positions of great power in the Empire." He leaned back in his chair, folding his hands together. "The Empire is no more than a memory," he said. "It would be a noble work to restore its greatness. But I have not brought you here to listen to an old man's dreams. Has Jean Sorel spoken to you of the enterprise in which we are engaged?"

Malchik found his gaze drawn to Sarl's face. He looked away swiftly. "The Heir told me that you would bestow that knowledge upon me, Mon Seigneur," he said, choosing his words carefully. He was aware that the elaborate phrases of the Doyen's speech hid an artful manipulation of words that could produce subtle inflections of meaning.

"He has done well," said the Doyen, nodding. "My son and I are of like mind in this. For three years we have suffered patiently while the strangers trespassed upon our lands. At first, we were lenient, taking but a few lives here and there, as a warning, yet they continued to build their accursed tunnel, defiling my property and disturbing the peace of the forest, which no impious hand had cut for hundreds of years." He rested his head on his hand. "It grieves me, boy, to see goodly trees hewn down, and mean, ugly edifices raised in their place. My fathers ruled in these parts long before the coming of the Great Cold, and so it has continued, from father to son, until my time. It has been my lot to see both the Wanderers multiplying like rats on the borders of my *domaine*, and the coming of hellish engines that spew forth fire and smoke from their entrails. I have sworn by the souls of my fathers that I will rid the forest of trespassers, and I will do so, if I have to kill them all." He glanced over his shoulder, towards Sarl.

"We know what will happen if we drive the strangers out," said the Heir. "Others will come to replace them. The Southerners will not leave us alone. They will send troops to enforce their will. It matters not. We are ready for them. We are raising an army to lance the evil at its source."

"This was my son's plan, and his thought. One by one, our enemies will feel the edge of our sword. We shall cleanse this land of its impurities. I see from your face, boy, that you understand me well."

Malchik hoped that his expression did not betray the growing dismay that he was feeling. "You can draw upon the power of the Goddess, Mon Seigneur," he said, trying to keep his voice neutral.

"That is our intent," said the Doyen. "She has felt the anguish of a mother as ungodly feet trample her sacred groves. It is she who has served us as a faithful Genius, killing the stragglers and the unwary for us. In return, we nave promised her far greater banquets of slaughter, and the souls of our enemies. Do I shock you, boy? Does it trouble you that one who calls himself a true son of Doxa can make such an alliance?"

Malchik had to choose his words with care. "It seems to me, Mon Seigneur, that you have weighed the honour of your house in the scale against the tenets of Doxa, and found one lighter than the other."

"You have a quick wit and a clever tongue, boy," said the Doyen. "I have not lapsed from the true faith, but Jean Sorel in his wisdom has shown me the benefits of nurturing this ancient power, which the ignorant call a goddess. No, boy. She is the *Genius Loci*, the spirit of the forest itself, which has called out to us for aid and made common cause with us in our hour of need."

Malchik's head ached. He wondered whether the old man believed his own words, or whether Sarl had convinced him by some piece of sophistry that there was no conflict between serving the Cold One and the Church.

"What, then, is your plan, Mon Seigneur?" he said.

"Did not Jean tell you? Even Masalyar lies within reach of our arm. When we raise our standard, the foe will fall before us like corn before the scythe."

"He has seen the crows, Mon Seigneur," said Sarl, leaning over the back of the Doyen's chair. "He knows how far our outriders have advanced. One day soon, those decadent citizens will look north and see a great shadow coming, descending upon them like a thunderhead."

"I—tremble at the thought of your might, Jean Sorel," said Malchik. As soon as the words were out of his mouth, he realised that they sounded ironic, but it was too late.

The Doyen gave him a smile that seemed to change his withered face. "You have nothing to fear, boy," he said. "So long as you give us faithful service, our countenance will be as the noonday sun, smiling upon you. For you have chosen the better part, and the curse of the Wanderers is lifted from you, as if it had never been. Though your blood will never be as pure as that of unstained lineage, your zeal as a convert will be rewarded fourfold, and your abjuration of error will bring you rejoicing to the feet of Megalmayar."

Malchik found himself looking at Sarl, and Sarl unmistakably gave him a wink. He glanced away hastily, fearing that his face would turn red. "I only regret that I came to Gard Ademar as a trespasser, Mon Seigneur," he said, warily.

"You could not know, any more than the strangers did," said

the Doyen. "They took no thought as to our ancient rights, but claimed a share of the forest as if it were lawless wilderness. In this, they have done no more than befits their ignorance and rapacity, as men do who are little better than brigands. Such recklessness deserves due punishment."

"But Jean Sorel has surely told you of the shamans that they have engaged to protect them, Mon Seigneur," said Malchik, privately hoping that this remark might embarrass Sarl.

"I have heard of their conjuring and their incantations, of their spells and other mummeries. They do not frighten me. I shall deal with them as I have always dealt with sorcerers. My Jean is adept at catching such jugglers. And when we have them, they burn like any other folk."

"Burn, Mon Seigneur?" said Malchik.

"We give them the mercy of the garrotte. Then their bodies are reduced to ashes. Not all seigneurs show such lenience."

Malchik bowed his head as if in assent, but his heart was far from compliant. He had to do something, and swiftly, before he became implicated in the deeds of this hideous family. He could not retreat into imprisonment and paint pictures, like Cluny. It was clear that Sarl had no intention of leaving him alone. He thought of his family, and tried not to imagine what would happen if Sarl ever laid hands upon them.

Yuda was singing as he shovelled wood from the tender into the firebox. Annat recognised the tune; it was the song Malchik had played at the feast of the Bear People, which seemed not a few days but months gone by.

"A *red* ship goes sailing out *on* the shining sea,
She *flies* on the dawn wind that *comes* in the night
I *stood* on the shoreline with a *lantern* in my hand
And the *flame* of the candle burning bright."

Yuda was stressing certain words as he plunged the shovel in amongst the logs, then heaved them into the firebox. Sometimes it was hard to hear his voice with the noise of the wind and the roaring of the engine; at other times, he sang out loud and clear. *Isabel's song*. Annat thought of the gentle ghost and wondered if she still followed them, watching over them as a benign but insubstantial presence. Though Yuda sang vigorously, the wistful nature of the words seemed to emphasise the uncertainty of their position, like a red flag waved in defiance against a thunderous sky.

"How will we know when we have reached the Castle of Ademar?" she asked Casildis. They had been travelling for about an hour, and had recently left behind the river plains with their knotted willows, to enter a swathe of darkly wooded hills, where the trees pressed up to the line on either side. Though the river still kept pace with them, frozen in its stony bed, the atmosphere was gloomy and oppressive.

Casildis leaned forward to pull on her shoes, which she had kicked off while she was sitting amongst the blankets. "I think that one of us should keep a watch, as soon as the land changes," she said. "It is strange to think that I will be approaching this time as an enemy."

"We used to have skis at home, but we never did it for fun," said Annat. "Only when we needed to go out beyond the village for supplies."

Casildis divided her hair into two long strands, and began to plait it. "I don't think we shall be skiing for pleasure this time," she said. "I hope that your father or my husband has made a plan for what we shall do when we come to the castle. My father the Doyen used to keep it stoutly guarded, but he may not think that needful in this world."

Having plaited her hair and fixed it in a crown on top of her head, Casildis clambered from the tender into the cab where she paused to exchange a few words with Yuda. Annat gave a little shiver, for their bodies when they stood close together still spoke the language of passion, even if they themselves were not conscious of it. She hoped that Govorin was too busy watching the line ahead to notice. But something told her that Yuda and Casildis, though they stood apart, were sharing a moment of warmth against the danger ahead, as if one had sipped from a cup of hot liquid before passing it to the other. When Casildis went to stand in the doorway, grasping her wide skirts with one hand to stop them flapping about in the wind, Yuda did not pause in his work to gaze after her, as he

might have done before. Whatever their feelings, they were
partners in an enterprise for which thoughts of desire had to be
set aside.

Annat too scrambled over the packed logs so that she could
watch the landscape passing by from over the top of the tender. Looked at head-on, it rushed past in a blur of dark green
foliage, forming repeated patterns before her eyes. Feeling
dizzy, she clung to the edge of the tender, her thoughts
whirling like eddies in her mind. She wished she had stayed in
the warmth of the *Rashim*'s house, where the *Golem* would
have been there to protect her, even though she was afraid of
it. The fear she confronted now had no face, only the outline of
Sarl's silhouette and a handful of names: the Doyen, the Castle
of Ademar. She wondered how Govorin, Casildis and Yuda
managed to master their terrors. She received no scent of apprehension from her father, even though he knew he was facing a fight. He was working too hard, driving out the
imaginings with each stroke and swing of the shovel.

The terrain before her slowly began to open out, and the
trees to grow thinner and further apart. Instead of the leafy,
close-packed firs, tall frames of oak, beech and elm rose in
solitary desolation out of the smooth snow, like candelabras
whose tapers had long ago burnt out, leaving them blackened
and empty. Casildis watched for a while, then left her place in
the door and with quick strides approached her husband, taking hold of his broad arm. Annat knew what this meant;
Casildis must have seen something reminiscent of the parkland
that surrounded the castle in the upper world. She saw Govorin
wind the reversing handle and stoop to pull on the brake lever.
As the train bowled to a halt, she felt her heart pummelling her
ribs like a fist. When the locomotive stopped, she was out of
the tender in an instant, joining the others in the cab.

"What are we going to do?" said Casildis.

"Go down there slow, to scout out the land," said Yuda. "We
need to get a view of the castle without them seeing us."

"We don't know for certain that Malchik's there," said
Annat, anxiously.

"I reckon we can be pretty certain he's there. Where else
would Sarl have taken him?"

Govorin gave a grim smile. "What troubles me most is where Sarl is now," he said. "He could be at the castle, or still on our tail. I'd be happier if I knew."

"You and me both, Mister," said Yuda. "I'd be happiest of all if I knew what he was thinking." He bit at his fingernails, adding, "There's one sure way to find out; wait for him to jump at us from out of the bushes."

"There are no bushes," said Casildis.

"But there are these damn trees. I don't like trees," said Yuda. Turning to Annat, he said, "You'd better stay close to me, Missis. I've got a bad feeling about this. I'd be happier if Sarl had tried to ambush us before now, by sticking a log across the line or rolling boulders down on our heads. I reckon he knows we're coming."

Govorin unwrapped the bundle of skis and ski poles, and divided them out. While he was doing so, Casildis put on her bow and the quiver with its few remaining arrows. The skis were designed for cross-country travel, with a simple toe-strap. Annat found that someone had provided a smaller pair to fit her. One by one, they jumped down from the cab and slipped their feet into the straps. She reflected that it would be hard to ski and fight at the same time, unless you were remarkably skilled, or were carrying a gun. Watching Casildis glide down to the foot of the embankment, Annat judged that she looked skilful enough to manage the skis and handle her bow. She followed, hesitantly at first, but found that her feet soon remembered the movements, and executed a smooth turn below the bank, confident that at least she could stay upright. Yuda and Govorin followed less elegantly, taking steps down the bank on the flat of their skis.

"You'd better lead, Missis," Yuda said to Casildis, who was scanning the landscape ahead, shading her eyes.

"I think this way is best," said Casildis, setting off at a diagonal towards the north-east. "The castle lies in a valley."

The four of them moved in a diamond-shaped formation, with Casildis in the lead, Annat and Yuda together in the centre and Govorin bringing up the rear. Mist hung amongst the trees and the sky above was grey as woodsmoke. It was soon clear to Annat that Yuda was an accomplished skier, sliding first his left and then his right ski along at a walking pace, and moving his legs into parallel when they came to a downwards slope. Govorin, who followed them, was more competent than graceful, but he did not lag behind.

They moved amongst the crucified trees, which seemed to grasp at the sky with desperate fingers. Casildis kept up a steady rhythm, sometimes striding, sometimes gliding along and turning at the end to see if they were following her. Her figure stood out amongst the trees with its dark, long-skirted coat and high-piled crown of hair. Annat poled towards her, glancing from time to time at the dells and hillocks over which they were passing, and reflecting that with the trees in their autumn leaf it could have been a beautiful place, which now seemed desolate and ominous.

At last they came to the edge of a wide, steep slope, which swept down into a crescent-shaped valley below. The castle that lay at the bottom was a whitewashed structure with a massive barrel tower at each corner, crowned by a cone-shaped roof of red clay tiles. Some of the windows were mere slits, but others were large and blank, set high in the wall and paned with glass. It was both a defensible castle and a chateau: a dwelling for a country lord who lived amongst his serfs. Casildis leaned on her ski-poles, gazing down at it.

"This is my father's chateau, just as you would see it in the Forest of Ademar," she said.

"It's not what I was expecting," said Govorin, rubbing his eye. "Somehow I imagined it would look more—sinister."

"I grew up here, remember?" said Casildis.

"It feels sinister enough to me," said Yuda, leaning on his ski-poles.

As he spoke, there was a cawing and a rush of wings in the air above them, as if they had disturbed a crowd of rooks from their nests. *A murder of crows* . . . thought Annat. The next moment, with the shrieking of a nightmare wind, a flock of black shapes swept down upon them, beating at them with bony wings, and clawing at their faces. Annat threw up her arms to shield her head, and glimpsed the others, staggering and slipping under the onslaught of black feathers. The birds were eyeless frames of bone and feather. Their cries tore the sky, and they beat against her, pecking and tearing. Though she shut her eyes tight, she could feel their beaks and raking claws, grating against her skin and probing her clothes.

She heard Casildis cry out in anger; opening her eyes, she saw the woman struggling to loose an arrow from her bow. Yuda was bowed down to the ground beneath a mass of wings. Govorin punched the air with his hands, striking out to right and left; a few carcasses had fallen at his feet. Caught in a cloud of pinions, Annat stumbled towards her father, struggling to sure the power within into her hands. Suddenly there was a lightning flash, a stench of singeing down, and the bird-cluster that clung to Yuda exploded. Bleeding from his cheeks and hands, he struggled to his feet, as the bodies thudded smoking to the ground about him. She saw Casildis loose a bolt into the screaming mass above them. The arrow flared and fizzled; it soared into the air, rending the cloud apart, and plunged to earth like a rocket, burying itself up to the flights in snow.

Yuda threw his hands out in a gesture of defiance, and the blue lightning crackled from his palms, surging towards Annat. She saw it earth in the feathered bodies around her, making them sear and smoulder. Suddenly, she was free. The cloud of cawing birds wheeled round them, gathering itself for a new attack. Once more, Casildis strung an arrow to her bow. She aimed high, deep into the heart of the block. The shaft went up like a flare, spinning in flight, and was lost to sight in the dark mass above. Annat ran to her father's side, staring at the sky, and saw the darkness lift, wheeling away to the east. Before she could draw breath in relief, arrows began to fall like rain. Yuda threw himself to the ground, pulling her with him. All around, Annat could hear the whining buzz of the shafts; one fell spent on the snow near her hand. She clung to Yuda's hand, willing herself not to be afraid.

—*It is the Cold One*, she thought.

He did not answer, but his fingers squeezed hers. The arrows whined and thudded around them, plunging into the snow. An arrowhead buried itself fin the sleeve of her coat, pinning her to the ground. Then she heard someone cry out, a man's voice, in agony. Shielding her head, she sat up, with

Yuda beside her. The shower of shafts ceased, as suddenly as it had begun. Govorin was on his knees, crawling across the snow, to where Casildis lay on her side, the bright hair spilling from her head. A black-feathered shaft protruded from her side, under her left breast. Yuda sprang up and ran to where she lay, turning her over on to her back. Casildis moaned, her fingers playing with the wood of the shaft.

"Mother, Yuda, what are we going to do?" cried Govorin. Yuda did not answer, but snapped off the arrow shaft and flung it away. He took Casildis's face in his hands, gentle and rough at the same time.

"Casildis!"

"Shot with my own arrow," Casildis murmured. Yuda drew his hand across her lips, and looked at his palm.

"No blood," he said. "You'll have to get her back to the train, Mister Govorin. If we wait here, they'll come down on us. I can feel them."

"You've got to heal her, Yuda."

"Soul Men, Sergey. You know what that means? You must get her away from here. Get out the arrowhead. I don't think it's entered the lung, or the heart. But there's no time for me to heal. Annat and I will have to face the Soul Men."

Govorin hid his face in his hands. "Damn you, Yuda," he said, softly. "I'll do as you say. But if she dies, I'll send you after."

Yuda straightened. "She won't die," he said, mirthlessly. He stooped suddenly, and kissed Casildis on the mouth. "Don't you die on me, woman," he said.

Govorin scooped Casildis up in his arms and struggled to his feet. She was a much lighter burden for him than she had been for Yuda. He gave Yuda a look somewhere between hate and despair, and turned away, beginning the climb back into the trees, leaving the skis abandoned on the snow.

—*Soul Men?* Annat thought.

Yuda nodded, pulling black gloves from his pockets. He went to retrieve his abandoned skis, and began to put them on.

—*Let's get out into the open,* kind. *Away from these fucking trees.*

They skied out on to the edge of the hill, poling along the

crescent-shaped valley to the left. Yuda kept glancing from the castle below them to the thicket on their left.

—*I can't sense anything,* Annat told him.

—*After a few years, you get to know the signature they leave. I'm sorry, Natka; I don't think we're likely to survive.*

—*But you destroyed those other ones!*

—*That was different.*

He began to glide down the slope, moving nearer to the castle. Its white walls gleamed in the cold light of the sky. A small black figure, he turned and waited for her.

The assault came suddenly, almost before she had reached him. Tall shapes in white cloaks and high white hoods with holes cut out for eyes seemed to rise up out of the snow. As they came gliding down the hill, Annat recognised the twisted force of their conjoined minds, and the stench of madness and evil. Yuda pulled her against him, and they stood back to back, kicking off their skis. The masked men began to run round them in an unending circle, weaving a violet torus of power. She heard Yuda swearing under his breath. He crouched down, snatched up a handful of snow, and shaped it into a ball. When he threw it at the force-field, it fizzed and evaporated in a puff of steam.

Annat became aware of another figure that stood aloof amongst the trees at the top of the slope. Focusing on him, she recognised Sarl, clad in a green cloak and a long green tunic, with a sword belted at his hip. Yuda had seen him too.

"I knew it," he said baring his teeth. "I hope Govorin got clear away."

—*What are we going to do?*

—*This.*

Crouching low, he ran from the centre of the circle towards the pulsing torus, and before Annat could cry out, he had flung himself against it. For an instant, the sky went black. There were screams, and flashes of magenta and crimson lightning tore the air. Plumes of flame shot up into the sky, and there was a smell of burning flesh. Yelling Yuda's name, Annat ran towards the place where she had last seen him, and stumbled over his body. His clothes were still smoking, and she smelled singed hair. She rolled him over and cried out at the sight of his blackened face. Then his eyes opened, and he raised his hand to wipe off the soot. The edges of his hair had frizzed up and burnt, and his garments were wrapped in ash, but he was unharmed. The Soul Men had not escaped so lightly. Two bodies lay charred and smouldering on the snow, and a third was alight, a running, crying human torch. Annat buried her face in Yuda's arm.

—*I thought you were dead.*

—*Don't you ever do that, Missis,* he thought, gripping her by the upper arms.

The remaining Soul Men were regrouping. Once again, they began to process in a circle round Yuda and Annat. He stroked her hair with a hand that stank of smoke.

—*See, we won't get away. I can't do that again. There are too many of 'em, and Sarl is in control. A sane shaman makes the gestalt much stronger.*

As he finished speaking, Annat saw the faint violet shadow of the ring of power begin to re-establish itself. The Soul Men were closing in, weaving their hands in complex patterns. Yuda slowly stood up and put his arm round Annat's shoulders.

—*All we can do is wait.*

—*What is going to happen to us?*

Yuda gazed up at the still figure on the hill. Sarl's face was like thunder.

—*This is a binding spell. I don't think he's planning to kill us right off. Unfortunately.*

The Soul Men drew closer, and Annat thought she could see eyes through the holes in their hoods. She clung to Yuda, trying to imagine how she might protect him. The wavering, humming ring was tightening about them like a lasso. Yuda was rubbing his face, wiping away smoke and sweat. She could hear him calculating whether he dared to break the circle again. He rubbed his hands on his trousers and raised them into a defensive position, counting the Soul Men as they circled.

—*D'you think you could fix on that one? The tall, thin one. He's the weakest.*

Annat put her arm across Yuda's back, understanding what

he wanted. He had exhausted much of his power in shielding himself when he snapped the torus. However, yoked to her, he might be able to weaken one of the links in the chain. Together, they sighted on the walking man. It was essential that they both fire at the same time or the energy would be diffused, too weak to break through the force-field. Annat stretched out her arm beside Yuda's, and heard him counting under his breath.

"Shoot on three," he muttered.

Annat kept her eyes on the tall figure for as long as she could. When he re-entered her field of vision, from the right, she heard Yuda start to count.

—Be ready to run, he thought.

Annat summoned up the power from her deepest reserves, feeling it throbbing in her arm. As Yuda shouted, "Three!" she let it flame from her hand, and it surged across the circle, fizzing and twisting round the blue bolt of Yuda's lightning. It tore through the wall of the ring, and earthed itself in the breast of the thin man, blasting him from his feet. The torus slipped and fell apart, and Yuda ran for the gap, dragging Annat with him. He sprang up the hill, making straight for the place where Sarl stood. And, drawing his sword, Sarl was coming to meet them. Once again, Annat sensed Yuda scraping up the wisps of energy, tensing them through his body into his right arm. Behind them, she could hear the feet of the Soul Men pounding the snow.

Sarl strode towards them. When he was only a few feet away, he flung down his sword and raised his hands in a gesture that mimicked Yuda's. Annat saw the red lightning branch from his fingers. Yuda answered with a silver-blue flame, and the two met halfway, fusing into a ball of sparks that toiled and struggled, bobbing first towards Yuda before it sank back towards Sarl. Suddenly, there was a puff of smoke. Yuda gasped, and Sarl took a pace back. The lightning ball vanished, leaving a vacuum in the air that sucked in on itself and disappeared. Annat heard the Deputy's laughter as he bent to pick up the sword.

"We are evenly matched, you and I," he said. "But it is no matter."

In the same moment, cold hands laid hold of Annat, and tore her away from Yuda. She saw him struggling in the grip of two Soul Men, but their joint powers were enough to pinion his waning strength. Sarl stepped up to him, smiling.

"Welcome to the Castle of Ademar, Mister Vasilyevich," he said. "I have special rooms prepared for such as you and your daughter. In case you were hoping to escape."

"What quarrel have you got with the *kind*?" said Yuda breathlessly.

"None, for now. But I do intend to keep her where her powers will be of no help to you—and of no danger to me."

He pointed towards the castle, and the Soul Men who held Yuda began to drag him down the hill towards its gate, with Annat close behind. Annat gazed up at the chateau's white face, and saw it as a beautiful mask that kept a skull concealed beneath.

Chapter 17

The Doyen of Ademar sat in state in his great hall, on a dais that raised him above his servants. As Yuda and Annat were manhandled towards the platform, through the crowd of retainers and men-at-arms, she was able to study the old man sitting in the gilded chair. The look on his face seemed remote, uninterested, but his eyes followed them as they were jostled across the room. He wore rich, strange clothing, unlike anything she had seen before; she had an intense impression that she had been conveyed into another century, though it seemed as crisp and fresh as her own time.

Annat and Yuda were brought to the foot of the dais and made to kneel before the Doyen. Annat kept her head bent and her gaze on the floor but Yuda raised his eyes to meet those of the old man. Though he was on his knees, he managed to seem proud, in spite of his burnt clothes and the soot that smeared his face and hands. He did not glare in defiance, but sat back on his heels, resting his hands on his knees. Annat could not help noticing the two rings he wore, the plain wedding band of gold, and the dark stone set in dull metal that the *Rashim* had given him.

Sarl came to stand beside them, and bent his knee to the Doyen, his father. The old man raised a jewelled hand.

"Are these the two you told me of, Jean Sorel?" he asked, in a voice cold as the north wind.

"These are the Wanderers that I have been pursuing," said Sarl. "And my men are bringing in the others, the black man and my errant sister Casildis, who has been sorely wounded."

—*Fuck*, thought Yuda, though his face showed no trace of emotion. Annat felt like weeping, but she tried to keep in the tears, she did not want them to know she was afraid.

"Have my daughter brought to the physicians, and let her husband be immured until I decide what to do with him," said the Doyen, waving his hand regally. "These two I give to you, Jean Sorel, to dispose of. Let the man be put to the torture to find out what he knows, and shut the maiden in a dungeon, to be brought to the stake in due season, when she has had time to repent of her errors."

Annat shot to her feet. "No!" she shouted. "You can't do that! My father is a good man. What gives you the right to harm us? We have done nothing to you. Even a criminal is allowed to know the charges against him!"

One of the guards lashed out with his arm, and knocked her off her feet. The Doyen leaned forward in his chair, resting his chin on his hand. "She does not know," he said, gazing down at her with hooded eyes. "Is it possible that our law means nothing to these outlanders? That they do not understand how grievously they have offended?"

Annat raised herself to her hands and knees, pain echoing through the left side of her face. "My mother was Aude d'Ifloras, the friend of your daughter Huldis. You can't ignore that!"

The Doyen sat back in his chair, and regarded her with a sombre look, studying her face. For a moment Annat thought he was going to relent, enough at least to tell them why they were condemned. "So Aude had a daughter," he said. "How strange it is for me to see three of the same household, the one a true son of Doxa, the others faithless and false. I have spared your brother, child, because he was anointed, and because he has made submission to me. You I cannot spare, though I pity your youth, for the holy chrism has not touched your brow, and you have made common cause with the Wanderers of Chorazin, who are under our edict."

Annat struggled to her feet and looked up into the old man's eyes. "My brother is alive," she said. "Is he here?"

The guard made a movement as if to strike her again, but
the Doyen held up his hand. "Let no man lay impious hands
upon the girl, for she has our blood in her veins," he said. He
gazed from Annat to Yuda and back. "I have chosen to spare
your brother the shame of seeing his family brought so low,"
he said. "Though he has made common cause with us, I do not
think him so unfilial as to rejoice at his father's capture. I myself will bear the news to him."

Annat felt strange and confused. In spite of his cruel orders,
there was nothing inhumane about the old man. He seemed to
have treated Malchik well, though she guessed that her brother
must have pretended to become the Doyen's adherent. She
could not blame her brother; that choice was not even offered
to her or Yuda, who seemed so calm. She decided to make one
last appeal. Her hand touched Yuda's shoulder. "Please do not
harm my father, sir," she said. "He will not speak for himself,
but I can speak."

She saw the momentary softness fade from the old man's
face like a withering leaf. If Yuda was steel, he was granite.
"No mercy for him, child," he said. "His doom is spoken. Take
them away."

Annat was seized and hustled from the hall, past the curious
stares of knights and retainers in their green livery. She did not
see what happened to Yuda. There was one face in the crowd
that looked at her with pity as the gaolers dragged her past; a
tall young man with dark hair and eyes stood amongst the rest,
fingering the hilt of his sword, and for a fleeting moment, his
gaze met hers. That look went into her soul. One man who saw
her as a human, not a Wanderer and an outsider. The youth was
not much older than Malchik, and she thought she traced a resemblance to the Doyen in his features. Perhaps he was another son, a younger son not so favoured as the Heir was, or
even illegitimate. That glance, that face, was like a cup of
fresh water pressed to her lips, to quench her thirst.

Once out of the hall, the men-at-arms took her to one of the
round towers, and down a spiral stair lit with pine torches.
They did not speak to her, but gossiped about household matters as if she did not exist. At the base of the tower, she trod on
flagstones strewn with dirty straw. The knights pushed her

down a narrow passageway, past a number of locked wooden doors, until they had almost reached the foot of the next tower. One guard paused by a green-painted door to unlock it with a key from a ring at his belt. The other kept his hand clamped round Annat's arm.

"See him?" he shouted into her ear. "That's Jacques the Gaoler. Keep him sweet, and he'll treat you nice. Otherwise, you can forget about food and water, and sit in your own shit."

Jacques the Gaoler pushed open the door. "This here," he said, slowly, "is a special dungeon that Zhan Sarl has prepared for the likes of you. So don't try no clever tricks, darling. Here you sit and here you stay."

"You can have her, Jacques, if you want. I'll see no one disturbs you."

"What would I do with a little stringy thing like that? 'Sides, the Seigneur said no one was to touch her. You remember that, Guyot, if you want to keep your head."

Guyot muttered under his breath, and shoved Annat through the door so that she fell headlong in the straw. She lay prone on her face, weeping, and heard the door slam shut behind her, and the key turn in the lock. As soon as it was closed, she felt the pressure of the walls bearing down upon her. Sarl had indeed prepared the room, binding the stone with another ring of force. She could see its violet light against her closed lids. She sat up, gasping for breath, feeling as if she were about to suffocate. At first, she could not believe that she had opened her eyes, for she was in total darkness. Then she caught sight of a faint line of red light showing below the door, and through the cracks in the planking. The door would be the weak link in the force-field, but even if she were able to get out, where would she go? There was no doubt that Jean and Guyot would be sitting on guard somewhere outside, and they might do anything to her if she tried to escape.

Annat sat up, clasping her arms round her knees. There was a particular smell in the cell, the odor of rotting straw, feces and damp. The cold of the place reached out to touch her like a dead hand. If only she had thought to bring the doll with her! Its comforting presence would have stayed with her, like a small seed of hope. But now they were all prisoners, Yuda,

Govorin and Casildis, and Malchik too, in his way. She buried
her face in her lap, trying not to think and not to cry. The
words of the Doyen's sentence repeated themselves in her
head. She was to be burned, and Yuda to be tortured. How
could it have turned out so badly? She had hoped, when the
Rashim gave them their presents, that he was offering them
each some magical assistance.

Annat slipped her hand into the front of her bodice, and
drew out the small metal box. She closed her fist on it, feeling
the coolness of its polished lid and metal sides. The *Rashim*
must have had a reason for giving it to her! She was convinced, in spite of what he had said, that he did possess some
foreknowledge of their fate. Surely he could not have seen her
withering in the flames, burnt at the stake. She tried to shut
from her mind the image of the wretched Soul Man, burning to
death as a human torch. The pain, the horror, as your own flesh
was consumed, with no water to put it out. No one deserved
that fate, not even such a man.

Annat could not believe that those men she had seen gathered in the hall would consent to her death, would come to
calmly watch as she was led to the piled logs, and say nothing.
But no one had protested against their sentence, no one had
stirred a muscle to save them. She stood up and began to pace
the cell, quickly judging its extent. There was a drain in one
corner, where the stench of urine and feces was almost too
strong to bear. Annat turned away from it, wishing that she
could stop herself thinking of water. Something the Doyen had
said puzzled her. "She has our blood in her veins." She wondered what he had meant. Her mother, Aude, had been a serving girl, a lady-in-waiting at best, but one of the Doyen's
servants, not part of his lineage. The image of the two girls,
Aude and Huldis, seemed to come to her quite freshly, as if it
were earlier that morning that they had walked out in the snow
together, laughing, arm in arm, while Aude carried the doll in a
sling hanging from her back. Annat felt the drifting sadness of
that long-vanished day, as she understood that her mother had
returned to the castle alone, weeping for the loss of her friend,
and that no one had believed her story.

The pain hit her like a stone in the midriff, and she fell to the floor. She curled up into a ball, clenching her hands. Knives were slashing at her, cutting out a string of paper dolls from her skin, and each doll was an image of herself. Doubled up, Annat squeezed her eyes tight shut. She was already at the stake, and burning. But she must not let them see what she felt; they must not know how much they were hurting her. She thought of the great light, the fire in the sky that came from His ring. Up there, above the clouds, rose the first of the Ten Sephirot, Keter, the Crown. The great sun looked down upon her with its numinous eye, the stare of the One as he gazed out upon Creation.

The agony stopped as suddenly as it had come. Annat gasped, feeling the cramps receding in her arms and her belly. She lifted her hand to wipe the sweat from her forehead. The thoughts she had just experienced were not hers; she knew nothing about a crown, or the Sephirot. She had never heard the words before. She staggered to her feet, retching a little from the after-effects of the pain. She groped her way to one of the walls, and leaned her burning face against its cool, moist surface. For a moment, she wondered if she were suffering the onset of a fever, for her mind had entered what seemed like a delirium. She felt a smarting in her hand; opening it, she discovered that she had clutched the small box so hard that its edges cut into her palm. And then she understood. It was Yuda's pain she was sharing, as they tortured him. The force-field in the room was not enough to sunder the bond between their souls.

"Oh no," said Annat, softly. She crouched down on the ground, slipping the cool box back into its hollow against her breast. She knew that this was only the first spasm, that more would come, and more. She tried desperately to think of a way in which she could send Yuda her wholeness, the cool of the dank cell and its soothing darkness. But instead, the pain returned to gripe at her, with raucous, cawing laughter, and she fell on her side on the floor, clenching her eyes shut.

There was a knock at the door. Malchik sprang to his feet, a rush of thoughts coursing through his mind. A summons had come for Cluny earlier that morning, but none for him, and he had stayed in the room, waiting, as his imagination played on the reasons for his exclusion.

"Enter," he said, and then hurried to open the door. The Doyen himself stood outside, with Cluny at his back, but there was no sign of Zhan Sarl. Malchik remembered at once to bow, and to stand aside as the old man limped into the room, leaning on his cane. As the Doyen hobbled to the single chair, Malchik tried to catch Cluny's eye, but the young man was staring resolutely at the floor.

"Come to me, boy," said the Doyen, easing himself into the chair with a look of pain etched into his features. "Cluny, shut the door and wait outside. Make sure we are not disturbed."

Malchik sat down on the floor at the Doyen's feet, and waited for his master to speak. The Doyen seemed to take a long time; he sat with his eyes closed, grimacing and rubbing his right leg. At last, he said, "Pardon me, boy. The cold of this place does not sit well with old wounds. You must wonder what has brought me to your chambers, rather than summoning you to mine. The reason itself is simple; I made a promise that I would tell you myself, and I never break my word, even when given to an infidel."

Malchik too felt the cold that filled the room, and seemed to enter his bones. "I am doubly honoured, Mon Seigneur," he said, and he was truly impressed that the old man had taken the trouble to struggle up the stairs from the hall, just to see him.

The Doyen sighed. "I thought I should be the bearer of the news," he said. "Jean Sorel is apt to be brusque in his manner, and you should not hear it from a lesser person. Your sister and father are taken, together with their companions; they are my prisoners."

Malchik heard himself gasp. The chill wrenched the color from his face, and he began to shake. The Doyen laid his clawed hand on Malchik's head. "As I thought," he said kindly. "This news has moved you, and it is right that it should. My eldest son has given himself up to the Cold One, and it seems that the price was the loss of all human care. Though I appreciate the sacrifice he has made, I fear that he would slit my throat without a second thought if it served his purpose. He is not the man I once knew. You, child, still keep some mortal kindness, and are saddened at the fate of your kin. But they must die. They are Wanderers and shamans, and I can show them no mercy, any more than I would to ravening wolves."

"Mon Seigneur—" Malchik began. He felt faint, and a haze of darkness passed before his eyes. "How was my sister?" he said, biting his lip.

"She is a maiden not without courage. I have often found that the women of that race bear themselves with more spirit than the men. I think it best that you do not see her. I will send word to the Biskopa in Yonar, so that he may come to preside at her burning. Be assured that she will not suffer; such victims are strangled before the fire is kindled."

Malchik came close to breaking down. He raised his hand to his eyes, knocking off his glasses. "Please excuse me, Mon Seigneur," he said. He wished he could find some hate in his heart against the old man, but all he felt was the Doyen's kindness, behind the terrible, mad words.

"In time, you will be reconciled to their fate," said the Doyen. "You will come to understand the justice of my judgement. I will leave you to your thoughts now, boy." He bent down to retrieve Malchik's spectacles from the floor, and handed them to him. "May the Mother herself bring you peace, and lead you to a reconciliation with the true way," he said.

Malchik struggled to his feet, and helped the old man to rise from his chair. He did not dare to look him in the face. He led the Doyen to the door, and felt the strength of that frail body against his arm. When he knocked on the wood panels, Cluny opened the door, and stood outside to let his father pass. A man-at-arms was waiting to conduct the Doyen to his chambers.

The two young men retreated within the room. There was a moment's awful pause, before Malchik sat down heavily on the floor, taking his head in his hands. "My God, Cluny, what am I going to do?" he said.

"I am so very sorry," said Cluny, crouching down beside him.

"Cluny—my sister—how was she?"

Cluny gave a small shrug. "I only saw her once, when she was hauled away from the dais to the dungeons. She seemed to me too young to burn at the stake. And your father showed no fear when he was taken away to the torture. That is all I can say."

"Torture?" Malchik whispered.

"Jean Sorel believes he should be made to reveal what he knows of our presence here, and of the pact with the Cold One. We—they—need to know what the strangers have learned. And he is a spy for the strangers."

Malchik seized Cluny's arm. "You understand, don't you, Cluny? I have to save them."

Cluny frowned, and his deep-set eyes avoided Malchik's face. "There is little you or I can do to ease their fate." He glanced at the easel. "In truth, there is one thing I could do. But you would have to bring them all here, to me, in this room."

"How could I do that?" said Malchik, wretchedly.

"I do not know—but if you did, I could use the painting to free them. But it is vain to tell you of it, and hurt you with hope. Your father and sister are in the dungeons; the black man is a prisoner of courtesy, though not in this tower; and my half-sister Casildis lies close to death, wounded by an arrow. They were taken trying to rescue you."

Malchik stood up. "I have to do something, Cluny," he said. "I was always the one who got others into danger. It's my fault that they were captured. Tonight, I shall try to discover where Govorin and Casildis are imprisoned. Will you help me?"

Cluny looked up at him, and managed a faint smile. "I think you know the answer to that question, Malchik," he said.

Annat lay curled up on the ground in the darkness, covering her face with her hand. There had been no pain for some time now, but all her bones ached and her skin was sore to the touch. She could not get comfortable whichever way she lay, and she could not sleep. She had no idea whether it was night or day. Perhaps a few hours ago, one of the guards had opened the door and pushed in a cup of sour water and a trencher of

cold, greasy meat. Seeing Annat doubled over on the floor; he
had gone away laughing to himself. She could not understand
how a person could become so brutalised that they enjoyed
seeing the suffering of others. After a time, she had drunk the
water, and emptied the dish of meat into the privy. It was more
than likely to be pork, given to her in mockery.

There was a ripple in the darkness. Annat did not stir, imagining that it was only the force-field re-establishing itself as
Sarl came close. Then, a faint, hoarse voice sounded in her
head, cool as the water that she had craved.

"Annat."

For a moment, she thought it was her father calling out to
her, but as she sat up, she became aware of a luminous, indis-
tinct figure in front of her. It was the form of Isabel Guerreres,
the murdered shaman, standing before Annat in her flowered
dress, her red hair glowing like a distant beacon.

"Isabel," she whispered, "how could you get in?"

"I have been with your father, Annat, but there is nothing
more I can do for him. So I have come to you."

She crouched down, and her faint hand strayed over Annat's
hair. Annat felt a stirring of coolness, like a gentle wind.

"Isabel, what can I do?" she said, wretchedly. "The force-
field in the cell keeps my powers pent up inside me."

"There is so little I can do, and without me, you can do
nothing," said Isabel, sadly. "I am scarcely more than a wraith,
a shadow with no substance, and one breath of the Cold One
can blow me away, like shreds of cloud."

Annat felt something hard within her bodice, pressing her
breast. As she reached in to pluck it out, she remembered the
Rashim's words. Dust from the *Golem*'s brow, to give substance to something insubstantial. She lifted the box tenderly
in her palm, gazing at the luminescence of the mother-of-pearl
lid.

"Isabel, if I could give you substance, would you be able to
break the ring of power?" she said.

Isabel gave a faint shrug. "If you could give me substance, I
could be both substance and shadow," she said in her soft
voice. "But I am a ghost. Though I can pass through stone
walls six feet thick, I cannot break iron manacles."

"Perhaps it is only a dream," Annat said to herself. "Perhaps I will wake, and find myself lying in my bed in Sankt-Eglis." Very carefully, she opened the little box. She could not see what was inside it, but she held it up and blew across its surface. A faint dust that glittered like mica rose into the air, and drifted towards Isabel, who gave a little shiver as it approached her. As Annat sat watching, a ripple went over the form of the ghost, and it began to fragment, breaking into colored pieces that floated in the air. Annat waited, gazing at the gently bobbing shapes as they formed and re-formed into small clusters. One glittered like a piece of silver, another was deep crimson as stained glass, and a third was a washed blue through which the light flowed like the distillation of a sunlit day. Annat held her breath, wondering if she were watching a dissolution, or the beginnings of a change.

Slowly, the fragments moved together and started to coalesce, their colors running into each other. Having formed a glowing, viscous ball, they began to spin on the spot, until watching them made Annat dizzy and she was forced to shut her eyes. There was no sound till the end, when a clear, bell-like note sounded, sweet as shattering icicles. When Annat opened her eyes, Isabel stood before her, still dimly radiant but opaque, a solid form with the colors and shadows of life.

Isabel sighed. "If only your pretty magic could give me back my life," she said, in a hoarse whisper. "But see, I am substantial. I have the body of a mortal and the powers of a ghost. Look!"

She reached out to the pale strands of throbbing violet that formed the torus of power binding the walls of the cell, and tore them asunder, flinging them away in flakes of burning blue. This time there was no fire or lightning, as there had been when Yuda broke the force-field. Isabel stood in a shower of purplish shards of crystal, which fell about her, dissolving harmlessly into the ground.

"Isabel," said Annat, softly. The pressure in her skull was gone, and she could breathe easy once more. The young woman's form stood gazing at her sadly.

"I wish I could destroy Sarl so easily," she said, "but the Goddess protects him."

"Isabel, can you get me out of here? I have to find *Tate* before they kill him."

"I think I know a way," said Isabel. A little smile traced her features. "This is not the first dungeon that I have escaped from."

And she stooped to pick up the pitcher of water that stood by the door, where Annat had left it.

There had been a feast in the great hall to celebrate the capture of the prisoners. The Doyen had presided at the high table, served by Cluny and other youngsters, while Malchik had occupied an honoured seat at his side. Sarl sat on the Doyen's left hand, eating heartily, while Malchik picked at his food, his mind full of horror and dark thoughts. The feast had seemed to last for hours, and all the entertainments, the jugglers and jesters and conjurors, only served to heighten the cold that welled up inside him, and remind him of his family, chained in the dark somewhere beneath his feet. He noticed that Sarl left before the feasting was finished, and almost asked leave to follow him, but he kept silent. There was nothing to be done for Yuda or Annat; guards, thick walls and perhaps strong magic would be used to bind them.

Late that night, Malchik lay sleepless on his truckle bed in Cluny's room. The same thoughts kept going through his mind. From what he understood, Govorin had not been shut in a cell, and Casildis was in the care of physicians, hardly a prisoner at all. He lay still, listening to the clock over the castle's central court ringing the hours, and when two o'clock had passed, he decided to make his move.

He sat up in bed, wondering if he ought to wake Cluny. But while Malchik might be able to escape through the painting, Cluny would have to remain, and Malchik wanted to draw as little suspicion upon him as possible. He clambered out of bed and put on his spectacles. He was wearing a long white nightshirt loaned to him by Cluny, and it was bitterly cold in the room, even though the stove was still burning. Malchik searched for a spare cloak, trying not to make too much noise, and drew it about his shoulders, shivering. He put on his discarded slippers, and, thus fortified, let himself out of the room on to the landing. Cluny did not stir.

Another door was set in the side of the tower, raised a few steps above the one that led to Cluny's room. Malchik knew it would lead into one of the connecting galleries that linked the four towers of the chateau. He opened it a crack, and peered into a long, wide corridor, lit with sconces on the walls, which appeared deserted except for shadows and the marks of moonlight from the clerestory windows in the wall that overlooked the inner courtyard. Malchik stepped down into the passageway, whose floor of stone flags was covered by a long woven runner that stretched from one end to the other. On his right stood a long range of closed doors. For a moment, he visualised himself opening each in turn, apologising and withdrawing his head.

There were four such galleries on each storey, and the castle itself stood three storeys high.

Malchik began to pace down the corridor. With flagstones for a floor, there were no creaking boards to betray him, and the carpet muffled his steps. He wondered whether all the towers were guarded. If there were sentries at the main portal, the question remained as to how many kept watch within the castle, and where they were placed. Sarl had not put a guard on the chamber he shared with Cluny, so the Heir must assume either that Cluny would keep an eye on his companion, or that Malchik himself was to be trusted. Time was of the essence, yet he still had little idea how to conduct his search. At the moment, he was heading for the Doyen's private apartments, in the south-west tower. There would certainly be a sentry on watch there, and it might be possible to ask him where the prisoners were kept.

When he reached the door at the far end of the gallery, Malchik hesitated. He had no idea as to what time the household would be stirring. His hand on the iron door-handle, he paused before opening it decisively. A lowered pike met his gaze, and a gruff voice challenged, "Who goes there?" Malchik stared at the shadowy face masked by a conical helmet with a long nasal guard.

"Friend," he said weakly, drawing his cloak tightly about him in an attempt to hide his night attire.

"What is the watchword for the night?" said the guard suspiciously.

"I've no idea," said Malchik. "I'm looking for the privies."

The guard levelled his pike, and said, "These are the Seigneur's apartments, boy, and no one but his kin may enter, or those who know the watchword. As for the privies, you'd better return to the north-western tower and take a turn along the other gallery. You'll find them on the ground floor of the north-eastern tower. I doubt you'll be the only one, after the feasting tonight."

"Lonely work, eh, guarding while others feast?" said Malchik, as he backed into the corridor.

The guard nodded. "Lonely work indeed, boy. At least the lads on the gates have each other to talk to. Even the gaolers get some cheer. But there's precious few of us night-watchmen. Why should they need us, when they have magic and suchlike to keep their prisoners safe? And now goodnight to you."

Malchik thanked him and apologised, retreating behind the door. He scuttled back along the passage to Cluny's tower, and let himself back on to the stair. There was another entrance opening into the northern gallery, and he hurried through, hoping his heart would stop thumping so fast. He shut the door after him with great care, and stopped, taking several deep breaths to calm himself. At least he had an excuse if anyone asked him why he was wandering the castle at night.

He now faced another row of polished doors on his left, and another range of high-set windows on his right. He was about to step down into the corridor, when something caught his eye and set his nervous heart thudding once more. Towards the far end of the gallery floated a tall figure in ghostly white. For an instant, he was certain that he had seen a ghost, until a moonbeam fell on the figure, and lit up a long skein of radiant fair hair. It was Casildis.

The woman came to meet Malchik like a phantom stepping through the bars of the moonlight. Her beauty in the twilight seemed unreal, as if she were the spirit of the Bright Lady visiting him. When they were a little distance apart, she stopped and regarded him questioningly. Malchik's voice choked in his throat.

"I'm sorry, I'm so sorry," he said.

"My husband is a prisoner of courtesy, but Yuda and Annat are in the dungeons," said Casildis, coolly. "I was shot and wounded until Zhan Sarl took it upon himself to heal me. But you have been received by the Doyen and are here as his guest—"

Malchik cut across her words, trying to ignore the hurt they caused him.

"We have to get out of here, Casildis," he said, feeling himself go red. "We have to find Govorin and bring him to Cluny's tower. Cluny knows a way to help us escape." Then he hesitated as something she said had struck home to him. "Zhan Sarl *healed* you?"

"I am ever his grateful servant," said Casildis bitterly. "But why should I trust you, Malchik? They tell me you have sworn fealty to my father."

"Casildis, you have to trust me. It's our only chance," he said, urgently. "If I stay here much longer, the Goddess will overpower me. But it's not too late—not yet. Please help me."

Casildis shook her head. "Even if I were to help you, Govorin is locked in a chamber and I don't have the key. And if he must stay, then so shall I."

Malchik took a step closer. Her eyes were beautiful, liquid and clear. Though they looked at him with mistrust, he felt he could place all his faith in this woman, and wager his life on her.

"If we don't do something while we have the chance, they are going to burn Annat," he said. "I swore fealty to the Doyen under duress. What choice did I have? Please take me to Govorin. I will not betray you. If you don't believe me, we can go to Cluny and he will vouch for me. But we have so little time!"

Casildis gazed at him. "I have to trust you, Malchik," she said. "I have no other hope. Only we two are free to walk the corridors of the castle. I will take you to Govorin, but hear this: if you betray us, you will die by my own hand!"

Chapter 18

Holding the pitcher in one hand, Isabel walked to the cell door and touched the lock. Before Annat's gaze, the metal deliquesced, dripping on to the floor where it fizzled and steamed. Just as she had destroyed the torus of power that ringed the cell, now Isabel had broken the one barrier that stopped them from leaving. Perhaps that was what she had meant when she said *the body of a mortal and the powers of a ghost*. Isabel raised her head to smile at Annat, and lifted a finger to her lips. If she had broken the lock, there would have been a loud noise; this way, there would be nothing to show how Annat had escaped but a thin, cooling puddle of metal on the floor.

Outside in the stone corridor, there was no one in sight, and no sound but the hissing of the pitch-pine brands burning in their iron sockets on the wall.

—*The gaolers are this way,* Isabel thought, turning to the left. —*Follow me, but keep out of sight. Their room is in the base of the tower.*

Annat followed her along the passage, glancing nervously at the blind cell doors on either side. She kept expecting Jacques or Guyot to emerge from a room and seize her. Isabel walked confidently, her head up, cradling the stoneware pitcher in her arms; Annat noticed that she was barefoot on the torn and dirty

straw. When they came to the tower entrance, Isabel made
Annat wait behind the door, and opened it cautiously. Annat
peeped through the crack between the hinges to see that a yellow light filled the small chamber beyond, where Jacques the
Gaoler and Guyot his mate were seated at a wooden table,
talking in low voices and playing cards. They looked up in surprise as Isabel stepped into the room. She must be a startling
figure to them, with her cropped red hair, the scarlet scarf
round her neck, and the short dress that scarcely covered her
knees. A slender waif with the face of a woman.

"What can I do for you, my darling?" said Jacques with
mock courtesy. "I don't remember your face from the kitchens.
And I always remember a pretty face."

"I have brought wine for you, on the orders of the Doyen,"
said Isabel softly.

Jacques and Guyot rolled with laughter in their chairs. "Not
that old story," said Jacques, wiping his eyes. "Someone wants
to escape, so they send us a girl with a jug of drugged wine.
Well, it doesn't fool me. Come here and give me a kiss."

"No, it is not that story," said Isabel, and she brought the
pitcher down hard on his head, smashing the clay to fragments. As Jacques slipped from his chair unconscious, blood
pouring from his scalp, Guyot leapt from the seat, too shocked
to call for the guards. Before he could recover his wits, Isabel
had dealt him a swift blow with the edge of her hand to his
upper lip, and he toppled forward, haemorrhaging from the
nose.

"Not that story at all," said Isabel. Annat gasped; she was almost tempted to laugh, the gaolers' fate had been so swift and
final. She crept out from her hiding place, to find Isabel wrest-
ing the bunch of keys from Jacques's belt.

—*Are they dead?*

—*Of course.*

Isabel straightened, the bunch of keys in her hand. She
gazed at Annat with sea-green eyes, thinking, —*How good it is
to have my form and my strength returned to me. Do you know
how long this change will last?*

—*I don't,* thought Annat in answer.

—*It means so much to me. But now to find your father.* She

paused. —*You must be strong. It will be no use to him if you cry.*

—*I'm strong.* Annat gave a small shiver of dread. She was not sure that she believed her own thought.

Isabel reached out to touch her arm, smiling sadly. —*Trust me*, she thought.

She shepherded Annat across the gaoler's room and through the door on the far side, which gave entrance to a passage much like the one they had just left. Annat trembled, sensing Yuda's presence even before they had found him. Without speaking, Isabel took her hand in a cold grip, and led her along the corridor until they reached the door to the last cell on their left. While Isabel was searching through the bunch of keys that she held, to find one that would unlock it, suddenly, with a faint exclamation, she pushed the door with her hand. It swung open.

As they stepped inside, Annat quickly took in several things. This dungeon was much larger than the one where she had been kept, and the force-field was down. Yuda was chained to the far wall with his arms above his head; he seemed to be clothed in scarlet. By the light of the sconces burning on the walls, she saw Zhan Sarl standing close to her father, too close. A shiver of revulsion went down Annat's back as she saw the other things that the room held: the brazier of hot coals, the branding iron and the knife. She did not want to weep, as Isabel had feared; she was gripped with terrible rage, and saw herself in her mind's eye seizing the iron and searing Sarl's insolent face with it.

But Sarl did not look insolent when he turned to see who had entered the dungeon. Though at first his features bore a strange smile, as he recognised Isabel all the color went from his cheeks, and he dropped down on his knees, shielding his eyes from her. Annat wondered at the reason for his sudden fear.

"It is me, Zhan Sarl," rasped Isabel, advancing across the room towards him. "There are some things even you can't kill. Remember this?" and she tore the scarf from her neck, revealing the ugly gash in her throat.

"Not you," said Sarl incoherently. "Anyone but you."

Isabel bent over him so that their faces were close. "So strong a shaman that I couldn't detect you," she said. "But now I am strong and you are weak. I can't kill you—that is forbidden me—but I can do enough."

She reached out and placed her hand on his breast. With a groan, Sarl slumped sideways, drawing up his limbs like a dead insect, and lay still. Isabel stepped over him contemptuously and approached Yuda, who had not moved since they entered the cell. He hung slack against the wall with his head bent, seemingly unconscious.

Annat slowly followed Isabel. She had to admit that Yuda was not wearing a scarlet suit; it was his blood. When she joined Isabel and tried to force herself to see him, the hot tears blossomed from her eyes. Without looking at her, Isabel gently laid a hand against the small of her back.

"We have to get him down from there," she said. "Then you can heal him."

"There's too much," Annat sobbed. "I think he might die before I finish."

Something gleamed in the darkness above Yuda's head. Annat blinked, and saw that it was the stone of the *Rashim*'s ring. It glowed in the dull light like a tiny coal, alive and burning. Isabel noticed it too.

"What is that?" she said.

"The *Rashim* gave it to *Tate*. He said it was a stone of little value."

"Perhaps," said Isabel. She stood on tiptoe and slid the ring from Yuda's finger. When it lay in her palm, it seemed to throb with vivid life, turning from red to orange to a swirling gold. Deep in its heart, Annat thought she could discern a pattern: a strange shape made out of ten circles linked together, and each one had a name written on it in *Ebreu*. She felt as if the circles were rising or she were sinking into the centre of the stone, so that she could read their names. She recognised the topmost from her delirium earlier that day, when she had shared Yuda's pain: Keter, the Crown.

"What do you think it is?" said Isabel.

"I don't know—but the *Rashim* must have given it to *Tate* for a reason."

Annat took the ring from Isabel and turned it over in her
hand, feeling it stir like a tiny spider. *Ten Sephirot.* Those were
the words that Yuda had used. It was as though he had been
trying to get a message to her, one that he could not finish.
Annat held up the ring and pointed it towards her father's
body, to see what would happen. At once, a golden glow blossomed from the stone, and the ten circles were projected on to
Yuda's body: Keter, the Crown, above his head; Daat, or
Knowledge, at his throat: Tiferet, Beauty, against his heart;
Yesod, the Foundation, at his loins; and Malkhut, the King-
dom, beneath his feet. Though Annat understood the meaning
of the names, she did not know what purpose they served. She
stood gazing in awe as the golden light washed over Yuda, and
even the congealed blood liquefied and began to seep back
into his veins. The wounds healed one by one, leaving dark
scars. He did not stir, and Annat wondered whether he was
aware of what was happing to him. Though his body and limbs
were covered in cuts, little by little, every one closed, and the
bruising to his hands and feet faded away.

"This is more than magic," said Isabel. "Your *Rashim* must
be a man of great power."

"The *Rashim* only said he had owned the ring, not that he
made it," said Annat.

At last the golden light dwindled, and the ring in Annat's
hand became once more a dull and lifeless gem. She closed
her fist on it, feeling its warmth. Yuda's slack head moved
back, and his eyes opened; their blackness seemed infinitely
deep. He straightened his arms and tugged against the chains
that held him, wrenching them from the walls without any sign
of effort.

"Yuda!" cried Isabel, short and sharp; it was the first time
she had shown any emotion. He lowered his arms, and his eyes
seemed to focus on the small woman.

"Is that you, Isabel?" he said, quietly. He stretched his limbs
and stepped away from the wall, coming face to face with her;
they were about the same height. He was naked except for a
dirty loincloth, and the dark marks covered his body, back and
front.

"What did they do to you, Yuda?" Isabel said in a voice full of pain.

He reached out to touch her face. "I never thought to see you again, Izzy. Least of all here."

Remembering the red scarf in her hand, Isabel swiftly tied it round her neck, to cover the wound in her throat. "I had unfinished business," she said, simply. "I am only a ghost."

"You don't seem like a ghost to me," he said, feeling the flesh of her arm as someone might fondle a cat. There was an inexpressible tenderness in the way he touched her, but none of the radiance of desire he had shown to Casildis.

"It was Annat who gave me substance, using the powder from her little box. It seems as if the *Rashim* of Chorazin foresaw what you would need."

Yuda glanced at Annat, who offered him the ring in silence. He took it from her and slipped it over his index finger. She felt in awe, both of the strength he had shown in withstanding the torture, and of the power she sensed in him now. It was as if he cast a new shadow she could not see, giant and golden.

"You were there, Natka," he said. "You stayed beside me."

"I couldn't help it!" Annat cried.

"But you stayed," said Yuda, quietly. He noticed Sarl's prone body on the floor, and added, "We'd better be moving away from here. Someone is sure to come looking for this Prince of Ademar. Unless they leave him to take his pleasure in private."

Annat shuddered. "He was standing so close to you—"

"Better not to think of it, Natka. Where shall we go, Izzy? This place must be crawling with guards."

"We should find Malchik. They have put him in a tower with the Doyen's bastard son. I made sure of him before I sought the rest of you."

"He may be wanting to stay," said Yuda, tightly.

"I don't think so, Yuda. I saw him, and his mind was troubled. The Cold One has not mastered him yet."

"I'd like to know how you plan to get us out, once we find the boy."

Isabel gave a quick laugh. "But it will be easy for us, Mister.

Have you no idea of your new strength? You wrenched your chains from the wall."

Yuda held up his right arm and examined the manacles hanging from his wrist. He snapped off the chain so that only the iron cuff remained. "So I did," he said, unsmiling. He stretched out his hand and grasped Isabel's in his, holding it up between them. "If I return from the Goddess's *domaine* alive, I'll pull this place down, stone by stone," he said. "I swear it by the blood they took from me."

In spite of her harsh words, Casildis took Malchik's hand in her warm grip, and led him after her as if he were a child. She passed down the corridor to one of the polished doors set in the outer wall of the quadrangle, which looked no different than the others. Tapping lightly on it, she whispered, "Sergey? Malchik is here."

Malchik heard the Sheriff's voice say, without a hint of animosity, "Has he come to pick the lock?"

"I don't know what to do, Mister Govorin," said Malchik in a tremulous voice. "Is there anything in there that might open the door?"

"Not without making a hell of a lot of noise," said Govorin ruefully. "I've got nothing with me but what's in my pockets— and this pendant the *Rashim* of Chorazin gave me."

"What's that?" whispered Malchik.

"In his place, I'd have given it to Casildis. I never thought to look inside the locket—he said it was a jewel—but I can't see that it'll be much help . . ." There was a pause and then Malchik heard Govorin say, "Well, I'm damned. There's a golden key inside. How's that for irony?"

"I still have the ball of twine he gave me," said Casildis, thoughtfully. "What if he could foresee our troubles, and gave us gifts that might help us? Perhaps you should try it in the lock."

"It's too small, my love. Like something made for a doll," said Govorin.

"Just try it, Mister, please!" said Malchik, soft and urgently. "I don't see what other chance we have."

There was a silence, followed by a faint rattling and clicking; then the door swung noiselessly open, and Govorin stood before them.

"Well, I'm damned," he repeated. "A pass key," before Casildis ran into his arms. They gave each other a passionate kiss, and Govorin stroked her head.

"Please hurry," said Malchik, fearfully. Though they had been careful to make little noise, he was constantly afraid that some restless sleeper might step into the gallery, or that a guard might pass by on his rounds. Govorin pulled the door shut, as quietly as possible. After a brief whispered colloquy, they hastened back to Cluny's tower, where they paused on the stone staircase, just outside the chamber door.

"We can't leave without Yuda and the *kind*," said Govorin.

Casildis folded her arms. "We'll need more than a golden key to release them," she said. "My father has had them shut in the dungeons, where there are gaolers—" She broke off, biting her lip.

"And torturers," said Govorin, quietly. "Sarl told me what he planned to do to Yuda. In some detail." He shook himself. "No matter. We have to try to get them out. It's better not to think about the risks. Are you up for that, Malchik? You don't have to come."

"I do, Mister Govorin," said Malchik, wretchedly. "I can't go back. Do you understand? If I go back now, it's to stay with Sarl and become like him."

Govorin patted his arm. "Good boy," he said, gently. "I know there's a struggle going on inside of you. Time we were moving."

They began to descend the spiral stair, with Malchik in the lead, his hand grasping the cold newel post. But before they had reached the foot of the steps, he came face to face with a sentry, who levelled his spear and demanded, "Who goes?"

Malchik stared at the metal leaf-blade a few feet from his stomach. Govorin was not many steps above him, and he had no idea whether the sentry had seen him.

"I wish to visit the prisoners," he said, in what he hoped was a voice of authority.

"And who may you be?" the sentry demanded, without lifting the spear.

"I am Malchik, friend of Jean Sorel," said Malchik, feeling his voice shake.

"The Heir has his own business in the dungeons, and no one is to disturb him," said the sentry, nastily. "There isn't a password for tonight. No one to be admitted, save the gaolers. He's got special prisoners down there, and he's giving them special attention."

Malchik felt faint. He swayed on his feet, grasping at the newel post, and the guard's face seemed to blur before him. The image of Sarl eating at the feast passed before his eyes. There was no alternative but to turn back, in the hope that the sentry had not seen Casildis or Govorin behind him. He was about to make his apologies when something happened that took him completely by surprise. Three small figures appeared from round the bend in the stair below, moving silently on the flagstones. Malchik twisted his face, trying to force himself not to react, but their mere appearance was so shocking that he could not help himself. Yuda was stripped to the skin, and his body and limbs were covered in dark, ugly scars that looked newly healed; Annat's eyes were huge, and her face seemed to have faded almost to the bone; but the third, Isabel, was human and solid, no longer a phantom.

"What're you looking at?" said the guard suspiciously. "Are you trying to fool me?"

Malchik stared at the hapless man, with three shamans behind him, and began to laugh wildly. He could not help himself. The sentry swung round, but he was already too late. A swift bolt of fire flew from Yuda's hand and caught the man in the face, lifting him from his feet like one struck by lightning. There was a clatter as the spear fell to the ground, followed by the soft thud of the man's body hitting the steps. Yuda rubbed his palms together, blowing on them.

"I think we came just in time, don't you, boy?" he said drily, as if he had been planning his appearance there for that very moment.

Malchik could hardly breathe. He kept seeing the pattern of wounds that snaked across Yuda's body. The small man stared up at him, as if expecting an answer to his question. Then

Govorin stepped out from his hiding place, and said, "My God, Yuda, what did he do to you?"

"He was inventive, I'll give him credit," said Yuda. "Shall we come up, or were you coming down?"

Malchik recovered himself a little. "Mister, I think Cluny can get us out of here . . . the Doyen's bastard son," he added, by way of explanation. "He said that if I brought you all to him, he could do something."

"I'd favour breaking out and killing as many of them as possible," said Yuda. "But I'm not in a forgiving mood. Let's meet this Cluny of yours, and see what he says. Unless you want to stay here with your new friends."

Malchik swore at him. He was not prepared for recriminations.

"Give the lad a chance, Yuda," said Govorin. "He's put himself in danger to help us. We'd better do as he says."

With Malchik leading the way, they climbed the stair to Cluny's room, and Malchik opened the door. He hesitated before speaking, then swiftly crossed the chamber and lit the candle beside Cluny's bed. Holding it up so he could look into the young man's face, he hissed, "Cluny, I've brought them all here."

The others filed into the room as he finished speaking. Cluny woke with a start and sat up in bed, gasping at the sight of his unexpected guests. "You did it!" he said, in a whisper. Malchik admired his composure, for it was a strange band of figures that presented itself in the flickering golden light of the single candle.

"Are you the young man who thinks he can get us out alive?" said Govorin, sceptically.

Cluny swung his legs over the side of the bed and seized the candle from Malchik, holding it high. He went padding over to them in his night-gown.

"My brother doesn't command the magic alone," he said. "I have only one skill that I know of, but it should be enough."

He strode to the easel and threw off the paint-stained cover. The picture beneath showed the stylised landscape under a sky of blue so pale that the color seemed about to fade into the air.

"How do you propose to get us out?" said Yuda.

Cluny looked at him gravely. "They will never discover how you escaped. I will add your figures to the picture, and you will find yourselves transported into that landscape and able to move away. When they come to look for you, the painting will be empty again. Even Jean Sorel will not suspect."

"But won't it take a long time to paint all of us?" said Malchik, glancing at his companions.

"That's the beauty of it," said Cluny, picking up his brush and palette. "A few shapes and daubs of color should be enough."

"Best paint me first," said Yuda, stepping forward. Cluny shook his head. "You must understand that you will find yourself outside, in the snow," he said. "And you, sir, are all but bare as a worm."

Yuda grinned. "They took my shoes. Took everything. Reckoned I wouldn't be needing them any more," he said. He clapped Cluny on the arm. "No need for the long face, boy. It wasn't your choice. And I don't need clothes right now. I'm still cooling down." Seeing Cluny's mystified look, he laughed. "Just paint, and leave the worrying to me."

Cluny turned to Casildis. "But you, sister, must borrow some of my clothes—and you must get dressed, Malchik. You cannot wear your night attire in the snow. While you are changing, I shall start to paint the others."

As he hurried to the garderobe to change his clothes, Malchik felt a strong pang of regret at the warmth with which Yuda had spoken to Cluny. He felt he had forfeited such friendship. He wondered if Yuda, like Casildis, would ever believe that he had not chosen to throw in his lot with the Doyen, except under duress. As he laced up the hose and pulled on his leather slippers, hoping they would be thick enough to keep out the snow, he tried to imagine how he might begin to approach the man, but nothing suggested itself.

When he emerged from the dressing room, Yuda had vanished and curious little stick-figure had appeared on the surface of the painting. In spite of his wretchedness, Malchik had to suppress a laugh. Cluny was working quickly, daubing an image of Isabel on to the canvas, using orange for her hair, red for her scarf and dots of color to mark the flowers on her dress. As soon as he had finished, Isabel took a step towards the picture and disappeared. As Malchik watched the image, he could have sworn that he saw the two small figures moving. Cluny had already squeezed black pigment on to his palette, and was sketching Annat, with two blobs for her eyes and a streak for her nose. Govorin stood observing the process with rapt attention, resting his chin on his fist. Cluny's hands seemed to move so fast it was hard to see them; when Casildis rejoined them, clad in one of her half-brother's better tunics over a pair of leggings that had seen several repairs, Annat was gone and Cluny had turned his attention to Govorin.

"I wonder whether they have noticed anything amiss yet?" said Malchik anxiously, rubbing his hands together. "Surely someone must have checked the dungeons by now and found the prisoners gone."

As he spoke, Govorin vanished into the picture, and only Malchik and Casildis remained. Cluny began to paint his sister before she had time to speak, stroking long lines of golden yellow on to the canvas to represent her hair.

"Cluny . . ." she said, starting forward, "thank you. I shall never forget this. I wish you could come with us."

"So do I," said Cluny, without pausing. He blocked in the blue of her tunic and the russet of her hose, keeping his eye on the picture as he worked. Casildis bent to press her lips against his cheek and was gone, leaving Malchik and Cluny alone to contemplate the small, jittery figures that now filled the frame.

"I can't say thank you properly," said Malchik, suddenly assailed by strong and strange emotions. "You don't know how much it means to me. To do this for us . . ."

Cluny gave a bitter laugh. He drew two circles for Malchik's spectacles, and dotted an eye with each. "You don't know how much it means to *me* to thwart my brother," he said. "He has to be stopped before he destroys us all. Maybe it's too late for that." He smiled at Malchik, pausing in his work. "I hope you find yourselves somewhere safe," he said. He splashed on the yellow of Malchik's hair and the buff of his tunic. "And I hope that some day, we can meet again as friends," he went on.

"We are friends," Malchik stammered. He stepped forward,

but Cluny was gone. He felt the rush of cold air against his face, and a strong scent of linseed oil and hemp. For a moment, he became the small caricature figure daubed on the face of the canvas, staring fixedly at his colorful companions. On the other side of his flat world was the tower chamber, curved like a lens, and Cluny's face looked in at them, huge and distorted, holding up the brush. Then with a faint pop, like bursting bladderwrack, Malchik fell out on to the snow and lay there in a heap, staring up at the others.

"Time we were moving," said Yuda, regarding his son with wry amusement, as Malchik waved his limbs feebly like an upturned beetle. Then he stretched out his arm and hauled Malchik to his feet, dusting the snow off his back with a rough friendliness that left Malchik almost speechless.

"You mean you don't . . . I don't . . ." he stammered. Yuda gave him a straight look.

"You got us out. I reckon that squares off the account, as far as I'm concerned."

Having quickly discussed what Cluny had told Malchik concerning the whereabouts of the scene in the painting, they set off across the blank, pure snow, heading in what they hoped was the direction of the river. Isabel was the only one who seemed to have any sense of the way they needed to take. They moved swiftly, with Yuda in front all but skimming over the surface in his bare feet, and the ghost-woman at his side. Several times she steered them to the left or to the right, until at last they mounted the top of an incline, to see the train a few hundred yards away, against a backdrop of leafless trees. It was swarming with the green-cloaked men of Ademar.

"Down," said Yuda, and they flung themselves flat on the snow. Annat crawled forwards on her stomach until she lay beside her father. She could just hear him using *sprechen* with Isabel in an exchange of thought more rapid and cryptic than any she had so far achieved. They were discussing ranges and lines of fire with surprising precision. She tried to count the men who were examining the locomotive, and decided that there were roughly ten of them. It was difficult to know whether they had been sent there some time ago to guard the train, or if they had just come from the castle in pursuit of the fugitives.

—*Nah, too soon,* Yuda sent to her. *Iz and I could finish this lot, no trouble, but we'd pancake the train. Have to get them away. You game? We'll run fast.*

Annat had difficulty keeping pace with the speed of his thought, but she sent him something like a fumbled nod of assent.

—*Good girl. You're learning. That's what it's about.*

He sprang to his feet, a strange and naked figure to startle the man below, and Isabel and Annat joined him. Yuda shouted in a loud voice, "Hey, goons! Fuck you and your master, the Doyen of Ademar," and accompanied his words with an insulting gesture.

There was an answering rumble of anger, then arrows began to fly and the green-clad men came hurrying across the snow towards them. Yuda was off, skimming over the snow as lightly as a deer, with Isabel and Annat spreading out in his wake. They ran east along the track, away from the train and their friends. Arrows flew past them, and someone hurled a spear, which crashed harmlessly to the ground near their feet. As they moved, Yuda kept up a stream of instructions from mind to mind. They veered to the right, climbing the slight incline that rose away from the line. Annat felt as if she were running on air; a yoke of power seemed to link her to Isabel and Yuda, so that she could keep pace with them, passing lightly over the surface of the drifts that clogged and delayed their pursuers.

As they reached the top of the incline, Yuda turned. He ordered Annat down on the ground. With Isabel beside him, he moved his hands in a complex gesture and sent out a surge of power that Annat had never seen him use before: a net of golden flame. Annat knew that he and Isabel had shaped it together, but the driving force was his. She saw the pursuing men stop in their tracks as the mesh came flying towards them; though they tried to stumble from its path, it flew down on them swiftly as a great bird, spreading its coils over them. The knights were caught in its bright snare. She watched them fighting against its threads, which seemed only to draw tighter upon them as they struggled. For a brief while she could hear faint cries, but they slowly faded away.

Yuda closed his hand into a fist.

—*Now we'll do the rest,* he thought.

Annat was a little afraid of his confidence. The change in him was palpable; since she had used the *Rashim*'s ring to heal him, his powers seemed to have grown in ways she did not understand. When he went past her, she felt the heat roiling off him like steam from the engine. It was as if he had been called back from the edge of death into a second term of life. As she followed him, some of his fierce joy communicated itself to her. He who had been the prey was now the hunter. Just as he would remember and bear the scars they had inflicted on him, he wanted them to remember his name and the losses he made them suffer.

Some four men-at-arms had remained close to the train, and Yuda had them in his sights. Annat saw their expressions of bewilderment and fear as they observed the fugitives returning alone, without their pursuers. They would not understand how this small man and woman and a thin girl could defeat armed knights. One of them raised a crossbow uncertainly, and another levelled his spear. Yuda grinned, a smile with all the kindness of a wolf.

—*I'll take the two on the left,* Annat heard him send to Isabel.

The killings were swift and brutally efficient. First Yuda made a scything gesture with his left arm, and a blade of blue fire flew from beneath his hand, whizzing across the space between. It sliced the two men through the midriff, cutting them down like sheaves of corn that collapsed and crumbled into dust. Then Isabel blew out of her palm a small flame that rose into the sky, dainty as a bird, to swoop down over the heads of the last guards, and engulf them in a sheet of fire that seared them to charcoal. The silence that followed ached, and Annat felt some pity for the lives so quickly extinguished. There was nothing left where the four men had stood but a pile of ashes, scattered across the snow.

—*I'd forgotten how it was to work with you, Iz,* Yuda thought.

—*It is good, Yuda, but it's over.*

—*How do you mean?*

—*I have to go now my task is done. I am still no more than a ghost that comes and goes like the mist. I can't stay with you to see the end of your journey.*

Yuda flung his arms round her to hug her close against him, hiding his face in her hair. There were other thoughts between them, but Annat did not try to hear them. She stood forlornly at a distance while Govorin and the others slowly emerged from their hiding place, trudging down the incline towards her. She did not need to ask what her father was feeling; his sadness had entered her own soul, and she grieved with him for the dead friend who could visit but never stay. The two shamans only separated when Govorin joined them; but Yuda still held Isabel's hand.

"There's your train, Mister Govorin," he said.

"I'm astonished," said Govorin, tersely. "I've never seen shaman-work like that before. I'm not sure I want to see it again."

"Nah," said Yuda. "But they would have killed us, or taken us back to Ademar to die."

Govorin shook his head, brushing off the powdery snow from his jacket. "They hurt you bad, eh, Mister?" he said, simply. Yuda gazed at him straight, as if they were two shamans, and gave a small nod in answer.

"And the *kind*," he said. "She shares what I feel."

As Malchik and Casildis joined them, Isabel said, "I must go. It is my place to wander alone."

"The music summons you," said Malchik, shyly. "The song of the red ship."

Isabel smiled at him. "Perhaps," she said, and leaned forwards to press a kiss on Yuda's forehead. Then she began to walk away from them, heading up the incline south of the track without a backward glance. Yuda stood gazing after her a long while, with Annat beside him.

Chapter 19

They had to wait while Govorin kindled the fire on the grate to heat the boiler. Even with Yuda's help to get it burning, nothing could hasten the work of making steam. While the two men laboured, Annat stood watching the woods with Malchik and Casildis, expecting every moment to see knights riding out of the dawn mist. Casildis alone seemed calm; when Annat began to shiver, she drew her close and wrapped her cloak round them both. Malchik was tensed as if to run, like a wild deer alert for predators. Seeing the white fumes of breath that issued rapidly from her brother's mouth and nostrils, Annat remembered that he now had the most to fear from Sarl and the Doyen. If they caught him, they would condemn him as a traitor and show him no mercy.

When at last the chimney began to emit a trail of cloud, Govorin pulled on the regulator and, with a defiant crescendo of steam, they began to move. Released from the need to keep watch, Annat rummaged amongst the pile of possessions in the tender until she found the doll, and sat clasping its rigid body against her with one hand. After a time, Malchik came to sit beside her, his hands dangling between his knees. His face had a lost look, as if he did not understand how he came to be where he was. The insight came to Annat that their captivity in the Castle of Ademar had hurt them all in different ways, and for Malchik, the distress had been to witness what had happened to his family and friends.

After a while, Casildis took over the firing from Yuda so that he could put on some clothes, and he came clambering back into the tender, observing Annat and the oblivious Malchik with a thoughtful look that had some concern in it. He put on a clean shirt and trousers taken from his pack, and discarded the loincloth. After searching for his *vyel*, he took it out of its case and sat down with it on his knees, fingering the strings until a slow tune began to emerge from under his bow. The skein of his music seemed to weave a cocoon of peace around Annat, though she could only just hear it above the noise of the locomotive. She knew that he was playing to heal a part of them that all the *Rashim's* magic could not touch. He was not going to tell her what Sarl had said and done to him, but with harmony he could soothe each of them in ways that words could never achieve.

She noticed that the landscape was beginning to change. They had left behind the wood of bare trees that filled the parkland around the castle and were climbing a slow incline cut into the side of a hillside, silvered with snow only in the crevices and ledges where it had found purchase. The river was sinking into the gorge below them, and a sheer precipice on their left fell down to the frozen water. It was a beautiful, perilous scene, through which dark birds wheeled and cried. Annat, who was sitting on the left-hand side of the tender, wriggled to the edge and peered over, still clutching the doll. The air was turning colder, with a frosty edge sharp as a honed scythe; but it also had a living freshness that Annat had not noticed before in La Souterraine. The sky was a breathless, deep blue, and the summit of the hill seemed to cut crisply into its surface, with a crest of white-crowned jagged rocks.

Yuda put down his *vyel* and crawled over to join her.

"Pretty, isn't it?" he said, after a while. Annat silently agreed with him. She noticed that his mind was refreshed, with a peace in it that seemed to echo the silence of the landscape. She glanced at him, and he smiled. It was the first unforced smile she had seen from him since they escaped from the castle.

—*How is it with you?* she thought.

—*I was going to ask you that . . .*

He leaned over the edge of the tender beside her, gazing down into the valley. The wind played with his black hair, sending it flying in all directions. There was a look of eager fascination on his face that almost reminded her of a young boy; though he had been riding the trains for many years, it could still delight him to come upon new scenery or an unexpected situation. A droplet of water formed at the end of his nose, and he grimaced and wiped it away. Annat laughed, feeling a sudden lifting of her spirits. Yuda might have changed, but he had not travelled so far away that she could not reach him.

—*I wonder how long it is until we reach the* domaine *of the Goddess?* she thought.

—*I need to speak to the Chief about that.*

He sat back and smiled at her again, more wryly this time. It made her wonder what he felt for Casildis, after everything that had happened since their night together. Though she doubted his feelings had changed, only the superficial levels of his mind were open to her, and his dark and inward thoughts were carefully hidden.

—*There are things I don't want you to know.*

—*I know that. But I have shared so much with you.*

—*We need some secrets. Zyon, kind, I'm your father!*

Annat looked up at him mutely, holding the doll against her chest. So long as it was not that he didn't trust her.

—*There are things even you are too young to know. Yet!*

Annat gave a small shrug of acceptance. What he was telling her made sense. But if he could not turn to her, with whom could he share the deepest, most painful thoughts? There was no certainty that he could turn to Govorin.

—*That was what he meant,* Yuda thought. *There were some matters a man didn't discuss even with his nearest friends. Maybe he expected them to understand. Maybe they didn't understand the way he'd hoped. Perhaps it as a little different for men, like that. Sometimes you had to manage alone.*

Annat thought she understood, though she was not sure she agreed with all that he was saying. The idea of such loneliness chilled her. In his place, she would have felt a need to talk, to share her feelings even if it were only to laugh off what hurt too much to explain. She watched him clamber down into the cab and touch Govorin on the shoulder. Govorin turned his head a little, and Yuda spoke to him quietly. She saw the Sheriff nodding agreement. Those two had been close for such a long time that, in spite of everything that had happened, Govorin was not going to turn Yuda away. The Sheriff was very different from Yuda, yet he was someone her father needed, a place of reliable stability. But she could not be certain that Yuda would confide in Govorin, any more than he had done in her.

While Yuda was talking to Govorin, the track reached a much steeper gradient. It was as if the unknown builders of the track, who had kept it running steady along the mountainside, had found a place where there was no alternative but to sweep up to the crest, or drive a long tunnel through the heart of the mountain. The locomotive began to struggle and Annat saw the two men in agitated conversation. She sat amongst the logs with the doll in her lap, and gazed at its painted wooden face. It was so long since it had spoken to her that she found herself doubting whether she had ever heard its voice. Stroking its yellow hair, she thought that it might have been intended as an image of Casildis. She bent over it whispering a mute apology to the image, and still as blood, the voice answered her at last.

—*Not much longer, Annat. We are coming to the* domaine.

Annat sat back in amazement, scarcely able to believe the words that she had heard in her mind. She gripped the doll, demanding of it in her heart why it had not helped them, why it had left them so long without a guide. The silence that followed told Annat she would not have the answer to the riddle soon. She sat with the doll on her knees, pondering what it had said to her, and wondering when she should tell the others. Yuda came climbing back into the tender, to occupy the space between her and Malchik.

"This is it, *kinder*," he said in a quiet, grim voice. "We have to lose the water-tank. And the three of us will have to get out and walk."

"But how will we manage without water for the engine?" said Malchik worriedly.

"We won't be needing it. We're not far from the *domaine*."

"How do you know that?" said Annat. "The doll just told me the same thing."

Yuda grimaced. "Since you healed me with the *Rashim*'s ring, there are things that I seem to know, Natka," he said. "I'll tell you more when we've crossed the pass."

He crouched down at the back of the cab and began to struggle to uncouple the water-tank. It was almost impossible with gravity working against him, but Yuda's new strength enabled him to do it. They stood together watching the tank racing back away from them down the track, until it jumped the rails and seemed slowly to spill over the edge, tipping its contents out in a hurtling stream. They watched it fall, turning in the air, and it was like being forced to witness the death of a friend. It flew down out of sight, and a little later they heard the roar of sound as it bounced off the mountainside, the noise of its ruin echoing amongst the hills.

"Come on, *kinder*," said Yuda. "We have to get off and walk. That way, if the train goes over, some of us may survive."

They jumped out one by one on to the side of the climb away from the drop; the engine was labouring, steaming slowly. Even Malchik managed the jump down from the cab, though he stumbled on the ballast below. Yuda stood by the trackside and shouted to Govorin, "We'll see you on the other side, Mister Sheriff!"

Annat saw Govorin wave as the train began to struggle up the incline, its wheels slipping and screaming. Yuda climbed down the ballast and led them away from the track, on to the broad curve of the hillside. He seemed to know where he was going; when the line and the drop beyond were out of sight, he found a stony path that zigzagged up the mountain, its grey imprint moving between the rocks towards a saddle in the summit above.

It was a slow climb, even for Annat. She had tied the doll to her back to leave her hands free. Yuda took the rear and helped Malchik along. Though with the solid rock to cling to her brother was less afraid than he had been facing a precipice, he still needed encouragement. Yuda had to show him where to place his feet, and kept hold of his wrist when they rounded the sharp, slippery hairpin bends. Annat hurried ahead of them, scrambling light-footed over the stones. She kept looking up at the light-strewn col, the pass above them. Sometimes she could not see it at all, when the hill threw out a shoulder of rock. At other times, it gleamed promisingly in the light, and she saw a window in the wall, like the one through which she and Yuda had gazed down over the forest: a peephole for the sun that she could not see.

Annat paused to look down on Yuda and her brother below. They seemed to crawl slowly over the barren rock, which showed a soft pale golden-grey under its powdering of snow. She had a strange uneasy feeling as she gazed at them that it would be the last time that she saw them together like this. She wanted to turn to the doll for reassurance, but it had retreated once more into its wooden silence. With a shudder that had nothing to do with the cold, she turned back to the path and began to mount it, feeling a chill about her heart. The mountain had seemed friendly, as if it offered its shoulder to her, but now she felt there was something menacing about the golden crags amongst which she clambered. The wind had given them fantastic shapes, eroding the soft stone into pinnacles and turrets; but some reminded her of human forms clinging to the slope, with holes worn into their faces instead of eyes. Annat was tempted to wait for Yuda and Malchik to catch up with her, but she hurried on, glancing from side to side and trying to fight the sensation that the rock formations were moving when she did not look at them.

The last stage of the ascent led her straight over a smooth, slanting outcrop. Annat used her hands and her feet to find her way up its surface. She could see the stone lens winking against the light, letting the sun flash through like a masked jewel. Up there a cluster of shapes and silhouettes gathered. Annat paused on top of the rock, her heart pounding. A shadow lay across the mountainside, but she could still make out the gleaming forms strewn across the ground: the soft, rounded glow of whitened skulls; the ribcages hollow against the wind; and the smaller pieces, vertebrae and finger-bones, scattered amongst the stones, all polished to a fleshless ivory. With a stitch in her side, Annat stood panting, shading her eyes against the light.

Up ahead, just before the entrance to the archway, stood a huge statue. It was carved into the shape of two women seated side by side, their faces worn and featureless, except for the hole of a mouth. Surrounding them were other figures, grey and golden as the fabric of the hills, with rough-shaped heads and craggy bodies, their blunt hands clutching axes and swords hewn from rock. As Annat watched, she saw them stir, and lumber towards her, as if the limestone ground had broken open and come to life, forcing its crags to walk.

—*Yuda!* she called to him, not daring to use her voice.

She turned, to see her father guiding Malchik up the last slope. He raised his head in answer to her call. Gripping Malchik by the hand, he led him swiftly over the brow of the hill, bringing him to stand beside her. Wordlessly, Annat pointed to the stone creatures. Yuda put his hand on her shoulder.

—*There's no way back,* he thought.

Slowly, the three of them advanced together up the shallow slope to the place where the statues sat. The stone men, who stood aside to let them pass, closing in behind them, looked as if they had been partly carved, partly assembled from lumps of rock; their faces were snarling masks with heavy brows and pebble eyes.

Yuda approached the feet of the statue. The two massive shapes sat side by side, linked hand in hand. The sinuous forms of their garments had been eroded and rubbed smooth by the wind.

"The twin Goddesses," said Yuda, so that Malchik could hear him too.

As he spoke, a voice, frighteningly loud, issued from the mouth of the right-hand statue, together with a cold mist. It was harsh, as if a raven were using human speech.

"You shall not pass!" it said.

Annat became aware that the stone people were closing in around them, brandishing their blunt weapons. Yuda pulled her against him, gazing up at the featureless face of the statue that had spoken.

"What do you want, Goddess?" he said, quietly.

"Before you can cross the Col de Pertuis, you must give me a life. Unless blood stains the feet of my statue, you shall all perish, both you and your friends who dare to scale my mountain."

"Shit," muttered Yuda, holding Annat tighter. She glanced round at the figures that surrounded them, whose blank faces did not change. A cold air came off them, as if they were breathing. They were the color and texture of the mountain, and there was no pity or human emotion in them.

—*We can't fight our way out of this*, Yuda thought.

The voice of the Cold One issued once more from the mouth of the statue. Annat watched the wisps of icy mist rising into the sunlit air as it spoke; the sound echoed off the walls of the pass.

"Give me the boy. His life is forfeit."

"No way," said Yuda, almost laughing.

"Then I will take the girl. Pure virgin blood is sacred to me."

Yuda turned to face them. His eyes were bright and his face had a hard look, as if he found the conversation with a stone deity ridiculous. He put Malchik's hand in Annat's. "Wait here. I'll deal with this," he said, under his breath.

Surrounded by the men of the crags, who pressed in on him from every side, Yuda approached the forms of the twin Goddesses. Annat was expecting to see him raise his hands and blow them asunder with a blast of the golden power he wielded, but to her surprise, he knelt down at their feet with bent head.

"Lady," he said simply, "let me be the one. Take my life."

As Annat cried out in protest, the stone men seized him and flung him across the feet of the statues, raising their weapons high. Malchik pulled his hand from hers, and they ran towards the crowd, but they might as well have attacked a wall. She saw Yuda lying there, gazing up at the masks, his face calm, then he turned away and shut his eyes. As the stone men brought down their knives, Annat hid her face against Malchik's chest, and he hugged her tight.

There was a rending crack as if the mountain itself had split apart. Lifting her head, Annat saw the statue above them split from top to bottom by a great fissure that severed the two seated forms. As she watched, the head of the Cold One snapped off and fell to the ground, smashing into fragments. A column of icy mist poured from the hollow neck. All around them, the stone men ossified where they stood; they were cracking and crumbling, falling apart. Dust rose from the ground, and the boulders rolled away, no longer human in form, but transformed to shapeless fragments.

Annat tore herself away from Malchik and pushed her way through the cairns of disfigured rock. She found Yuda lying motionless at the feet of the statue, blood on his face and shirt. Annat flung herself across him in a blind prostration of grief, aware of nothing. She guessed that, because he had been willing to die, he had destroyed the spell that kept them from crossing the pass. She felt Malchik's touch on the back of her neck, and heard him crying. Then she felt Yuda stir beneath her. She sat back pushing her hair out of her face, and saw her father open his eyes.

"Not dead yet?" he said, with the beginnings of a smile. He sat up slowly and reached out to touch her face. "Looks like something went wrong."

"I thought they had killed you," said Annat.

Yuda swung his legs down so that he was sitting on the massive feet of the statue. "Not this time," he said, gently. He glanced up at Malchik and added, "I'm gratified to see you both so upset. But we'd better be carrying on."

As he stood up, brushing off the stone dust, Malchik suddenly dropped down on his knees and wrapped his arms round Yuda's waist, hiding his face against him. Yuda looked down at him in astonishment, then distress.

"Boy," he said, helplessly. "Malchku, don't."

"You were gong to die for us. To die," said Malchik in a thin voice.

Yuda gazed at his son with a strange expression. He

stroked Malchik's head and held it to him with fierce tenderness. "It doesn't matter, boy," he said steadily. "It's over. No one died."

Suddenly, he looked across at Annat. She was not shut out from this moment, though passed between him and Malchik. She was the one to whom Yuda showed the depths of his anguish. He did not need to explain his love for her, but what he felt for Malchik ached like an open wound, an old wound that had never healed.

"Do you understand, Malchku? I was ready. Sometimes you have to be ready," he said. Freeing himself from Malchik, he crouched down facing him, and took his face in his hands. "You mustn't kneel to me, Malchik. It tears my heart. A Wanderer doesn't kneel."

Annat watched the two men amongst the stones. She went over to them and touched Yuda's shoulder. He managed to smile at her and, between them, they helped Malchik to his feet. Linked arm in arm, the three of them walked away from the fallen statues and the broken stones, until they reached the archway. On the other side, the path swooped down, and they saw the light glinting off the brasswork of the train on the line below. It was waiting for them.

—*I'll tell Govorin myself, when there's time,* Yuda thought.

—*He knows you better than we do,* thought Annat. She wanted him to feel her wonder, though she could not be as frank as Malchik. —*He knows what you are capable of.*

"We've known each other a long time," said Yuda, looking at her. She knew then that she had seen part of his secret self: not just his love for Malchik, but the devotion he could show to those he cared for. And she was as dear to him as her brother, though he would never need to make the same clear gesture. She was a shaman, and he had expected her to understand what he felt without speech.

They said nothing more during the long descent, and they were very quiet when they rejoined Govorin and Casildis. The Sheriff gave them a quizzical look as he described how he had nursed the train up the gradient; once or twice, he had been afraid that it would slip back or jump the tracks. Yuda

listened without speaking, nodding occasionally; he looked
very tired.

As the train moved off, he stayed in the cab with Govorin,
and Annat and Malchik settled themselves in the tender
amongst the wood, unwilling to say anything to each other.
The engine was running along the side of the mountain, balanced between the rock and the empty air. From time to time,
it glided through tunnels hollowed from the naked stone, and
its echoes reverberated about Annat as it thundered along.
The track zigzagged along the edge of the hills' great shoulders, above the gorge that the river had carved. They were
heading due west, and light from the sun sparkled off the icy
cliffs opposite, catching them when they escaped from a tunnel and glinting off the engine's brasswork. When Yuda came
climbing back into the tender, to occupy the space between
Annat and Malchik, she felt oddly shy and could not look
him in the face.

"We'll be stopping in a while," he said quietly.

Malchik blinked. "Where?" he said, glancing uneasily towards the drop on the far side of the train.

"Where there's somewhere for us to sit down," Yuda reas-
sured him. "But we need to talk. All of us, not just we three."

"The Cold One," said Malchik, almost to himself.

"What is it, boy?" said Yuda, leaning back on the chunks of
wood.

"Sarl is using her to drive out the trespassers from the forest. And the crows have already come to Masalyar. They are
ready to attack."

"He said something similar to me," said Yuda abruptly.

"Sarl spoke to you?" said Malchik in astonishment.

"Oh, he lavished quite some time on me. He wanted me to
know how important my failure was. To understand it fully, as
he saw it. He was excited by the thought of my despair." He
sat up and smacked his hands together. "I hope I disappointed
him. You see, boy, Annat and I are linked. She feels what I
feel. She was there in the darkness like a small candle that re-
fused to be put out. All I know of you, Malchku, is that you're
alive. But that knowledge was as important to me as Annat's

flame of hope. Whatever Sarl might say, I trusted something in you to resist him. Do you get what I'm saying?"

Annat noticed that her brother was crying only when he took off his spectacles to wipe his eyes. "I think so," he said.

"Something good, boy. It's important for you to remember that, because the trouble isn't over. You carry the seed inside you, and if Sarl didn't succeed in making you surrender to it, be sure the Cold One will try." He snapped his mouth shut, then added, "I've said too much. But there's a lot to say, and I'm damnably hungry."

Govorin stopped the engine when they reached the top of a plateau with the drop on one side and a snow-covered shelf on the other. They dismounted from the engine and built a fire to boil water for *chai*, sharing out what was left of their rations. They still had pemmican, and a little of the food that the Wanderers had given them, which the guards seemed to have ignored. They spread the bedrolls on the snow to sit on, and enjoyed the first time by themselves for several days. Even Casildis no longer complained of the taste of the pemmican.

They were high above the valley, in thin, bright air, with the fire burning hot and the black engine behind them. In spite of the cold, it was like sitting beneath the awning of a high blue pavilion embroidered with birds. While they huddled in their cloaks and coats, Yuda alone sat barefoot in his shirt-sleeves, seemingly untroubled by the ice on the wind. When he had finished eating, he fetched a cigarette from his pack, lit it and inhaled deeply with an expression close to rapture.

"Zyon, that's good," he said. "At least Sarl didn't know that I'd do anything for *tabak*."

"I'm glad you left room in your pack for some spare trousers," commented Govorin. "I wasn't looking forward to a journey in the company of that loincloth."

"It served its purpose," said Yuda, grinning. "I should have given it an honourable burial."

"Cremation was too good for it," said the Sheriff. They shared a smile and fell silent; Yuda fetched out a burnt twig from the fire, and began to draw patterns on the snow. Annat leaned forward to try to see what he was drawing, but could only make out meaningless scribbles.

"One of us is going to have to talk, Yuda," said the Sheriff. "Shall you begin, or shall I?"

Yuda blew smoke. "I'll say my piece when you've finished, Seriozha," he said, simply.

Govorin leaned back, folding his arms across his broad chest. "Well," he said, slowly, "Yuda and I have got something to share with the rest of you. I think Annat knows this already, but we're coming to the *domaine*. It could be over the next hill, or a little further. We don't know whether the track will take us all the way there; we may have to do some walking. But it's the end of our journey. Though I don't rate our odds that high, I think we have a chance." He shook his head. "Over to you, Yudeleh. I've told them the easy part, you tell 'em the hard stuff."

"Govorin's right," said Yuda. "When we set out, our purpose was to bring Malchik home. It's been some time since we realised that wouldn't be possible. The five of us have to confront the Cold One, and that means we have to tackle Sarl. Death feeds the Cold One, and she's hungry. Torture feeds her, suffering feeds her—but she only becomes more famished." He paused, looking at them each in turn. "While I was with Sarl, I went on a shaman's journey. I travelled inwards. He tried to break me, not just with wounds, but with darkness and magic. He drove me to a place beyond pain, and there I saw things, secrets and shadows, that I had never dreamed of. When Annat found me, and healed me with the power of the Ten Sephirot, I travelled from the lowest depths to the highest heights. I don't have the words to express what I saw, but the fire burnt me to cinders and renewed me." He paused again, studying his hands, which rested on his knees. "And one of the things I learned was like a memory, burnt into the walls of the castle. I saw them, Huldis and her friend, together. I saw the magic they did, and how Huldis was snatched away. But when I saw the face of the other girl, I knew her. It was my Aude."

"I saw them too," whispered Annat.

"The old man told me that Aude was his daughter. A bastard like Cluny," said Malchik.

Yuda shook himself. "It doesn't seem to have stopped him condemning Annat," he said.

"My father has no respect as to persons," said Casildis. "He would condemn his own son if he thought it just."

"When we've finished with Sarl, somehow, sometime, I'm going to return to the Castle of Ademar," said Yuda, softly.

"I wonder about Cluny," said Malchik. "I hope he wasn't punished for helping us. I hope they didn't find out."

"You know Sarl's mind better than any of us, boy. Can you tell us where he is?"

Malchik shook his head. "Not now that I've defied him. All I know is that he wants to destroy me too. And I know—" He broke off.

"You don't have to say it, Malchku," said Yuda. "Sarl had his own reasons for hating me. It was himself he hated, me he had to destroy."

"You knew?" said Malchik painfully, raising his eyes to Yuda's.

"For a man like that, such a feeling is worse than his own death. They can't accept any weakness, any evidence of their own vulnerability."

Annat thought of the look on Sarl's face when she had seen it in the torture chamber. A kind of starved ecstasy that had frightened her with its nakedness, though she had not comprehended its meaning. She picked up the doll and dandled it in her lap, wondering whether the hounds of Ademar were yet on their scent, or whether they would look up to see the crows flying overhead, like a flock of evil angels.

Govorin echoed her thought. "I don't suppose we've shaken him off for good," he said.

"I doubt it," said Yuda.

"He has to kill a shaman to bring back the Cold One," said Malchik. "But in order for it to work, the shaman must die in the Rotunda, at the heart of her *domaine*."

There was a silence before Yuda said, "I can see a problem there, boy. We need to get at the Cold One in order to set you free. That means we want the same thing Sarl wants. And one of us has to die."

"No," said Annat, loudly. Everyone looked a her. "Not you, Yuda. I won't let you."

She had scarcely finished speaking when they heard a voice, loud and cheery if somewhat hoarse, shouting, "Hallo, the camp-fire! Mind if I join you?"

Yuda sprang to his feet, with Govorin close behind him, but there was no sign of the speaker. Annat noticed at once that he had spoken in Sklav rather than Franj, though he spoke it badly.

"Where are you, Mister?" Govorin shouted in answer.

"Come out where we can see you," said Yuda, feeling at his belt for a knife that he no longer wore.

There was a pause, and then a tall, jaunty figure appeared, climbing up on to the track from the east. He wore a Railwayman's overalls and a spotted kerchief tied round his neck, and Annat recognised him at once; it was Zarras, the ganger who had died in Yuda's surgery on their first day in Gard Ademar.

"Friend approaching," he shouted in his croaking, injured voice, and waved his hand. There was nothing corpse-like about him, though his face seemed pale under his tan. Govorin and Yuda froze.

"Zarras?" said the Sheriff. "Is that really you?"

"It's me, Chief," the dead man agreed. "Hope I didn't give you a start."

"A start? Man, you're dead! I went to your funeral! What are you doing here?"

Annat hugged the doll close, as if it could warm her. There was something both sad and comical about the arrival of the dead ganger, who seemed so unsurprised to find them there.

"Greetings," he said, as he approached Yuda and Govorin. "The others sent me to find you."

"Others? What others?" said Govorin excitedly. Then he slapped his thigh and exclaimed, "By the Mother, that's it! It was you building the line!"

Yuda, with a cautious look, held out his hand to Zarras, who took it and shook it warmly. "I'm sorry we never did get to meet, Mister," he said. "But your face is the last thing I remember from my life. You got me an easy death, and I don't like to leave debts unpaid."

"Are all the others here?" Govorin demanded. "St-Paul, Razumovsky and the rest? Some of them went years ago."

"We're all here, Chief, but we thought I should come up alone to warn you. There's a bit of a problem up ahead, see."

"Never mind that—call the others! It would do me some good to see their faces, even if they are dead. Then you can tell us about this problem."

Zarras smiled. "I'll call them over, Chief," he said. "It's a strange thing how we came to be here." He tipped his hat to Casildis, then walked over to the line and stood on the very edge of the precipice, where he cupped his hands to call, "Come on, lads! The Chief wants to see your ugly faces!"

Govorin and Yuda turned to each other, sharing an incredulous laugh.

"Were you expecting this?" said Yuda.

"Not exactly; but who else would build a Railway line through La Souterraine?"

There was a sound of falling rocks and some swearing, before six more figures, bright in the Railway's red and blue, clambered into view over the edge of the track. They were a motley gang; some marked with the wounds that had killed them, some pale and thin, while a couple were brown-skinned and merry, as if they had never died. With Zarras in front, they came shambling over to the camp-fire and greeted Govorin with a certain shyness; Annat tried not to look to closely at a bearded man who had half his face shorn away, though the other half looked cheerful enough.

"Thank you, lads," said Govorin. "I'd hoped you might get some peace in death, without me to harry you!"

"It's not your fault, Mister Govorin," said Zarras, who seemed to be their spokesman. "As we died, each of us found himself in La Souterraine. We didn't know where we were, and we went on building the line, because there seemed no reason to stop. In the beginning, we weren't sure if we were dead or alive. But, if I say so myself, we did a sweet job of it!"

"All done without an engineer," said Govorin, grinning. As he shook each man's hand in turn, Annat was impressed that he did not flinch from their disfigured faces. "You're a credit to the Railway, lads, though I must say it's hard you never got a day off for being dead!"

A small, wiry man with a gap-toothed grin spoke up. "And we didn't get paid no wages either, Mister G!" he said.

"We'd never have made it this far without you," said the Sheriff, more seriously. "Sarl would have caught us long ago if we'd been on foot, or even on horseback, God forbid! But why don't you join us? I'd offer you food and *schnapps*—you've got a little left, haven't you, Yuda—but I figure you can't have it!"

"The fire is welcome, Mister," said Zarras. "Seems like in this place we can never get warm."

Casildis made room for the little group of gangers, and they settled themselves around the fire, holding out their hands to its heat, and casting hesitant glances towards Annat and Malchik. Several of the men tipped their hats to "Missis Chief," as they chose to call Casildis; like her husband, she seemed to know them all by name.

The gangers might be dead, but their company was a relief. It was not long before Annat began to get used to their strange appearance, just as if they had been men who were alive and disfigured. She laid the doll carefully on the snow and drew nearer to the fire, hoping to hear their stories. They too seemed eager to hear the whole tale of the journey, and were fascinated by Yuda. They were intrigued that he seemed not to feel the cold; they could not get close enough to the fire, basking like lizards in its warmth, and rubbing their hands over the burning logs. Govorin, having recovered from the first shock of the encounter, was chatting away with them like old friends. Yuda, who did not know them, was less talkative, but Zarras seemed to have a special regard for him, and was politely questioning him about the powers of a shaman. Soon Annat rose from her place and went to slip herself between Yuda and Casildis, so that she could hear what they were saying.

"Who's the little maid, Mister?" said Zarras. "She does have a great look of you."

Yuda glanced at Annat, then put his arm round her shoulders.

"This is my daughter, Mister Zarras," he said. "She'll be a powerful shaman one day."

"I was just telling your father, Missis," Zarras said, "we've reached the end of what we can build. Up ahead there's a deep chasm, and the bridge that crosses it is made of bone. We can't lay sleepers on that."

"How will we get across?" said Annat.

"I reckon you'll have to go on foot, though it looks a flimsy path to me. But I figure it's meant to keep folks out rather than help them over."

"Is the Goddess's *domaine* on the other side?" Annat asked.

"Seemingly it is, though none of us has tried to go across. We don't want no truck with any Goddess, or not with the Cold One, leastways. Some of us have seen too much of her already."

"What are you going to do now the track is finished, Mister?" Yuda asked.

"Reckon we'll stop here till you come back," said Zarras, matter-of-factly.

"It's good to know that someone is guarding our backs. You could give Sarl and his knights something to think about."

Zarras's face broke into a grin. "Now that's a sweet thought, Mister," he said. "Sweet as a nut. He has to cross the Bone Bridge, same as you."

"But he's got horses," said Yuda, pulling Annat against him. "We can do many things, but flying's not one of them."

As he spoke, there was a ripple of laughter from Govorin and his former gangers, and someone started to sing. The words were in Sklav, and one by one the dead men joined in as best they could, though some had voices thin as reed flutes. Govorin's bass formed the backbone of the song, and after a murmur of recognition Yuda joined in. Though Annat had heard him sing before, once again she was surprised by the deepness of his voice. She leaned against him, wondering where he found the spirit to sing when their future was so doubtful. Like many Sklav songs, it was a melancholy air, yearning for a lost motherland; the Wanderers sometimes sang such melodies about their return to Zyon, though they had left it so long ago. She watched Malchik across the fire, listening; like her, he did not know the tune or the lyrics, but they still had a powerful effect, summoning up a nostalgia that was not their birthright. Yuda gave her shoulders a squeeze; he too had been born in Neustria, not Sklava, but he shared some of the culture and the dreams that united Govorin and his co-workers. He reminded Annat in his thoughts that it was a song for anyone exiled from home, who longed to return. The gangers would not see their homeland again, but there was some hope, however small, that Annat might return to hers.

Chapter 20

The train began to glide slowly down the track, with the dead men walking on either side of it. Yuda and Annat stood side by side on top of the tender, as if they were riding in a triumphal chariot. Above them, clouds spread out like a fan shaded the liquid blue of the sky; ahead, the rocky landscape unfolded as they passed from one curved mountainside to another. The wind had fluted the jagged pinnacles of rock until they were as complex as lace: strange, delicate festoons of stone overhung the precipice, casting antic shadows that fell across the train as the hidden sun moved westwards. There was just enough wind to lick Annat's hair back from her face and rustle her skirts; she felt as if she were riding across the dome of the world, gazing down on its map spread out below her. She held the doll in her arms, with its face staring ahead, so that it too might watch where they were going. Below her, she could see Malchik sitting upright and alert on his throne of logs, and Casildis shovelling wood into the firebox, while Govorin drove the train with a steady hand, watching the line up ahead.

The chasm came to meet them suddenly; the precipice curved round to the right and disappeared into the distance, heading south as a long rift valley that cut them off from the other side. The track followed the curving shoulder of the land

for a little way, before it petered out, ending in a pair of
buffers. Govorin brought the train smoothly round the curve
and applied the brakes so that the locomotive rolled neatly into
place. Casildis straightened, rubbing the small of her back, and
smiled up at Annat and Yuda where they stood on the roof.

No one said much as they set to work gathering and loading
up their belongings. They left the bedrolls and the blankets behind. Casildis put the water-bottles into her pack, while Govorin took the remaining food. Malchik slung his harp across
his back, and Yuda kept nothing but the *vyel* and a pocket full
of cigarettes. Annat watched them, hugging the doll to her
chest. They were all making a tacit assumption that they would
not need much once they entered the *domaine*; from there,
they would either escape, or die.

One by one, they climbed down from the train and skirted
the edge of the drop until they reached the bridge, where the
dead men waited for them. Annat noticed that Malchik leaned
against the side of the train, feeling his way with his eyes shut,
until he was able to walk in the middle of the track, away from
the precipice. They gathered in a small group on the narrow
ledge of stone, gazing at the bridge that spanned the crevasse.
As Zarras had observed, it was fashioned out of bones, a slender structure with a narrow walkway and no handrails. It
looked as though it would scarcely carry a man, let alone a
railway engine. Though the span was short, it was not short
enough for anyone to cross at a single bound, though a man on
horseback might manage it.

"This is where we leave you," Govorin said to Zarras. He
laughed in his beard. "Possibly in a downwards direction."

"We'd better cross one at a time," said Yuda. "I doubt if the
bridge is strong enough to carry two."

"I don't think I can do it," said Malchik, his mouth trembling.

"Yes you can, boy. Just keep your head up and look at the
other side. I'll go first, so you can see how it's done."

Without hesitating, Yuda stepped out on to the bridge and
walked swiftly across without looking down. Annat saw the
fragile structure shaking under his weight, and wondered how
it would carry someone like Govorin.

Yuda beckoned her. "You next, Natka," he said, commandingly. There was nothing she could do but go. She looked down at the whiteness of the bones, her heart pounding, and then remembered Yuda's words. When she raised her head, he was smiling at her, and his confidence in her reached out like a strong hand. Annat took the first step on to the bridge and once she had begun, there was no turning back. Her legs trembling, she ran across without looking down, feeling the bony structure dancing beneath her feet. She kept her eyes on Yuda, but it seemed a long time before she ran into his arms, to find herself shaking and sweating on the other side. It was only then that she dared to glance down into the narrow chimney of rock, which seemed so deep that she could not see the rocks below. Yuda hugged her.

"Well done, *kind*," he said. "I knew you could do it. I wish I was as confident about Malchik."

As he finished, Casildis was already stepping out on to the bridge. She walked painfully slowly, keeping her gaze just ahead of the place where she had to set her feet, but her balance was good, and she moved steadily, keeping her arms spread out on either side of her. Yuda gripped Annat's wrist almost too hard, watching the woman and willing her to stay upright. Suddenly, Casildis leapt forwards and crossed the last yard at a single bound, leaving the bridge swaying and dancing behind her. Yuda swallowed air and went to meet her, seizing her arms to keep her from overbalancing on the edge. He guided her back on to the broad ledge without speaking, watching every step that she took.

"I'm all right, Yuda," said Casildis, laughing breathlessly. "You can let me go now."

Malchik and Govorin remained on the other side, amongst the huddle of dead gangers. Annat could see that her brother was trying to argue with the Sheriff; but at last, he turned round, got down on his hands and knees and began to feel his way out along the span, which swung and jiggled under his weight.

"Oh God," said Yuda. "I don't think I can watch this." But he went to the end of the bridge and began to coax Malchik forwards. Annat felt sick as she watched her brother edging his way across the slats, moving one hand at a time. He gripped the edges hard, too hard, and the bridge swayed, bowing like a catenary as he neared the center. Malchik stopped, and Annat could see that he was panting hard.

"Don't stop, boy," said Yuda. "It's only a little further."

He stepped out on to the bridge, holding his hand out towards Malchik. There was a faint cracking sound, and the sinews that held the slats together at the far end came apart. For an instant the bridge seemed to hang suspended, and then it slammed down out of sight, with Malchik clinging to the pathway. Yuda fell like a stone.

Annat screamed. She ran to the edge of the cliff and bent down, peering along the line of the bridge. Yuda was just below her, hanging on by one hand, and Malchik was under him. As she watched, her father turned in the air and took hold of the bridge with his free hand. Annat thought that he would scramble to safety, but instead he began to edge downwards. He caught Malchik by the scruff of his tunic and, clutching the bridge with one hand, began to climb.

"He'll never make it," gasped Casildis.

"Shut up!" said Annat. She crouched on the edge, willing Yuda on as he had done for her. Only the new strength he had gained since she healed him enabled him to carry Malchik's weight. She could see that her brother was hampering Yuda; he still clung on to the struts of the bridge, and it was all Yuda could do to curse him into letting go. Her father hung by one hand, and Annat could see the bone slats tensing beneath the weight he carried. At last, Malchik began to move slowly upwards, and Yuda let him go for a brief instant in order to haul himself back on to the ledge. He lay on his belly next to Annat, and reached over the edge of the stone as far as he dared go, holding out his hand to Malchik.

"Take my hand, boy," he shouted.

Malchik had stopped again. He was about a yard from the top, and Yuda's hand dangled just above his head. He only had to reach out and take it. Annat could see the bridge swinging slowly under his weight. At any moment, it might snap from its hawsers and plunge down into the chasm.

"Take my hand!"

"I can't. I'll fall," Malchik groaned. Yuda edged out still further and gripped one of Malchik's hands by the wrist.

"I've got you, boy. Now let go!"

Malchik still clung to the struts, his eyes closed. Yuda tugged at his wrist, and at last Malchik uncurled that hand. His palms were bleeding. Yuda took a grip on his hand and began to pull. Slowly, Malchik edged upwards, his weight supported only by his purchase on the bridge and Yuda's grasp. Annat saw and heard the hawsers that held the bridge beginning to ease apart. Yuda rose to his knees and with a great heave pulled Malchik over the edge, dragging him on to the ledge as the bridge finally severed from its moorings and fell clattering into the chasm below.

Yuda dragged Malchik towards him and bent over him, clinging to his back as if he were afraid to let go. His shoulders were shaking.

"Zyon, boy, I thought I'd lost you," he muttered. Malchik lay sprawled on the stone, his face buried in Yuda's lap. He seemed more dead than alive. Yuda stroked the boy's head, roughly, a couple of times, and then got to his feet, helping Malchik to stand. Annat could see her brother shaking all over. Yuda guided him inland, away from the edge, and made him sit down with his back to the cliff wall. Then he turned to Annat and Casildis.

"We have a problem," he said.

Govorin was stranded on the far side of the ravine, amongst the gangers; there was no way for him to cross. Yuda stood on the edge and shouted to him. "You'll have to stay there, Mister. Wait for us."

Govorin waved ruefully. "Me and the boys will prepare a reception for Sarl," he called.

"We'll come back, Sergey, whatever happens!" Casildis shouted.

Yuda turned to her with a grim face. "I hope you're right there, Missis," he said, softly.

Govorin blew a kiss to Casildis, which she pretended to catch in her right hand. Then they waved goodbye to the Sheriff and his companions, and set out along the path that would take them inland, towards the *domaine*.

Annat had picked up the doll once more, and she held it in her arms as they walked along the ledge that led away from the chasm. Yuda took the lead, and she was behind him, with Malchik following her, still feeling his way along the rock wall like a blind man; Casildis was last. The ledge had been cut in the naked stone, and it was less than a yard wide. Above them, the rock wall rose high and sheer, speckled with the droppings of birds. Below was a free fall down to the frozen river. The height did not frighten Annat, but challenged and exhilarated her. She watched Yuda's back, observing how confidently he strode along the narrow path. His mind was focused on the destination ahead.

After a while, the path began to climb the side of the cliff. At first, it rose steeply, and Annat sometimes had to use one hand to guide herself over the rocks. She saw Yuda ahead scrambling round a sharp hairpin bend, where the track doubled back on itself. From here on, it climbed the side of the mountain in a series of zigzags, and the hillside itself sloped inwards, giving an illusion of security. Annat was able to glance down to see her brother's toiling progress below, while Casildis waited patiently behind him. Annat herself was able to move much faster, clambering after Yuda with one hand against the rock. From time to time, her father would pause to check on Malchik's progress; once he made to turn back, but Casildis signalled to him to continue; she was content to guide Malchik's steps alone.

At last, the path reached the top of the ridge. There was a second sheer drop on the other side, and the path danced perilously along the narrow summit, weaving its way amongst the startling chimneys of rock configured into delicate shapes by the wind. Yuda waited for Annat to join him on the ridge, and she saw from his face that he too found only excitement in the dangers of the climb. She was out of breath by the time she reached him; he stood alone on the summit, with the wind blowing out his hair, as steady as if he stood on an open plain. When Annat reached him, she found that he was gazing out across the rippling pattern of the gorge below. On the opposite side, fantastic shapes and pinnacles mimicked the rock towers of the ridge; just behind was a shimmer of blue, which might be grass-covered hillsides, or a distant sea. There was no trace of any snow.

—*I'd say it was worth it just to see this,* he thought.

—*It's like flying.*

They stood side by side, gazing out over the empty space, briefly distracted from the purpose of their journey. Not far below, Malchik was toiling up the zigzag path, helped by Casildis. Yuda looked down at his son with a troubled expression, but he did not wait long for him. Instead, he set out along the ridgeway, climbing up to the first crest of rock, which gave some protection from the drop on the right. Indeed, the path was less threatening than it had seemed at first; the cliff on the right formed a steep scree, which ended at a narrow ledge before plummeting out of sight to the slopes below. Annat followed Yuda, keeping close on his heels. With his bare feet, he had an extra grip on the stone, and he swarmed up the rocky outcrops with the ease of a monkey. In spite of the seriousness of their purpose, Annat took a childish pleasure in hurrying after him, and when they reached the foot of the stack, they paused, sharing a smile.

It was hard work traversing the ridge, with climbs up to the level of the chimneys followed by cautious descents to the path. From time to time, Annat would glance back towards her brother and Casildis, who were still some way behind, crawling along the track and slowly mounting the pinnacles like two moles in the daylight. The wind sang above her through the eroded pipes and crannies of the stone chimneys, making a mournful sound. At last, however, the footway began to descend from the summit, weaving its way down the ridged spine of the hill towards a new valley. Very faintly, far below, Annat made out a silvery-green raft of meadows, traced with the long windings of a rock wall. Beyond the wall was a mass of dappled dark green, and Annat realised with a shock that she was looking at the *domaine* of the Goddess, spread out below.

The climb down from the mountain was much slower than the ascent. Annat and Yuda toiled along the stony path that wound over the side of the hill, sneaking between outcrops of rock and doubling back on itself to emerge above a scree or plunging downwards over a series of uneven steps, some so high that Annat had to jump. Below them, the planar landscape shimmered like a mirage beneath the haze of low cloud; as they descended, its details grew clearer, and Annat could see the dark shadows of the complex alleyways that formed the maze and the glassy dome of the Rotunda at its center. She paused to gaze, her heart thumping loud, and Yuda stopped a little way below her. They were within sight of their destination, and the touch of the sun had transformed it from something threatening into an enchanted garden, which seemed to beckon and encourage their approach.

"I wonder if there's a gate?" said Yuda aloud. Annat did not answer; fear turned her mouth dry and her stomach hollow. Yuda glanced back at her with a questioning look; he had come to rely on her instinct for danger when he himself knew no such fear. Annat sat down on the path, nursing the doll on her knee. "Perhaps we should wait a bit, to let Malchik catch up with us, she said, gravely.

"Perhaps we should," said Yuda, gazing down at her. "I knew Casildis would make a calmer guide than I would. I'd have lost patience long ago."

"He's always been afraid of heights. He never even climbed the cliffs at home."

"It's not surprising. Just before I left your mother, I dangled Malchik over a cliff to give her a fright. It was then I realized I had to leave; I was turning into a monster." He turned away from her, and she felt the sharp edges of regret and grief.

"You never did that to me," said Annat.

"Your mother only cared for Malchik. You looked too like a Wanderer to make her happy. That's why Yuste adopted you. But Aude doted on Malchik. Poor *kind*."

He looked up to the place where Casildis and Malchik were slowly descending; Casildis walked in front while Malchik came down bumpily on his bottom. Yuda sighed. "I thought I was so clever," he said to himself. "And look at him now. But he's done it; maybe in his own way, which isn't all that graceful, but he has done it."

Annat scratched her leg; her woollen stockings were itching

at her. "Malchik does try," she said. "I think he'd do anything to please you."

They waited until Casildis and Malchik were within hailing distance before setting out again. The track was less steep than it had been higher up, and Annat and Yuda moved swiftly, jumping light-footedly over the stones and uneven boulders. The hill spread out beneath them like a broad belly, and scraggy plants began to appear in crevices in the rock, small thorny bushes and clumps of thistle to scratch the unwary. Annat did not envy Yuda his lack of shoes, but he seemed quite skilful at avoiding the thorns, pausing once only to extract some spines from the pad of his foot. After a while, they began to pass amongst ragged mounds of gorse and the first scrawny, wind-thrown trees butted up out of the stony earth, coarse and frayed and as grey with dust as the rock. The path was now broad and shallow enough for Yuda and Annat to walk side by side, and they trudged along, glad of the shelter from the wind.

The slope curved smoothly down to meet the tree-line, and the first dark pines came shouldering forwards to meet them, bringing a still gloom that was strange after the harsh clear light of the mountainside. They walked between the green shadows, on a meandering path of light that dipped in and out of the shade. No bird calls came to interrupt the silence, only the high rushing of the wind through the tops of the pines, which emphasised the sinister loneliness of the place. Annat and Yuda walked slowly and cautiously, like intruders; there was an air of waiting, as if at any moment something might spring from amongst the trees.

They had walked about a mile along the wandering track when it opened on to a broad grass avenue, bordered on either side by mighty yews. Each tree had been clipped into a shape: there were towers and castles, ships and windmills, beasts and monsters. The dark forms with their polished leaves loomed above Yuda and Annat like rows of guards holding back the crowd from a procession. The avenue descended the hill as far as the eye could see, and at the foot Annat could just make out the hedge that bordered the wall of the *domaine*.

"So, we're nearly there," said Yuda, sounding suddenly

tired. Annat glanced up at him as they walked along. Except for Malchik and Casildis, they were the only living creatures for miles in all that wilderness.

"Are you ready?" she asked him.

"We'll find out when we get there," he said, grimly.

The cold sun seemed to peel open a strip of golden green before them. They passed between the shadows of the yews, stepping swiftly through the long grass. The wind could not be heard down here, and it might have been a pleasant place had it not been for the ever-present sense that something watched them and waited for them: the mind of the Goddess. Yuda put his arm round Annat's shoulders; they hurried along, feeling that the shade was a friend and the sunshine their enemy. The sun, which they had never seen, was the spy of the Goddess; it trained her gaze upon them, two tiny and insignificant figures in that vast landscape, dwarfed by the crouching yews and the tracts of empty forest beyond.

Once or twice, Yuda looked back to see whether Malchik and Casildis were following them. Now they were on more solid ground, the pair were beginning to catch up. Ahead, the tall hedge did not seem to draw nearer, but rather to increase in scale and detail. Annat could see the twining briars that formed it, a mass of stark tendrils and long thorns. She was not surprised when Yuda broke into a run, and they dashed the last few hundred yards hand in hand, impelled by a sense of urgency that forced them to confront that ugly barrier, rather than endlessly drifting towards it as it grew in height and density. Behind them, Casildis and Malchik too began to run, and the four of them arrived before the high mass of the hedge almost at the same time. They stood in a row, gazing at the thick wall of thorn, which looked as deep as it was tall. Some of the spikes grew six inches long; there was no way to penetrate it without an axe.

"This is the entrance," said Yuda, gazing up at the top of the hedge.

"Do you believe we could climb over?" said Casildis.

"We'd be torn to pieces," he replied. Annat sensed him pondering the problem. They could walk along the boundary, to see if there were a place where the hedge grew less thickly; or they could try to enter here. "Any chance your doll could help us?" he asked, still inspecting the close-packed briars. Annat shook her head. The doll was silent, but Annat was aware of a presence within, which knew of their plight; it would help them if it could.

"There's only one thing to do, then," said Yuda, glancing round at them. "The rest of you stand well back. That includes you, Natka," he added, feeling the question in her mind.

Annat backed away, following Malchik and Casildis, to stand watching her father as he stood before the hedge, feeling the palms of his hands. He was fathoming the height of the briars with his gaze, as if taking the measure of an enemy. Though Annat knew what was coming, nothing prepared her for the heat and force when Yuda extended his hands and sent out a burst of white flame. It tore into the hedge, seizing on the dry tendrils and scorching them to twisted ash. While Yuda jumped back, the whole mass went up in a golden, roaring, dazzling hell, a mass of fire that seemed to beat against the distant sky, sending up a great tower of smoke. Yuda came to join them, wisps of steam drifting from his hands; the fire had not touched him.

"That was, er, impressive," said Malchik drily. "Now we only have to get through a wall of burning thorn."

Yuda laughed, pretending to cuff his son. The fire was spreading away from the original flash-point, catching in the tender-dry wood. Ahead of them, the briars seemed to writhe in agony, twisting as the flames consumed them. The heat of the blast had been so intense that in places the stems had not had time to burn; they had been seared to charcoal in an instant, and they were falling, crumbling under the weight of the collapsing tendrils above. A blackened hole was appearing in the hedge, emerging from between two balks of flame: a place where there was nothing left to burn. Annat could see that the wall beyond was buckling, dragged down by the creepers that had been rooted in it, and the calcifying power of the flames. As she watched, the hedge yielded to the fire, losing its shape as one by one the stems caught fire or stiffened into ash. The blackened remnants lay strewn on the ground, smoking, and the earth beneath was burnt white.

"Time we were going," said Yuda. He turned away from them and approached the thorns, which lay in a sprawling, tangled heap of blackened branches and cinders. He kicked the pile with his foot. There was a clear gap in the hedge, and the stones beyond had collapsed, leaving a fissure framed by uneven edges. They had breached the wall of the *domaine*.

One by one, they followed him through the opening, stepping out on to the short turf that lay beyond. They found themselves standing in a sunken alleyway that passed between overhanging arches of sweetbriar to end against the entrance to a great maze. Its walls were carved from box and living yew, growing more than six feet tall. Beyond them rose the dome of the Rotunda, balanced on tall stone columns. The scene was beautiful and tranquil, like the deserted garden of a great house whose inhabitants had gone indoors to seek shelter from the sun; but here the sun gave out no heat. Annat felt a foreboding far more intense than anything she had experienced when climbing in the mountains above, or walking through the forest. She turned to Yuda, and he said, softly, "We're looking at our death."

They stood in a row, gazing down the sunken path bowered with unseasonal roses. There were no bees humming to charm the stillness; it had the breathless, empty silence of a mortuary where the dead lay, serene and hollow, awaiting the embalmer. Annat felt the chill air against her skin like an unwelcome touch. Even the flowers had the waxen look of funerary ornaments. There was no life here, only the preserved illusion spread out to cheat the senses.

"Shall we go?" said Malchik, nervously.

Without answering him, Yuda began to walk slowly along the sheltered avenue. Annat scuttled after him, hugging the doll's wooden body tight against her chest. There were shadows here, cast by the intricate shapes of the climbing roses, which seemed frozen in time. She felt that time itself had been peeled away, leaving nothing but stasis. It might take them for ever to each the end of the avenue; or they might age as they passed down it, until their bones fell and crumbled into the grass. The procession of flowered arches appeared endless, each one shedding the same scent of sweetness that was close to decay; they all seemed to draw Annat closer to the embalmer's slab, offering her a winding sheet and a coffin filled with perfect blooms. She saw herself in her mind's eye laid out, pale and lifeless, holding a white rose against her breast; preserved for the view in a glass-covered casket.

Yuda's hand touched the small of her back. "Try not to think about it," he said. When Annat glanced at him, she saw instead a broken form covered in blood, the mouth open and the jaw slack. Yuda squeezed her shoulder, and the reality of him broke in upon her; he was alive and walking beside her, and they were halfway down the avenue.

Up ahead, at the end, was the green wall of the maze. In between stood a circular sunken lawn with a sundial at its centre. Yuda and Annat approached the sundial and paused to study the gnomon and the shadow it cast; the finger lay upon mid-of-the-day. Yuda caressed the lichened stone with his fingertips.

"I wonder how many years it's shown that time," he said.

"Everything has stopped," said Annat, looking up at him.

"I think time stopped here when the Cold One was exiled," he said, glancing at her.

"What about us, *Tate*? If we get back to the outer world, how much time will have passed?"

Yuda gazed at her with sad eyes. "We can't tell, Natka."

He traced the rim of the dial with his fingers and bent to read the inscription. " 'The sun's majesty will be darkened when its face is revealed once more.' "

"We can't see the sun now," said Annat. "We've never seen it."

—*The sun is the gift of the Bright Lady*, said the doll, soft but distinct. Yuda straightened and Annat saw from his face that he had heard it too.

"No sun, no change and no time," he said.

When Malchik and Casildis joined them, they began the walk down the second half of the avenue together. Surrounded by her friends, Annat was no longer troubled by images of death and loss; but the lingering sadness remained. She was not very surprised to see Yuda take Casildis's hand; they walked together, lost in mutual silence, watching the entrance to the maze as they approached it.

The four of them stopped just outside, and Casildis reached the tiny ball of twine the *Rashim* had given her from her pocket. "This will help us find our way back, if we need to return," she said, tying one end to a twig in the hedge. The maze looked more inviting than menacing; they could just make out the shady path that turned to the left inside the entrance, carpeted with short green turf. They followed Casildis, who clasped the ball of twine in her fist, into the first alleyway. It seemed to curve gently to the right, ending at a blank wall of privet and a concealed turning. They walked to the end of the alley, where they had to turn right, and the path promptly doubled back on itself. It did so several times, before opening out to offer identical ways to left and right. They hesitated at the junction before choosing the right-hand path, which began to curve promisingly towards the centre.

An hour later—or perhaps it was more—they were lost. The intricate weavings of the maze had carried them back and forth, and several times, to their dismay, they had passed lengths of Casildis's twine that had been left earlier. They tried retracing their footsteps, rewinding the delicate ball of thread, until they found themselves at the junction where they had made the wrong decision; there they would follow another route, only to discover at its end the gold glimmering like tantalizing spider's web amongst the bushes. They stopped together at the base of a weathered stone statue showing a nymph balancing the world-globe lightly on her shoulder. Malchik bent to read the inscription while the others stopped to discuss where to go next.

"My thread is here," said Casildis, fingering it, "but I'm sure we never came this way. I don't remember any statue."

"As this is a dead end, you would have rewound your ball of twine," said Yuda, tightly.

"There's some more writing on this plinth," said Malchik. "If only I could make it out." He tried to trace it with his fingers. "'Come Death and quench the something flower, That guards the stillness of the Hour . . .'" The rest of it has worn away, but the word looks like 'frozen.' A frozen flower?"

"Come on, boy," said Yuda. "Don't waste time over that thing."

"We have to go back the way we came," said Annat, glancing back down the alleyway, which seemed ominously shadowed. The chill and stillness here had acquired an air of menace that she had not noticed in the outer reaches of the maze.

"I think there were three openings at the last junction," said Yuda. "And this is the third we've tried."

Slowly, they began to walk over the short grass, which carried the impression of their footprints in its springy turf. Malchik lingered, still puzzling over the writing on the statue. Annat hurried ahead, beginning to feel a sense of panic. She hoped that Yuda was wrong, and that they had not explored all the turnings at the last fork. Perhaps they would have to return to an earlier junction, to set off in a different direction. She wished that her mind did not seem full of fog and confusion. She could scarcely remember the turns they had taken before that last division of the way, let alone whether they had explored all its passages.

They stopped again to take their bearings when they reached the crossroads. Annat turned back to meet the others, no longer sure which route to follow. She saw Yuda hurrying towards her, grim-faced, with Casildis behind him, carefully gathering in the golden twine. There was no sign of Malchik.

"Why isn't Malchik with you?" she exclaimed, darting to meet them.

"I thought he was following me," said Casildis, glancing back.

"Damn the boy, why can't he keep up?" said Yuda, impatiently. "At least we can't lose him down a dead end."

As he spoke, there was a long, high-pitched cry from the direction they had come, but it was not Malchik's voice; it did not sound human.

"Zyon," said Yuda, and he began to run back up the alley, with the others close behind him. As they ran, the sound echoed again, and this time it seemed to have a mocking note. They rounded the curve in the wall of yew, and came face to face with a thick green barrier growing across their path. Annat was sure that it had not been there before. There was no sign of Malchik, and the statue of the nymph had disappeared.

Yuda threw himself against the barrier, clawing at the mingled leaves of box and yew, but to no avail. The hedge seemed as solid and thick as if it had grown there for years. Yuda swore, cursing himself, Malchik and the Cold One. There was nothing he could do; Malchik was gone, as surely as if the ground had opened and consumed him whole.

With Malchik's loss, the last trace of hope seemed to have been stripped from Yuda, and he went at the task doggedly, but without joy. Neither Annat nor Casildis knew how to comfort him. They returned to the crossroads and selected another path. It seemed to all of them as if it no longer mattered which turning they chose, when the Goddess was altering the maze around them. They walked in single file, with Yuda at the front and Casildis in the rear, pausing only to confer when they faced another choice. It was a laborious process that found them often retracing their footsteps, and all the time the clear sunlight never changed, casting its noonday shadows across them as they walked to and fro.

At last they sat down to rest in an arbour sheltered by the branches of a pear tree, which bore a full shroud of blossom. Yuda leaned his chin on his hand, not looking at the others, and Annat played listlessly with the doll in her lap, wondering how long they had been caught in the mid-day stillness. She had asked the doll to help them, but it had not answered her. After a while, Yuda turned to Casildis, who was sitting next to him.

"What do you think, Missis?" he said, almost aggressively. "Which way should we go?"

"All ways look the same to me, Yuda," she said. "I think the *Rashim*'s gift has failed us. The traps left by the Goddess are too cunning."

"I am so tired," he said. "With all my powers, I can't think of anything."

"Lie down and rest," said Casildis. "What harm can it do? We won't find Malchik any quicker by driving ourselves to death."

Yuda lay down with his head in her lap, and she stroked his hair with her long fingers.

"The Goddess won't hurt him," he said, thinking aloud.

Casildis sighed. "But that's not what troubles you," she said.

"We could have been here for years," said Annat, looking up at the pale blossoms overhead. Their frailness made them less ominous than the waxen roses. They spoke of transience in the midst of all that stillness.

"What if she's taken his mind?" said Yuda. "I don't know how to get him back."

"Perhaps you will find a way," said Casildis.

"You are beautiful," said Yuda, focusing on her face. As Casildis raised her fingers to his cheek, Annat reached up to pick a sprig of the dangling blossom. It snapped off easily in her hand, and she lifted it to her nostrils, wondering if there would be any trace of scent left. She held it cupped in her palms, seized by the overwhelming sadness of the place. Fragility and change were the true substance of life, not this perfect preservation. She watched the spray withering in her hand, dropping petals that slowly turned to a grey dust. She blew it from her palm, thinking that she understood something. There had been no change in this place for years, but she had wrought one by picking the flowers. She sprang to her feet, scattering the last of the dust.

"I know the answer," she exclaimed.

"What's that?" said Yuda wearily, rolling his head towards her.

"Nothing changes here, nothing dies, and nothing is born. Only the maze keeps reshaping itself around us. But we are alive, we change and we can die. Where we come from, the sun rises and sets. Once we remember that, the maze should reveal itself to us as it really is."

"Annat is right," said Casildis. "Nothing could be this perfect after three years of winter—let alone twenty-three. It must be an illusion."

Yuda sat up and pulled Casildis against him, kissing her forcefully on the mouth. As she pushed him away, protesting gently, he jumped to his feet and caught Annat by the hand.

"What a fool I've been! All this time it's been staring us in the face—but it took my clever daughter to see the truth. Look!"

All around them, the maze was changing. The petals

dropped like snow from the pear boughs, withering into fili-
gree skeletons. The leaves fell in showers, and the tall hedges
shrank and collapsed, revealing little by little a sad wilderness
of brown foliage and rotting trunks. The grass mouldered beneath their feet, shrivelling away to reveal dank patches of
moss clogged with dead leaves. At last, the garden's true state
could be seen; it was a ruin, overgrown with weeds and brambles that had died themselves, leaving behind their carcasses,
saturated with winter rain. The feeble sunlight shone wanly
over the scene of decay; the three of them stood under the bare
branches of the pear tree, and only the petals that had strewn
their hair did not wither away to dust.

Chapter 21

The walls of the Rotunda rose a short distance away. Seen from close to, it was a massive structure, its dome supported on Corinthian columns hewn from white marble. The curved walls were made of stuccoed plaster, and in many places the stucco had begun to crack and fall from the bricks beneath. Nothing could mask the awesome beauty of the place, which stood amongst the ruin of the maze like one of the ancient temples of the Kadagoi, fractured by time but still maintaining the ghost of its former grace.

Yuda kept hold of Annat's hand. He glanced at Casildis, and the three of them set out without another word, picking their way amongst the tangles of brown yew, and fallen briars. Without its glaze of perfection, the maze no longer had the power to threaten them; there was nothing left but a lingering melancholy for its lost grandeur. They walked purposefully towards the Rotunda, skirting the heaped piles of thistle and brambles, and the silence was like the saddest music in the world, lamenting fallen splendour and withered hopes.

They passed along the wall of the Rotunda, gazing up towards the skyline of the dome, until they came to a door, set beneath a grand marble portico, which had long ago been filled in to leave only a small entrance below. Releasing Annat, Yuda was the first to step through to the gloom beyond. The others followed him, and paused together in the chill twilight, waiting for their eyes to become accustomed to the darkness, while the crooning voices of doves drifted down from the unseen roof above.

The circular space was empty except for a ring of statues set back in the shadows between the columns. In the centre was a tall dais on which stood a double throne, but only one of the seats was occupied. The form of a woman sat there, her head covered by a white veil, with a silver crown above it; she sat motionless with her back to them, slumped forward in her chair, in the attitude of one long dead.

"Lady," said Yuda quietly, but his voice pierced the stillness, "where is my son?"

There was a silence before two figures stepped from the other side of the throne; one was Sarl, and he had his arm round Malchik's shoulders. The boy's eyes were blank and staring.

"Malchik!" cried Annat.

He will not answer you," said Sarl, quietly. "He has looked into the face of the Goddess, and he is one with her, as I am."

Annat heard the cry of grief in Yuda's mind. He gripped her arm like a drowning man.

—*But it can't be true,* Tate. *Surely we can get him back?*

She thought into silence; Yuda did not answer her.

"Leave while you may, Vasilyevich," said Sarl. "You can do nothing here."

"I came to save my son, to destroy the Goddess—and you," said Yuda. "That leaves two things that I can do. And I'm not alone."

"What, with my sister and that child? You could not save yourselves from the Soul Men, let alone stand against the Goddess. Turn back, Vasilyevich, and take home your defeat. I need not kill you now."

The flare that sprang from Yuda's hands lit up the drum-shaped chamber, bringing the statues round the walls to flickering life. The radiance grew to envelop Malchik, Sarl and the figure on the throne, like a bubble of light that increased in brightness as it swelled to fill the space. The vault of the dome cracked with a sound like the earth breaking, and still Yuda stretched out his arms, as if to engulf the whole world. Annat crouched down, shielding her eyes, and Casildis clapped her hands to her ears; they saw Sarl recoil, his mouth open in a soundless cry, while Malchik slumped down on his knees like a rag doll.

"Forgive me, Malchku," whispered Yuda.

The bubble burst, and ribbons of fire trailed across the walls and ceiling of the Rotunda; the interior filled with smoke. Sarl had fallen back against the steps of the dais, his clothes smouldering on his body. Without a glance in his direction, Yuda strode across to Malchik and knelt down beside him, cradling the dead boy in his arms. And the Goddess came.

Her presence manifested first as a slow chill that brought tendrils of mist arising from the ground, but soon ice was forming on the walls and creeping across the floor, throwing out tentacles to bind Yuda where he sat, and curling over Sarl, licking at his wounds with frosty tongues. Annat began to shiver, clutching the doll against her chest. She saw Casildis standing alone, her head raised as if in a trance, her long hair stiff against her back in rime-covered strands. No snow fell, but the air seemed to crack with the breath of winter, and ice crystals issued from Annat's mouth, as if she was exhaling jewels. The Goddess closed her grip upon them, shutting out the last glimmer of light from the dome, as even the hidden sun was eclipsed by her rising shadow.

"Lady," gasped Sarl. The skin on his face was burnt black, and his hands were raw; but like busy needles the shoots of frost crept over him, sheathing him in a silver carapace that moved with him like a second skin.

The temple was filled with the presence of the Goddess: dark and cold and more deathly than winter. Once more, Annat felt the hopeless silence of the mortuary, a stillness that promised no new life. As she watched, the shape on the dais stood up stiffly, and turned to face them. Too chilled to cry out, Annat stared at it in numb horror. The skin of the face had a smooth, luminous whiteness as if it had rotted long under water, there were black holes where the eyes should have been, and the mouth was a brown line. The figure began to descend the steps until it stood just above the place where Sarl lay.

In her mind, Annat heard the voice of the doll, so weak that she could hardly make out the words.

—*Set me free, Annat!*

—*But how do I set you free?* Annat begged. There was no reply.

The mouth of the Cold One opened on a cavernous darkness. "Destroy my enemies," she said, in the voice of a snake.

Sarl rose to his feet, armoured from head to toe in silver mail. Though Annat could see the raw flesh beneath the transparent sheath that clad him, he seemed to feel no pain. He stretched out his arm and a spear of ice fell into his grasp; brandishing it triumphantly, he walked down the steps to where Yuda knelt, still holding Malchik's body. Annat struggled to move, but the freezing shackles held her fast. She was clamped to the ground, bowed over her doll. As Sarl came to stand above Yuda, her father let Malchik's form slip down to the floor. Turning his head to look up at Sarl, he said, "What kept you so long?"

As Sarl raised the spear to plunge it into Yuda's heart, Casildis, with a cry of rage, tore free from her bonds and flung herself, bleeding, across the room. She seized the haft in both hands so that the point rested against her own breast.

"Kill me first, Zhan!" she shouted. "Show me you have the strength to do it. For I swear by the Bright Lady you'll have to kill us both."

"Step aside, Casildis," said Sarl, trying to wrench the spear from her grasp. Yuda stood up and took Casildis gently by the shoulders.

"Not you, Missis," he said. "This is between us, he and I."

Casildis turned on him, shielding him from Sarl with her back. "You have a daughter living!" she yelled. "Don't you care what the Cold One will do to her when you are gone?"

"Kill them both," said the voice of the Goddess.

Sarl raised the spear as if to transfix Casildis and Yuda together, but his hand shook. Annat watched her father gazing up into the woman's face, warmed as ever by the touch of her beauty.

"My son is dead," he said, obstinately.

Annat sent him a flood of thought, begging him to stay, showing him the shards of her own grief, and asking him to remember her. She saw Yuda glance towards her and saw from his eyes that, for all his pain, he would not desert her; a few words from Casildis had reminded him how much he cared for his only daughter. He laid his hand on Casildis's shoulder and said, with a smile that was both sad and bitter, "The woman's right, Zhan Sarl. You'll have to skewer us both." He grasped Casildis by the waist and pulled her against him, thigh to thigh, burying his face in her hair. Sarl stepped back.

"I cannot do it, Lady. I cannot kill my sister," he said. The spear in his hand broke into splinters of ice that fell to the ground at his feet.

Yuda pushed Casildis away from him. "I'm not your sister, Zhan Sarl," he said. "And I can kill you."

He stretched out his hand as Sarl had done, and plucked a fiery weapon from the air. As a glowing disc like a shield appeared on his arm, two bright blades dropped into Sarl's grasp, and he rushed at Yuda, who swung to meet him, wielding a sword of flame. The two men clashed like a hammer striking an anvil, and sparks and shards of ice flew from their blades. Yuda knew his own strength and his weakness; he did not stay locked with Sarl, but darted back, mocking him with speed and lightness of foot. When Sarl strode after him, he returned to the attack, searing the icy armour with tongues of flame. Sarl spun, cursing like a man plagued with a gadfly, but Yuda was always just out of reach of his whirling swords. He moved with the grace of a dancer, crossing the slippery floor on sure feet and luring Sarl to follow him, only to turn and sting the Heir's flesh when he went too near. The blood flew from Sarl's arm as the sword raked him, and he swore at Yuda, demanding that he stand and fight like a man. Annat saw her father laughing, quenching his anger and pain with every stroke; he parried Sarl's answering blows, sending them glancing from his coppery shield.

She found that she could move. The web of icicles that bound her to the floor had begun to melt in the heat from the combat. At last she understood that the doll contained the spirit of the Bright Lady, trapped there when Aude and Huldis summoned up the Cold One; knowledge that seemed to come too late to save them. She lifted the doll close to her face, and begged the Goddess Artemyas in her heart to reveal how Annat could set her free. She sensed that the answer was easy, but the doll could not tell her; Annat would have to guess that final step.

Yuda and Sarl were circling each other, crouching like wrestlers. Annat could see Sarl sweating as the armour melted off him. Yuda ran at him, yelling a wordless cry, and once more the cold iron clashed with the flaming steel, sending up sparks in a white shower. Having led Sarl a dance, her father began to press him, cutting a cat's cradle of light between the glittering blades. It seemed as if, with his new strength, Yuda was almost a match for Sarl; he parried the mighty strokes with his shield, riding the blows that fell unceasingly like the hammers of a smelting engine.

Annat struggled to her feet. The Cold One stood immobile on the steps, her dreadful face without expression. Whoever fell first, she would feed on his soul; and if Sarl won, she would take Annat and Casildis as her own, or destroy them. Annat moved towards the combat, seeing her brother's motionless body lying close to the steps of the dais. She felt hate rising within her that his life could be carelessly reduced to nothing, as if he did not matter. She saw her feelings reflected in Yuda's face and the glow in his eyes. He had no thought for his own safety, only the task of killing Sarl.

Both men were bleeding and the fresh blood spattered the floor, glistening in the light. Annat wondered how Sarl could have got close enough to Yuda to wound him. She watched her father taunting the tall warrior, not with words but with quick movements that sent him wherever Sarl was not. As the two men fenced across the floor, feinting at each other with flickering blades, Casildis watched from the steps of the dais, hope and longing in her eyes; she would have liked to fight at Yuda's side, to bear him company in the unequal struggle. For Sarl seemed invulnerable. Though Yuda had cut him, he showed no sign of tiring; the ice-armour re-grew to cover his limbs, and he seemed to rise above the slighter man like a silver giant.

Yuda was losing patience. His shield had been hacked to pieces, and he flung it away. He moved the sword to his left hand and struck at Sarl with his lightning, playing it from his hand like a whip. Sarl cut the lightning cords asunder and bore down on Yuda, who jerked the steel from his right hand with a twisting stroke. The two remaining blades clashed edge on edge, and the men were caught, snarling face to face. Sarl strove to bow Yuda to the ground, but Yuda slipped from beneath him like an eel and almost stabbed him in the face before Sarl's rising sword hooked the weapon from his hand and sent it clattering across the floor.

As Sarl lunged at Yuda, cutting a gash in his shoulder, Annat gave a cry of pain and alarm, only to see her father ride the blow and sting his way free with a dart of fire. He shook himself, and once more spun the radiance from his ring, whirling it towards Sarl like a red-winged bird. As the man staggered back, Yuda went after him, only to be suddenly caught and impaled by the sword in Sarl's left hand. Yuda stayed on his feet, but his dark head dropped forward. As Sarl wrenched the blade free, he fell at last, lying suddenly broken on the marble floor.

"No!" Annat yelled. She dashed the useless doll to the ground, shattering it into brittle fragments, and flung herself across the room to where Yuda lay. Casildis was there before her, lifting the man's head into her lap. As Annat fell down on her knees beside them, she saw the slow rise and fall of Yuda's breathing, while the blood ebbed out from the wound under his breastbone.

The Cold One descended the steps, to stand just above them.

"His soul is mine," she said.

Yuda's eyes opened. "The boy is with me," he said, in a whisper, but quite clear. "Tell her she can't have us."

"She knows," said Casildis, stroking his hair.

The door swung open, banging back on its hinges, and a wind came howling into the chamber, stirring up the rags of mist and smoke. When Annat raised her head, she saw the figure of a man standing in the doorway, black as midnight; it was Govorin.

"You're not the only one who has a champion, Goddess," he shouted as he strode into the hall. Sarl turned slowly, the sword bleeding in his hand, and the darkness gathered about the two men so that they could hardly be seen except by the flames that smouldered still on the walls and the ground.

Annat could hear a humming in her ears, like the voice of many bees. It was not a lament, or a song of death. It spoke to her, murmuring soft words that she could not quite distinguish. She reached out and laid her hand over Yuda's wound.

"Not this time, Natka," he said, softly. "I'm finished."

"No," said Annat, baring her teeth. "I'm not letting you go."

The golden song came to her from the warmth of long summer afternoons, when they were flying home to their hive, laden with pollen. All the time it was growing in strength. Annat bent over Yuda and the power clothed her hand like a glove, reaching down into the wound with honey threads. Busy as spiders they spun, weaving and healing, closing torn veins and drawing injured cells together.

Govorin met Sarl in the centre of the hall, wielding a knobkerry fashioned from ebony. Just as Sarl was clothed in an armour of ice, Govorin was naked except for a coppery sheen that seemed to wrap him from head to foot; and Sarl's power could not pierce it. With a face like a thunder god he struck, and the sword shivered to pieces in Sarl's hand. Yuda turned his head to watch the two fighting, and spoke again, his voice a whisper.

"You know what this means, Natka; you've done it," he said.

Annat scarcely heard him, caught in the spinning of the golden twine. She felt the heat flooding through her like music, a song that wove itself out of the language of the bees. Stubbornly she crouched over Yuda, willing him to heal and wielding the power that had risen to fill her from the fragments of the broken doll. She had only needed to smash it, here in the Rotunda, to free the Bright Lady from her prison.

"Don't die, *Tate*; you mustn't die," she said. He did not answer. She saw Casildis's slender hand resting on his hair, and felt the flame of his life flickering inside her, like a candle about to go out.

Behind her, Govorin gave a shout. He was driving Sarl before him, but the Cold One had given Sarl a new sword. Steel clashed on wood as the two men strove together. Like Yuda before him, Govorin was laughing, but his eyes were cold with rage. He seemed to burn like a black coal filled with fire, and while he prevailed, the dim flame lingered in Yuda, though he lay still and his eyes were shut. Annat felt Malchik's presence in the air, hovering, and she knew that he waited between life and death. She took Yuda's slack hand in hers, fearing that she had done all she could, and turned to watch the fight on which all their lives depended.

The warriors were drawing nearer. There was no quarter, only the clash of their weapons. Annat saw that Sarl's left arm hung useless by his side, broken by the mighty staff of ebony. Govorin whirled it round his head for a killing blow, but in that moment his foot slipped on the bloody floor and he went down, falling at Sarl's feet. Casildis cried out as Sarl straddled him, raising his sword high ready to drive it home, when suddenly Yuda raised himself on his elbow and sent a last, luminous jet of fire straight into Sarl's face. There was a flash, a shock and a burst of black smoke; the jolt threw Sarl across the room, where he crashed against the wall, and his skull split open, spraying dark matter. As Sarl slid to the floor, Yuda sank back, curling his hand against his breast, and his head went slack on his shoulders.

Annat saw Casildis bury her face in her hands. She felt a pressure on her shoulder, and knew that Govorin was behind her.

"I'm sorry, Natka," he said. "I think he's gone."

Annat bowed her head. There was nothing in her mind but a wide, aching emptiness, not even the faint trace of a candle-flame. But the soft whispering of the bees went on unceasingly, and now it was growing stronger. She lifted her hand to touch Govorin's, unwilling to answer him and give up hope. She felt tears running down her cheeks, splashing on to her hand and Yuda's wound. Too late for her father; he was dead, and the chant of the bees would not rouse him from the stone

where he lay. She heard Casildis speak, and her voice seemed
to come from a great distance.

"No, Sergey, you're wrong. You must be wrong; the Bright
Lady is here . . ."

Annat turned her head. She saw the shimmering figure, like
sunlight reflected from water, mounting the steps of the dais
until it reached the place where the Cold One stood. The
Bright Lady touched her sister's shoulder, and as she did so
the shell fell apart, peeling back like the skin of a snake, to reveal a beautiful form, all moonlight and shadow, with a trail of
starlights in its hair. Overhead, the darkened sky above the
dome grew light, and the sun threw its full splendour down
into the ruined hall, its intensity veiled by the marble of the
vault.

Yuda opened his eyes; they were darker than the empty sky.
Annat had healed him, or the Bright Lady had, through her;
but she did not think that he would thank her for it. He had
been with Malchik, in a place where she could not go; now he
had returned alone, to face the knowledge that his actions had
destroyed his son.

"*Tate*," she began, squeezing his hand. The flame was there
once more, constant and unwavering.

"It's all right, Natka," he said, and she felt the strength of
his fingers. "I've come back."

"Is that you, Vasilyevich?" said Govorin, leaning forward
across Annat.

"Did we kill him, Sergey?" said Yuda, smiling faintly.

"You did, Mister. You killed him, and saved my life."

Annat sat back on her heels, feeling strange and hollow
without the doll to fill her arms. The twin Goddesses sat side
by side on their thrones, holding hands, like mid-day and midnight yoked together. It was not possible to see their faces,
only as shadowy gold like the sun half-eclipsed, and a deep
blue changeable moonlight. No words were spoken, but the
Goddesses inclined towards her, seeking to know what she
wanted. She sensed them smiling at her behind the sunlight
and the shade, offering radiant gifts: a share of their wisdom,
peace, happiness. Annat could not return their smiles. The only
thing that she wanted was for Malchik to be alive, and for

Yuda to be made whole. Without her brother, life would be hollow, forever twisted and broken. The Goddesses did not answer her, but the Bright Lady rose to her feet and clapped her hands. At her signal the Rotunda filled with music, not the murmur of doves or the drone of bees, but the sound of voices that were almost human, whispering and chanting a thousand liquid notes. Annat found herself looking round her for the source of the singing, but instead she saw with a shiver that the statues round the walls were beginning to come to life, stepping down from their niches one by one and approaching the dais in the centre. As they moved out of the shadows, Annat saw in astonishment that they were not stone figures at all, but living men and women, who stretched their limbs and rubbed their joints to ease the stiffness of long disuse.

Govorin looked round him incredulously. "I don't believe it," he said. "Does this mean we've done it; done what we came for?"

Suddenly, the singing ceased. The Bright Lady was descending from the dais. She made her way through the throng like a candle illuminating a dark hallway, until she stood before them. Seen from close to, her form seemed made out of a continual play of light and flame, from buttercup yellow through gold to a deep molten red. From time to time, her eyes were visible, like stars or shadows or patches of foggy blue. As Yuda turned his head to look at her, she bowed to him; to all of them. She held up her left hand as if to pluck a fruit from a tree, and a golden apple appeared in her palm. With a liquid gesture, she cast it to the ground, and it rolled across the floor, spinning and turning, until it came to rest where Malchik lay. To Annat's astonishment, Malchik slowly rolled over, sat up and reached out for the apple. He picked it up and took a large bite from the golden flesh. As they watched, he seemed to turn from ashen grey to vivid color; Annat saw the sudden rich brown of his eyes and the red that flushed his cheeks. Apparently unconscious of anyone else, Malchik went on eating the apple, taking generous mouthfuls and chewing vigorously. The light in the dome glinted off his golden hair, and his hands, which had been pale and lifeless, regained their natural color.

"Boy," said Yuda, in a weak voice. He did not release his

grip on Annat's hand and she knew that, even when his mind was filled with the shock of Malchik's return, he had not forgotten her. She was so confused with the sudden joy of the moment that she could not think straight. Malchik noticed them and scrambled to his feet, the half-finished apple in his grasp. He came towards them with a puzzled expression on his features, and Annat wondered how they must look huddled together on the floor in their damp, dirty, bloodstained clothes. Her brother knelt down beside her, studying Yuda, and suddenly held out the remains of the apple to him.

"You should have some of this, Mister," he said seriously. "It's good."

Yuda lay still, gazing at his son and the proffered apple. Then he reached out and took it from Malchik, turning it over in his hand.

"Some things can't be mended, Malchku," he said.

Malchik sat back on his heels. "Eat it, Mister," he said, frowning. "I'm alive."

Yuda bit into the apple, and swallowed painfully. The change that came over him was not as swift or marked as it had been in Malchik, but he sat up slowly, releasing Annat's hand.

"Zyon, boy," he said, "I thought I'd lost you."

"We thought we'd lost *you*, Vasilyevich," said Casildis. Yuda glanced at Govorin, who nodded in assent.

"Annat healed me," he said, showing her the shadow of a smile.

One by one, they helped each other to their feet, to find themselves surrounded, at a little distance, by a crowd of awed and uncertain strangers. Most of them seemed to be villagers from Gard Ademar; but there were a few Railway People amongst them. Casildis gave a small cry and ran towards one girl, a gilt-haired beauty who shrank from her touch.

"Huldis! I am Casildis, who was your young sister."

"What has happened to me?" said the girl. She looked no older than Annat, and it was plain that she had not aged at all during her time in the Rotunda.

"Huldis," said Yuda to Govorin.

"I can't believe it yet, Mister," said the Sheriff. "If this is our victory, why does it feel like defeat?"

"It cost us dear enough," said Yuda. He tossed the apple in the air and caught it with one hand. "But I think I'm beginning to believe it."

He held out his free hand to Annat, and suddenly she ran to him and put her arms round him. She knew he was right; she was only just beginning to realise that Malchik was truly alive, and her father healed. She was not sure that she dared to feel happy after so much pain. But she sheltered under the wing of Yuda's relief, as he turned back from death and felt the sun warm his face.

Casildis was approaching, leading Huldis by the hand. She bowed low to the Goddess.

"Thank you, my Lady," she said. "You have granted all my wishes. All that are permitted."

Annat guessed that she was referring to Sarl, whose broken body lay where it had fallen in the dust by the wall of the Rotunda. Even the Goddesses could not restore him to life and take away the years when he had done evil to serve the Cold One. But he had been Casildis's brother and he had spared her; she was admitting her sadness that he alone could not be redeemed. The Bright Lady lifted her shimmering hands over Casildis's head, as if to bless her. Annat found the shy Huldis glancing at them curiously, herself and her father, Malchik and Govorin. The pale, pretty features reminded her a little of Sarl, but with none of his brutality. And her eyes were like those of Casildis.

As Casildis joined them, bringing her sister, the four of them gathered together. Malchik, unasked, put his arm across Yuda's shoulders, and was not rebuffed. Casildis smiled at them, but a little sadly. She stretched out her hand to Annat and said, "Natka, this is my sister Huldis, your mother's friend. See, Huldis, Aude had a daughter—and a son. And this was her husband. All of them came here to set you free—and Govorin, my man."

Huldis glanced timidly from one to the other. She was slighter than Casildis, and her face was pale after her long imprisonment.

"Is it true?" she said, almost in a whisper.

Yuda touched Annat's head. "This one looks more like me, though there's a likeness to her mother, if you look carefully," he said. "But Malchik is the image of Aude."

"She wasn't so tall," said Huldis, blinking at Malchik, and Annat realized that, however hesitantly, she was making a joke.

"We have a problem, Casildis," said Govorin, folding his broad arms across his chest. "This lass belongs to Ademar, but I can't see us getting too warm a welcome if we take her there."

"Huldis needs time," said Casildis firmly. "She has lost twenty-three years, yet is still a young girl. I was a child when she was taken from us, and Zhan a kind brother. I cannot send her home to live amongst strangers. She understands that Aude is gone, and that a long time has passed while she stayed here a prisoner. I need to take her to a place of safety, a place where she can live quietly until she has gathered up the pieces of her life."

Annat spoke up. "What about us, Mister Govorin?" she said. "Can we go home?"

"Home?" said Govorin thoughtfully. "The Mother knows what we'll find when we return to Gard Ademar. With the Doyen inhabiting both worlds, he may have razed the place to the ground in our absence. Our home could be smoking ruins."

"I'd like to get out of this place," said Yuda, with a grim smile. "But they say a Wanderer has no home. I want to return to Chorazin and give the *Rashim* back his ring; if he lets me, I'd like to stay there awhile, with the *kinder*. They too need time and a place to heal, Annat especially. Since the old man hopes to reverse the miracle and return to the outer world, he may need someone to protect him when he gets there."

"Chorazin," said Govorin, fingering his beard. "It used to lie on the far side of the forest from Gard Ademar, not a long way from the castle. Wherever you go, Yuda, I mean to go with you. I'm not letting you out of my sight again for a while. You nearly died on me there, and I couldn't have that."

"We should all go together," said Casildis. "Huldis isn't

ready to face my father yet. If the *Rashim* will give us sanctuary, I think we should shelter there."

"He may no be so happy with that," said Yuda tersely. "The Doyen accused him of stealing Huldis."

"But from there I can take her to safety amongst the Women. As their priestess, I must tell them what has passed. And find Mari Reine . . ." She broke off, lowering her gaze to the ground.

"My wife is right, Yuda," said Govorin, with a rueful smile. "None of us can go back to Gard Ademar, not right away. When the Doyen finds out we've killed his son and heir, he'll be after revenge. I doubt if he'll care much that we did it to rescue his daughter. If the *Rashim* will have us, we should hide out in Chorazin, at least until we know which way the wind is blowing. It may be that from there we can get a message to our friends, and find out whether the village—and my tunnel—are still standing."

"So be it, Mister Govorin," said Yuda, smiling back at him. "You're the chief. I just hope the *Rashim* finds us welcome guests and not a nasty surprise."

The Bright Lady came to stand amongst them. Now, for the first time, she spoke; the word was "Chorazin," and her voice echoed softly like a memory of music. Yuda bowed to her, as Casildis had done. "Our thanks," he said. "*Shkineh*, Bright Lady, Child of the One."

The Goddess raised her hands, and again the strange voices began their plangent song. The Rotunda slowly vanished like mist from around them, and the six of them found themselves in a small walled garden, where a fountain played in a marble pool, and a great tree cast shade across the short grass. It was mild as an early spring day, and leaf buds were showing on the overhanging branches of the tree. Beneath the trunk was a chair, where a man sat reading, wearing a long violet caftan edged with fur, his glasses resting halfway down his nose. It was the *Rashim*, and standing just on the other side of him, with a shocked expression, was Hadass.

"Look, *Tate*, it's started to rain people!" she cried.

The *Rashim* folded his book shut, not forgetting to mark the place, and raised his head, pushing the spectacles down still further so that he could peer over the top of them.

"It has indeed," he said, smiling in his beard. "The first spring day, and 'the flowers arise from the earth,' in the words of Sha-almi."

Hadass ran to greet them, then stopped, seemingly awed by their torn and bloodstained attire. She glanced over her shoulder for her father, who stood up, removing his spectacles altogether and placing them in the pocket of his caftan.

"We are not spirits, Hadass, it truly is us," said Annat, releasing Yuda and stepping forwards.

"A long journey," said the *Rashim*, approaching and looking at each of them in turn. "And now you have come back to Chorazin. Is it today that my prayers will be answered, and the city return to the outer world?"

"We are hoping you might know the answer to that, *Rashim*," said Govorin. "The Bright Lady sent us here, straight from the heart of her *domaine*. As you might have guessed," he added, glancing down at his translucent copper armour.

"Will we be welcome amongst your people, *Rashim*?" asked Casildis, hesitantly. "I have brought back my sister Huldis, who was a captive of the Cold One. I dare not return her to Ademar for fear of what the Doyen might do. For Sarl, the Heir, his son, lies dead, slain by Vasilyevich."

"Yuda ben Mordechai," said the old man, turning to face him, "did you use the ring I gave you?"

Yuda held up his hand, and the ring flashed in the sun. "I have come to give it back to you, *Zaide*," he said. The *Rashim* shook his head.

"Keep it," he said. "The ring is yours. I have looked into its heart many times and seen worlds beyond worlds. But now that its power has changed you, it belongs to you alone."

As he spoke, there was a rushing sound, as if a wind had sprung up to shake the branches of the tree. Standing together, they all looked up at the sky. Clouds poured overhead, raw sunsets came and went, and nights flashed by with a whirl of stars. Annat felt Yuda take her hand. They stood side by side, watching the sky change, as the planet Rogastron and its three moons grew slowly fainter. Little by little, the constellations altered and grew familiar; the sun that raced across the sky became white and fierce, settling at last high above the branches that sheltered them. Stillness followed, before the birds began to call again, uncertainly. Annat looked up at her father's face and at Malchik's beyond.

The *Rashim* was the first to break the stillness. "My children," he said, "the day has come, and Chorazin lies once more amongst its ancient hills. I have not welcomed you, but I bid you welcome now, both *Dzuzukim* and Wanderers. I know that you have saved my people, and ended the Cold One's reign of winter. You may dwell amongst us until the time is right, and live with us as friends and neighbours."

"We will protect you, *Rashim*." said Yuda. "Last time the Doyen sent his men to harry you, there were no warriors to defend you. But I and my brother here, Govorin, will make sure that if he comes again, the odds are weighted more strongly in your favour."

"I hope it will not come to that," said the *Rashin*. "But your presence gladdens me more than any armour or engines of war. For though twenty years and more have passed in this world of ours, I do not think time it will have tempered the Doyen's hate against us."

"Since he lives in both worlds, we don't know how long he will have known of Sarl's death," said Govorin. "But we can guess that he will be seeking our heads. As outlaws, we may find your city a welcome hiding place."

Suddenly, Casildis sat down on the grass, as if her legs would no longer hold her up. "Forgive me, *Rashim*," she said, lifting her hand to her face , "but it has been a long day, longer than any I remember."

"*Meine Tate*," said Hadass reproachfully, "we have kept our guests standing when they have just done the hardest work in the world. Let them sit here with you in the garden while I send Yosef to prepare food, hot water and fresh raiment."

"Sitting sounds good to me," said Govorin, lowering himself to the ground beside his wife and beginning to break off the upper parts of his body armour. "I can't remember the last time I sat down without some horror coming to interrupt me."

"Forgive me, my children," said the *Rashim*, restoring his

spectacles to his nose. "In my joy I had forgotten how far you have travelled and the great perils you have seen. Old men are forgetful, myself more than most. Go on with you, Hadasseh, and find the *Golem*—but see that he does not flood the kitchen floor again!"

Flashing a smile at Annat, Hadass darted into the house. The *Rashim* subsided into his chair beneath the tree with a thankful sigh, and Annat shared his relief as she sank down on the springy grass. Malchik promptly folded himself up beside her, saying, "My legs feel like toffee!" Yuda and Huldis were the last to relax. Yuda stretched out full length on the ground, his hands behind his head.

"Why did you say a Wanderer has no home, Mister?" Annat asked him. "I want to go home. I want to see Yuste."

He turned his head in her direction. "But where is your home, Natkeleh?" he asked. "Is it with *Bubbe* and *Zaide* in Sankt-Eglis? Or in Masalyar with Yuste? Or with me?"

Annat could not answer him at once. "I don't know," she began. "I don't know where I live any more. I miss the Black Train."

Malchik stretched out his long legs in front of him. "I think I know what Vasilyevich means," he said, thoughtfully. "When you've been on a journey like that, somehow you don't quite seem to belong in this world. Part of you gets left behind in the strange world, and makes you want to go back there."

"The boy's right," said Yuda. "The curse of the Wanderers is to be restless. We're always harking back to some lost place— the Old Country, or Zyon itself. And we have been in La Souterraine, and left a part of our souls there. It would be strange, Natka, if you knew where you belonged."

"I belong with you and Malchik," said Annat promptly, as if to prove him wrong. She saw him smile, covering his eyes with his hand. Instead of speaking aloud, he sent her a thought.

—Maybe that's the right answer. I don't know. Just for now, I'm happy to be here in this garden, with my friends around me and no danger threatening. He paused. *—Because I don't think our journey is finished.*

"What do you mean, Yuda?" said Annat quietly, and Malchik gave her a startled look.

Yuda rolled over on to his stomach, feeling in his pocket for a cigarette. He pulled out one that was crushed and wrinkled, bent it into shape and put it in his mouth to light it.

"I suppose you get to know how it feels," he said, looking from one to the other, "when you've won your first battle but it's only the start of the war."

Malchik nodded. "I think I understand, Mister," he said.

Annat drew up her legs and wrapped her arms around them. Gazing intently at her father, she knew that he was right. They might have vanquished the Cold One, but somehow that victory had opened up another, unknown vista before them. There would not be leisure for her to go back to being a child again. She had seen and learnt too much, and broken her doll.

Jessica Rydill lives in the West Country with her collection of slightly unnerving dolls. She became obsessed with the department of Drome after volunteering for a French workcamp in 1980, when she encountered some of the places mentioned in this book. Her interests include myth, dreams and East European music.

PENGUIN PUTNAM INC.
Online

Your Internet gateway to a virtual environment with
hundreds of entertaining and enlightening books
from Penguin Putnam Inc.

***While you're there, get the latest buzz on
the best authors and books around—***

Tom Clancy, Patricia Cornwell, W.E.B. Griffin,
Nora Roberts, William Gibson, Robin Cook,
Brian Jacques, Catherine Coulter, Stephen King,
Ken Follett, Terry McMillan, and many more!

**Penguin Putnam Online is located at
http://www.penguinputnam.com**

PENGUIN PUTNAM NEWS

Every month you'll get an inside look at our upcom-
ing books and new features on our site. This is an
ongoing effort to provide you with the most
up-to-date information about
our books and authors.

**Subscribe to Penguin Putnam News at
http://www.penguinputnam.com/newsletters**